1

THE CAVERNS OF CRACKLEMORE

— BOOK 1 —

The Great Charming

JACE SCHWARTZ

This is a work of fiction. Names, characters, places, and incidents
either are the product of the author's imagination or are used fictitiously.
Any resemblance to actual persons, living or dead, or locales is entirely coincidental.

Copyright © 2023 by Jace Schwartz

All rights reserved. No part of this book may be reproduced or used in any manner without written permission of the copyright owner except for the use of quotations in a book review.

First hardback edition October 2023
First paperback edition October 2023

All illustrations copyright © 2023 by Mikaila Schwartz
Cover and interior design by Erik M. Peterson

ISBN 978-1-955051-27-9 (hardback)
ISBN 978-1-955051-28-6 (paperback)

Published by Punchline Publishers
www.punchlineagency.com

www.studiojandm.com
Instagram: @schwartzjace

For my children,
who remind me to play and tell stories every day

CONTENTS

1 The Secrets of the Plink Family   1
2 The Storm and the Dive   19
3 The Golden Singer   29
4 A Long Way from Lily Ridge   51
5 The Tour of Valor   67
6 The Hoaxbite and *The Emerald Egg*   105
7 The High General Sir Vector Cottley   123
8 The Surprising Sketch of Remaine Plink   135
9 The Monkeywood Witches   151
10 Harbor's Hand   167
11 The Bird Cage and the Bird Lady   185
12 Rawthorne Manor   201
13 The Hollowfiend's Hunt   210
14 Lichenbluff Castle   229
15 Mr. Lecky Wooling and the Garden Chest   243
16 Baublers and Charmers   265
17 Vulcutta's Song   281
18 Visitors and Invitations   297
19 The Crack in Time   309
20 The Secrets of the Rawthorne Family   341
21 The Brumaloss   361
22 Finale of Fangs   383
23 The Beasts of Doromund Venerack   391
24 The Great Charming   411
25 The Caverns of Cracklemore   425

CHAPTER 1

THE SECRETS
OF THE PLINK FAMILY

EVERY FAMILY KEEPS ITS SECRETS and the Plink family is no exception.

The Plinks kept many secrets, in many places, but one secret—their most treasured—they kept especially well-hidden, out of sight, tucked away from the world, in a watery cave not far from their home. It was not hard to keep the secret there. That was where they had found their secret and that was where their secret would stay.

Truth be told, the Plinks of whom this story concerns had not actually found their secret at all. They had inherited it from the Plinks before them, who had inherited it from the Plinks before them.

It had become legend as to who, exactly, had discovered the underwater grotto first, but a few things are known: the discoverer was, to be sure, a Plink, and he bore the mantle of a poor fisherman, a mantle which, along with the secret in the cave, he would also bequeath to every generation of

Plinks to come. Most certain of all, whenever that day was, and whoever that man was, he had discovered the secret network of caverns as a result of following an impossibly fat, and tantalizingly rare fish with scales like liquid sunshine.

The man and the fish were a perfect match, for it is a rare kind of person who bravely pursues a mysterious fish into the throat of an even more mysterious coral tunnel with no promise of air around the bend. But the fish was *very* fat, and it shimmered with scales so golden the whole thing might as well have been made of coin, and that was good enough reason for what's-his-name Plink, desperate for a fresh catch, and even more desperate for a jingle in his purse, to risk a little lack of air.

As surely as the sun sets over the Pearl Sea, the risk paid off. What opened before this particular Plink as he chased the beautifully plump fish deep into the belly of the seaside cliffs, was a hidden haven for the exquisitely buttery fish now known in Windluff, simply, as butterfin. The butterfin made their home in the vast, underwater maze of connected grottos and hidden caverns all of which sparkled from the delicate shafts of light that had pierced through the rocky exterior. Until this moment, the butterfin remained there undiscovered. The Butterfin Caves were a gemstone find; a golden yolk hidden within the unassuming shell of the southern cliffs of Windluff.

In the years to come, butterfin would prove themselves as elusive as they were delicious, as slippery as they were savory. But given enough time, a patient Plink would always find luck bubbling up in the waters of their secret caves. Eventually, a gorgeously round butterfin would present itself, almost joyfully, knowing its oversized body would soon be tossed into a cauldron steaming with yet another Plink secret: a white sauce so creamy, so buttery smooth, and so mouth-watering, its recipe was never committed to writing for fear of its secret being stolen.

Plainly, this was the extent of the Plink legacy: a very fat fish and a very buttery sauce. And though the Plink recipe managed to keep the family afloat drawing crowds of hungry dock dwellers with appetites for butterfin, the truth is, it all never quite amassed to anything that might help them become more than what they were: a family of poor fishermen. For generations, the Plinks made their homes on the royal docks in the Salt District of Windluff, on the southwestern coast of the Isle of Moorington, serving sloppy butterfin to the other sea-beaten dockdwellers.

Fishermen came and went, the tide rolled in and out and in again. Years went by and time saw the meandering and unremarkable growth of the Plink family tree. But despite never growing into anything more than what they were, the secrets were always passed on with relish. The hidden caves, the fat fish, and the family recipe—small, golden tokens of pride for the Plinks, tokens they shoved in the ragged pockets of their fishing togas; secrets to keep them going when storm clouds gathered and life felt weathered. And the Plinks at present were a particularly weathered bunch.

They lived in a house like a water-logged wine barrel that, like all the other homes on the docks, rose and fell with the tide. It was a small, rickety tower held together by rope and rusty nails. The pools of water on the kitchen floor never really dried.

But it was neither their painfully tight quarters, nor their dreadfully low funds that made them some of the most weathered Plinks on record. Rather, it was two notable things that beat them down.

Firstly, three of them (and soon to be four) were ill.

Eventually, throughout the Cracklemore Isles, all are taken by Frostblood, some sooner than others, but inevitably all by their final years. Approaching the end of those years were Deeno and Millie Plink. Frostblood was sadly seeing to the end of their sanity, unfortunately, and well overdue was their time to sail East to the Colony Gardens where the elderly at last find relief until their final breath.

Their son, Philo Plink, was, by all accounts, of an age where Frostblood should hardly be affecting him at all. At least that's what all the healers had told him once he began showing devastating symptoms six years ago. Deeno, Millie, and Philo, these were the three ill Plinks. By anyone's standards, it was Philo Plink who, after his strange accident that brought on his case of Frostblood, suffered most severely. Sadly, it was also Philo Plink who had surpassed his parents in deterioration.

No doubt all of the aforementioned is why Fortis Plink, Philo's wife, found herself feeling perhaps more weathered than any of the others. All had fallen on her.

Fortis was an elegant woman, a "fallen star," as Philo used to call her, who from a life of nobility, condescended to join the Plinks on the docks. At the time her rebellion felt wild, adventurous, and, on the most romantic of evenings, when Philo would whisk her away to the Butterfin Caves, as harmless as a late-night snack. It was for love she defied her father's wishes to live the life of a noblewoman. She was written out of her father's will and disowned entirely, but she still felt she had gotten the better deal, because shortly after becoming a Plink, Fortis became a mother. She felt that life couldn't possibly get any sweeter.

And if it weren't for that fateful night of her husband's accident, perhaps she would have been proven wrong. Perhaps it would have gotten sweeter for many years to come, like an aged vat of butterfin sauce. Unfortunately, though, Fortis had been right. Life would not be getting sweeter. Frostblood had come early for her beloved husband. Things were turning bitter.

It is Philo's mysterious accident, an event that no one was willing to talk about after the fact, that brings us to the second reason this family found itself so worn out. The Plinks, in true Plink fashion, were a family of secrets. Some secrets were hardly worth mentioning, and some were as fat and juicy as butterfin. But there comes a point, in one way or another, when the pressure to keep the secrets becomes too strong. The internal dams inside the Plinks were beginning to crack.

Not even the youngest Plink, a boy by the name of Remaine, was immune from keeping secrets.

It was not always that way. In his younger years Remaine had nothing to hide. He led a simple fisherman's life; he learned to swim before he learned to walk. The gritty feel of sand under his feet was more familiar to him than the tickle of grass, the taste of salt water more common than bread. It was all humdrum and routine and entirely secret-free for little Remaine. In fact, he would have had no need to keep secrets at all if it weren't for his sister.

Five years his elder and a prodigy from birth, Silome Plink positively reigned. She was a queen among peasants. Everything she touched turned to gold—or butterfin. Never had a Plink been more celebrated in all the family history than Silome, who, at the age of eight, speared her first butterfin. Despite their generously rotund form, mature butterfin are devilishly tricky to spear, but before Silome Plink, they seemed to bow in reverence and offer themselves up. Even with her own petite size, she cast a gigantic shadow, one in which her shrimpy little brother, Remaine, was forever destined to walk.

At first, when he was very little, it was just the games they would play. Silome would tease him, he would cry, she would laugh, and then she would win. Every time she would win. One time, in a challenge, she took a bite out of a raw fish. Before he could even try it, Remaine was barfing into the Pearl Sea.

But over time the borders of Silome's reign extended beyond games. She also provided. At sea she was a legend, and there were times when Silome, despite her young age, single-handedly kept the family business afloat with her catch. If Remaine wished to have anything glorious for himself, away from Silome's ever expanding domain, it would have to be kept secret. And where better to keep a secret, Remaine thought, than a long-forgotten corner of the Butterfin Caves.

For years Remaine had kept his secret there, and for years he had been adding to it.

Thus, our story begins on his twelfth birthday when Remaine Plink surfaced in that forgotten corner of the Butterfin Caves and gasped for air. He treaded water for a moment, just enough to catch his breath, then he climbed the cave's wall, scaling the reefstone with scrawny wet limbs—a slippery business demanding his total focus, especially with today's catch slung over his shoulders.

Like butterfin, reefstone was native only to the coast of Windluff. Reefstone wore a dull, pale gray mask, but when cracked open, it shone a brilliant interior of blue and orange rock. A few brightly colored patches on the wall, worn down over years of the boy's climbing, guided him up to his secret perch.

A hole in the rocky wall let in a single shaft of light, like a sword. The light sliced through the air and then bounced off the rippling water, sending warped rays dancing about the cave. Remaine climbed to the ledge and approached the hole. He squinted back the glare and peered outside to find a lone, white sail. The family boat waited for him. He had time.

The perch on which he stood, all ten square feet of it—was the boy's secret. Or rather, the perch was the place where he kept his secrets—thousands of them.

On the walls of the perch, Remaine had carved images of Igniro the Great Mariner. Tall and proud, Igniro gripped a trident. That was how he killed the Pearlback.

The secret mural told of Igniro's adventures according to Remaine. And though no one was there to tell him so—he made sure his family never saw it—the drawings were quite something. The large portrait of Igniro especially, by any standard in the Cracklemore Isles, was an advanced rendering for a boy of twelve.

He picked up a favorite rock lying nearby and added a few more strokes to the mariner's form. Then he put a few more details into the larger mural, the one where Igniro was riding the Pearlback before spearing it through.

Remaine stood back to admire his work yet again. Per his tradition, he stood firm, planted his fishing spear on the ledge and rose to his full height. Then he sucked in air and puffed out his bony chest, emulating the tall, strong Mariner as best he could.

Then he felt hungry. He plopped down, swiped a clamlet from his stash in the corner, cracked it open, and popped it into his mouth.

Never could anyone find a stronger contrast to the mighty Igniro than the puny Remaine Plink. Remaine's floppy, mostly wet hair was the color of dirty sand, and his eyes were the color of ocean rain. His scrawny, squid-like body was pale and freckled, giving him the appearance of a sculpture haphazardly molded from the sands of a Windluffian beach.

Though he was still quite small, Remaine had grown several, violent inches the past year, leaving him even more awkward than before. The three togas he owned no longer fit him, and his knees and elbows were always getting tangled up in the rigging.

But despite the cosmic gap between him and Igniro, this corner of the cave was where they had their adventures, back-to-back, tridents in hand. Right here worlds opened. Igniro sailed the two of them across fearsome seas. On those voyages, always in Remaine's imagination, on this tidy little perch, beneath the encouraging stare of the Great Mariner who never breathed a critical word against him, Remaine Plink was brave.

Though he would never admit it, these little made-up stories were the most important things to Remaine Plink. Out there, beyond the caves, he drowned in a sea of Plink gumption—his cowardice an anchor around his feet. In here, on this perch, Remaine Plink took flight; in here, he was not a coward at every turn.

Tossing the clamlet shell into the water, Remaine reminded his hero casually, "It's my birthday today."

Igniro stared.

"And for just once, I'd like to win."

Igniro stared inquiringly.

"I know, I know. I've been in the cave for hours and still I—"

A sudden splash echoed from deeper within the cave, jolting Remaine.

"That'll be Silome!" whispered Remaine. "See you!" He had only meant to pop by his hideout for a moment, but somehow (or like always, in truth) he had gotten lost in his imaginings and had forgotten why he was in the caves in the first place.

Remaine stole one last glance at the day's catch, crammed inside his bag of netting. He had high hopes it would be enough, but the splash had made him nervous. He flopped the bag over his shoulder, and it hit his back with a *shlpat*. Remaine took three deep breaths, held the third, then dove into the water, leaving his secret perch behind.

Cheeks ballooned with air, Remaine wormed his way through the familiar coral maze, popping up at familiar air pockets along the way to catch another breath. In the final stretch of the labyrinth, he pulled himself along for nearly a full minute until, at last, the open ocean spread out before him.

One thing that was not a Plink secret, although Remaine wished it were, was that Remaine Plink was petrified of open water. His family often found opportunities to grumble about the matter.

Remaine kicked hard and swam skyward until the surface broke and the fresh air greeted him like a sigh of relief.

He spun around in the water searching beneath his feet, treading furiously. The sun was setting. He wanted to win. It was his birthday after all. But Remaine knew *she* would be right behind him. Taking another big breath, Remaine swam with renewed vigor.

The boat was waiting for him. Ever faithful, *Lady Vex* was a humble little sloop, a single-masted beauty that had been in the family for a thousand years, at least that was what grampa always said with a wink.

Out of breath, Remaine came to the sloop's hull and began to climb. With a final swing of his leg, Remaine rolled onto the deck, his net of fish landing with a slosh. His mother squatted next to him, smiling. All around her face spilled her frizzy, sandy curls as she leaned toward him.

"Where is she?" panted Remaine, coughing up water. "Did I beat her?"

His mother did not respond, but there was a sparkle in her eyes. Remaine sat up to the undeniable sound of someone climbing aboard after him—the sound of his sister—in second place.

Flinging herself over the rail, just seconds behind him, came the small, yet remarkably strong frame of Silome Plink.

Normally, the sight alone of her imperious presence would twist his insides. Today, however, a grin as broad and proud as the horizon stretched across Remaine's face.

"Five for arriving first," came a tired voice from the stern of the sloop. Deeno Plink, his grampa, extended five fingers from a hand so hardened and old, so knotted from a life of grappling with rigging and nets, it almost looked to be made of wood. His bald head, tan and splotched, shone in the setting sun like the oily shell of a brown chicken's egg.

Remaine smiled at the sound of his grampa's voice, knowing it had taken him an inordinate amount of "fish sauce," as his gramma called it, to rally for his birthday week.

"Well done, Remaine," Grampa added, then shouted in Silome's direction, "Shark! Second place? Isn't like you!"

Much like a shark, Silome's face was impenetrable—impossible to read. She wore her stoicism heroically. With the same commanding air, she reached behind her into her pack, grabbed her first fish, flinging it onto the deck with a juicy slap. It was a small, white thing with a gray smudge on its side.

"A cloudtail! That's one for Silome!" Grampa Deeno exclaimed, and even Gramma roused herself enough to applaud in Silome's direction.

Gramma Millie was a wispy-haired old woman whose battiness betrayed her age even more so than her husband's splotched head betrayed his. She leaned next to Remaine, wrapped in her own blanket. "Oh, hmm, but can your brother reply?"

Really this was the most his grandparents had spoken in weeks, and Remaine was grateful for the rally. This week was special.

"I can reply," said Remaine, still catching his breath. He reached behind him and grabbed the slimy tail of the first kelp guppy. Its pale brown body landed on the deck with another slap, this one a bit louder.

"Kelp for three!" shouted his grampa.

"Kelp for three!" they all echoed.

Next Silome retrieved a smaller, pink fish.

"A lilabelly for one!"

"Lilabelly for one!" echoed Gramma Millie.

His mother did not echo, though. She rolled her eyes and said more slowly, with crisp enunciation. "A *lily barebelly*." When she could, she labored to correct the lazy Plink tongue—a task as hopeless as saving a sinking ship, she would say.

"Cloudtail for three!" Gramma Millie shouted.

"No, Gramma, we already said that," said Silome.

"Remaine?" asked his grampa.

Remaine produced his second kelp guppy, Silome followed with her own kelp guppy. That received a cheer as well as a few murmurs. Finally, Remaine produced his third and final kelp guppy which was met with enthusiasm. With his five-point lead for arriving first, the score was fourteen to five, and an impossible sense of hope began to rise.

"I'm out," said Remaine.

All eyes fell on Silome. The shark remained unreadable as she glanced around. Then she reached behind her, with both hands this time. Remaine's heart sank.

The round, golden body of a butterfin hit the deck like a stroke of fate.

"The shark bites again!" coughed their grampa. "Fifteen!"

Gramma Millie licked her lips as if they were smeared with garlic butter. "Just in time for tomorrow's batch," she purred, closing her eyes once more.

Then Silome shot a look in Remaine's direction, a look that wormed its way right into his belly.

As a rule, Remaine Plink was not a boy who hated anything. He disliked it when the rigging got tangled up in knots and it was his job to untangle it, and he really did not like it when low tide brought with it the smell of decay. He did not like crunching down on tiny bones when he ate fish, and he very much did not like losing to his sister. But something Remaine Plink could not stomach in the slightest—the *one* thing he did hate—was the face of patronizing pity emanating from his older sister when, at that moment, she reached into her net once more.

A second butterfin hit the deck, and Remaine was sure that even the long-dead Enchanters gawked in their graves. For a moment, frozen in time, Remaine could only be grateful Silome had not gone easy on him. He would never be in danger of that.

What a fool he was to have convinced himself turning twelve would somehow enable him to finally claim victory over Silome in something. *Anything*. He should have known it would not be that easy.

At least not yet. Remaine's long-awaited twelfth birthday was finally here. This time tomorrow, when the Great Charming gathered on the horizon as it always did with every full moon, he, along with everyone else of age in the Cracklemore Isles, would finally be Charmed. Remaine would at last become a man.

For the entirety of the return journey home, all the way back to the Salt District Docks where the Plink home bobbed about, fastened in place by a web of old anchors and seaworthy knot work, Remaine allowed his sister to bask in her glory as she always did.

Silome had already experienced the Charming. She had the benefit of having the magic in her veins every day now. All he had to do was be patient. One more day.

At dinner, later that night, Fortis Plink wiped her mouth and said, "Well, Remaine, we have one gift for you this year, but—"

"—Not till tomorrow." Remaine finished with a smile. "I know." He remembered when Silome had turned twelve and she had to wait to get her gift, too. He risked the question he had been thinking about all week. "Do you think Dad will be there for my Dive tomorrow?"

His mother sat across from him and looked down at her plate, as did the rest of them, sitting smooshed together around the small table. The crooked window hung open and the never-ending seagull cries echoed outside. The house rose and fell like a lazy buoy, but none of them really noticed.

"I don't—" she hesitated, then, forcing herself to look at him, continued, "I don't think he'll be able to wake up, Remaine." She brushed her gray-streaked curls out of her face and managed to front a smile. "Not till after the Charming."

Remaine looked down and gave a nod.

Grampa cleared his throat. "We'll see there to be you Dive, boy."

"Yeah," smirked Silome. "I'll see there to be you dive too, Rem."

"All right, all right," said their mother. "We'll all *be* there to *see* you."

"Thanks, Grampa."

After dinner came the traditional birthday dessert pie of sweet bread rolls with tangy-ink filling. It was another old recipe, made specially for Plink children on their twelfth birthdays.

The first wash in the Great Charming was reason enough to celebrate and eat sweets. But the Plink family held even closer to their heart another secret celebration, and the anticipation of the Plink Dive wiggled around in Remaine's belly like a barrel of tadpoles.

The premise was simple: after the Charming came—now filled up with the strength of the Old Enchanters—the young Plink takes to the sea with nothing but a traditional trident. Their task: to spear a single fish. That fish, according to Plink legend, marks them for life. All the wisdom they'll need, all the markings of their person, the traits of their character, *somehow* all of it is symbolized (and every Plink will swear by this) in that first catch following the Charming.

Remaine's sister, unsurprisingly, yet nonetheless impressively, managed to spear a fireshark, and no creature beneath the waves could have been truer to her character. She was a fireshark in every way.

So even though the mood was suddenly dampened by the cool reminder that Remaine's father, sick in bed in a loft above the kitchen, would not be there to witness his Dive, Remaine still fell asleep that night, rose the next morning, and passed the next day on the docks with his mind hazily fixed on the magical storm fast approaching. Like that storm in the distance, a day lay on the horizon, Remaine had no doubt, when he would at last savor the sweet taste of victory over his sister in a game of Fish Count.

Later that evening, a crack of thunder tore through the sky so loudly everyone could feel it. A blanket of reverence fell heavily over *Lady Vex* as the family boarded her and headed back out to sea. As was their custom, they steered their humble vessel to the same place they had been the night before, the ocean-sprayed base of Mariner's Cliff.

Mariner's Cliff was the highest point in Windluff. Its grassy knoll towered hundreds of feet above the city. Remaine eyed the cliff carefully as *Lady Vex* bobbed nearer. The moonlight shone ghost-white on its pale wall. The ruins were clear tonight.

Most of the ancient statue of the Great Mariner had crumbled and fallen from the cliff face, but fragments of that colossal figure still clung to the cliff as if the ruins were flowers blossoming among the ferns and vines.

As dockdwellers, the Plinks had no real need for learning much more than the family trade. But Fortis Plink came from a different sort of family. She insisted her children digest *something* besides fish, so once a year, usually during the winter when the fish were sleepiest, Remaine and Silome were forced to attend a lecture or two from the professors.

For one of these lessons, Remaine and Silome had gone out to sea early one morning. It was a horribly frigid morning. The ocean spray pierced the students like needles. Remaine's teeth chattered so hard he feared they might chip. He huddled together with the other seven-year-olds beneath wool shawls, gazing off the port side of the ship with a line of professors standing behind them. Of course, Mariner's Cliff was nothing new to Remaine—he had seen it all his life—but to some of his peers, it was their first sighting of the thing from the viewpoint of a ship.

"Now that piece there," shouted one of the adults, pointing a cold, purple finger into the air at the pile of broken ruins near the surface of the waves. "You can see, just there, all that remains of the Great Mariner's feet. Do you see the ankle bone? And that! Most think that bit up there is what we have left of The Great Mariner's royal robes, wrapped around his right arm—just there."

The professors went on with their story, and Remaine, even at seven, had been very skeptical. Igniro the Great—*his* Igniro—looked very different than the mariner described by the professors. Anyone could plainly see the crumbling bit halfway up the cliff was not the remains of some old robe. That bit was a shield. Or at least what was left of one.

Where everyone else saw only remnants, Remaine Plink could envision all of Igniro Ravillion, The Great Mariner of Windluff. Once Remaine tried to tell his family what it felt like—to see the tales of Igniro flash before his eyes—how his imaginings sent the hair on his arms standing straight and the way his gut would flutter, and his chest would pound at the thought of the ruins coming to life to leap into the sea. The family's reaction, a mixture of confusion and annoyance at learning what was distracting a young, able-bodied fisherman from the family business, solidified in Remaine his decision to forever hold it as his secret.

After hearing the hour-long lecture about Igniro's accomplishments, boring laws he had written or fancy cities he had founded or other forgettable stuff he had done, Remaine decided to keep *his* Igniro to himself, a secret hero whose likeness was better depicted on Remaine's wall in the Butterfin Caves.

Tonight, from the deck of *Lady Vex*, Remaine stole a glance at Igniro again, but only for a moment did he envision the trident, the wild hair knotted with salt, the heavy-browed gaze fixed on the horizon. Instead, and as if by Igniro's invitation, Remaine turned his gaze out to the horizon, too. As they did every month, countless ships had taken to the sea to receive the Great Charming. Across the deep waters of the Windluff coast and spread out with great stretches of open water between them, they waited. On land, too, everyone was preparing themselves. Those fortunate enough to live on Lily Ridge were clinking wine goblets as they stood on expansive balconies that overlooked all Windluff. They could see it all—the Pearl Sea and her horizon, a bluish line blurring in the storm clouds of the Great Charming.

In fact, in every village and city in Moorington, across the country's entire archipelago– and in every last secret cavern, every citizen in the Cracklemore Isles over the age of twelve, was fixing their eyes outward to see the approaching storm from whichever direction it arrived.

"Here," said Silome, not taking her eyes off the wall of dense clouds. She bumped Remaine's arm and offered him a sloshing, leather pouch. "For luck. I made this batch."

Remaine thanked her and took a drink of the tea. True to Silome's character, the tea was almost unbearably strong. He winced and shook his head. She rolled her eyes and gave him a slap on the back.

Then his mother drew near, her curls swirling around her in the peculiar, unsalted wind, as she clutched her shawl.

"All right. I think it's time, then. Here. Wipe your mouth. And…" she reached inside folds of fabric and removed a small, wooden box. "Happy late birthday, Remaine."

Remaine dried his chin with the back of his hand and took the box from her.

He already knew what it was, and yet at that moment it sounded as if the whole world had gone silent, right down to the bellowing thunder. He opened the box as if he might wake a sleeping baby inside it.

Somehow, seeing its simple contents softened the blow of his loss against his sister yesterday, and lessened the pain of his father's absence tonight. It even made up for the time he told his family about the stories in his head. Maybe it even made up for all the times his family had looked down on him, wondering if he'd ever rise to the Plink name. In that moment, Remaine could picture Igniro's proud face once more because at last Remaine had a vial of his very own.

He reached into the box and removed the small glass bottle. It was a perfect fit in his hand. A simple cork stopped it at the top and the glass had swirling characters etched into the side. He recognized the swooping "R" at the beginning of his name, and the towering "P" of his family name, but after that, it all looked like a mess of scribbled lines. His poor mother—she had tried so hard to instill letters into her children, but like most dockdwellers, Remaine was blowing bubbles in tidepools before he was talking, and he had never quite learned to make sense of the alphabet. Still, the meaning of the markings was clear enough: *Remaine Plink of Windluff*.

Then silently, stealthily, the light shifted. The skies darkened as they filled with huge purplish pink clouds. This was no natural storm, not with its vivid colors and strange, melodic thunder that sounded as if it was played by an enchanted, celestial harp. Remaine filled his lungs again. His skin tingled. The storm enveloped all of them and for a moment the Plinks could do nothing but stand and stare in awe.

Remaine's mother placed her hand on his bare shoulder.

"You get the best seat this time," she whispered. She gave him an affectionate kiss on the cheek and motioned him to the bow of *Lady Vex* where his sister had stood when she experienced the Great Charming for her first time as well.

"All right, spread out! Spread out!" Fortis said, her curls whipping about. Despite the practical limitations of obeying Fortis aboard *Lady Vex*, centuries of sacred ritual kept them all obedient to her orders, and so they all found what privacy they could.

Every month, with the full moon, no matter who you were or where you were, the storm always came and washed itself over Cracklemore. But only after twelve could you *breathe in* the Enchanter's Charm; only then could the Great Charming fill you.

Later, when it was all over, Remaine would look back on this last moment before the swirls of thick mist swallowed up the family boat, probing his memory for the smallest clue to make some sense of just what went wrong. But in that moment, as the Great Charming arrived, not in his wildest nightmares did Remaine imagine anything could ever go wrong. Despite the secret adventures and endless worlds of his mind, Remaine had not the imagination wild enough to fathom the truth about his own world—a world where the Great Charming was aware of an unknown secret held deep inside Remaine's body, a secret Remaine himself was not yet aware of.

CHAPTER 2

THE STORM AND THE DIVE

REMAINE'S MOTHER ALWAYS SAID it was bad manners to watch someone breathe in the Great Charming. By this she meant it was impolite to watch the part that follows the Charming, the part where one breathes out all the bad bits. The bad bits were known in the Cracklemore Isles as the Old Cold. If it weren't for the rushing in of the Great Charming—these bad bits would very quickly grow into Frostblood, all of which is very personal. If Fortis Plink could not refine her children's language nor interest them in letters, she could at least insist they follow Cracklemore custom and practice good manners by respecting the privacy of the ceremony. No need to discuss it.

Lightning shot across the sky like white lace, and thunder rang out with lilting harmony.

A grin spread across Remaine's face as the warmth of the Charming embraced each of them. All he had to do was wait.

But as is often the case with children, waiting was very difficult, so

Remaine Plink broke the rules and peeked over his shoulder to steal a glance at his family.

They were scattered about the small boat. Each Plink, faces turned to the sky, allowed the rain to wash over them with eyes closed. His mother and his sister sat similarly at opposite ends of the deck, arms wrapped around their knees, while his grandparents appeared to be sound asleep at the stern.

Then they all inhaled deeply. The Charm filled them. It was a pure, clean sound, like stretching in the morning.

Remaine watched closely as they each then lifted their own vials to their lips. As silent as death, on the wings of their exhale, out came the Old Cold—a blueish gray mist, like tendrils of painted air, slipping from their mouths and floating along their breath like weightless snakes. Each Plink channeled the serpentine mist of the icy curse into their vials.

Thrill pulsed through Remaine at the sight of it. He wiggled back into position and squeezed his eyes shut. It was his turn.

The warm rain continued to fall on him happily, easily, and he held his shiny new vial tightly with slippery fingers. He waited. He squirmed. He waited some more, until, at last, the air around him… changed.

The mist dissipated and the crisp coastal breeze returned.

It was somewhere in that first moment of goosebumps prickling up his arm that Remaine Plink realized, slowly at first—as slowly as you might realize you are, indeed, in a nightmare—that nothing, *nothing at all*, had happened.

But that was ridiculous. Of course, something had happened. He lifted his vial to his lips and gave a heavy exhale. Perhaps he needed to get it started. But nothing came. *Could this be true?* With his right hand, he brushed his left arm. It was still wet from the storm. He glanced around, the air was still thick, and still violet, but there was no denying it, the clouds were moving away, making their way inland,

and Remaine Plink had been left behind. The Enchanters... their Charm... somehow—and Remaine clawed in in his mind to figure out how—somehow, it had passed him by. He was unable to receive it.

He began to shake, and a realization as crushing as the sea itself began to fall on him. Musical thunder chimed in the distance as if the Enchanters were mocking him in song, leaving the sky dark and his spirits even darker.

He felt suffocated when he finally stood to face his family. Not a one of them broached the invisible sacred boundary of privacy. Remaine always felt inclined to practice good manners, but now he clung to them with gratitude. No one said a word. They stared at him. Remaine blinked in return. The choice to tell or not to tell rose before him like the terrifying Pearlback out of the waves, and he sensed that his very survival hinged on which course of action he took. Should he tell them something was wrong with him? His was already the smallest, most insignificant little life, drowning in the unfathomable depths of Silome's shadow—a life of pretend adventures in a secret little cavern with no actual courage to show for it. He could not bear to give the family another reason to see in him a Plink failure. Remaine stayed silent.

Silome approached, her eyes ablaze with superiority; Remaine looked away. This was it. He knew it. She could see through him. She always could.

Then she thrust the old, rusty family trident into his hands.

"How do you feel?" she asked quietly.

Remaine risked a glance into her piercing gaze and found a genuine curiosity in them.

"Good." He lied. Then he climbed onto the railing of the boat.

He knew the approximate depth of the water beneath *Lady Vex*, but in the darkness, it looked as if it could have been a thousand feet deep. He tried not to think about it. His teeth chattered as he stripped down to his underclothes.

"Now, listen to me, young man," said his grampa. "In through your mouth, out through your nose."

"No, no," hushed Fortis. She patted Deeno Plink on the shoulder. "In through your nose, out through your mouth."

Grampa coughed and scratched his shiny head.

The world was quiet, and the surface of the water was still. Remaine could at least be grateful for that.

"Three deep breaths." His grampa tried again to give the boy advice. "And fill up those lungs, Remaine, and hold on the third! You need full lungs down there!"

"Thanks, Grampa." Remaine said over his shoulder.

Then his gramma added, "But if you need to go deeper, then you'll have to let some air out through your mouth and—"

"—No, no, no—through your *nose*," corrected his grampa, then he looked at Fortis to verify his own sanity. She smiled. He continued, "But n-not *all* your air, boy…" his eyes squinted, as if trying to recall a distant memory.

"—And if you take a breath down there," Gramma Millie sang out, waving her hands around, "It's all over. ALL OVER!"

"All right, you two," said his mother, as she gently guided them back into a resting position. She had endless patience for Remaine's rapidly aging grandparents. "Thank you. Remaine's been swimming his whole life, he knows how to dive." Then she approached her son.

"You're a Plink fisherman now, son," she said quietly.

"After the Dive, you mean," replied Remaine, giving a hard swallow and looking over the edge. This was it. All he had to do was spear a fish by light of the moon at the base of Mariner's Cliff. The trick was in choosing the right one. And that was tricky enough *with* the Great Charming. *Was it even possible without?*

He felt as though he might puke.

"You'll be fine, Rem," said Silome.

Remaine sucked in a deep breath through his chattering teeth, their rattling now louder than the fading harmonic thunder.

Remaine calmed himself enough to take three deep breaths. Time slowed on the third as he held it, and without so much as a drop of the magical strength he had been promised his entire life, he kicked off *Lady Vex* and dove into the dark waters of the Pearl Sea.

He allowed himself a few seconds to feel the shock. Once his body absorbed the cool blast, he opened his eyes.

It was a world of inky midnight. His heart began to pound. Still, the Great Charming always came with the full moon, and the full moon always brought her dropping silver shafts of light in ethereal columns. At least he had that.

Remaine released a few bubbles from his nose and allowed his body to sink lower into the blurry underworld. Small, reflective comet-tails darted out of his path, only to curiously circle back and nibble his toes as he kicked downward.

His eyes began to adjust. Lurking in the deeper darkness, much bigger, darker shapes kept their distance as Remaine stayed his course. A few cloudtails floated by, unaffected by his presence, and the all-too-familiar shape of the lean, striped fireshark could be seen circling in the foggy background.

Releasing pressure from his ears and a bit more air from his nose, Remaine continued to kick, sinking lower and lower into the black water. He scanned the reef line with the limited scope of the moon's light. Orb-like eyes peered out from dark burrows.

The pressure began to build in his chest. Remaine knew he had less than a minute to spear his fish. A familiar archway in the reef appeared before him. Remaine took comfort in the tangibility of it. The hovering shapes of several dark fish underneath proved promising. He only needed to be still, and they would come to him. At least that's what he had been taught. Then again, he had also been told that he would receive the Great Charming when he turned twelve.

Did the fish only come to the twelve-year-old Plinks *because* they were Charmed? Maybe the fish could smell it. Remaine began to panic. What if the fish couldn't smell him! Remaine kicked off from a piece of reefstone and ventured underneath the reef arch to get into position, praying some sea creature would take pity on him and sacrifice itself on the tip of his trident.

Suddenly, every fish around him, big and small, darted away. Remaine whipped his head from side to side, releasing a curtain of bubbles. Wait. Where did they all go?

What he saw next sent a wave of nausea through his entire body. The strange thing disappeared in a blur as quickly as it came, but it was enough to squeeze his lungs. Beneath his feet, far below, the entire sea floor seemed to move. A huge expanse of gray, no doubt the ruinous fragments of the Great Mariner which had crumbled over the years, somehow moved in a slow, underwater landslide.

Diver's Spin! Remaine had experienced it before, but never like this.

Horribly disoriented, Remaine propelled himself backwards, releasing precious air in an involuntary shout of surprise. He clawed upward. His lungs began to scream, his head began to pound and Remaine inhaled a costly gulp of water. He cried out involuntarily and a cloud of bubbles swirled around him.

Blackness swallowed him.

He awoke, his body overcome by a fit of choking. He coughed, then wretched, then coughed some more, his lungs rejecting the water, salt and acid burning his throat. With each inhale, he imagined a rolling wave slapping him indifferently in the face, forcing water back down his throat. Remaine kicked out of instinct, but he heard his sister shouting "Remaine! Stop! You're on deck, Rem. Stop! You're on deck."

He opened his eyes. His grampa sat him up and gave him a hard slap on the back. Remaine gagged up more salt water, then crumpled into a shivering ball, arms wrapped around his knees.

"What happened?" Remaine choked. His throat was blazing, and his voice was like stone.

No one answered. Silome knelt beside him. Her face betrayed her—she was a thousand leagues away. Silent. Horrified? Embarrassed? Ashamed? The impenetrable shark.

He glanced around at the rest of his family. They stood motionless; a shared, dumbfounded look stamped on their faces. His mother had covered her mouth with a delicate hand. His grampa stood as rigid as the cliff behind them. All their mouths were closed in tight lines and their eyes pierced Remaine's heart right through in the way his own trident should have done to a stupid cloudtail or fluppy guppy.

He shivered beneath their scrutiny, wishing he did not understand. But his trident lay beside him, its point gleaming, completely clean and devastatingly fishless.

He was the first of his family name to fail the Plink Dive.

"I didn't—" he began, "th-the ocean floor—it—it *moved!* It—"

Even the memory of the sea floor shifting and spinning made him nauseous again.

"Diver's Spin..." said Silome quietly.

"Y–Yeah," said Remaine, "well, sort of... it... it was different—it was so much worse. The whole ocean floor, I saw it m—"

"—Boy," said his grampa, and Remaine wished he could forget only minutes ago he had called him young man. They locked eyes. His grampa wanted to say more. There was an agonizing pain on his face, but Deeno Plink merely shook his head.

The burning in his eyes came suddenly, and without even the slightest bit of self-control, tears poured down Remaine's cheeks, still wet with the ocean water. If he wiped them away, they would no longer blend in with the rest of the water on his face, so he kept his hands frozen to the deck. But his mother knew him too well, and he could see her eyeing his cheeks where the river of tears shone.

"All right," said his mother, "that's enough. Up. Come on, up to your feet now. Breathe it out, and let's be done with it. Quickly now." She fussed with his soaking wet tunic as if to dust it off then held out her palm. The family watched in silence. Remaine was frozen to the spot as his mother reached into his pocket and removed his vial for him. "This is what you do now, right Remaine? Every time, yes?" Her words were curt and hurried, betraying her embarrassment to even talk about something which should be known. She uncorked his own vial and held it up, like a mother might feed an infant. "You've been Charmed now. You have the strength now. Come on, breathe out the Cold, and let's go home. We'll sort it all out tomorrow."

The tears in his eyes dried on the spot, and he felt the blood in his cheeks dry up, too. His cheeks paled, and his breath caught in his throat. Everyone was watching him. He did not know what else to do. Had anyone noticed the vial was empty?

He had no such luck.

"But…" Fortis Plink looked down at the vial. "Where's—"

He opened his mouth, but his sister, to the boiling of his blood, spoke first.

"He didn't breathe any out," she said, almost under her breath. Her eyes were wide, and they were darting between the vial and her younger brother as if he were transforming before her eyes into a horrible monster. "You didn't, did you? The Charming… you didn't…"

She said it as if she were sealing his bleak and miserable fate for all eternity.

"Don't be ridiculous, Silome," his mother said. "We were all here. It came and went."

"Did you see him breathe?" Silome replied quickly, her jaw set hard. "He was at the bow." With every word she grew in stature, towering over him like a giant. "It didn't work on you." There was a passion rising in his sister, and Remaine wanted to scream. It felt cruel, the way she cornered him. Was it not enough that she so easily embodied every good thing the Plink blood had to offer, while he was left to flounder and fail?

"No," he said, and somehow saying it made it all too real.

There was another gasp across *Lady Vex*, and Remaine found he almost preferred the terrible, disappointing silence he had endured only moments ago.

"It's... unheard of," breathed his grampa. He rubbed his shoulder with a gnarled hand, his gaze boring a hole into his grandson. "You're... you're of age—the Great Charming—it always comes..."

Then one by one, each Plink began to furrow their face at him as if horrified by what they were seeing, all except Silome who, much to Remaine's irritation, looked as if she were about to dissect him. There was almost a smile on her face, her eyes wide with sick fascination, and the sight of it made his insides turn.

"We'll speak no more of it," whispered his mother, glancing over her shoulder. There were no ships around for miles, but she fidgeted, suddenly paranoid. "Does everyone understand? Not one word—not until we get to the bottom of it. And—" she made sure to lock eyes with each person, then her gaze fell back on Remaine and Silome, "not one *word* of this to your father. He *mustn't* know."

Her face contorted in a strange, painful sort of way, then she reached up and adjusted the rigging.

A numbness consumed Remaine as they sailed home in silence. He did not feel anything as his grampa, with no discretion, exhaled more of the blue, Old Cold into his own vial, his body shaking, little moans coming from his gray mouth. Remaine forced himself to look away when his gramma, too, crumpled into a lethargic huddle once again, silent and somber.

Only moments ago, the storm had given the family reprieve, but now Remaine had triggered something dark within them. A sharp knot formed in his gut at the thought of his grandparents. They should have set sail already, off to the Colony Garden in the East with all the other elders to live out their days in peace. But they hadn't. They had wanted to stay in the Cracklemore Isles, and battle the Old Cold a few more years, just to see their grandson come of age, to see their grandson Dive, to see him become a man. Each day their aged minds and frail bodies had paid a price. Each night they slept longer, yet more fitfully. But they had made it. Remaine had come of age, and with a flourish, he had crushed them. They would depart for the East in disappointment.

Remaine fought his way from *Lady Vex* into the Plink home, a pulsing ache gripping his chest and throat as he climbed the old rope ladder to his bed. His body rattled as he dried himself off and crawled under the quilt his gramma had made for him, back when he was a bright and promising newborn. He ignored all Silome's attempts to speak with him.

In bed, a realization, like an old, barnacle-ridden anchor sinking deep into the depths of his stomach, fell on Remaine as he understood, somehow, that his childhood was forever lost in the Butterfin Caves. Now, as a man—or the failure of one—he would find nothing but disappointment in Igniro's gaze. Suddenly, the precious secret of his hidden perch paled in comparison to the secret he must now keep hidden in his pocket.

Remaine, by some miracle, eventually fell asleep that night, but his mother, who lay in a larger loft below her children, did not. She was kept awake by her own secrets. Secrets she had successfully kept under lock and key for over a decade. But tonight, her son confirmed, the seams of her secrets like the seams of her old house were tearing apart, and the water was rushing in.

CHAPTER 3

THE GOLDEN SINGER

FORTIS PLINK'S TIRED FACE was the first thing Remaine saw the next morning. As she came into focus, he heard her hushed voice.

"Wake up, Remaine. Shh."

He sat up in his loft and rubbed his eyes. His mother was perched on the ladder which led up to his and Silome's sleeping quarters. Only her head was visible. She held her finger to her lips, and with her other hand rubbed his knee. "Sorry to wake you so early," she said.

Silome gave a loud snore next to him.

"I want you to come with me this morning, all right?"

It was too early to think. He nodded.

Her head disappeared as she descended the old ladder. Remaine lay back down, gave an enormous stretch, then followed.

The entire Plink home was a leaning, creaking tower of water-logged lumber. But, if one stepped with care, it creaked less. When he landed in the

kitchen, he heard his father cough above him. Remaine paused, listened, then stepped with extra care.

It had not taken long for the fisherman, Philo Plink, to win Fortis Diaquinn's heart. As Fortis told the story, she was unable to resist Philo after that day he juggled three fish to get her attention. One of them had not been dead, and the living fish flopped its way off the dock when he dropped it, earning Philo a smack in the head from Deeno Plink.

Philo had winked at Fortis. Fortis had smiled at Philo. Before too long, Fortis was learning how to dive, and discovering she loved nothing more than how tightly Philo gripped her hand when, at last, she worked up the courage to explore the Butterfin Caves.

When Fortis spoke of those days, she did so in a dreamy sort of way. Their love was young and secretive, hidden in the Butterfin Caves away from her father's watchful eye. Thus, life had felt charmed, and the hard stuff seemed a thrill. Even when her father disowned her, writing her out of his will—it rolled off Fortis' back. Her first dose of reality came with her first night spent in the Plinks' bobbing-cork-of-a-home.

"Ah," she said the next morning, green with nausea. "This is what you meant by a life dictated by the whims of the tide."

As there would be no Plinks allowed in the Diaquinn home on the hill, Fortis had been welcomed into the house on the sea. It took some getting used to, but eventually she did get used to it. The gentle rocking, she claimed, proved helpful for sleep.

On this morning, Remaine followed his mother's lead in her effort to protect the family's sleep. Still drowsy himself, he sat down on a chair at the table—the only one that didn't creak—and yawned as his mother fussed about the place.

This was the family common space, with a sink, stove, and an old, wooden table with four, mismatched chairs. There were cushions to lounge on. The ceilings hung low and there were suspended fishing nets strung about like spiderwebs that provided extra storage. The nets were his mother's idea, and though she spoke little of herself, she did take special care to remind the family of her nets when the house became untidy.

Fortis knew where everything was and had personally seen to the much-needed organization of the Plink home so many years ago. Even now, the only reason every square inch of this home had been scrubbed clean (though in appearance it didn't look like much) was because of Fortis Plink. "Put things in their proper place and peace will come to all," she would preach.

His mother handed him a mug of a clear, palish yellow liquid. The steam of the lemon tea tickled his nose. He sipped, and as his sleepiness began to fade, so returned the memory of the day before. The way his mother chewed her lip and avoided his eye contact confirmed his catastrophic failures were on her mind as well.

Fortis tied her wild blond curls back behind her neck. Her tresses had always been her crowning glory. Normally she allotted a few early-morning minutes for a time of quiet lament, brought on by the sight of wiry silver strands now intermingled with what used to be a cascade of pure gold. Her silent mourning would then give way to a few seconds of cursing. "Time," she fussed, "such a villain he is!"

This weary woe was a smokescreen for much deeper fears.

Once the liveliest Plink of the bunch, Remaine's father now lay sleeping above them, his shallow breathing ragged enough to be heard from the kitchen. His eyes were sunken, his hair thin and balding. Since his accident, it was to Philo Plink whom Time had proved to be most villainous. Yet, Philo slept best on the nights of the Great Charming, and that is why Fortis and Remaine kept particularly quiet this morning. With any luck, Philo would find some restoration over the next few days.

A single, flickering candle illuminated a woven basket piled high with neatly folded laundry. It leaned at a dangerously low angle next to the sink. Fortis tightened her shawl about her neck and grabbed the basket, followed by another matching basket, this one empty, which she slung over her back.

"The sun will be up in a couple hours," she whispered. "If we hurry, we can be back before the rest are up."

"Where are we going?" he yawned again.

"Come along, Remaine."

A loud squawk from behind her nearly sent the basket flying. Fortis jumped and whirled around. Remaine's heart leapt, and he sloshed the hot tea onto his wrist.

"Ouch!"

After a long, anxious moment, hearing only the soft exhale of Silome rolling over in bed above her, Fortis took a deep breath and scolded the family Songbird—a seagull named Chicken who was hardly worth the title of Singer.

Silome had named the bird Chicken after finding him comfortably nestled on a bowl of eggs his first morning at home with the Plinks. Purchasing him a decade ago had nearly drained the family savings, and he was one of the cheaper Singers.

Fortis glared. Chicken blinked his beady black eyes.

His mother softened. Poor Chicken. Time had not been good to him either. His mangy feathers stuck out at odd places and his neck was crooked. He had been faithful, and he did try so very hard.

Fortis extended a hand and patted Chicken's old head and whispered, "If they wake up soon, tell them we'll be home by breakfast." The Singer blinked again then buried his face in his feathers.

Fortis nodded to Remaine, beckoning him to follow as she opened the front door. They were met by the hum of waking commerce on a bed of morning mist.

The royal docks were a city in and of themselves, a planked network of floating homes and docked ships, all connected by zigzagging avenues of wooden walkways, ramps, stairways, and bridges. The docks' barely organized chaos was another thing Remaine's mother had been known to critique under her breath. But what his mother launched audible diatribes against with fervid passion, what she never got used to and what she still found positively unbearable, was that every square inch of the docks reeked of fish.

If there was one thing Fortis Plink prided herself on, it was her unique ability to scrub her home completely free of the reek of fish. Her skill of successfully removing the putrid aroma of fish from any kind of fabric had earned her a reputation as a miracle worker. The "Sorceress of Soap," some Windluffians called her. Her refusal to succumb to the filth of the Fish Trade had therefore brought her employment. When she was not needed aboard *Lady Vex*, Fortis Plink moonlighted as the best laundress in the Salt District.

Fortis made her way from apartment to boat to house to shack, dropping off bits of sparklingly clean laundry along the way, Remaine in tow like a little duckling. She knew her customers and their garments like every Plink knew the caves beneath Mariner's cliff. With each delivery of clean laundry, Fortis would add the dirty stacks left outside to the basket on her back.

They visited with Miss Leela, a tired, single mother of three to whom Fortis always gave a discounted price, then they said hello to the Worther brothers who were always first out on the water, and usually last to leave; more than anyone else in the Salt District, the Worther brothers smelled like the bottom of the ocean.

Fortis whispered, not for the first time, "it's the Worther brothers, and the noses they offend daily which keeps us going, yes Remaine? Clean laundry is of immense, societal importance."

A few skeletal cats scurried about their feet in search of rats and the whole expedition was set to the tune of seagull-cries; the rhythms of a morning on the docks. Fortis looked up at the sky and quickly measured the dawning light. They had made good time. Picking up the pace, she headed north up the Docks to the edge of the Salt District until they came to a humble little row of apartments.

Fortis knocked on the green door with the rusty knocker shaped like a flower. On the other side there was the sound of shuffling and a strained holler. Eventually the door opened to reveal Remaine's mother's dearest friend, Cressa Merchant.

Draped in flowing yellow fabric from head to toe, Cressa embraced Fortis, cocooning her inside the folds. Remaine was next. Cressa pulled him into her skeletal frame, burying his face in curtains of yellow. Then she pulled him back to get a good look at both of them.

"Precious Plinks," she smiled. Her gaze lingered on Fortis and her eyebrows raised with concern.

"Oh, don't look at me like that, you old woman," said Fortis. "You look just as tired as I do. Can we come in?"

Rather than bright with the zinging scent of soap, Cressa's house was foggy with the aroma of herbs, dirt, and seaweed, hanging about the room—organized by Cressa's standards but not, to be sure, by his mother's. And yet, despite the jungle-like atmosphere, Fortis found it comforting, somehow. It was why she came here so often.

"Tea?" asked Cressa.

"Yes, actually, but not for me."

Cressa flashed a look at his mother, who glanced down at Remaine. He knew, instantly, it was the sort of thing grown-ups do when they want to be careful of little, listening ears.

"Philo's... fine," said Fortis. "You know. Some days are... worse than others."

Cressa put her hands on her hips and turned to Remaine, "And how are *you*, young *man*?" Her eyes twinkled. "Forgive my manners, precious—I haven't said congratulations *or* happy birthday yet! Twelve, Charmed—and the Plink Dive—how did it go?"

Remaine gulped. Any sleepiness still lingering in his head quickly evaporated. His stomach gave a horrible sick lurch, and his throat felt tight all at once. He looked up at his mother. She was pale.

Cressa's gaze darted between them. "Fortis? What is it? What's the matter?"

A torturous silence hung for a moment before Cressa came to the rescue. "Remaine, I almost forgot, would you go upstairs and cut me three or four good strips of the pink kelp? You'll see the big clump drying by the window." Cressa handed him a small plain knife.

Relieved he would not have to watch the agony on his mother's face any longer, Remaine followed her orders, marching up the rickety stairs to the next level. This level was half as small as the space below, and yet doubly crammed with stuff. In the corner, by the window, though, a big pink plant presented itself. Its bottom was in a big bowl of water, and its tops were hanging out the window—big pink ribbons with yellow splotches. Remaine stepped over to the plant loudly enough to make his mother feel he was busy, but still keeping himself quiet enough to eavesdrop.

"What do you mean nothing happened?" asked Cressa.

"The Charming—he never got it. He still hasn't—he hasn't breathed out the Cold."

"He's the proper age…" Remaine heard Cressa respond.

"Yes," continued Fortis. "Cressa, have you ever heard of this? Has anyone ever come for medicine for something like this?"

More silence.

Remaine cut a strip of the pink kelp off in a blundering, loud sort of way.

"No, Fortis."

"Philo was right," Fortis whispered. Remaine could hear the emotion bubbling up in her voice again. Her voice lowered, and he cupped his ear to listen.

"He s–said that night—the night he came home," Fortis' voice was trembling. "He said the curse would come for the Plinks. We would live to see it. You remember it too, Cressa. What if this is it? What if Philo was right?"

Remaine had been asleep the night of his father's accident. No one ever spoke about it, at least not anymore. Silome had been awake. She was only eleven, but she had seen her father's arrival. It used to give Remaine nightmares when Silome described it to him. Eventually he asked her to stop talking about it. But he was still haunted by the picture in his mind—his father bursting into the door, drenched in rain, screaming about the Berylbones, and the East, and never wanting to go back—and the curse, the curse, the curse.

Finally, Cressa asked, "What will you do? How can I help you?"

"I want you to look at Remaine," Fortis said. "Just see if there's anything obviously wrong with him, would you?"

"Oh, Fortis," breathed Cressa. "Of course I will, Honey, but I don't—"

"—and if you find something, you can't say a word. If you *don't* find something... not a word. If it's Frostblood—"

"—Fortis. Frostblood never comes to children."

"He's not a child anymore, Cressa. He's twelve. And he doesn't have the Charming."

Another beat of silence. Remaine coughed loudly and cut another strip of kelp.

"If he has Frostblood, they could take him East, Cressa."

"If Frostblood does take him, Fortis, he'll find relief in Colony Gardens, and—"

"—I won't let them!" Fortis snapped, so suddenly it made Remaine drop the knife. His cheeks burned. He started to tremble.

"You know what Philo said, all those years ago, Cressa. The curse of the Berylbones—it came from the East—Philo can't bear the thought of going back there."

"Fortis," Cressa said, trying to keep her voice steady. "Colony Gardens may lie in the East with Pylon Crag, but the Gardens and the Crag are not the same place."

"I know," Fortis breathed. "I know. But you don't hear Philo at night, Cressa. You don't hear him cry out in his sleep, begging me to protect him—to keep them from taking him aboard the eastbound ships. It's all the same to him, and—and now Remaine—and—"

"Shh," Cressa patted Fortis' knee. "We don't know anything yet. If this is the curse of the Berylbones, then, soon enough, Remaine will display symptoms of Frostblood. And then we'll know. Until then, let's stay calm."

Remaine heard his mother sniffle. "He's so young…"

"We'll start now. With tea. I'll do what I can to help stave off the Cold's effects, and with any luck, he'll receive the Great Charming soon and this will all be for naught. Come. Let's give him a look, shall we? All will be well. Remaine! Have you found that kelp!"

Remaine jumped up, nearly sending a large pot filled with what looked like dead moss toppling to the ground.

"Coming!" he hollered back.

When he came down the stairs, it was like stepping into a room filled with lingering smoke from a fire he had caused. The two women gave him false smiles.

Cressa stood and began moving around the room, forgetting about the pink kelp. Remaine set the cuttings on the table. His mother cleared her throat.

"Remaine," Cressa said. "Come over here, would you? It seems you've grown six inches since we last met, I want to get a closer look at you!"

Remaine stood before her. Cressa smiled, tapped his head, then began to poke and prod his cheeks, opening his mouth to look inside, and lifting his brows with her thumbs to look into his eyes.

"My have you gotten handsome," she feigned, as if she weren't poking around for signs of Frostblood. Remaine pretended back.

"Thank you."

"Remaine," she said, a bit more carefully, though she was quick to flash him a light smile, "Could you please swish this around for me?

When you're done—and I know this sounds strange—but, could you then lick this leaf right here?"

"What?"

"Oh, I know, I know—so strange. So silly. But you know—this leaf here has a way of showing us what's on the inside of our bodies when we lick it. Odd, huh?"

"Why do you want to know what's on the inside of my body?"

His mother spoke suddenly. "Remaine, please, just listen to Cressa."

Remaine did as asked. The plant tasted like old driftwood.

"Good boy," said Cressa. "Now. About your Dad's tea!"

Cressa began cutting strips of dried sea plants and tossing them into a bowl. Her small home, alive with nautical fauna, generously supplied her with ingredients from every corner. After severing a final strip of something gray and wiggly floating in a clear bowl of water, Cressa dropped all the ingredients into her mortar. Then she vigorously mashed the mixture with the pestle.

It was Remaine's mother who changed the subject with a genuine question, much to Remaine's relief. He was not sure how much longer he could bear the torture of their invisible concerns leaking out from their quick glances with one another.

"Have you heard from Estin?" asked his mother.

It was Cressa's turn to break composure. Her expression changed in a subtle way, but Remaine could tell the question had poked a sore spot.

"What? What happened?" Fortis stood to her feet.

"I received a message yesterday afternoon," said Cressa. She stopped mashing the tea and her gaze flashed back to Fortis, then out through the cracked window and along the zigzagging docks. "From the duke."

Fortis gave a hard swallow. "Duke Hegs contacted you? Why?"

"I—I've been requested at the Royal Suite in three days' time," Cressa's chin gave a slight quiver, but she steadied herself. "The duke said the prince has explicitly requested an audience with me before he begins duties for the Tour of Valor."

"The *prince*?"

"There's only one reason the prince would want to meet with me," Cressa's voice cracked. "Estin's been—"

"—Oh, Cressa, it doesn't necessarily mean something bad, it could mean—"

Fortis stopped herself. Cressa's large eyes were filling up with shiny water. The two women embraced.

Fortis rubbed Cressa's bony back, and said, "Never did I witness such warrior-like strength than when Estin and Silome fought us before bedtime."

Cressa chuckled and gave a sniff. Fortis smiled, thankful for the lift in mood.

"Oh, they were absolute terrors, weren't they?" said Cressa, pulling away and wiping her face. "Scurrying about the place like little rats, destroying everything, hiding in everything. I swear they knew their way around all this stuff by the age of five better than I do now. Not you though, Remaine." Cressa pulled away, smiled at him, and patted his head once more. "Always one to do as your mother asked, huh? Quiet little man, you were. Mind elsewhere."

Cressa returned to her work. She divided the contents of the mortar into two bags. The first she sealed and handed to Fortis. "For morning," she said, scribbling a tiny sun on the side of the parchment.

She swiped a tall glass bottle, piled an inch high with jet black leaves with bright green spots. She removed a single leaf and held it gingerly in her hand. She then sliced a miniscule corner of the leaf and ground it into dust between her fingers. Of that dust, she took a fraction and allowed it to drift into the second bag of tea. "For night," she said.

Remaine knew a single petal of gruggleroot could put someone to sleep for a week and three petals could kill a grown man. And yet, even the potent plant had fallen nearly ineffective over the years for his father's restless night.

"You seem to be running low," Fortis said, eyeing the near-empty bottle.

"Yes," Cressa replied, "fiendishly difficult to find. I've discovered I can't keep to my regular spots like I used to. I have to go deeper to get the good stuff."

"The world is discovering your secrets," Fortis said. "The powerful properties of aquatic plants. Who knew?"

"I knew," she said. "I've always known."

They both sighed at the same time, and by the misty expression twisting both their faces, Remaine knew he should busy himself in the corner once more.

"It's finally come for me, hasn't it," Cressa whispered.

"What?" asked his mother.

"Loneliness."

"You're not alone, Cressa."

After a few lingering laments about their gray hairs and their grown babies, after trying in vain to ignore the obvious problem of Fortis' youngest child and her withering husband, and after puzzling over Cressa's summons from the Duke of Windluff and Prince of the Cracklemore Isles, Fortis and Remaine left the house of Cressa Merchant.

Not far from Cressa's home, at a small, dead-end pier known as the Cleaning Clump, where the scent of dead fish had a life of its own, Silome Plink slid a blade across the belly of a bright purple fish as if through melting candle wax. She twirled the knife between her fingers and made another artful incision. Her fingers practically danced with finesse, and she combed them through the fish's insides with the satisfying de-boning sound. *Pop-pop-pop.*

Remaine observed with pathetic self-pity. Ranking high among things Silome did with sickening ease, gutting fish was near the top.

He stared down at the poorly butchered flounder before him. Its dead eyes stared at him in mockery. Remaine winced, then continued hacking away, making a complete mess of his station.

When he was younger, Remaine cried at this part. Only his mother had been patient. "We call it cleaning, Remaine, because that's all it is. Put things in their proper place and peace will come to all."

His mother's aphorism had helped a little. He learned to see the blood and guts and everything else as a mess that just needed cleaning. He was like his mother in that way.

After an uncomfortable morning at Cressa's, his mother had found they had spent more time than planned. So, Fortis had hurriedly sent Remaine off to the Clump to meet up with Silome while she returned home to care for his father.

Silome asked about their outing, but Remaine refused to talk about it.

"She just wanted company I guess," Remaine lied.

The two young Plinks worked in a crouch next to other ocean tradesmen, catching, counting, and cleaning.

"Thirty-three," said Silome, wiping her forehead. This was how Silome was like their mother—the way she sighed and wiped her forehead after she finished a task. But in every other way it was the gritty, Plink blood which ran through her veins like flaming hot magma.

"That's plenty, right?" asked Remaine.

"Should be."

The Plink siblings tossed their cleaned fish into their net packs and slung them over their shoulders, sending loose scales and fish slime running down their backs. It was yet another thing Remaine disliked, although he pretended not to mind it at all.

Silome squinted down the broad, planked walkway of Salt District Avenue and frowned at the noisy crowds.

"Busier than normal," said Remaine, raising a hand to his brow.

"The prince arrives this week," said Silome, scanning the commotion. "Ah, well. It's low tide anyway."

Remaine read her mind. The Otter Ropes would be much faster.

Silome led the way to a nearby post, not far from the Cleaning Clump. The water sloshed against the barnacle encrusted posts below. She walked right to the edge of the dock, unhooked a knotted rope from the post, and without the slightest show of hesitation, flung herself from the platform.

Remaine squirmed at her effortless exhibition. He had never seen his sister show any sort of fear. He swallowed. The terrifying jolt of swinging twenty feet from the docks' edge onto the small rowboat below, like everything else, had never come easy for him.

Everything sneered in a particularly fierce way at him today—Cressa's examination, the fish gutting, Silome's graceful leap from the height of the docks, and not least of all, the hollow clink of his empty vial, still tucked away deep in his pocket.

Last night he had a nightmare, too. He was in a dark, foggy world and the Great Mariner had risen up like a mountain out of the water and scolded him among a crowd of a thousand generations of Plinks, all of them golden fat with kissy fish lips. When he woke up, sweating, he had checked his vial in desperation, but his fears were realized again at the sight of its crystal-clear, bone-dry interior. Remaine was an aberration.

Unhitching another rope, Remaine peered over the edge to find Silome waiting for him below in an old, leaf-shaped dinghy named *Baby Vex*. He jumped and swung in a broken arc, like a haphazard pendulum, eventually dropping awkwardly into the rowboat, giving it a rock that almost tipped them both into the water.

"Easy, Rem!"

"Sorry."

There was a silent tension wedged between them. He could feel her looking at him, but he kept his eyes on the water.

"Do you want to talk about it?"

"No." he said.

"You'll be fine," she said. Her statement was about as comforting as a hug from an actual fireshark. Still, he was thankful she left it at that. She stood, grabbed the taut line strung parallel to the water, and began to pull.

Only exposed during low tide, the Otter Ropes ran the length of the docks' underside in a massive grid system. The ropes reeked like an army of unbathed seals, and they were only used by locals who wanted to avoid foot traffic (and who were also brave enough to endure the smell). Fortis Plink had often said that she would rather die than pull herself along "the latrine lines," as she called them, and to tell the truth Remaine felt the same. The horrible little dock spiders crawling underneath only added to the discomfort. Silome was indifferent to all of it.

They worked together to pull themselves along the roped channel, the dingy beneath them sloshing along happily. Above them a world of commerce boomed and clamored, a world that found its epicenter at the Brineymore Round, where all Otter Ropes came together.

After a short while of pulling themselves along, the two Plinks arrived at an enormous shaft of sunlight, a hundred feet wide, piercing through a hole in the wooden planks of the royal docks above.

Hundreds of rope ladders hung down from the circular rim of the hole in the docks. Remaine tied up the dingy while Silome gathered the fish packs. Then they climbed.

Suspension bridges arched across the open circle at the top, and hurried traders bustled along, the occasional fish fell from head-balanced baskets. Open shops dotted the rim of the trading circle, and a stream of people swept them up as soon as they reached the top. They began to walk clockwise with the current, passing shops of every kind.

One shop glistened with luxury items like silks and jewelry. Remaine had no memory in his twelve years of life of ever having stopped there. They passed a shop filled with nothing but cheeses, and another with fresh vegetables from the farms in the Roosterhall Valley. Another shop sold glass vials ready to be freshly etched with a name.

Remaine had always peered in there with excitement, now he looked away in private shame.

The Round was decorated with traditional statues of the ancient Enchanters of the Ravillion bloodline. They adorned all of Moorington, and the rest of Cracklemore for that matter, having been peppered throughout the Isles over the past few millennia by the Enchanters who founded the world. Over time the statues had cracked, and bits of stone had fallen off; the ones in Windluff were particularly weather-beaten. Still, the pale stone figures had become traffic markers in the bustle of the Round, and Remaine followed the flow of foot traffic, passing a female statue with a chipped nose. On her open palm she held an indistinct bird, her strong frame draped in flowing fabric. This statue signaled that Silome and Remaine had arrived at the aviary.

A wooden archway framed an interior of bright light streaming in from every angle. At first glance the shop appeared to be open to the outside, but the sunshine came through a thousand old glass panes and windows, all somehow fused together to create a large, wonky, sphere-like greenhouse.

From the warped floorboards to the dirty glass ceiling, the Brineymore Aviary was bursting with Songbirds.

These weren't the lovely kind of Singers, either. Those were reserved for the aviary in the city center. These birds were hand-me-downs of the magical fowl, the rejects, all of them doing their job, but only just. Scruffy birds with wiry feathers huddled together on bespoke perches of washed-up driftwood while others cuddled in nests made of old fishing gear. Crammed into every nook and cranny was an explosion of lush greenery, and where any room was left, little bowls of water and shallow baths glistened in the sunlight.

The smell of bird droppings was, at first, overwhelming, but intermingled with the ever-present odor of fish just outside, it blended together in the nostrils of the average dock dweller until it disappeared. There was no getting used to the sound, however.

"I'll see you at the shop!" shouted Silome over the shrieks and squawks spilling out into the Round. An orange bird with one leg screamed right next to Remaine's ear.

"What are you doing?" he shouted back.

"Just League stuff," said Silome. "It'll only be a second. Here." She unslung her net-pack from her back and tossed it at Remaine.

Remaine watched as Silome pushed her way into the feathered world of the aviary with confidence. The more expensive the bird, the farther its wings could carry it, and the longer your message could be. Tradesmen and tradeswomen shoved past one another looking to find a Singer who could reliably deliver their messages across Cracklemore, and Silome disappeared into the shop with the best of them to find one who could take a message all the way to the Weatherlee mainland.

It was a marvel to Remaine how accomplished his sister was. When she was just thirteen years old, she had caught the eye of a nobleman from Ravillion Bay who had been trading in Windluff for the summer. It was the perfect combination of luck and skill, and later that week the nobleman recruited Silome into the League of Young Traders, an elite training program for young adults ready for more opportunity. Every summer Silome would disappear for a month or so, usually to Ravillion Bay, and when she returned, Remaine would have to hear all about it.

With a little less pep in his step, Remaine walked, past the aviary, then past another shop, more opulent than the others, and run by a man wearing black robes with red ties. His hood was red, his face stoic, and behind him were other healers of identical appearance.

Healers mostly treated Frostblood as best they could, but the sickness always came to the elderly, and on the rarest of occasions, it came earlier in life. Remaine gulped, haunted with vivid images of his father, and the several times the healers fruitlessly came to his home. He hurried past the shop.

A familiar squawk rang out among the crowd as he came, at last, to the Plink shop.

"Hello, Chicken," smiled Remaine, patting the family's Singer.

The bird bobbed and pecked hospitably. Behind the counter, a tiny figure with her back towards him was hunched over a cauldron of thick, bubbling cream. The swirling steam smelled of butter, garlic, lemon, and a few other secret things.

"Have you cleaned them?" asked Gramma Millie, extending a hand behind her, careful to keep her nose inches from the sauce. Most of the time she slept, but when it was time to prepare butterfin, a force, sometimes even more powerful than Frostblood, pumped through his gramma's veins.

"Yes," said Remaine, coming around the counter with the two packs of cleaned fish. He began to help her unload, separating Silome's prized butterfin from the rest.

"Now, butterfin over there, son," said his grampa who, Remaine just noticed, was on his hands and knees behind the counter, scrubbing something off the floor. He stood to help Remaine, gruffly separating the fish. The command was superfluous, barked as if Remaine was doing this for the first time.

Silome came along shortly, and no sooner had she arrived did Chicken let out an ear-splitting squawk. He hopped onto the counter, taking center stage. Then he opened his beak, his eyes went blank, and he lifted his wings as if to take flight. His body stiffened, like he was made of stone, and from his skinny throat spilled the voice of their mother, Fortis Plink.

"If they wake up soon, tell them I'll be home by breakfast," came the whisper of their mother from inside the beak of the bird.

Then the voice was gone, and the bumbling spirit of Chicken returned to the bird's body as he nestled into his nearby nest, a clay bowl lined with old rags, pleased at having delivered his message.

"Chicken..." muttered Silome, rolling her eyes. "And when were you supposed to deliver that message, eh?"

"Early this morning," said Fortis Plink, appearing from behind them. She shook her head at Chicken. "I don't know why I even try anymore. Ah well. Glad he failed in his duties—I was with Cressa longer than expected. You would have been left waiting. Your father was still asleep when I got home," she sighed. "I was hoping to bring him along today."

Just a few days ago, Remaine wished for nothing more than his father to wake up. Naively he had hoped he would even wake up in time for the Dive. That way he would have seen Remaine finally earn his place. Now he felt relieved that his father had continued to slumber away. Every hour his father slept was another hour free from the disappointment that would come in learning Remaine's secret.

Fortis hauled onto the counter a bag full of vegetables, recently purchased from a few nearby shops. Wordlessly, Millie Plink began to organize them.

Once or twice a month the Plinks came to the Brineymore Round. When Remaine was younger, they practically lived there. But with the decline of his father and grandparents, the family could only manage the one time. It took all their energy, and any more it required a good washing from the Great Charming to get Deeno and Millie Plink out of the house.

"Chicken," Fortis said, fixing her gaze back onto the family Singer, "what are we going to do with you?"

"Crusty old bat..." mumbled Millie, still bent over her butterfin cream.

"I am not!" hollered their grampa.

"No, not you!"

The two tended to the butterfin while the rest of the Plinks assumed their roles within the shop. But they had not a single customer before something highly unusual happened.

From the top of the Round, where the roofline kissed the sky, a great screech pierced through the commerce. It was distant, and at first it almost rang out unnoticed, but as it sounded a second time, heads turned upward.

Flashing like a golden medallion, the Singer which had let out the screech was hovering over the round, its large metallic wings beating the air. The iconic bird of Hubert Hegs, Duke of Windluff, slowed the foot traffic of the Brineymore Round, as curious dockdwellers looked on to see what message the duke would be sending here.

It was not unusual for the duke to send his Singer to deliver messages—in fact, it was Hubert Hegs' preferred way of communicating, probably because he had grown too large to comfortably travel. But to see the glittering bird down on the docks, at the Brineymore Round, was striking to say the least, and no one was more surprised to see the golden bird dive bomb into the Round than Fortis Plink.

Remaine did not notice his mother shift her weight, nor did he hear her breath catch in her throat at the sight of the bird. Remaine watched in surprise along with everyone else as the bird descended like a shooting star.

"What does *he* want?" Silome said, crunching into an apple.

The bird lifted its wings, catching the wind, elegantly gliding down. Then, to the surprise of every person in the Brineymore Round, the Singer of Hubert Hegs circled through the air and landed right at the Plinks' stall.

A few passersby hurried out of the way as the massive gold bird beat the air into a breeze around them. Ignoring them all, it trotted to the Plinks' counter where it hopped up, its talons scratching the polished wood. Chicken shook like a newborn puppy beneath the great bird's shadow.

Each Plink looked at one another, but only just; the bird demanded their attention. His belly was the color of fresh cream, and his head sprouted an ornate plume of vanilla feathers which cascaded down onto his golden back in a cockatiel fashion. He was, undoubtedly, the most iconic Singer in Windluff.

The bird fidgeted for a moment, eyeing Fortis from head to toe, cocking its head from side to side. It clicked its shiny black beak a few times, then suddenly the bird's movements changed from twitchy and bird-like to smooth, slow, and calculated like a cat's. Its beak unhinged like a drawbridge. Its wings slowly spread, as if about to fly. Then, bubbling up from deep in its belly, came the soft, frothy voice of Hubert Hegs, Duke of Windluff and the greater Moorington Isle.

"Miss Fortis Plink," said the duke. This was followed by a gentle little cough, then a whirring sound as the man cleared his throat. "Excuse me. Miss Fortis Plink, please come to my home tomorrow morning for sunrise tea. I would like to discuss with you a few things of…" the voice paused, but the bird did not change form in the slightest. "… of great importance. Please bring your son with you, if you don't mind. Oh. And a plate of your famed butterfin. I've been informed by a trusted source it's something quite special. Let's see… yes… I think that's all. Right. See you then."

The bird left the shop, and the Round, leaving nothing but a single golden feather behind, with which you could have toppled every last Plink.

"Charms and cheese!" said grampa. "What's that about?"

Remaine stared at his mother. Her face was white. He himself felt as if he might throw up. What could Hubert Hegs, the Duke of Windluff, want with him? His gut twisted even tighter with a horrible thought. Did the duke know about his… abnormality?

"I don't know," Fortis said, trying her hardest to make her tone light. "I can't imagine."

In truth, Fortis was imagining several things, and as she was a very intelligent woman who had a clear memory of the past, she knew she was not far off. She excused herself, saying, "I had better get back to your father."

Outside the Brineymore Round, Fortis Plink walked home, head down, chewing the inside of her cheek. The Royal Docks were more alive than ever, making ready for the prince of the Cracklemore Isles. Seagulls screeched, water sloshed against the docks, sailors barked orders as they tossed ropes and buckets of crab, yet all the while Fortis's mind was entirely elsewhere. For all she knew, the docks could have gone silent, because all she could hear was the soft voice of Hubert Hegs still echoing in her head, leaving her oblivious to the world around her, oblivious even to the smell of fish.

CHAPTER 4

A LONG WAY FROM LILY RIDGE

EVERYTHING CHANGED FOR REMAINE after the double catastrophe of the non-existent Great Charming and the failed Plink Dive. Barely two days had passed since that fateful night, and he found no relief came with the passage of time. It only got worse, his feeling of strangeness, and his only wish was to be in his cave. At first his imaginings soured. No doubt Igniro was disappointed in him, too. But it did not take long for Remaine to find solace returning, once more, inside his head. In his imagining, Igniro brushed the dust off Remaine's shoulders, pulled him up to his feet, ready to embark on another adventure. Of course, the ache to escape into these stories was, as usual, only compounded by his family.

When the family had returned from the Brineymore Round, their voices hummed amidst the scraping sound of spoons to wooden bowls at dinner, though not a one of those voices addressed Remaine directly, that is, until Silome said, "You hungry or what, Remaine?"

Her question drew attention to his absence of appetite, at which point he caught his grampa staring at him, one bushy eyebrow hiked high, which he lowered when Remaine locked eyes with him. His mother's response was worse. When he didn't eat, she made him tea, insisting he drink the whole thing on the spot under her close supervision. The expression on her face made Remaine feel as though he were inflicting real pain on her every time he came around, so after dinner he tried to keep to himself, lingering in vacated places, which were mostly outside, even aboard *Lady Vex* as she bobbed indifferently next to the tense home.

Remaine tucked himself in early that night in an attempt to spare his family his presence. He heard them whispering below, but only a few words were exchanged before his mother silenced everyone. The following morning, though, he caught more of it.

He pretended to be asleep as more whispers swelled. Only his father, still asleep in his own loft, remained ignorant to the hushed exchange.

"Shh! Keep it down."

"Oh mother, please," said Silome in a half-hearted whisper. Then he heard a familiar *thwock* sound. Silome was throwing her darts into a favorite target on the wall. No doubt she had hit the center.

It was still dark outside. The sun would be up soon enough, but for now, a candle lit the kitchen below, and its soft glow bounced gently off the cargo nets draped from the ceiling. Remaine's peeking eyes were entranced by the light as he lay still in his bed, eavesdropping.

"I don't want him to hear, Silome."

"Which him?"

Thwock.

"I don't think *either him* can hand—" his mother paused and sighed. Remaine could not see her, but he knew she was rubbing her temples. "Neither of them can handle any more right now, all right? So please… just… keep it down."

There it was again, in Remaine's mind, the picture of his father's accident. The rain had been falling like black needles, Silome said. His father had burst through the door like a criminal on the run. No one could understand why he had fallen to the floor, nor why he had been shaking and sputtering nonsense, nor why he had come home so soon, nor why he kept clutching at his chest. But he had. And their family had never been the same. Now he lay asleep, still oblivious to Remaine's abnormality.

"What did Cressa think?" Silome asked, casually.

"She doesn't know what to think," whispered Fortis.

"It's all that daydreaming, Fortis," said his grampa. Remaine heard the chair scoot across the floor as Deeno Plink sat. His hand hit the table. "He's never been *here*. That boy's always *here*…" Remaine heard a quiet patting sound which he knew to be his grampa tapping his own head.

Another memory came to Remaine.

He held the net on the side of *Lady Vex* but Mariner's Cliff held his attention. It was coming to life in his mind again, and the Mariner was diving into the water—the water which concealed his mortal enemy—the Pearlback. But the beast was out there, on the horizon, where the water's cloak reached its limits and the Pearlback was surfacing, exposing its serpentine head. Igniro was on the hunt. Remaine's mind pictured the legendary beast as clearly as he pictured its slayer.

Witnessing the adventure had slackened Remaine's hand, and he did not notice that the net had silently slipped from his fingers. Nor did he notice his family barking at him—not until Silome gave the side of his head a loud SMACK!

The smack had thrown the imaginings right out of Remaine's head, the cliff had returned to its ruinous state, and the horizon had appeared crisp and undisturbed once more. Remaine suffered the vocal blows of his family all that day—he had lost them a good catch, not to mention valuable time, as they had devoted the rest of the day to retrieving and untangling the net.

But somehow, the bliss of the tale had sustained Remaine beneath the familial onslaught. The exhilaration of seeing Igniro leap from the cliff was stronger than shame's torture.

Now, though, he wasn't so sure.

Presently, as he heard his grandfather bemoaning the inside of his grandson's head, Remaine noticed the old man's voice strain. Somehow Grampa's whisper was louder than his regular speaking voice, "It could be he just wasn't... *ready*."

"Oh, Deeno," said his mother. "What do you mean *ready*?"

"Well, I don't know!" replied his grampa, who pronounced 'well' like 'wool'. "It finds you at the close of childhood, don't it? Which has always ever been twelve, but maybe some..."

"Who?"

"I don't know, just... some. Others. Maybe there are others who stay... a certain way... till later."

Thwock.

"What?" asked Silome. "Stay what way?"

"I don't know... *childish*?"

Remaine felt like one of his own cloudtails, sloppily gutted right there.

"Perhaps," confessed his mother, "But I can think of plenty of childish twelve-years now fully charmed."

"Besides, Remaine's childish, but not *that* childish," added Silome. Remaine was genuinely surprised to hear his sister come to his defense. He listened as she yanked her darts out of the wall, and said, "I'll swim naked to the Brineymore Round and back if the Great Charming finds Remaine more childish than Tarquin Pellatrim, or Barnsy Heel. Or *Jileanna Hegs*!"

There was a beat of silence at the mention of the name Hegs.

"Relax, mother. You can't honestly think that the golden whale knows about Remaine."

"No," whispered his mother. "Of course not." He heard his mother fuss about the kitchen, then say, "I'm going to wake Remaine, now. We have to go. Please, everyone, not a word about all this. Let's just… make it through today."

Silome gave one last *thwock*. Then his mother's head appeared once more.

Remaine pretended to wake up.

"Come along, Remaine. You're with me again, today."

About as far from the Docks as one could go without leaving the city limits of Windluff, East Hill shone above the city like a diadem, and its crown jewel was an immaculate avenue named Lily Ridge, whose inhabitants were as crisply manicured as the hedges that bordered their estates.

The pale gravel gave a satisfying crunch beneath his sandals as Remaine followed his mother out of the carriage. It was the first time he had ridden in a carriage, and if his mother had not looked so painfully severe during their journey, he would have smiled, and maybe even enjoyed it.

The lane was dotted with shrubs clipped in perfect spirals, and every blade of grass stood upright, not a one growing out of line. The statue-saturated gardens were as foreign to a Plink fisherman as the Colony Gardens were to the bloom of youth. To Remaine, Lily Ridge was all a marvel, but to his mother, it was the stuff of her childhood.

Fortis held a plate filled with butterfin, covered by a humble wooden bowl turned upside down. Holding it on her left forearm, she used her right hand to comb through her curls. As they approached two attendants standing guard at a gate of swirling iron, she quickly whispered.

"Remaine, be quiet unless the duke addresses you, you understand?"

He fidgeted.

"Can I help you?" asked one of the men. He was wearing crisp, uncomfortable-looking clothing.

"Fortis Plink," she said, "and her son, to see... Duke Hegs."

The attendants checked a neatly rolled scroll, then the gates unlocked with a *click*. They swung open to more white gravel twisting in an uphill stream, punctuated on either side by lemon cypresses. The road brought Fortis and Remaine, both breathless, to the front doors of Hegs Manor, an architectural statement of white stone, edged and capped and outlined in all the right places with bronze, like icing on a gigantic, white cake.

Two more servants dressed in customary black liveries greeted them at the door. Between the two stood the estate manager and butler of Hubert Hegs, a small, rat-like man who followed his master faithfully.

"Miss Plink," bowed the man. It was not so much his appearance as his twitchy movements that made him seem so entirely murine. "And Remaine Plink." He ushered them both inside.

A round room with a high ceiling opened before them. Hanging on the walls and displayed on a number of marble plinths at the far end, demanding their immediate attention, were many shining medals and honorariums.

It only took a second for Remaine to understand what they were. The life-sized portrait of Hubert Hegs helped his discovery. The entire room had been devoted to the awards given to the duke during his days of valor. Beside the gilded display and the portrait—which showcased a much younger, much slimmer Hubert Hegs—and perched on an enormous ring of gold, sat the Singer of the duke like a living piece of art at home among the collection. The morning light fell through the windows and kissed with great affection the golden display of metal and feathers. The Singer clicked at the two of them, then cocked its head to the side, bored.

The twitchy butler spoke, "The Lord Hegs will be down short—"

Just then a voice rang about the chamber like a trumpet gone flat. "Oh! They're heeeere, Papa! Finally!" Jileanna Hegs approached slowly, with a propriety so forced it nearly broke the seams of her opulent dress, giving Fortis and Remaine plenty of time to digest her appearance. And what a picture of indigestion it was.

If one squinted, and cocked the head, and could somehow see beyond the poorly painted eyes and the smudged red paint sloppily applied to the lips (with no real attention given to the shape of the mouth) and if one could somehow unsee the two dozen scarlet bows clinging to limp strands of generously oiled hair, one might uncover a rather pretty thirteen-year-old Jileanna Hegs. For now, though, the overly made-up, bizarrely long-necked teenager glided towards them in an obvious effort to channel the persona of a mature lady of the manor. A broad grin stretched across her face, making her poorly painted lips look even more like two red jellyfish than they already did. "Admiring Papa's awards?"

Fortis Plink dipped her head and bent her knees. "Good morning, Lady Hegs."

Remaine bowed slightly. He and Jileanna had interacted only a few times, during their days at lecture, and each one of those interactions was confirmation to Remaine that the Salt District was a very long way from Lily Ridge. Jileanna might as well have been a different species.

Jileanna gave a squashy clap. "I *adore* it when people call me that! Papa says now that I'm a woman, I ought to expect repex… espect repe…" she took a deep breath then let out a heavy laugh, leaning on the closest plinth before trying once more, "expect respect."

Fortis smiled. Remaine tried.

"Right you are, Jileanna." It was a man who had spoken, but his voice was so delicate, so light and airy, so velvety and sweet it turned the stomach like an over-rich cake.

The man was Hubert Bellow Hegs. He was the Duke of Windluff and everything about him was over-rich. With a body like a humpback whale, Hubert Hegs lumbered into the room, bearing heavily down on a jewel encrusted cane to compensate for his weak leg. On his shoulders he wore the customary feathered epaulettes which marked him as a city chairman. The golden color of the feathers matched his Singer, his awards, and his robes, which hugged his midsection fiercely.

"Miss Fortis Plink," huffed Hegs through labored breathing. Each word frothed and bubbled in his cheeks before spilling out. He smiled, revealing a line of very small teeth, then wiped a bead of sweat from his miniscule forehead, framed by a line of thinning orange hair. "And young Remaine." The duke eyed him in a way that made Remaine feel as if he was about to be eaten. "So good of you to come. Ah, I see you brought us some goodies. Poolish?"

The butler, Poolish, took the platter from Fortis and then scurried off with such speed he seemed as if he had stolen the plate of food from her and was now taking it back to a hole in the kitchen wall.

"Shall we?" Hegs hummed.

Jileanna released another heavy giggle as Hegs led them through a series of archways out onto a balcony that overlooked the whole of Windluff.

From this perspective, the top of Mariner's Cliff was half as high and the reefstone roofs of the city gleamed below them, and beyond the sea wall, shone the royal docks.

"Please sit, Miss Plink. Remaine."

"Thank you," Fortis said, sitting at a small table of twisted bronze, topped with a silky lace cloth upon which perched bone-white teacups and matching saucers. The table was set for four. Remaine's mother sat opposite the duke, and Remaine sat opposite Jileanna. The Plink butterfin sat in the center of the table.

Fortis smiled. "And thank you for sending the carriage. The journey up the hill would have taken us half the day."

"Not at all," said Hegs. He closed his eyes slowly and bowed his head magnanimously.

Remaine fidgeted amidst the finery. His feet barely touched the floor, so he swished them quietly beneath his chair, hands tucked under his thighs. A white-gloved servant poured the tea. His mother took a sip, as did the duke. Jileanna took a rather loud slurp, which she acknowledged with another loud laugh. She batted her eyelids, plastered with thick maroon paint.

The sun rose behind them, increasing the temperature tangibly. Remaine's mother readjusted in her chair.

"Did you have a good summer?" Fortis finally asked. "I'm sure a duke keeps busy."

"Indeed," Hegs said into his tea. "A party here, a chairmen meeting there…" He sipped with supple grace, then made himself more comfortable in his seat, an agonizing spectacle given the proportions of his bountiful size and the limitations of the petite chair which groaned courageously beneath him.

"Sometimes," he continued, "I wonder if I am the man for the job. But then a decision is made, and another, and another, and pretty soon I see all my decisions have been like scaffolding—precise, crucial, all to the construction of our noble Windluffian society—the betterment of which only buttresses the honor of the good Ravillion name. Then I think to myself—Hubert Hegs, you were *born* to do this."

Fortis sipped her tea. "Mmm."

Jileanna, inspired by Fortis Plink's refined touch, at once sat up straight to mimic her. "Mmm," she murmured, fluttering her eyes again.

Hegs inhaled deeply, emotionally, then with eyes again half-closed, and as if his words were being recorded as poetry for future generations, he breathed, "And I bear the heavy weight of my duty with a humble and determined heart."

He smiled and shook his head as if he had been caught giving his own golden robes to a poor street urchin. Then he sipped his tea, and the ensuing silence gulped them all down again.

A knot in Remaine's stomach began to tighten in the stillness.

Why had they been summoned here? He felt it was possible that at any minute the duke would be asking for his vial, embarrassing him for being Windluff's greatest failure. In addition to his worry, Jileanna's constant attempts to make eye contact with him made him feel horribly uncomfortable, and he wished for nothing more than to leave. He supposed his mother must have read his mind when she finally asked, "I don't suppose you'd be willing to get right to it, Duke Hegs?"

"Please, Miss Plink, I think we both know you can call me Hubert." He paused, then added, "And I assume there's no harm in me using your name as well?"

"Of course, of course. So, why am I here, then…" her mouth twitched, "Hubert?"

Hegs tightened his lips. "I see we won't even enjoy tea, then."

His mother said nothing and with another curt smile, she took another sip. Remaine glanced up at the duke and found he was looking down at him. Remaine diverted his gaze at once over toward Jileanna, which felt worse yet. He finally resolved to look down at his knees.

"Fine, then," the duke chuckled, waving his meaty fingers through the air like a fan of cream-filled pastries, "Let's have it your way. We'll move quickly." Hegs wiped his puffy lips with a lace handkerchief and closed his eyes, like a man about to pray. With pious reverence, he spoke.

"Fortis, as a mother you must understand the natural worries that go with being a parent. At first you are concerned with the child's nourishment—their survival—then once you've sorted that out it's the child's development. Their minds, their place in the world, their character. Then you blink, they've grown, and you realize there's little left that you can do."

Fortis held her cup close to her mouth, studying the duke.

"All this worry," he continued, "eventually stacks up on itself like the stones of a great fortress until it's no longer bearable and someone *else* must manage the estate. Our children must become... both caretakers of *and* refuges for someone else's love and worry."

Jileanna's bejeweled limbs jangled as she wiggled in her chair to fix her posture. She straightened her back and somehow elongated her neck even more. She daintily dabbed her lips, smearing the paint on them further.

"I'm sure you've guessed by now," the duke continued, twisting his girth around to face Fortis squarely, "I'd like to speak with you about the arrangement of our children's marriage, Fortis."

His mother choked. Remaine's cup and saucer collided so violently in his hands he feared he had cracked them clean in half. Fortis's face turned cherry as she coughed.

"Surprise!" Jileanna clapped, swaying back and forth, her long neck like a ship's mast in the wind.

"What?" Remaine managed to squeak out.

"M–marriage? Our children?" Fortis pressed, clutching at her chest, still recovering from the tea which had gone down violently.

"Yes, companionship." Hegs' dove-like coo had a bite of annoyance. "I trust you and your fisherman must know something of it." His orange eyebrow reached a new height, fully colliding with his hairline. Tapping his daughter's leg, he added, "You'll find no fault in me for pursuing it for my Jileanna."

"N–no... no fault at all, Hubert. But—"

"Good. Then you must know it is Remaine Plink on whom my daughter has set her eyes. And, of course, I've assured her your son feels the same way, no doubt."

All the force of incoming high tide could not have washed the amazement from both of their faces. Remaine stared at the duke, blinking, trying to understand the duke's declaration.

"I..." he began, but there were no words. He looked at Jileanna, who was either very good at pretending not to notice their shock or was actually oblivious to it. She slid her fingers into her oiled hair, twisting a tight ringlet around a finger. He gaped at his mother, who gave him a severe look which could have meant any number of things. Safely, though, it meant to keep quiet.

"Hubert," said Fortis, "my son is… well… he's a *dockdweller*… he's a *Plink*. Arranged marriages only…"

"Take place among nobility, yes, yes, I know." Hegs' gaze wandered off the balcony. "And yet, on occasion, a swan chooses to condescend to a seagull, as you well know."

Fortis's face flushed. "I admit you've caught me off guard, Du—Hubert. But surely you must know, especially in light of your present allusion, I of all people am not one to hand my son over to someone in an arrangement. If it is not something he wants—"

"—Tell me, Fortis, what do *you* want?"

The question effectively squeezed Remaine and Jileanna right out of the scene. But they were not out of it, they were in it, forced to listen to the grownups converse in their cryptic way.

"Me?" she stumbled, "But, what—"

"Am I to understand that you, yourself, are drowning in happiness down in the Salt District? The Sorceress of Soap has no qualms with her charmed existence?"

Fortis blinked, and her mouth, previously ajar with surprise, closed into a small, straight line.

"I thought not," Hegs purred, triumphantly. "Your father was a chairman of the reefstone trade, Fortis. Durable, reliable stuff. In just the past five years Ravillion Bay has requested a small fleet's worth of the stuff for work being done in Mirror Pass! The Cracklemore Isles are shot through with blue and orange—the color of coin, as I recall Count Diaquinn calling it. And we all know he suffered no shortage of *that*. You and I both know of the piles he left behind—I imagine they haunt the occasional daydream of yours? I think, if you ask me, the swan married the seagull, yet often she misses the lavish comforts of the freshwater lakes."

His mother's hands began to tremble, so she set them to smoothing out the folds of her skirt. Then she asked, without looking at Hegs, "And what is it, exactly, that *you* want, Hubert?"

"I already told you. The marriage of my daughter with your son."

"Me to him!" said Jileanna zealously, flinging her long bony arm across the table to point at Remaine. Her heavy voice, coupled with the sound of her clashing bracelets, startled Remaine.

It was Fortis's turn to raise her eyebrows. She kept her tone even. "I've already told you, Hubert, my son bears the Plink name. Your family's reputation would be tarnished by a union such as this."

None of it really made clear sense to him, but Remaine did know, vaguely, of what his mother spoke. He was a dockdweller. That's where he belonged. On the docks. People on Lily Ridge belonged on Lily Ridge. He pictured the gleaming, spotless display of Hegs' honorariums and medals, and tried to see it all covered with fish guts.

But the tranquil smile on the duke's face as he looked out over Windluff suggested something different.

"Which is why I inquired of you as to your desires, Lady *Diaquinn*," said Hegs. Remaine had heard his late grandfather's name before, but never had someone called his mother Diaquinn. She was a Plink.

Hegs continued, and once again spoke in the mysterious, cryptic way. "You'd do well to think long and hard about those desires. If Jileanna were to be married into the Plink family, well, its current state could use some… improvement." His pink, watery eyes glinted like a cat's.

"Its current state…" his mother repeated.

Hegs sipped his tea and again turned his gaze out over the city and across to the Royal Docks. Seagulls screeched from below—the sounds of their whole world rose up to them in their cries.

"And what, precisely, are you proposing, Duke?" asked his mother.

Remaine gawked at her. She wasn't actually considering this, was she? *A marriage? To Jileanna Hegs?*

Hubert Hegs smiled wickedly. "You've fallen a long way from Lily

Ridge. What's his would be hers—which of course is nothing. But what's hers would be his… and yours, Fortis. I will take you in. Here. Back home to Lily Ridge."

"You mention only me."

"You and your children, of course. I will secure your son a position in a less… aromatic trade. Your daughter will leave labor and enter into good society as is fitting for a young lady…" (Jileanna batted her eyes in approval at this) "and your name will be lifted from the muck of the eternal swamp in which it is currently mired, forever destined, and the Plink name will mean something great after I arrange for its exaltation."

"Its exaltation?" Remaine asked.

Hegs blinked in Remaine's direction for what felt like the first time in hours.

"I *am* the royally appointed Duke of Windluff and the greater Moorington Isle, young man. As I said, I bear the responsibility with a humble and determined heart. Cleaning up a ruined reputation is all in a day's work for me."

"It sounds like you intend to scrub the Plink reputation clean of its very essence," said Fortis. "And of the members which make up its heart. What becomes of my husband in this gracious offer of yours?"

Hegs smiled at her, then leaned forward. He removed the upside-down wooden bowl from the plate of butterfin, washing them all in the delicious smell of creamy garlic butter. Then he picked up his fork with a grip so delicate Remaine could not help but marvel at the grace. It was like watching five baby seals synchronize themselves to cradle a flower between them. After a moment of turning the fish over, he stabbed a particularly juicy chunk and placed it on his wide tongue where it was rolled away, disappearing inside his mouth.

Hegs closed his eyes. "Mmm," he sighed.

He stood up and lumbered heavily to the edge of the balcony, gripping the banister. Then, after a moment, as if he had taken a short nap and had woken refreshed, he spoke again with a voice frothy and light once more.

"I have it on good report the Plink butterfin is something of a delicacy on the docks."

"Um... yes... it is", said Fortis, scrunching her brow at the change of subject.

"I've been made aware that His Enchanted, Prince Xietas Ravillion, wishes to partake."

Fortis and Remaine stared at one another, dumbfounded.

"We've made all the arrangements. The Plinks will serve the prince and his men at the Tour of Valor in two days' time."

"T–two days... Hubert—I—we—"

"To the prince?" Remaine gawked.

"Isn't it *spectacular*!" clapped Jileanna, fanning her face with delight. "The *prince*!"

"I trust you will not refuse His Enchanted?" said Hegs sweetly.

"Of course not," said Fortis. Remaine could tell his mother was reeling from the explosion of information lying in pieces all around them. "It's just that we—" began his mother, "well—I mean—butterfin can be hard to catch—"

"See that it's done, Miss Plink. We wouldn't want the royal family disappointed." Hegs' tone was final, cold, and suddenly, both Fortis and Remaine knew there was no room left in the conversation.

Remaine had gone numb, yet by some miracle managed to stand to his feet as his mother did so. He tried to mimic her movements in keeping composure.

Jileanna stood too, and gave a huge curtsy, bumping her elbow on the table on the way down.

"Thank you for tea, Duke Hegs," said Remaine's mother. "If that's all, we will let ourselves out."

She grabbed Remaine's shoulder and pulled him along.

"You can't survive alone, Miss Plink," said Hegs, before they were out of earshot. "The frost in Philo's blood is well known. Don't forget, I was there. I remember that voyage well—the way your foolish husband got himself into trouble."

His mother paused stiffly, and Remaine did too. He looked up at her face, but she was elsewhere. Her gaze was distant and glazed.

"It's been six years," continued Hegs, "but it might as well be sixteen. There's no hiding it. Your fisherman won't last much longer—and the time for your elders to refuse the Call of the East has expired. This, too, is known."

When they were at last alone in the carriage and descending Lily Ridge, Remaine asked his mother, "Mom, I don't have to marry Jileanna, right?"

Fortis reached for her vial with a shaking hand, then brought it to her lips, releasing a stream of freezing breath. The blue, wispy snake spiraled from her mouth then spun itself into the bottle. She corked the top firmly. A calmness fell upon her. She leaned forward.

"Let's focus on the Tour, Remaine. How does that sound?"

He nodded slowly, pretending it helped.

"For now, let's keep all this hushed, yes?"

He stared at her.

"I'll sort the pieces out—not to worry." She chewed her lip and stared out the window as they lurched along down the hill. "Put things in their proper place and peace will come to all," she whispered to no one really, then she flashed him a quick smile. "Let's get out on the water."

CHAPTER 5

THE TOUR OF VALOR

NEVER HAD THE PLINK FAMILY felt more resolved to catch fish than they were the following day. Work began before dawn.

Lady Vex was the first out on the water, her stern cutting through the glassy surface, still untouched by the daily winds. The peaceful film which covered the Pearl Sea was pierced, rather violently, by the determined Plinks who lined the bow, spears in hand, and nets slung over their backs.

The Plinks had never before been summoned to the banquet table of the royal family, and the sheer magnitude of the summons forced all but Millie Plink into the water. Even Fortis, who—she realized upon taking her three deep breaths—had not dived in several years, leapt from the side of *Lady Vex* determinedly, her mind on nothing else but the capture of the coy butterfin, swimming somewhere in the labyrinth of the Butterfin Caves.

Most notably, the significance of the situation had even brought life to fragile Philo Plink. Though he could not dive, he forced himself into the water to help with the netting, and by mid-afternoon, the Pearl Sea had thoroughly washed his Plink skin, and there was a hint of life back in his eyes.

"Remaine," hollered Philo. "Hold this here, will you?"

Remaine watched as his father struggled to tread water as he worked to tie the net off. It was one of the more basic tasks, but it proved a challenge for Philo. Reluctantly, Remaine swam over to help. Remaine was anxious to help but nervous to draw near for fear of what conversation might come. His fear was not without reason. Within a minute of helping his father, the both of them silently kicking beneath the water as they fought to keep their heads and shoulders steady, Philo asked Remaine the dreaded question again.

"So, you still haven't told me, Remaine," Philo coughed, as a bit of water splashed into his face. "What did you catch during your Dive?"

"Hey! Remaine!" Silome shouted from behind, and Remaine quickly whirled around to find her hanging on at the side of the boat, feigning a scene of struggle to hoist her pack of fish from the water. "Help me out!"

Remaine said nothing to his father and kicked away speedily.

"Thanks," Remaine mumbled. His sister had been oddly supportive of him lately, and he found himself, perhaps for the first time in his life, thankful for her presence.

"Can't hold him off forever, Rem," she said quietly, pushing the fish pack up with ease. Remaine did not even have to help her in the slightest.

This was how the previous day had gone too, and Remaine knew his sister was right. His father had woken up before lunch yesterday, and for the following six hours, it was all his father could do just to keep his eyes open, to eat, to drink, to listen to the world around him. His mother had placed a bowl of clamlets in front of Philo, as she always did. He cracked them open mindlessly. Something about it kept him calm and focused. By evening, his father was coming-to, and Remaine could sense his awareness growing. Remaine managed to scurry off to bed and fake sleep by the time his father asked about Remaine's Dive.

"You'll have to ask him yourself," he had heard his mother say. His grandparents had kept silent too, retiring to bed early as well.

Remaine had made it a point to wake up as early as he could, scarf down a piece of bread, then make his way out to the docks to prepare *Lady Vex* for the day at sea, just so he would not have to linger in the home alongside his father.

Philo had then approached Remaine during their voyage out to Mariner's Cliff, and Remaine had managed to dodge the question by pretending to see a butterfin, which brought the boat to a halt. After no fish was found, Remaine slipped to the opposite end of *Lady Vex*, putting as much distance between himself and his father as possible, and the very moment *Lady Vex* arrived at the family fishing spot, he took to the water.

After Silome's aid in drawing him away from their father, Remaine dove once more, and this time made his way to the place he had been dying to get to since the night the Great Charming passed him by.

Remaine closed his eyes and lay back on the wet rock. A nap on his perch—it might be his only true escape. Somehow, within a week, his entire life had collapsed in on him. Not that it was anything worthwhile to begin with, but now it was truly, terribly worthless. Dive-disaster and potential allergy to the Charming aside, was he really going to have to marry Jileanna Hegs? Remaine barely understood the point of getting married anyway—it all gave him a squirmy feeling still. Why him? What did she see in him anyway? Maybe if he showed her his empty vial... maybe *that* would repulse her...

He was about to drift away into one of his stories—perhaps the one where he and Igniro dive fearlessly to the bottom of the sea—when a voice came from behind.

"The elusive hideout," she said, and Remaine nearly cracked his head open on the low rocky overhang trying to get up. He whipped around and found his sister wringing out her dripping wet hair.

"Silome!" was all he managed to sputter. Much to his horror, she was examining his mural.

"No wonder you don't catch anything, Rem," she said, eyes locked on his work. "Unbelievable." She said this last word almost to herself, hands on her hips. "You did all this?"

He stared at her, frozen with embarrassment. What would his family say if they could see the proof of their theories? He was, indeed, lost in another world.

"How long have you been at this?"

Remaine hesitated then mumbled, "I dunno. Five years or so. Sometime after you started traveling with the League of Young Traders."

Silome looked at Remaine with a guilty expression. He knew she couldn't help being so good at everything. What was she supposed to do when a bunch of fancy folk showed up offering to mentor her at some posh university once a year for a month or so? Naturally the whole thing made the Plinks swell with pride. For the past five years they waved her off to learn more, make connections, bring glory to the Plink name.

It had yet to amount to anything, though. That's what Remaine told himself when he'd escape to the cave and draw pictures.

"You're not bad," said Silome, casually. His stomach turned a bit. The shark never dangled compliments except to bait the smaller fish. She stroked the lines of the mariner's wild hair, her face a mask of convincing appreciation.

"You won't tell them, will you?"

She looked at him with eyes which matched his almost exactly in color and shape, then she said, and Remaine believed her when she said it: "No." She even looked like she wanted to say more, instead she turned back to his mural.

"What did Hegs want with you?"

"I dunno," he lied. He was glad he and his mother agreed to not talk about that part of tea with Hegs.

Silome eyed him critically.

Then he asked, "What's wrong with me, Silome?" The question leaked out of his mouth without his permission, then drifted over to his sister, impossible to retract. He did not like talking with Silome about anything which drew attention to the chasm between the two, and here he just gave it to her so freely, the opportunity for ridicule. And again, Silome surprised him.

"If you don't receive the Great Charming, Remaine, I think you'll still be all right."

A stinging sensation in his eyes made him look away. A terrible lump swelled in his throat. Not eager to explore why it was there, he simply nodded, grabbed his net pack, and stepped up to the edge of his perch. Remaine glanced over his shoulder. "Thanks for keeping my secret."

"I've known about this place for a while, Remaine." Silome shook her head as Remaine paused. "It's not like you're subtle. I've just kept my distance."

"Why?"

"I can respect you've got secrets, Rem. Now, come on. I caught enough butterfin for the both of us."

Remaine dove into the water.

The Ravillion dynasty had a very long, very peaceful reign in the Cracklemore Isles—so long, in fact, most people had lost count of exactly when their reign began.

The university professors boasted knowledge of some recorded inauguration five hundred years prior. But if one asked any regular mud-covered layperson, say, Deeno Plink, for example, the Ravillion bloodline was at least ten thousand years old.

The royal family, made up of His High Enchanted, King Ignis Ravillion, and the king's son, His Enchanted, Prince Xietas Ravillion, was a very busy family.

Of their many responsibilities was the annual Tour of Valor, delegated to and overseen entirely by the prince. The Tour was an endless current of recruitment, and the prince's itinerary always brought him to Windluff at the end of summer just as the leaves on the trees of Roosterhall Valley, and those dotting Lily Ridge, hastened to change color, zealous themselves to participate in wearing the ceremonial red with all the rest.

The long, realized peace of the Ravillion reign, despite its effortless appearance, was hard-earned, which is why the royals were so busy. Their family recalled the cold years of war and death, the days which saw the quakes that resulted in the Cracklemore Isles, formerly a single land. So, they worked tirelessly to ensure those days of bloodshed never returned, which is why the recruitment tool of the Tour of Valor was born and the red was donned.

The Tour of Valor tent had been erected at the highest point in Windluff, atop Mariner's Cliff. It overlooked the city, the royal docks, and even Lily Ridge. For leagues out to sea it shone like a dazzling ruby lit by a thousand torches.

A line of horse-drawn carriages streaming with red flags peppered the serpentine road leading up to the cliff. What was a duty for Xietas Ravillion was a festival throughout Windluff and all of Moorington, along with every other city in Cracklemore visited by the Tour. Thus, the nobility arrived, one by one, bedecked in rubies and red silks as crimson leaves swirled around the clifftop in celebration.

Off to one side of the Tour's tent sat a much smaller tent. Besides its customary red color, it was altogether designed to disappear from view. No torches lit it from the outside, and its inhabitants were instructed to stay inside until the proper time. To the members of Windluff's highest echelon, it was invisible to the senses unless, of course, they came close enough to use their noses.

A plume of steam, infused with lemon, garlic, and butter, among other things, drifted off plates and filled the unassuming tent. The smell had a power of its own, evinced in the burst of life which flowed through Millie Plink, once again bent at the waist, nose inches from the creamy, butterfin dishes. On any other night, she and Deeno would be fast asleep by now. But even with the tumultuous turn of events with their grandson, it was the call for butterfin, and the chance to serve the crown prince of the Cracklemore Isles that brought new brightness to their eyes. Occasionally Millie would plunge a crooked pinky into the sauce, lick it, smack her lips, then move on to the next dish to do it again. Now and then she'd put her pinky into Deeno's mouth. They would both nod and move along to the next dish, all the while muttering to themselves. The other Plinks stood by, holding their breath, awaiting orders.

Under the strict surveillance of Fortis Plink, the butterfin workstations had been meticulously ordered. They usually were, even if they were only serving at the Brinymore Round, but tonight, even the bricks beneath the tables straightened up beneath her gaze.

Behind Fortis Plink's spotless scene, however, the rest of the long kitchen tent had been given over to the erratic chaos of the Oswich family.

All afternoon the Plinks had worked in their corner of the kitchen tent amid the mayhem. The Oswich crates, filled with live chickens that morning, had been slowly depleted of their contents as the day wore on in order to prepare the dishes for the chairmen and other nobility. Where the fully functioning Oswich circus had taken up residence behind the Plinks, chicken feathers and feces now filled the tent with a smell far worse than fish—a smell so vile that Remaine's mother had commented on it more than once, and a smell so terrible that it had earned a continual stream of curses from Gramma Millie.

"A plague on chickens!" she mumbled repeatedly into her apron, and "The Cold Old freeze 'em dead!"

"I think you mean Old Cold, Gramma."

"DEAD!" she barked.

"It looks wonderful, ladies!" bellowed Harlo Oswich, the eldest son. He and his five scarecrow-like brothers lived on the other side of the hill in the Roosterhall Valley. Pale, dirty faced, all of them with the same tangled grayish hair, they danced about as if their limbs were held up by strings. Harlo was chasing a loose chicken past the Plinks. Gramma Millie took a deep breath.

"Don't mind me!" Harlo shouted. "Sorry! Sorry!" Harlo seized the chicken by its legs and held it upside down. It made a valiant attempt at another escape, noisily, alongside Millie Plink's head. Her thin hair parted like shallow water just above her ear as the chicken flapped away.

"They're faster than you think!" Harlo laughed. "And more slippery than your fish, even! I certainly won't miss the chase."

"Miss it?" said Fortis, "Harlo, are you—"

"—Volunteering. Yes!" he could hardly hold in his thrill. His bird's-nest hair whipped about his face as he flashed her a grin. "The boys are all old enough to help with the farm now."

"Your family must be very proud," Gramma Millie said curtly. Harlo and his chicken had clearly worn out their welcome.

"Oh boy, are they!" exclaimed Harlo.

Remaine stole a glance at the other Oswich boys. Like the Plinks, they were helping prepare the plates as well, and something told him they would greatly miss their eldest brother.

"I hear your butterfin is quite special," said Harlo.

Millie Plink let loose a loud exhale.

"Tell me what's in your sauce and I'll tell you what's in ours," he grinned.

"Do you know what all this is, Master Oswich?" said Remaine's gramma with more lucidity than he had seen in years.

Harlo watched as she smoothed the sauce with the back of a spoon. He shook his stringy head.

"Neither does anyone else," Millie looked at Harlo and gave him a terse smile. "A Plink secret. But if you hang that chicken any closer to my head, there will be one ingredient in here that we'll all know about."

Harlo's face hung blankly before her, the chicken still elevated between them. He lowered the flapping bird to his side and returned to his messy end of the tent.

"Good," said Millie, hands on her hips. "Cover the plates and keep them warm. I've done my part. All I ask is—"

"I do the talking," said Fortis, placing a hand on Millie's shoulder. "Don't worry."

"Good," said Grampa Deeno, "because you's the only one that's ever been in there before."

"You *are*," corrected Fortis, gently. "That was so long ago I hardly remember it, Deeno."

"Long ago is better than never. All our bellies will turn to water in front of them fancy lords. You at least have seen inside the tent."

"You've both done wonderfully," Fortis reassured them. "I'm sure the prince will love it."

But Remaine saw the nerves tighten across his mother's face.

Once the lids had been placed, Remaine peeled back a corner of the heavy red entrance-curtain to have a peek outside.

The sun had set over the crisp horizon. A field of hilltop grass rippled like water. Nearly a stone's throw away stood the massive sister tent to the one he stood in now. The tent for the Tour of Valor. It towered above them, perched atop Mariner's Cliff like a sentinel pyramid. Its blood red color had gone dark with the setting sun, but where its base had been lit by spiraling iron torches, the vibrancy of the red shone like fire.

The final carriages were arriving now, and with them the last of the chairmen, all their shoulders feathered with customary epaulettes, and the nobles of the city who would be dining in the tent. Among them was the Pellatrim family.

The Pellatrims came from a high-born pedigree, and every one of them dazzled. Torrin, the eldest Pellatrim, had joined the guard so long ago Remaine had no real memory of him. But Remaine knew Torrin's younger brother, Tarquin, who stepped out of the carriage alongside his regal parents. For as long as Remaine could remember, Tarquin Pellatrim was one of those boys who looked ten years older than his peers. Even tonight, though Tarquin was exactly Remaine's age—freshly twelve years old—he looked as if he might be eighteen. Their brief interactions in the annual lectures proved to Remaine he'd never find a starker opposite. From a young age, Tarquin had undergone private combat training, as had his older brother. Both Tarquin boys, like their father, were of strong blood and built like lions, with shining blemish-free skin and golden hair and eyes like bronze shields.

The Pellatrims strutted confidently into the tent.

At that moment, a gaudy carriage with an ivory finish produced what appeared to be a very ripe, very large cherry, followed by the twig from which it fell. Remaine's stomach tightened, and had Silome not been standing right there, he would have let out an audible moan. Hubert Hegs and his daughter, Jileanna, fell into the scene in a blinding display of ruby silk.

At the entrance of the tent, six royal guards, also decorated in the customary crimson, bordered the opening. They bowed their heads to the duke and his daughter. Jileanna replied with a dramatic curtsy. The Plinks watched as Hubert Hegs limped forward, heavy on his cane, to greet the guards. Even from their fair distance away, they could hear him laughing with the men.

"Poor Hegs," said Silome dryly, "wedged so tightly in his glory years. Forever stuck. Now he's just…" she paused as Hegs clearly motioned towards his leg, almost certainly breaking into his very tired and tragic monologue that told the tale of his heroic sacrifice that led to his injured leg, and so on and so forth. "He's just… a peacock."

Remaine watched as Silome rolled her eyes and returned to Gramma and Grampa who were still fussing over the butterfin and keeping the plates warm. Remaine felt a tug at his arm and turned to find his father standing beside him.

"Remaine," the voice was hoarse, and barely audible above the kitchen frenzy. "Here, son."

His father produced from behind his back a lump of familiar red fabric, patched in several places. For as long as Remaine could remember, his father had donned this red dress shawl for the Tour of Valor.

Everyone other than the nobility celebrated the Tour down at the sea wall, cheering on the parade of new recruits as they sailed away. Then came the music and the dancing, and the fireworks—bright red sparks that spilled and showered for hours. The fireworks were the best part of the whole tour.

"Your gramma made it for me when I was your age. It'll fit big—did me. But you'll grow into it. It's a… it's time you have it, I think." He smiled at Remaine in a strained sort of way. A genuine concern lived in that smile. He bent his head forward as his father fastened the shawl around him. Only when he looked up did he notice his entire family watching them. Their faces were tragically hopeful, as if the donning of his father's shawl would suddenly fix everything that was wrong with him. He smiled up at his father, then over at his family.

"Now," his father said, "tell me. Your Dive. What did—"

The seam at the tent's entrance flew open suddenly to the scarlet spectacle of Hubert and Jileanna Hegs, followed by the duke's ratty manservant.

To her credit, Jileanna had made every effort to appear as glamorous as her father. On her arms and her neck, she had bedecked herself with hundreds of golden bands and sparkling rubies which slid and clattered every time she wiggled. Her cheeks were saturated in a violet powder, and every feature of her face had been outlined in thick black paint. Hegs made no effort to introduce anyone to anyone, instead, his eyes zeroed in on Fortis and Remaine.

"Ah, Miss Plink. How delicious our timing is. And young Remaine." Hegs' gaze slid down from Fortis' face, landing briefly on Remaine. He said nothing more to the boy. At least nothing with words. After a prolonged beat, Hegs added, "I've come to give the food a quick inspection."

"My Lord Duke," said Deeno Plink. He and Millie wiped their hands on their aprons which they then clumsily and quickly removed to reveal their formal red attire. "You're more than welcome to see the dishes. I didn't realize you was inspecting."

"I usually don't," said Hegs. "But this year feels special, I think, given the Plink debut." Hegs quickly eyed Fortis before scanning each Plink, his gaze lingering the longest on Philo.

Then the world became very still as the large mass of Hubert Hegs bent over each plate, swelling in size as he breathed in deeply the butterfin aroma. All was silent as they watched his enormously round backside move sideways making its way from plate to plate—silent, save for one voice.

"It smells so wonderful, Remmy," breathed Jileanna Hegs. She had cozied up so close they were touching from shoulder to ankle. She stood nearly a foot taller than Remaine, and her neck arched over him like a palm tree. "I could eat every one of these plates!"

Remaine forced a smile in her direction.

"Remmy, have you gone to the Palace of Pools to pour out the Old Cold yet?"

Once the Old Cold was collected into vials, citizens of Cracklemore would visit the Palace of Pools to wash it all away forever. Remaine had never been inside Windluff's Palace of Pools, and with his empty vial, he probably never would. He shook his head. "No. Not yet."

"Good. Listen, how about tomorrow, you and me—"

"I think this will work out splendidly," cooed Hegs, spinning from the plates of fish to face the rest of the Plink family. "His Enchanted eagerly awaits his dinner. After you have served you may watch the rest of the ceremony from the back. Oh, and the prince asked for another plate to be made for a special guest backstage, so be sure to give that plate to Poolish here and he'll see it delivered. All clear?"

Every Plink, save for Fortis and Silome, who both appeared up for the task, stared with frozen expressions.

"Good. Poolish, lead on. Jileanna, shall we?"

The mousy manservant bowed before Hegs, his hands clasped firmly behind his back, and began to back out of the tent. Hubert and Jileanna Hegs followed him. The Plinks covered the plates with crystal domes before assembling them all onto rolling carts. Fortis counted quietly to herself, checking and double-checking the amount. Silome fell in beside her to triple-check. They began to walk out of the tent, following Poolish, the duke, and his daughter.

Remaine felt a tap on his shoulder. He turned to discover his father at his side, head drooped.

"Anyway, Rem, I'm sorry I missed your Dive."

"Remaine. Philo." Fortis called to them from behind. "It's time."

Remaine whispered a quick prayer of gratitude. He knew he would eventually have to tell his father. But not tonight.

A crisp, coastal wind kissed Remaine's face as he left the humid kitchen-tent.

Poolish moved quickly, too quickly for a family pushing carts of delicately plated butterfin. Still, they hurried after the hunched little man around the backside of the ceremonial tent, finally piercing their way through a back corridor of overlapping fabric. They made their way along the dark passages of rich, red drapes. A slit in the fabric revealed a spectacular inner world of gold and chandeliers. Hundreds of candles cast a warm glow in the vaulted canopy, reflecting a thousand times over in the countless rubies which shone from long elegant necks, or in the case of Hubert Hegs, a thick, jeweled belt that he already appeared to regret wearing judging by the way he kept re-adjusting it. Then the scene was gone in a flash as the Plinks continued to shuffle through the corridor to the back.

A few moments later, the darkness was flooded with light once more as a figure burst through the curtains, nearly tackling Fortis.

"King and *crab*!" bellowed their grampa, nearly tumbling over.

But the startled family quickly recovered at the sight of Cressa Merchant.

"Cressa!" said Fortis, louder than she intended.

"Shh!" hissed Poolish, his face screwing up in alarm.

"I saw you all coming in and I just had to sneak over!" said Cressa. Her thin face stretched wide in a smile. She positively glowed. Remaine could not remember a time seeing her this happy, and certainly not within the past year since Estin left.

"Cressa, where have you been!" whispered Fortis, a laugh escaping her at the sight of her elated friend. "I haven't seen you since you were summoned by the duke."

"Oh, Fortis," she cupped Fortis's face in her dark hands. "And my Plinks," she pulled Silome in for an embrace, then Remaine. "I was invited to dine and stay at the Royal Suite. I've been there all week. Oh, just *wait* till you see! How *wrong* I was! Just wait till you *see*!"

She kissed Fortis on the cheek, wishing them all luck, refusing to divulge any more for fear of ruining the surprise. Then she was gone in a swish of fabric as the curtains closed behind her.

The Plinks wheeled their carts carefully into a dark chamber lit by one, skinny shaft of light which seemed to cut the small space in half. The light came from the stage, and so, the Plinks stood in the wings, waiting.

Poolish held a finger to his lips, eyes wide and blinking. Never had a man looked so serious. His concern was superfluous, though, because every Plink stood paralyzed with nerves. Not a one of them would have dreamt of making a sound, especially as the chatter in the tent died down leaving nothing but an expectant stillness.

Music came next. The small orchestra was just visible from their place backstage. Remaine watched as the bows slid up and down, bringing to life the familiar anthem of the Cracklemore Isles. Most of the room remained hidden from view, but the front row was quite visible. Hubert and Jileanna Hegs rose to their feet, followed by the rest of the men and women. Their attention turned toward the aisle behind them, and Remaine waited with anticipation, knowing the prince had entered the tent.

The first down the aisle, stepping into view, was a small band of royal guardians, their usual gold and turquoise raiment traded in for scarlet, just for tonight. Remaine recognized one of them, the eldest Pellatrim, Torrin.

Behind the royal guardians lumbered a man who could not be mistaken to be anything other than their leader. The High Winged General Sir Vector Cottley was, without question, the largest human being Remaine had ever seen. He imagined if the general were the paternal type, he would be able to hoist Remaine up and cradle him like a baby. But by the looks of him, and the scars which split his face, this man was a far cry from fatherly.

Compared to the next figure, however, the high general was practically maternal.

Whether it was his gait, like an upright cobra, head held high, slithering forward, or his slanting brow and the way he interlaced his long fingers, Remaine imagined the prince's royal advisor—grand pinions, they are called—could only have been about as friendly as the snake he resembled. Unlike the hulking men in front of him, the prince's grand pinion was abnormally thin, and even more abnormally tall, and his eyes reflected the candles in a way even the rubies couldn't. He, too, had traded in his customary gold and turquoise garb for red robes, and slid in among the rest to prepare the way for another.

As quickly as the prince's entourage had slipped into view, they soon slipped out, leaving the small opening in the curtain to be filled, in full, with Prince Xietas Ravillion. The prince was unequivocally different in every way.

Whether five hundred years or ten thousand years, there was, of course, a singular reason why the Ravillion Dynasty had achieved such an expansive peace and had enjoyed such universal praise. Enchantment flowed through Ravillion veins more strongly even than the enchantment that comes to all in the Great Charming.

Heads dipped low in reverence, but not too much for fear of missing a moment. No one blinked, no one looked away, and not until the prince ascended the stage and turned to face the crowd, inviting them at last to sit, did anyone seem to even breathe.

"Good evening," said the prince. "And welcome to the Tour of Valor!"

A crashing applause tore through the tent, and the prince joined in as well. Remaine watched, mesmerized, as his crown sent beams of light dancing around the room. Though not as large as his general, nor as tall as his grand pinion, Prince Xietas Ravillion was somehow stronger and more commanding—a superior warrior, a lion next to house cats. He had dark, cropped hair beneath a humble, but fortified silver crown. And like all Ravillions, his silhouette was marked by his companion Singer, perched atop his shoulder—a massive, storm-cloud gray harpy eagle with a head as big as a dog's. Beneath the Singer's girth, any normal man would have hunched, but the prince stood tall and proud.

"Good evening, Windluff, and all who have traveled across Moorington," he said in his longer, smoother accent, cutting through the applause and praise, "thank you for the warm, Luffy welcome."

Prince Xietas smiled, then extended a hand. A goblet was placed there by the snake-like pinion right on cue. The prince raised the cup to his lips inviting the room to do the same.

"And don't you all look magnificent in red."

There was no applause at this. The prince's jaw hardened, and his brow raised sympathetically. The crowd was silent and serious. Remaine could see, at the front table, Hubert Hegs' meaty hand move from his belt to his heart.

"We don the scarlet dress for two reasons, don't we?"

Everyone bobbed their heads, their somber eyes locked on the prince. "We proudly wear the color of the blood of the warriors we've lost."

Light mutterings; a few sniffles.

The prince took his time, walking to the side of the stage where a large torch blazed gloriously. "And the heat of the red—" He paused, clutching his red cloak and holding it up, letting the flame wash over it, "—reminds us we will not be taken by the Cold."

The somber cloud evaporated in an explosion of cheers.

"Before we honor our Winged Warriors, though, we must feast. I am starving."

The prince flashed a handsome smile, and the crowd went wild. Everyone laughed, and some hollered, "Hear, hear!" or "I'm hungry!" and Hubert Hegs stood to his feet altogether in affirmation.

"In keeping with tradition," the prince said, "as we dine, we will enjoy a little entertainment, provided this evening by my loyal and brilliant advisor, Grand Pinion Lyme Stretcher of Thousand Falls."

Stretcher coiled over in a bow, his red robes pooling about him.

"Right!" the prince said, clapping his hands. "Dinner!"

At this, Poolish gave the Plinks a signal that looked either like a slit across the throat, or a motion for them to move. Remaine gulped, but Fortis nodded confidently, pushing her cart, the first to stride through the curtain's opening. One by one the Plinks followed suit, and suddenly they were on stage, blinking in the candlelight, while Poolish disappeared further into the shadows with the extra plate.

As the Plinks approached with their carts, Remaine saw the prince taking his seat in the center of the stage while Lyme Stretcher took his seat on the prince's right. The high general sat on the left of the prince, and the royal guard flanked three on either side.

These were the men who would feast on Plink butterfin tonight, and every last one of them looked hungrily at the small band of fishmen from the Salt District, as if they might forget themselves and eat the fishmen instead.

Fortis moved gracefully, leading the family to the prince, first. They had discussed it for an hour the night before, how they were to bow in a particular way, serve the food in a particular order, only make eye contact if invited, then hold the contact until the prince broke it first. They had discussed it thoroughly, and yet it was suddenly all gone from their memories. Up close, the prince radiated with an air of palpable power. Remaine's feet felt heavy, his hands tingled. Every one of the Plinks had gone pale before the prince, moving strangely, awkwardly, slowly. Had it not been for Fortis, the only Plink among them with a trace of instinct for how to conduct oneself in the presence of power, the Plinks would have lost the game right then.

As for Fortis, her bow was low, and the sight of it reminded Remaine of her lecture. He bowed too, and the rest of his family followed suit. All was quiet, then, as Fortis rose to begin the transfer of the covered trays from cart to table. Remaine knew his part. For now, he was to stand back. His mother alone would handle royalty.

"Ah," the prince said with a smile as Fortis removed the covering. The steam carried the buttery scent upwards. "Butterfin, is it?"

Fortis bowed her head. "Yes, Your Enchanted. A local delicacy, and our family special."

"That is what I hear. And from a good friend of mine. I have been looking forward to this. Plink. Am I saying that correctly?"

Every Plink cheek flushed pink. Fortis bowed her head slightly.

"Thank you, Plinks. Your name will be remembered."

Remaine did not feel his limbs at all after that. He hardly remembered serving the guards to the prince's right. At some point they said something to him, and he said something back, but when his mind finally returned to his body, he found himself in the darkness of backstage once more and Poolish was leading them to a small dining table that had been prepared for the family still within view of the stage. Six small plates of Oswich chicken and vegetables waited for them.

"Eat. Quickly." Poolish hissed. "And *watch*—for the slightest need, the slightest sign of discomfort, desire—an empty glass, a fallen spoon, a second helping…" Poolish's eyes were fixed on the stage as he laced his fingers together, then pulled them apart, then wove them together again.

Once they were seated, Remaine's mother leaned over and looked down the line at the stunned Plinks. "Well done!" she mouthed. "Well done!"

But there were no true congratulations just yet, even Fortis knew that.

Unable to touch their food, to blink their eyes, the Plinks leaned forward with bated breath, watching as the prince cut into his butterfin. No one was to take a bite until the prince chewed and swallowed his first.

He lifted the butterfin to his mouth. He chewed—slowly, thoughtfully. He closed his eyes, inhaled, and took *another* bite.

Millie let out a small whimper. Deeno's cheeks filled with air he refused to exhale.

The prince smiled and shook his head slightly. Then he stabbed a third piece of butterfin, and held it up, pointing his fork towards the opening in the curtain. He looked directly at the Plinks and smiled, then stuffed the bite of fish into his mouth with relish.

Millie collapsed into Deeno's lap. He fanned her face and wiped a single tear from his eye. "Of sails and songbirds…" he said breathlessly. "I never…"

Remaine grinned widely as he saw his parents embrace. His father popped a clamlet into his mouth happily, a rare sight. Even Silome cracked a small smile before stabbing her fork into her piece of chicken and lifting it up whole. All at once, Remaine's appetite swelled in his stomach like a great big bubble. He grabbed a bread roll and stuffed it into his smiling mouth. It had been a horrible week, but tonight… tonight was good.

They had only been eating for a few minutes when applause broke out, welcoming Grand Pinion Lyme Stretcher to the stage. Even the prince set down his fork to clap. From their shadowy corner, the Plinks followed suit.

The pinion brought silence with a single motion of his slender hand. Then from the folds of his red robes he produced an old lantern.

There was nothing spectacular about the lantern. Its top and bottom were made of gold, humbly molded into a simple design. Its glass was blackened around the edges and the fat, half-melted candle inside flickered as Stretcher held up its light.

Then he snapped his long, spidery fingers, and everything changed.

A loud crack ripped across the tent. Something shifted. Remaine felt it deep in his belly. Then he noticed the shadows.

The poised expressions of the Windluffian nobility had changed—eyebrows were raised, mouths had fallen open, and the shadows, cast about them by the thousand other candles in the tent, had shifted and shimmered. The lights above were moving.

All the flames, as if lopped off their candles by invisible knives, had separated from their waxy bases, and began to float towards the stage.

Stretcher opened the little glass door to the lantern with a tiny squeak. Then the flames rushed in, at least as many as could fit, with the rest left to orbit around Stretcher like bees around a hive. The lantern burned as bright as the sun and, with nothing but an odd little hum from Stretcher, they burst out again, a million little flames thrown about the stage, hovering at different levels in the air.

People began to ooh and ahh from the audience. Some cheered and applauded, but backstage, Remaine became a statue. He had never seen magic like this.

Stretcher snapped his fingers again.

At first it all seemed random, but as Stretcher began to speak, the small, floating tongues of fire split and spread out, some glommed onto others and grew in size, while others flitted about or shrank until a definitive scene came to life. The flames began to form the shapes of different figures and their surroundings.

Then Stretcher spoke.

"Before the land cracked and caved and split beneath our feet, the Cracklemore Isles were joined as one and the Ravillions reigned in peace." Stretcher paused as the drops of light formed the shape of a throne, where a king sat, and perched on his shoulder, a Songbird.

"The Winged Dynasty."

Another boom of applause. Remaine clapped too, and his eyes darted to the prince, who watched stoically from his seat. The prince took another bite of his butterfin.

"The peace was challenged… the *Berylbones*!"

From the edge of the stage, a fraction of the huddled flames grew brighter, their tops no longer flickering, but blazing now an icy blue. As Stretcher continued, the blue flames gathered together to form the silhouettes of tall, speared warriors who collided with the yellow glow of the king and his subjects in a blaze of green.

"*Boy!*" hissed Poolish.

Remaine blinked and looked up at the mousy man, suddenly hunched over him. "The prince! He's requested *more*!" Poolish's eyes blazed with a fury bright enough to rival Stretcher's lantern.

Stunned, Remaine forced his gaze away from the dazzling display of candlelight to find his mother replenishing two of the guards' plates on one end. His sister and grandparents were at the far end of the table doing the same for the other guards.

Remaine looked at his father, who had a hand placed to his forehead. Remaine knew the look well—if he moved, he would be sick.

"*Move!*" said Poolish, shoving Remaine forward.

The prince welcomed Remaine warmly, nodding to him with

a courteous smile. His deep, dark eyes glanced from the show over Remaine's shoulder, then back to Remaine's face.

Keep eye contact. All right, now collect his plate—wait! Eye contact again! Freeze. All right—move again. The plate. WAIT! Eye contact!

With trembling hands, Remaine collected the prince's used plate which had been cleaned almost spotlessly. Remaine turned around to place the tray on the cart, and in doing so, noticed his mother looking at him, her eyes wide.

At the same moment, the high general cleared his throat behind him, all the while a thousand yellow candle flames danced about his head.

"And so, our horizons must be protected!" bellowed Stretcher. The audience cheered. Orange light collided with blue in a splash of heat and color.

His mother was mouthing something to him. Remaine froze, eyes wide, desperate to understand. She tried again.

"*Don't. Turn. Your. Back!*"

Remaine whipped around, suddenly aware of what he had done.

The prince was smirking at Remaine. He gave Remaine a wink, but the massive bird on his shoulder was unraveling Remaine from head to toe. The black, bottomless eyes of the harpy bore into his very core, and then the bird disarmed him all together. It stretched its neck out, swooping its head down and towards him as if to eat him.

The prince stirred, curious. The high general next to the prince also noticed and twisted in his seat.

Stretcher's voice sang from behind, "And we celebrate the valor of the men who volunteer!"

The crowd cheered again; the room grew suddenly bright as the floating flames swelled in size for the grand finale. At this, the bird retracted its neck, coiling back into position on the prince's shoulder. The tension waned. Trembling, Remaine bowed before the prince, and without even giving him the chance to make eye contact, threw a plate of fresh butterfin on the table and backed away. Then Fortis was there, dressing the fish, refilling the prince's goblet, bowing, and backing away with her son and until the both of them, and the rest of the Plinks, were hidden backstage once more.

Poolish gawked at Remaine, horrified. The other Plinks shifted uncomfortably. Remaine gave a hard swallow and looked over his shoulder, expecting to see the stage on fire because of his actions. He was relieved to find, instead, Lyme Stretcher returning to his seat, the candles around the room topped once more with their flames, and the prince, casually poking at the butterfin with his fork once more.

They all breathed.

Before too long, the prince took center stage once more. The room filled with applause, and as far as Remaine could tell, all memories of his impropriety had burned away like the wicks of the candles.

"Lords and ladies," the prince said, "We train our men of valor for many years before they are strong enough to travel to Pylon Crag to face the endless tide of Berylbone invaders. Our men must rank from Shield to Sword, and keep their position through the trials, before they can go with us. For some, this takes a decade. For a rare few, half that. Which is why, I am delighted to celebrate with you, tonight, an absolute anomaly."

Whispers sizzled throughout the tent. The Plinks looked at one another, puzzled. Poolish managed to compose himself from the embarrassment he felt on Remaine's behalf earlier and peeked his head around the curtain.

"One of your very own, a 'Luffy', as you say—"

Some chuckled. "Aye!" shouted some others.

"—has confounded the best of us in the East. In just one year, he has proven himself formidable; his talent, unparalleled. Only one year after volunteering and he has returned home so you all may bear witness to this unprecedented advancement as we grant him, tonight, the new rank of Sword."

The people were leaning forward in their seats now, searching for anyone among them who might have a clue as to who the boy could be. It was unheard of, Remaine knew, for anyone to return home within five years—but a *single* year?

That's when Remaine saw her, there, practically hidden among the jeweled guests in her simple red frock, and altogether inconspicuous, except for now, her eyes wide with motherly pride. He knew exactly who it was.

"Please welcome along with me, Estin Merchant!"

The tent erupted once more in celebration. The Plinks huddled around the opening in the curtain. A glistening tear rolled down Cressa's cheek. Even Hegs appeared intrigued by the promise of the picturesque warrior who strode onto the stage.

Estin Merchant was categorically transformed. If the prince had not said his name, Remaine doubted any of the Plinks would have recognized the formidable figure before them.

His shoulders, plated in full, ceremonial armor, had nearly doubled in size, and on his head was a regal helmet, cleverly formed in the shape of the king's macaw. A heavy red robe concealed his form, but extending out from the center, Estin held his hands open, palms up. Resting on his gloved fingers was a long, aqueous blade with a silver hilt bejeweled with emeralds.

Estin knelt before the prince, lifting the sword above his bowed head as he did. The prince, whose back was towards the Plinks, held very still, allowing the moment to be treasured by Estin and the audience.

"Estin Merchant, of Windluff. The valor of the Winged Dynasty, carried on by his High Enchanted, King Ignis Ravillion of the Cracklemore Isles, has been found in you. No longer merely a Shield, a defender among the royal guardians, but now a captain, a shepherd, a prince yourself among your fellow brothers. This evening I, Xietas Ravillion, Chosen Winged Warrior of the royal guardians, Prince and Heir to the Enchanted Throne, your loyal ally and brother, hereby grant you, Estin Merchant, the rank of Sword."

The prince removed the blade from Estin's hands and with a single, elegant stroke, sliced the cape from Estin's shoulders.

"Rise."

Estin rose to reveal the traditional Ravillion colors of turquoise and gold splashed atop a canvas of ceremonial armor. The crowd was beside itself.

Suddenly, Remaine's mind found its way to his secret cave. He and Igniro stood together. Igniro, with his salt-encrusted hair and weather-torn toga, guiding the way for Remaine, his courageous young ward. Together, in Remaine's imagination, he and Igniro had sailed through hurricanes, fought off Berylbones in the East, and speared Pearlbacks right through.

Tonight, he drank it in—the glory of Estin Merchant, draped in the Ravillion colors, as the room showered him with adoration and pride. Estin held his chin as high as Igniro the Mariner.

"Hard to believe that's the same little boy who ran around with Silome." The voice came from his father, pressed close against the curtains. Philo Plink stared out at Estin in equal fascination. "I'm proud of that boy," he said, "always saw him as one of ours."

His father's labored breath brushed the top of Remaine's head. Then Philo Plink added, "All these boys turning into men... and my son, one of them."

The blood drained from Remaine's cheeks, or it flooded them, he wasn't quite sure which, but his breath caught in his throat as he braced for his father's next words.

"We might not all be warriors, Rem, but tell me, son," whispered his father. "What was your catch, eh? Tell me about your Dive."

Remaine could redirect reality away from himself, he could imagine worlds and adventures as easily as breathing, but creating illusions for *others*—giving them the slip—that was Silome's gift. It was the cleverest thing in the world when she used her words to spin tales, and somehow it was also always exciting. Even when she lied to their parents, it was always just to cover up an adventure she had had out in the docks past curfew. In the end, her tales always only ever bolstered her reputation.

But Remaine's insides turned to water whenever he attempted to tell a lie of any real consequence, which is why he all but felt himself leave his body to witness himself from the outside as he turned to his father, looked him in the eyes, and said, with a mouth as dry as the Cracked Desert, "I didn't... I didn't catch anything, Dad."

Philo blinked down at Remaine, as if he had spoken in a foreign language. Politely, he asked, "What?"

Remaine shook his head, "I'm sorry, Dad. I choked."

Philo's blank face revealed very little about what was happening in his mind, but Remaine saw a slight flutter in his fingers as he reached for a clamlet to crack, and he was all too aware of the small undeniable spasm that flicked from his eyebrow down to his cheek.

His father mumbled something in a quiet, scratchy sort of way, his eyes darting back and forth.

"What?" Remaine asked, regretting it, instantly.

"The curse," his father breathed, cracking a clamlet violently. He didn't bother to eat it. He dropped the whole thing onto the ground. "The curse!"

The prince's voice saved Remaine as its booming command drew all eyes back to the stage.

"Windluffians are full of secrets!" the prince smiled, holding up Estin's hand into the air. The cheering swelled. "And I'm greedy for more. We await, now, tonight's volunteers! Who among you, here now in the new year, will volunteer to follow in young Merchant's footsteps? Old and young, come forth!"

The clapping continued then waned. The elegant guests, most of whom were themselves a far cry from warrior material, turned to look over their shoulders excitedly. Some sipped from their cups or snatched the opportunity to stab at food on their dinner plates some more. Still, not twenty seconds passed before a shout came from the back.

"Tarquin Pellatrim!"

Remaine watched as his young peer ran through the crowd, fist in the air. He was strong, and agile, and he trotted up the steps to the raised platform like a well-trained horse.

"Another Pellatrim!" the prince smiled. "Tarquin, is it?"

The boy jutted his square chin in the direction of the prince.

"Mm Hmm. Now the test," said the prince. "Does Vulcutta approve?"

The confident face of Tarquin faltered as the enormous gray eagle with its massive talons perched atop the prince's shoulder side stepped closer to Tarquin. The bird ruffled its feathers, then craned its massive head forward to stare closely. Tarquin took a small step backwards. Then, regretting his retreat, he squared his shoulders to face the eagle head on. All was silent.

Remaine had never heard of the bird denying a volunteer. But he knew the prince queried the bird's judgment with every boy or man.

The bird let out a shriek that raised the hair on the back of Remaine's neck, then it unfolded its wings like enormous, feathered sails. The tent shook with celebration.

Estin crossed behind Tarquin and stood next to the prince. The two of them stood side by side as Tarquin faced them both.

"Today," continued the prince, "Tarquin Pellatrim, you are the newest recruit among the Ravillion Royal Guardians. Should you prove yourself worthy in our travels to the East Emeralds, you will be granted the rank of Shield upon our arrival. From there, the path of valor is veiled. Do you accept this task?"

"Yes," said Tarquin proudly, throwing a quick smirk over his shoulder in the direction of his elder brother who sat at the table on the stage. Torrin Pellatrim was stoic, but a glimmer of pride shone in his eyes.

Estin spoke. "Then we welcome you, Tarquin Pellatrim, and—"

But no more words came out. It was as if they got caught in Estin's throat. Estin even raised a hand to his mouth, as though he intended to help retrieve them. But something else came out instead.

The vomit exploded from Estin. It cascaded down in a gleaming, chunky flow from his own mouth to the golden face of Tarquin Pellatrim.

The room gasped. Tarquin's eyes squeezed beneath the putrid shower which, as everyone backstage noticed at once, was the color of Plink butterfin.

Had a hurricane blown in from the Pearl Sea and toppled the tent over, no one would have noticed. Every shocked mouth was covered, every wide eye was locked on the prince and Estin beside him, who appeared to be inches from keeling over. Save for Tarquin, who lifted a hand to his face to wipe puke from his eyes, the whole world stood motionless.

Poolish was the first to move. In a way only a rat could do, he turned his head slowly over his shoulder to look at the Plinks, big ears like oars on a boat adjusting course. The rage emanated from him like a steaming hot spring.

"What... did... you... *do!*"

His voice was barely more than a whisper, but Remaine felt his ears might burst with every word. He was not alone.

The Plinks looked at one another, then slowly, one by one, they began to unravel.

"I..." Millie Plink had never looked so ghostly in her whole life. Her eyes darted about, desperate for answers. "I don't..."

Deeno staggered backwards. Philo began to shake.

"We..." Fortis tried to speak to Poolish, but even she was at a loss. "We didn't do anything dif–different, we—"

"Shh!" Poolish interrupted, his attention diverted back to the stage.

The prince was muttering something to Estin, which was soon understood by all as permission for Estin to excuse himself. He did so at once, leaving the way he had come. Cressa excused herself at the exact same moment, disappearing into the shadowy curtains.

"Well," said the prince. "The attention was a bit much for young Merchant—not used to being so celebrated." His words floated up and over the crowd, lightening the mood in the room instantaneously. "And a *very* warm and… aromatic welcome to you, Tarquin." The prince laughed, dropping a hand on Tarquin's shoulder, realizing only after the fact that the instinct to do so left his hand soiled in vomit. He lifted it slowly, regrettably, allowing the puke to drip from his fingers. "Right… uh…" He held his hand out, then in a single move which threatened to give every one of them a heart attack, he turned to look backstage.

A mousy squeak chirped from Poolish's mouth, and suddenly he was scurrying on stage to greet the prince. Again, the whole tent watched in awe as the unconventional scene unfolded. Poolish wiped the prince's hand, bowed half a dozen times in the process, then retreated backstage.

"We'll certainly remember this Tour forever, won't we?" laughed the prince. Then he sent Tarquin off to the table behind them where several guards welcomed him, the first of whom was Torrin Pellatrim who sniggered as Tarquin approached.

Then the prince motioned for the high general to join him to replace Estin.

The mountain of a human marched beside the prince, and within moments another volunteer, Harlo Oswich, had come, a little awkwardly at first, given the need to sidestep the puddle of vomit. But it didn't matter, for no sooner had Harlo Oswich squared his shoulders, did he find himself before a very sick, projectile vomiting high general.

At the sight of the second man puking on stage—this one more like a volcano erupting—a few screams issued from the audience, and Remaine watched as three women near the front actually fainted.

The prince's tranquility evaporated. "WHAT in the *island of*—"

But his words were lost, because a second stream of puke fell from the general, directly onto the prince, filling up the bowl-like space created by his silver crown.

All turned to chaos.

The prince staggered back, shouted something indistinguishable, then hurried off stage in the opposite direction, his eagle screeching after him.

 The rest of the men on stage were standing now, clutching their stomachs, covering their mouths, but all in vain.

Butterfin vomit flowed like a bountiful river in the tent of the Tour of Valor, even Lyme Stretcher, despite his attempt to keep composure, let loose his vomit like a python who realized halfway through his meal his prey was too big for his body.

Now it was Poolish's turn to faint, and almost on top of him fell Millie Plink.

"Sink the sun…" murmured Deeno Plink. He gulped, and reached for Fortis who steadied him.

Remaine had always considered his mother a rock among shifting sand. No matter what life threw at her, no matter what his father's condition, and in spite of her departure from her previous life, no matter what came her way—and certainly a lot had been thrown at her—she was always steady. But even she began to break at the sight of all the vomit, and her melting expression turned Remaine's legs to jelly.

"Come on, quickly," her voice quavered. And then she was hurrying onto the stage with the tray of water-filled goblets. "Remaine, Silome, grab those rags!"

Butterfin had always been a delight for the nose—Remaine had always reveled in the delicious, buttery smell which could transform the dank smell of fish into something magical. Now the smell brought tears to his eyes and his throat tightened threateningly. He gagged as he hurried around the stage, aimlessly dropping rags on puddles of puke. One of the soldiers grabbed for a rag from Remaine's hand, but his efforts were useless. Remaine and all the rags he held were drenched in vomit before he even had a prayer of blocking the spray.

The man crawled away on his hands and knees while Remaine groped about for something clean to wipe his face with. He was inches from vomiting himself when someone pressed a clean cloth to face, helping him wipe away the rancid stench.

His father's face was twisted in a sour expression. He looked awful. But he helped Remaine as best he could, his hands shaking.

"Dad…" Remaine said. The tent had exploded with panic-stricken activity, and the noise was so loud Remaine had to all but shout. "Dad maybe you should sit down, you—"

"Silence!" bellowed a voice from the front of the stage. "SILENCE!"

Hubert Hegs stood precariously on a dry island of hardwood, surrounded by oceans of cream-colored bile.

His uncharacteristically loud outburst caught the attention of most, strangling the shrieks about the tent.

"Please, everyone, do not panic. What we have here is a clear case of food poisoning. Now, please, calm yourselves so we can sort this out."

The lords and ladies in the room straightened up at once, clearly embarrassed by their emotive display.

"Poolish. Please contact the healers at once. Could the sick individuals please take a seat? Everyone else, remain standing if you don't mind."

The division in the room could not have been clearer. The mass of nobility which spanned the length of the tent stood upright, turning back and forth in search of the sick. But it became obvious the sick individuals were all together, all on stage.

"There we have it," said Hegs. "If you ate the Oswich chicken tonight, all is well. If you had… the Plink butterfin," Hegs let the words fall from his mouth more slowly in his usual, purr-like way of speaking, "then it appears you've had some rather bad fi–"

Torrin Pellatrim gave a loud hurl from the back, pressing a fist to his mouth. Hegs leaned on his cane and glared at him over his shoulder.

"I think we've all learned a lesson tonight. Some things are simply not good to eat."

At this, Hegs turned to eye the Plinks, all of whom stood frozen about the stage, covered in vomit, pale as a milkmaid's apron.

There are moments where you cannot fathom how things could get any worse, because you are absolutely certain you have reached the lowest of circumstantial depths. That is how Remaine felt. He felt as if every important eye in Windluff was looking up, though *down*, to be sure, at his family.

But his father, who began to shake violently next to him, only to topple over with a loud cry, proved Remaine wrong. It could get worse. Much, much worse.

The Frostblood reared its ugly head in technicolor as Philo Plink clutched at his gut, shrieking hoarsely. Remaine dropped to his knees, clutching his father's hand, clueless as to how to help. Then his mother was there, and his sister, and his grandfather.

"CURSE IN THE EAST!" his father shrieked. "A CURSE UPON ME! A CURSE UPON MINE!"

The Plinks, and their butterfin, and the sea of puke in which Philo thrashed were the sole focus of Tour of the Valor. A few people gasped at the display of Philo's illness. Fortis Plink's face turned a brilliant shade of rose, and she made no attempt to pull the curtain of curls back as she leaned over her husband.

Silome, in true shark fashion, erased all emotion from her face. Her eyes became diamonds, cold and hard, and no one could stop her momentum.

"Mom, Grampa, grab his legs!" Silome's voice was a whisper, but it might as well have been a scream measured by how much command she managed to pump into the words. "Remaine—grab his other shoulder. *MOVE!*"

"I think we had all better clear out now!" The family could hear the duke directing from the stage over their shoulders. "Could the small council stay, though? Yes, Pellatrim—good. Bork, Ivystone, yes, and Wishmile?"

Someone from the crowd yelled something unintelligible.

"Move!" hissed Silome, trying to get them all off the stage.

"Ah, no Wishmile, then," said Hegs. "Do see he gets in bed, poor sensitive thing. Ah! Plinks!"

Remaine's stomach, already taunting him at the back of his throat, heaved at the sound of Hubert Hegs' voice. He saw his mother close her eyes, willing the duke to disappear.

"A word, please," said Duke Hegs.

When he took his eyes off his father, Remaine found the tent of the Tour of Valor was already emptied of most of its guests. Richly decorated tables and elegant plates still shone with food and drink. The candles were all still lit as if the party were about to start, rather than clearing out. Several people were coughing at the back, and the acidic smell of regurgitated fish was so strong in his nose he feared he might faint. Sympathetically, he feared for his mother's nose, too.

A small crew gathered around the duke, pressing silk squares to their noses. Bork stood next to Hubert Hegs. He was not nearly as large as the duke, but the way he carried all his weight in his belly alone made him feel, somehow, a rival in size. Viscountess Ivystone stood tall with prickly pride, making both Hegs and Bork seem rather boyish in her presence. And last were the Lord and Lady Pellatrim, two of the most strikingly beautiful creatures by anyone's standards.

"Well, what's to be done with them, then?" asked Lady Pellatrim first. Her voice was choked with fury. "My Tarquin—the most significant moment of his life—ruined because of this *dockdweller*." She pointed a long, well-decorated finger at Fortis.

Remaine did not know it, but there was a time in their youth when this woman and his mother would play together upstairs while their parents spoke of coin downstairs. Now Lady Pellatrim acted as if Fortis were as low and forgotten as the bottom of the sea.

"Locked up!" barked Bork. His perfectly round belly rose and fell like a buoy.

"Tried for treason!" said Ivystone. "Conspiracy against the crown!"

"That's not true!" yelled Silome, standing upright.

Ivystone held a gloved hand to her mouth, scandalized by Silome's brashness.

"We couldn't care less about the prince!" Silome spat.

"N–no!" stammered his mother, her voice shaking with horror. "What she means is it was an accident. I promise you—"

"What, do you promise, Miss Plink?" came a voice from behind them.

All turned, then bowed, at the sight of the prince. His shortly cropped hair had been rinsed, and his outer cloak removed. He appeared altogether fine, and his demeanor shone with usual Ravillion radiance, something which could not be said for Grand Pinion Lyme Stretcher who stood shakily at his side, glaring in Fortis's direction.

When no one spoke, Fortis swallowed and answered his question. "I promise you—we meant no harm. Butterfin has always been our livelihood, Your Enchanted, we've never seen it turn in the stomach like this." She bowed her head again, shaking her curls slowly.

"Fortunately, I have a strong stomach," said the prince. "An effective conspiracy would take much more than that."

"My prince," said Lord Pellatrim, standing upright, smoothing out his thick, glossy hair. "As a former member of the royal guard, I ask you to consider the shame this debacle has brought on the noble call of valor and see to a punishment which fits the severity of the crime."

"Thank you, Pellatrim," sighed the prince. "But you need not defend the guard. Its honor cannot be marred so easily. Hegs," he added, turning his attention to the duke, strangely silent thus far, "what do you think?"

"Honestly," said Hegs, "I agree with Miss Plink."

The Lord and Lady Pellatrim gasped. Bork's belly bounced so high the force of its dropping nearly sent him falling forward. Viscountess Ivystone let out a noise like the hiss of a cat.

"It's a case of food poisoning," said Hegs with his frothy, bubbling coo. "A rather bad one, to be sure, and no doubt we've learned our lesson. Of course, we should have expected as much from a dockdwelling family with little hygienic practices…"

If he weren't somehow defending them, Fortis Plink would have unleashed choice words.

"But I do not blame Miss Plink," Hegs frowned. "Nor her offspring, as she comes from a nobler, more trustworthy breed." He readjusted his grip on his cane and added, "However, I cannot speak for her well-aged elders and," he cleared his throat, "her… demonstratively deteriorating husband."

As if on cue, Philo Plink, who had been quiet for several minutes, let out a shriek and gave a great shudder, his whole frame tightening into a ball.

Hegs coughed. "Honestly, I think none of them are truly capable of conspiracy. Impropriety, absurdity, stupidity? Yes. Without question… but not conspiracy."

The grand pinion whispered something in the prince's ear. Fortis could see the prince fighting for composure at the smell of his advisor's breath.

"Quite right, Stretcher, quite right. Thank you." The prince straightened up and began putting on gloves. "The parade is already forming, and I still intend to keep with tradition and set sail before dawn. I don't have time for a full-fledged investigation, though I have recently acquired a foolproof method of means for drawing truth out of subjects warranting suspicion. Hegs, if you think Miss Plink's family is the type, we can give that a try. If so, you may go with me to my ship, and I'll arrange the questioning before we cast off."

"Means of drawing out the truth, you say?" asked Hegs, his brow twitching slightly. He shifted, like he had an itch, then bowed his head smoothly. "Your wisdom is ever increasing, my prince, but no, I do not think this necessary. I'll keep a close eye on the Plinks, but for now, I think we can all call this for what it is: rotten fish." He looked at Fortis and smiled with oily lips.

Nearly every minute of that evening would be seared into the memories of the Plink family for years to come. With horror they would recall the smell, the sights, the tingling heat of unwanted glares. But perhaps the most horrific thing to recall, and they would do so often, was that the family left the tent entirely alone that night, defeated and deflated in spirit, struggling and slipping in vomit, all but dragging Philo, without a single helping hand from a single sympathetic soul. They would remember rousing Millie, fanning enough wind in her face to recruit her brittle strength in aid, then they would remember hauling Philo out the back side of the tent, piling into the carriage that had brought them beaming with pride to the top of the cliff, only to be riding home in scandalous shame, smelling of sour fish and curdled cream.

And though the rest of the Plink family did not notice, two other particular moments above all the rest would also be burned into the memory of young Remaine.

As the carriage jostled home, Remaine was forced to watch as every Plink except him, one by one, took out their vials and breathed out the chilly cold which coursed through their veins from the trauma of the night. One by one they calmed themselves, even Philo finding comfort in the arms of Fortis, and one by one they all, inevitably, stole glances in Remaine's direction as his father, trembling, inquired, "W– why isn't R–Rem–"

"Shh" said Fortis, holding Philo's head to her chest. "Not now. Rest."

This was the first moment that Remaine would carry forever.

The second came later that night, as Remaine lay awake, staring out of the small round window at the foot of his bed, squashed between the floor and the low ceiling.

He sat up and rested his chin on his knees, wrapping his arms around his legs, trying to ignore the smell of puke still emanating from the bottom of his feet despite having wiped them off. Out of the tiny window, the royal docks sparkled along the coast, and at the far end, a stream of Luffies celebrated, making their way to the prince's ship, blissfully unaware of the disaster that had happened in the tent of valor earlier that evening. Somewhere out there, Tarquin Pellatrim and the other boys, already heroes in their family's eyes, would soon be waving goodbye to their adoring fans.

Visions of the Great Mariner flashed before Remaine, and even as he looked out the foggy window, he could imagine Igniro down there on the docks, beckoning to him, calling him to adventure.

He's never been here, Remaine could hear his grampa saying. He pictured Deeno Plink tapping his old bald head and saying with disdain, *that boy's always here.*

The Igniro in his head stood mightily on the end of the docks.

Then, as clearly as he saw the Great Mariner, he pictured Tarquin, growing up strong, standing alongside Estin and the rest, the prince bestowing a trident in his hand as Defender Prime of Windluff. The cheers for Tarquin and for the prince, for Estin and for all the royal guard—they all echoed so loud inside Remaine's head he almost covered his ears.

Here, though, in the silent Plink home, with no sounds save the uneven, labored breaths of his father above him, Remaine saw his own destiny just as clearly, and it was as bleak as the bottom of the sea. If not a perpetually disappointing life as a Plink Fisherman, his fate would be an arranged marriage to Jileanna Hegs.

And so, the second moment of that night, which Remaine would remember as the moment that changed his life forever, was his exhilarating yet horrifying decision to unravel his arms from his legs and crawl quietly to the end of his bed. He would remember, forever, the careful, silent breaths he took as he crept. And he would remember with such clarity, as clearly as he could envision Igniro calling him to bravery, his childhood home disappearing as he snuck from his bed and out through the window.

He would remember the rush of fire in his chest as he pulled himself silently along the Otter Ropes with shaking hands. And he would remember how in that burst of sudden madness, or rush of genius, he had not stopped to think about bringing anything with him save his empty vial, hidden deep in his pocket, and his father's red shawl still wrapped about him.

CHAPTER 6

THE HOAXBITE AND THE EMERALD EGG

BENEATH A SKY EXPLODING WITH RED FIREWORKS, Windluff had come alive. The cobblestone streets vibrated with stomping feet, moving to music emanating from unseen instruments lost within the teeming crowds. The rhythm rippled through the sea of bodies, making the populous move in waves, all crashing towards the central avenues for the Tour's parade like a winter storm on the beach.

Peppery smells drifted out from the kitchens, luring the hungry mania. Chunks of meat and vegetables were piled high on skewers, made to look like Berylbones speared through by the javelins of the royal guard. Artisans sold valor-themed paraphernalia to children, all dressed in the brave scarlet, play fighting with play swords against invisible Berylbones.

Everywhere one turned there was a blast of red smoke or a spray of red sparks or the fluttering of a red flag, and in the midst of it all, the city had grown as dull to anything that wasn't in the spirit of celebration as it had grown excited about everything that was.

This is why no one paid any real attention to the faces of the six soldiers that had turned the color of rotten seaweed. Despite their central position within the parade, their ghastly appearance was lost on the crowd. No one seemed to notice the faces of the high general

Sir Vector Cottley or Grand Pinion Lyme Stretcher, as they leaned on one another, like a boulder upon a stick, valiantly trying to prevent themselves from vomiting as their carriage rattled down the road. None but the nobles of Windluff, who could not usually be bothered to accompany the parade all the way down to the royal docks anyway, were aware of the food-poisoning catastrophe that had transpired in the tent a couple hours prior. As oblivious as the crowds were to the disastrous end of the show, so they were equally oblivious to the sickly green hue of the prince's men, and the sour stench still lingering on their clothes, as they rode miserably through the city.

The prince alone, who had survived the scene mostly unscathed, held the crowd's attention all the way. He waved and smiled and paused on occasion to shake a few hands, and with every one of these gestures the crowd exploded, like another one of their fireworks.

This was also why, as the prince and his men descended from the top of Mariner's Cliff, all the way down into the city proper, out to the sea wall, down the zigzagging road built into the wall's side, coming at last to the royal docks of Windluff, no one noticed a scrawny little boy emerge in a small dinghy, from beneath the docks.

All eyes were trained on the starboard side of the prince's glorious vessel, *The Emerald Egg*, and its long, majestic gangway illuminated by twenty tall torches. The crowd was completely unaware of the port-side of the vessel. That side was hidden in the dark cover of night, and it was on that side where Remaine Plink, having abandoned his tiny dinghy, and having swum over to *The Emerald Egg*, was now climbing up its side.

Somewhere inside of Remaine there may have been a small little voice, inviting him to at least stop for a moment to think, to pause and put an ounce of flesh on what was hardly even a skeleton of a plan. But it was as if a different spirit possessed him—maybe the spirit of the Great Mariner himself—and Remaine scaled the dark side of the massive ship. On more than one occasion, his hand or foot slipped, nearly sending him back into the water. But eventually the Plink blood proved strong enough to keep him stuck to the vessel until he finally swung himself over the railing of the portside of the ship, landing with a clumsy, soggy flop upon the deck.

An oversized heap of cargo was nearby, and Remaine scrambled over a few crates, quick as a cat. He found an opening in the massive pile and managed to wiggle himself into it. A small gap in between two large chests made for a peephole. Remaine peered out.

The Emerald Egg was a dream ship. It would drop any Plink jaw, without a doubt, and had it opened its own jaws, it could have easily consumed a vessel such as the *Lady Vex* a thousand times over. The figurehead of *The Emerald Egg* was masterfully carved into the bow of the ship to look like Prince Xietas' harpy eagle and was dragon-like in its proportions. Remaine had stowed away in a small, pristinely polished city, a city populated by row upon row of crimson-clad crew.

Luck befell Remaine. The stationed guard and crew stood with their hands clasped behind their backs, all of which, at present, were turned to him and his hiding spot. They stood in neat rows and every eye was turned starboard to the gangway as the prince's entourage at last came to the end of the dock and began to board.

Luck, unfortunately, did not provide him with any further ideas. But he had come this far, hadn't he? It had felt like a calling, or a feeling—he didn't know which, but he could not stop thinking about Igniro and Estin and the prince. He saw in the prince, and his men, a future he had never seen before tonight. It had never occurred to him this could be *his* path. He had to speak with the prince. Then the spirit of his mother nudged him; it would be bad manners to interrupt the moment, what with the crowds still cheering and waving. He would have to wait.

The first group of men began to climb aboard. Remaine watched as Tarquin Pellatrim, cleaned of all remnants of vomit now, was first to step off the gangway and onto the deck of the ship. Remaine could not believe that he and Tarquin Pellatrim were the same age. The few times they had been in lecture together, Tarquin had made an easy target out of Remaine. "Dinky Plinky," he had called Remaine, as he towered over him with his intimidating height and his bizarrely muscular frame, even then at the age of ten.

Behind Tarquin came Harlo Oswich, looking like a happy scarecrow, entirely unaffected by the dramatic finale of tonight's show. Following these two came twenty or so other men, some more advanced in years than others, but all of whom Remaine did not recognize. They had apparently volunteered without great pomp and circumstance, stepping up after the Plinks had ruined the show.

Behind them, though, unfolded the unpleasant sight of a sickly pale group of men, all suffering from the effects of the bad butterfin, who practically crawled rather than climbed aboard *The Emerald Egg*, one by one. It had clearly been a long journey from the tent to the ship, and now that they had arrived, it was evident the men desired nothing more than to lie down.

What had happened? Remaine had been sick from fish before—every Plink had. It was yet another rite of passage for a fisherman. But *never* with butterfin. And why, oh, why did it have to happen tonight? A twinge of guilt gripped his guts. No doubt his mother would be flogging herself for weeks, and his grandparents would probably sleep for a month, waking up more exhausted than when they had closed their eyes. Silome, he knew, would go stone-cold silent for days, and his father… Remaine swallowed and ignored the thought. He took comfort in knowing he was right to leave and that his presence around his father would have only made things worse.

The prince boarded next. His face bore the unmistakable furrow of a less-than-satisfied man forced to endure an unpleasant situation. Still, he appeared as regal as the heavens, and with a matching grace he turned to face the crowd who met his gesture with praise. The prince gave a simple wave.

Then, turning to the crew and with a subtle flick of his wrist, the prince sent the men into motion. Another minute passed of light-footed steps and quick, volleying shouts which echoed overhead from every corner of the ship as the crew confirmed the ship's readiness to set sail.

The prince wasted no time. Remaine heard nothing of the few, muffled words the prince exchanged with the men surrounding him. Then he crossed the deck, which seemed to stretch on for miles, until he came to two glossy double doors towards the stern. He exited the scene, accompanied by Lyme Stretcher and the high general. The doors shut behind them.

It was not long before the ship began to move with a familiar lurching sensation. Men in more formal attire ushered the new recruits through another set of double doors to the fore of the ship and they all disappeared below deck. The remaining crew on deck climbed rigging and manned stations, and aside from the watchkeeping orders shouted into the quieting night, Remaine was left in silence to himself, arms wrapped around his legs, chin resting on his knees, hidden in a pile of crates.

Then, like the fading of memory, or a life, Remaine peered out on the glittering city of Windluff, and watched with a strange feeling in his belly as the only place he had ever known began to shrink in the distance. He did not remember ever closing his eyes.

It was only when a bear claw of a hand grabbed him on the back of his neck did he even realize he had fallen asleep in his little hiding spot.

A gruff voice bellowed. "AVAAAAAST! STOWAWAAAAAY!"

Remaine could not see the man, or monster, who held him by his ankle now, entirely suspended in the air. It was still dark. Windluff was nowhere in sight. The stars shone overhead, or from Remaine's perspective, *underchin*, by the thousands.

"What's this?" hissed another voice, and Remaine could see its owner approach. It was the slender, lizard-like form of Lyme Stretcher who had managed to recover a bit of color to his face. "A little thief?"

"A Luffy dock rat by the looks of him," said the man behind him. "Worth little more than a proper *tossing*!"

Remaine felt his body swing forward as his captor made a motion to the taffrail.

"W–wait!" shouted Remaine, but there was no stopping the man. As the railing came closer, Remaine managed to feel the sharp stab of regret. Then he was hanging over a black sea. He let out a scream.

"Nothing like a good drowning to teach you a lesson, rat!" shouted the man, and Remaine could now see it was the high general. He loosened his grip, and Remaine dropped a foot.

"Steady, Cottley," Stretcher's voice brought the momentum to a halt. The high general tightened his hold on Remaine's ankle. "His Enchanted is to be made aware of all who come aboard his vessel."

Remaine's vision spun as the huge man swung him back over the deck. He dropped the boy without warning. Remaine's face collided with the deck and his body crumpled in a lanky heap all around him.

Whether fear or pain kept him motionless, Remaine did not know, but he did not move.

"You had better stand up, thief," said the grand pinion. Remaine's eyes were tightly shut, but he could tell from the sound that the man had drawn near and was towering overhead. "I will escort you to the prince's chambers. Now."

Once more, Remaine was picked up effortlessly by the general, only this time, it was by his hair.

"Ah!" he yelled out as the large man dropped him onto his feet.

"Silence!" the general sneered, kneeing Remaine in his back. "Move!"

Remaine stumbled forward, nearly colliding with the cobra-like pinion who was getting his first good look at Remaine.

"*You?*" sneered the man.

Remaine gulped.

"Come to confess? Follow me."

The grand pinion turned smoothly and strode away. Though he was aware of their stares, Remaine did not look left or right at the watchful crew, instead he kept his eyes on the hem of the advisor's robes.

The anticipation of approaching the prince's cabin was enough to make Remaine faint. Suddenly, with excruciating clarity, he managed to ask himself what he had been thinking. Of *course*, the prince will kill him. Of course, he will *hang* him, right here on board the ship! There will be no glory and honor to bring home to the Plinks. What was he thinking! Surely this was the stupidest thing he had ever done!

They had not quite reached the double doors when the doors swung wide.

All the mutters and whispers around the deck fell silent as Prince Xietas Ravillion stepped out from his stateroom.

"What's hap–" the prince stopped at the sight of Remaine. His brow furrowed.

"Your Enchanted," said the grand pinion, bowing low. "We've caught a Windluffian stowaway. A thief—none other than the fish boy who served the rotten dinner this evening."

The prince studied Remaine slowly. He blinked a few times. His eyes narrowed.

"Brave of you, boy, to attempt a robbery aboard *The Emerald Egg*." Prince Xietas' voice was as strong as iron, but it flowed like water. Everyone held their breath at the sound of it.

"I–I'm not—I'm not a thief," Remaine managed to say. He risked a glance up at the prince and found him staring down hard.

The general kicked him in the rear-end. A hiss of disapproval came from the royal advisor at this brazen oversight of decorum. "*Your Enchanted!*"

"S–Sorry!" blurted out Remaine. "Your Enchanted. I–I'm not a thief, Y–Your Enchanted." Remaine knew he had only seconds to defend himself before someone suggested something drastic. "I've… I've come to join the guard!" he cried.

A nasty sneer rippled across the deck. Then outright laughter. Remaine's cheeks flushed redder than they already were.

"He lies," growled the high general, squeezing the back of Remaine's neck. "I'd no sooner believe it if nana's nana fancied herself worthy of the guard. *I say we toss him!*"

"You know, Cottley," said the prince, still eyeing Remaine. "Not everything needs to be tossed. Still," he squatted down, eye-level with Remaine. "I'm not opposed to a tossing, if the circumstances call for it. Explain yourself, boy."

"I'm—I'm *really* sorry!" Remaine's voice was hoarse, and he hung his head back down towards the deck of the ship, exasperated. He was as surprised as anyone to hear his declaration to volunteer. It was as if the whole night had bubbled up into his mouth and with tears in his eyes he added, "My family—we're—we're all really sorry, I promise. We didn't know! It was an accident!"

No one spoke. Countless eyes crawled over him like a million mosquitos on his skin. He fidgeted and looked around. He saw the Pellatrim brothers, both of whom glared in his direction, their strong arms folded in front of their broad chests.

To Remaine's surprise, there came another voice from behind him. It boomed loudly, thick with a sing-song accent and it drew everyone's gaze, even the prince's.

"Surely this little creature isn't capable of too much damage, eh?"

Remaine turned to see the man. His size was striking, and Remaine thought in someone's imagination he might even be related to the high general, though his broad smile disqualified him from that. His red hair and beard were wild and wreathed his face like the fiery mane of a ferocious lion. He stood beside another man, much smaller and less distinct, but in whom Remaine sensed the greater authority of the two.

The grand pinion was put off by the boisterously loud question.

"Curse these addresses of sacrilege! You dare address your prince so informally, *privateer?*" He had a venomous shine in his eyes and said the last word with a particular bite. "This is *His Enchanted* prince! And it seems your watchful presence—your promise to protect him—is not as promising as we had hoped. A stowaway managed to sneak aboard!"

"Forgive me, wizard, I haven't a salt's pinch how he slipped past us."

"Mmm," said the prince, clearly less perturbed than his advisor. "Tell me, boy. How *did* you come aboard my ship without anyone noticing?"

"I—" truthfully Remaine did not know if he had an answer to satisfy. "I just... climbed aboard... on the portside?"

A beat of silence.

"It was dark!" he added quickly, suddenly overcome with the need to make sure the red-headed man suffered no blame because of him, "—just before you weighed anchor."

"Hmmm," said the prince with a thoughtful chew of his lip. "Unfortunately, my *wizard* is correct, Mr. Chince."

The redheaded man blushed. "Forgive me, Your Enchanted."

Prince Xietas turned now to the smaller man who stood slightly in front of the man with the red lion's mane. The smaller man was plain, with muddy brown eyes and sun-tanned skin. He stepped forward to distinguish himself from the girth of the red headed giant. At his heels, Remaine noticed, was an enormously fat gray cat, winding itself around his ankles, and on his shoulder perched a bird, a blue Steller's jay with an unruly spike of feathers along his skull. The man was skinny and, Remaine guessed, perhaps forty years of age.

The prince's words were commanding, but he kept his tone even as he spoke. "The shadows, Captain Rawthorne, are your designated realm of observation. Every blind spot. I hired you because of your reputation with blind spots." The prince, who had been squatting to get a closer look at Remaine, stood now to face the man in full. "What have you to say?"

"My prince," said Captain Rawthorne, bowing his head. His blue jay readjusted its footing. "I can only ask forgiveness."

His voice felt too soft for a Captain's, and too hoarse, as if he were sick. In contrast to the redheaded man beside him, Captain

Rawthorne's accent ran along the same long grain as the prince's. "We had kept a vigilant guard along the portside all night, except for—" he rubbed his forehead thoughtfully, "the boy must have slipped aboard just as we were preparing to set sail—as we weighed anchor. Just like he said." The man dipped his head, confessionally. "I do admit there would have been the smallest window of opportunity."

"Which he seized," said the prince. "Clever."

Remaine's cheeks flushed. His dumb luck had been interpreted as strategy.

"Perhaps there's more to the thief than meets the eye," added the prince. "The most dangerous kind of thief."

Remaine gulped. "N–no, no, Your Enchanted—" Remaine looked up. He made eye contact with the prince, regretted it, then broke eye contact with the prince, which he regretted even more. Remaine shook his head. "I promise, it was ch–chance. I had no plans. I promise. I just came because I wanted to join the guard—and I wanted to say sorry, for my family—and, well, I guess, I ran away, and now—"

"Your family's poor preparations warrant severe punishment!" snapped Lyme Stretcher.

"Nearly killed me!" gagged the enormous general clutching at his neck that was the size of Remaine's torso.

"Yes, thank you," said the prince, lifting his hand slightly to calm them both. "I've spoken to Duke Hegs and he has assured me it was nothing more than a pitiful mistake. I do believe him—the *Plink* family, was it?"

Remaine nodded.

"And your name?" asked the prince.

"Remaine."

"Well, Remaine," the prince continued. "You'll be relieved to know that I think the Plink family is harmless. I do not think they cooked up any plot against me."

Remaine shook his head with zeal. "No, sir."

"You climbed aboard by cover of darkness, Remaine. Did you also leave your home in the same manner? Does your family know you are here? How old are you?"

"T–twelve," said Remaine, gulping down a wad of guilt. He shook his head again. "And no, Your Enchanted. They don't know."

It was the large, redheaded privateer who spoke next.

"Would you like us to send for a ship, my prince, to take him back?" His voice boomed so loud it made Remaine jump. "Clearly the boy doesn't belong here."

"Aye!" said the general. "Or let's break him in two and toss him! Save us the trouble of calling for another ship."

At this, the prince locked eyes with Remaine, and this time Remaine did not, could not look away. Deep in the dark pools of the Enchanted Prince of the Cracklemore Isles, a magnetic pull drew out his words. "I–I don't want to go back. I came because I wanted to join the guard."

There was another ripple of laughter, though more muffled than the first and more short-lived this time. The prince appeared thoughtful.

"I see an honest desperation here," he said at last. "And I am not the type to deny honest desperation. But first, let us clarify a number of crimes."

Prince Xietas issued a shining longsword from its sheath with such grace and speed it could have been mistaken for a flash of lighting. In a single, elegant stroke, he brought the blade beneath Remaine's chin where it touched his skin like an icy finger. He held Remaine in this precarious place, but returned his gaze to the privateer crew, "First, the boy is quite small," (Remaine heard both of the Pellatrim brothers snicker at this) "and your explanation, Captain Rawthorne, satisfies me. Crime number one is pardonable; a simple mistake, I think."

Captain Rawthorne and the redheaded giant bowed low at this.

"Still," continued the prince in a matter-of-fact tone, neither cold nor warm, "you'll understand my need to *ensure* the truth. Master Stretcher?"

Stretcher gave a wicked smile and bowed as well, then he slithered away, disappearing into the prince's cabin. The time dragged on as everyone glanced around at one another in silence, but eventually, Stretcher returned carrying a glossy black box. He bowed low and extended the box to the prince, who gently lifted the lid and removed a small, ivory object. The shape and details of the object were unclear, as the prince enclosed it in his hand entirely, but Remaine had noticed an unmistakable pointy end.

The prince strode over to Captain Rawthorne who held himself stiffly in a veiled, stoic sort of way. Then, as if they were simply exchanging goods at the market, the prince said casually, "We call it a Hoaxbite, Captain Rawthorne, and it's rather new. And handy. I trust you'll take no offense?"

"Of course not, my prince," said the captain, bowing slightly. "Might I ask what you intend to do?"

"No," said the prince. Then as smoothly as he wielded his own sword, the prince grabbed the wrist of the captain, turned it over so the top of his forearm faced skyward, and without so much as a warning, jabbed the small, ivory colored object into Rawthorne's skin.

The privateer captain winced, but only just, quickly re-establishing his statue-like demeanor again. Blood trickled along his wrist as the prince held the object firmly in place. Then it was over and the prince removed the object from the captain's skin.

"There," said the prince, exhaling. He smiled. "That's done. Now. Tell me once more. Was it an honest mistake the boy slipped past your notice?"

Captain Rawthorne gave a hard swallow and squeezed his muddy-colored eyes shut, as if suddenly dizzy. When he opened them, his gaze darted from Remaine to the prince only once, then with deep sincerity, he said, "Yes, my prince. An honest mistake."

"And there you have it," said the prince with a smile. He looked at Lyme Stretcher who appeared less than enthused.

The prince returned his gaze to Remaine. "But there is one more crime—that of the fish."

A few men grumbled in agreement and out of the corner of his eye Remaine could see that several had not yet regained their color.

"It would not be the first time someone has made an attempt on my life, boy," said the prince. "It's never wise to lie to a Ravillion. But especially not when I have this." The prince held aloft his trinket. At the prince's invitation, Remaine repeated the same movements as Captain Rawthorne, extending his wrist to the prince. Unlike the captain, though, Remaine winced and quite loudly exclaimed, "Ouch!" when the prince jabbed him with the same ivory object. A small trickle of blood ran down his wrist. Remaine felt something course through him, like a word on the tip of the tongue, or a wisp of a thought barely remembered. He could not move. He could not blink.

"So, tell me," the prince said, each word as calm as an autumn pond. "Did your family try to poison me tonight?"

The dark, cosmic eyes of Prince Xietas seemed to bore into Remaine's every thought, and Remaine said, more calmly than he could have imagined possible, "No, sir."

"The boy could be ignorant to the family's schemes," hissed Stretcher, leaning toward the prince's ear.

"True," said the prince. "Either way, the boy is harmless." The prince smiled and looked straight at Remaine. "To the best of your knowledge, your family meant me and my men no harm, it was truly by a stroke of luck you avoided the surveillance of my privateers, in coming here you wished to express apologies on your family's behalf," he paused, eyebrows raising thoughtfully, "and, perhaps most fascinating of all, you are truly a dock dweller of Windluff, hungry for valor and glory who wishes to join the guard? Did I get all that right?"

Remaine blinked, surprised to hear it listed out like that. If it weren't for all the stares and glares, he might have found it a great relief to have it all spilled out there into the open. He nodded.

"Tell me, Remaine," continued the prince, who appeared to be in no kind of rush. "Why did you not volunteer back at the tent?"

Remaine paused. Truthfully, he had never considered the Tour, not consciously anyway. If he were ever to be heroic, it'd be on his perch, with Igniro by his side. Tonight was the first time he saw his worlds colliding—the adventures in his mind with his everyday life—and it had taken him all night to see it. It had taken tea at Hegs' house, and his father's fit at the Tour, and the sight of Estin, and the presence of the prince, and the mystery of the grand pinion's magic, for Remaine to see this new path before him—a path like Igniro's. If he took this path, it would be like coming up from the Plink Dive with a whale speared on the end of his trident.

There was one looming trouble, though. He remained uncharmed. His mother's face—the way she had twisted it up and kept everything quiet and dragged him from place to place as if he were in trouble—it all but confirmed to him he was, somehow, responsible for all this mess. The curse his father screamed about—the Berylbones he saw in his nightmares, the Frostblood, the Old Cold—somehow Remaine was the manifestation of the curse itself, whatever it was. It was an unbearable weight, and to the prince, alone, Remaine wished to confess all. If anyone could help him receive the Charming, it would be the prince.

But what about Stretcher and the general? What about Tarquin and Torrin? There they stood like hungry dogs ready to devour him. All of it was impossibly difficult to try to explain here, and frankly, too confusing to sort out.

"I–I don't know," he finally breathed, as honestly as he could. "I never considered it, until tonight."

"*After* your rotten dinner lay strewn about the stage?" sneered Lyme Stretcher.

"Yes," was all Remaine could say.

The prince stood. "Where is Merchant?" he asked.

"Here, my prince."

Remaine turned around. As Estin stepped forward out of the crowd, he locked eyes with Remaine briefly, but it was enough for Remaine to see shock—or horror, he was not sure which—on Estin's face.

The prince spoke airily. "You Luffies are a resilient folk, I see."

Estin forced a smile.

"Perhaps we've found our next prodigy," chuckled the prince, clapping a hand on Remaine's shoulder. The general grunted at this as the prince added, "Though I am not sure."

"What about the ceremony!" a voice blurted out. It belonged to Tarquin Pellatrim, who already looked at home among the other guards. Only his petulance betrayed his age. "What if he's not worthy!"

There was a noise, then, and Remaine was startled at how loud the flapping of wings could be. The prince's eagle, having been absent, suddenly appeared on his master's shoulder as if summoned by Tarquin's words. The bird leaned forward as it peered at Remaine, who gulped, unable to look away from the bottomless eyes and the hooked beak. Up close the prince's Singer was as big as a small child.

The bird jumped from the prince's shoulder and, to the amazement of everyone on board, landed on the deck directly in front of Remaine. Startled, Remaine sat up, then fell backwards onto his elbows. The bird, suddenly more predator than Singer, climbed upon Remaine's chest with its talons extended like daggers, cutting through the red shawl and digging into Remaine's skin. Remaine's elbows gave out and he fell flat on his back, trembling beneath the weight of the enormous bird.

Remaine whispered to no one in particular. "H–help—" The prince, the only one who really was capable of helping in this situation, watched with a concentrated fascination, frozen in place. The bird dug its claws in and took another step forward, this step taking him onto Remaine's throat—drawing blood. "Ah! Help!" gasped Remaine.

The bird froze, then, and placed its head near Remaine's mouth as if to listen to his shallow breathing. For Remaine, this lasted for an eternity, at least until it ended. Then the bird returned to the prince.

Xietas Ravillion turned to face Tarquin, his red cloak swishing. At the same moment, his silvery eagle screeched. Tarquin's mouth closed in a tight line, startled.

"Vulcutta listens for valor, young man—for the heart of those who will serve the Ravillion name well. She has found both you *and the Plink boy* to be of great use to the protection of the Cracklemore Isles and to the service to the Winged Throne."

A slight glare lingered in Tarquin's gaze as the prince moved on.

"The boy will be needing a place to get some rest, I think." The prince jerked his chin in the direction of his guards.

"I'll take care of it, my prince," said Estin, who stepped forward without hesitation.

"My prince," said the privateer captain with the hoarse voice. "Do you think perhaps we might let the boy's family know—they'll be wondering about—"

"Quite right, Captain Rawthorne," said the prince. He extended his arm, and suddenly his Singer was there, attentive. "A message for Duke Hubert Hegs, of Windluff." The bird fidgeted slightly, but her eyes remained spellbound by the prince. "Duke Hegs, you'll be delighted to know another Windluffian is aboard my vessel, eager to bring glory to crown, country, island, and family," he smiled at Remaine, "the young Remaine Plink. His arrival was unconventional, but we'll keep him aboard. Please inform his family of his whereabouts. I think they're in the dark."

Vulcutta exploded upwards after this, swooshing away over the deck, and disappeared within seconds.

"Rest there, my love!" shouted the prince after her. "Make sure he feeds you!"

With that, Prince Xietas turned his back on the crowd and disappeared into his stateroom.

The gathered crowd began to disperse; the privateer captain studied Remaine for a moment, then he and his crew returned to their posts. All at once, Remaine went from being the target of every critical eye on the manifest, to being practically invisible in every way. Wordlessly, Estin led him down through yet another set of double doors and down the staircase spiraling Remaine belowdecks.

The ship's belly was bigger than any Remaine had ever been in. Surprisingly high ceilings ran the length of the chamber, all a dark, oily canvas of polished black wood. Silver sconces in the shape of harpy eagles punctuated the curved, horizontal beams around him, and from the ceiling, hung in neat rows, were hammocks of soft, embroidered cloth.

Estin marched Remaine to the very back. "Here's where you'll sleep," he said, motioning towards the closest hammock which hung near a round, stained-glass porthole. The black waters of the Pearl Sea were smooth. Starlight reflected in fragments through the mosaic.

"This row's for Luffies," said Estin.

Nearby Tarquin Pellatrim slouched into his hammock, making sure to glare openly at Remaine.

When Tarquin finally looked away, Estin grabbed Remaine's arm tightly and whispered into his ear so quietly he barely heard.

"What are you *doing*, Remaine?!"

Remaine's eyes grew wide beneath the looming terror of the fully-grown Estin Merchant. In Estin's eyes burned a rage unlike any he had seen from him before.

"I–I told you—I came—"

"Remaine, *look* at you!" Estin hissed, and his brows raised in regret the moment he saw the color flood Remaine's cheeks. "I didn't mean—I just meant—the royal guard is not an *adventure* you go on. This isn't one of your stories, Rem."

A brotherly affection returned to Estin's gaze. Remaine recognized it and a watery glaze filled his eyes. He said nothing.

Estin blinked at him, dumbfounded. "Y–You… you just ran away without telling anyone?"

Remaine did not reply.

Estin's jaw tightened. He looked around and took a deep breath, his mind clearly racing. He looked as if he wanted to say something else, but he just swallowed. "Go to bed. You need sleep."

Then he turned and left, disappearing behind the long row of swinging hammocks.

Remaine Plink climbed into his new swinging bed, the rocking of the ship not unlike the rocking of the Plink home. As he closed his eyes, he saw his family and began sorting through images of each of them waking up, adjusting, probably comfortably, to Remaine's departure. He rolled over. His father would probably feel much better now that Remaine was gone. Remaine grabbed at his father's shawl, still secured around his neck. He thought of his mother, next, and was surprised to find hot tears stinging his eyes.

Tarquin Pellatrim was already happily snoring.

CHAPTER 7

THE HIGH GENERAL SIR VECTOR COTTLEY

THE NEXT MORNING, Remaine's stomach growled like a caged lion. It gave a great, audible roar as he entered the dining hall, and it was then Remaine finally paid attention to it, realizing it had been a very long time since he had fed the mad beast.

The smell of potatoes, eggs, and bacon had found him a bit earlier and drawn him from his hammock, down a dark passage of shiny black wood, around a corner, and up a short flight of broad steps. Then came the sound of silverware and chatter, and the sight of dawn streaming in through a long, impressive row of stained-glass windows.

Everything belowdecks of *The Emerald Egg* was grander than any building Remaine had ever been in. He took a seat at a shiny polished table bolted to even shinier varnished floors.

Someone approached from behind and a small plate of sausage slid into view.

"Eat this," said Estin, walking around to face him. Estin Merchant, no longer in ornate ceremonial attire, wore a clean white tunic with silver stitching, a well-made leather belt with a sword secured, and crisp leggings tucked into boots. Remaine had never worn boots; all his life, his toes had either gone free or they had been bound only by the thin straps of sandals.

"Thanks," said Remaine, stabbing a sausage with a jewel-encrusted fork. If he weren't so hungry, he might have taken the time to appreciate the taste. Instead, he quickly scarfed down two sausages. Estin stood guard, wordlessly. He stared hard at Remaine with dark brown eyes.

"Estin," sighed Remaine. "I'm fine."

"You'll need your strength, Remaine," said Estin, eyeing him pathetically as if he were a crippled farm animal. Remaine's blood felt hot.

"I left my mother at home, Estin. I don't need you to play her part."

Estin's mouth twitched, and at once Remaine regretted his words. It was unfair of him to resent Estin's help, but he was here now. He would have to stand on his own eventually.

"We've passed the Inky Delta," said Estin, gazing out the windows. The ship rose and fell gracefully and, Remaine noticed, moved very quickly.

"Already?"

"An hour ago," said Estin. "If we keep our speed, we'll leave Moorington behind this evening and arrive at Kipswitch before tomorrow." Then, more to himself, Estin added, "Windluff's getting farther and farther away."

"Morning!" chirped another voice. Harlo Oswich, with his floppy mess of pale hair and gangly limbs, was already taking his seat at the table. Remaine noticed he, too, was still dressed in the same red garb as he had been last night, and it dawned on him once more he had nothing here. He thought he might ask Estin about this, but he was distracted at watching Harlo shovel eggs into his mouth with a large spoon that could only be the serving spoon. "Eggs," said Harlo. "Just like home."

Remaine felt an odd little stab in his stomach at the mention of home. His stomach growled once more, and he decided he was still hungry, so he added some potatoes to his plate. Estin sat down next to Remaine and Remaine noticed Estin's leg bouncing nervously.

"Wanna eat something?" Remaine asked.

Estin shook his head, not looking at Remaine. His eyes darted around the room. He paused, then, and said, "Here they come."

Mouth still full of food, Remaine looked up to see the broad silhouette of Torrin Pellatrim, huge and thick, dressed in white, and behind him, smaller, but equally warrior-like nonetheless, Tarquin Pellatrim, himself still wearing red.

"Merchant," nodded Torrin, his voice as thick as his neck.

"Pellatrim," said Estin.

Tarquin stepped heartily in front of his older brother. "I just wanted to say no hard feelings about last night, Merchant." Tarquin's voice was much more refined than Torrin's, and more intelligent sounding too. Tarquin extended a strong forearm, offering Estin a hand.

Estin hesitated, then shook Tarquin's hand, "Oh... right. Yes... sorry about all that." He had the grace not to look toward Remaine, whose butterfin was the cause of Estin's torrential downpour of vomit upon Tarquin's head.

"Not your fault, Merchant," said Tarquin, smirking. "I see you're getting Plink here ready for today," he raised his eyebrows quickly. "Torrin's told me all about it. I've been ready for years."

"I'll bet you have," said Estin.

"What's today?" asked Remaine.

Tarquin chortled and gave Torrin an elbow. Torrin returned a wicked grin and folded his arms across his chest. "Guess you're not getting him ready, huh?" smirked Tarquin. "I'm sure it'll be a great surprise for him, then. Anyway, Merchant, I'd like to request a personal lesson from you. My brother's told me all about you, and I think you'll find I am ready for your training."

Estin forced a smile and said, "See you up there, boys."

He excused himself from the table and strolled out the same doors Remaine had come through. The Pellatrims sneered at Remaine, then followed suit.

Estin and several other men of higher rank lined up the new volunteers in orderly rows on the polished deck as if they were the day's catch. Remaine stood near the port-side railing, an ornately carved masterpiece of dark wood traced in silver. Poor *Lady Vex*, she was more driftwood and patchwork, and could have been stashed away in one of the cupboards aboard *The Emerald Egg*. With every passing second Windluff was drifting away from Remaine in more ways than distance.

Estin shouted from behind the line. "His valor and courage, High Winged General Sir Vector Cottley." The heavy footfall of the general was the only noise audible, save the sloshing of the waves. Cottley walked through the aisle like the king of the sea, every inch of exposed skin etched with scars like glorious testaments to his past victories.

He spun on his heel as he came to the front and motioned for them all to be seated.

"When we arrive at the East Emeralds," he began, his voice a rocky whirlpool of gravel and salt, "you will be tested and trained. Pushed. Pulled. Beaten. But made *strong*."

As he spoke, the general eyed each row of the new recruits slowly, making sure to linger a moment too long on each face.

"Some of you will do fine," he said. "You have strong minds. Good frames." He was like a tiger among wide-eyed and trembling cubs.

"Others will have to fight to keep up." His gaze lingered a bit longer on the thin, wiry frame of Harlo Oswich, but Oswich appeared oblivious.

When the general came to Remaine, his stare lasted an age. It made Remaine nervous, and he fought a strong urge to leap into the waves and swim away in search of any cavern to hide in.

"And some of you," said the general, still focused on Remaine, "might not make it at all."

Remaine swallowed.

"Lostil, Timson, Merchant." With each name the general snapped his fingers. "To me."

The three men of Estin's rank, like trained hounds, marched to the front and silently began to aid High General Cottley in the removal of his outer armor. The pieces dazzled as they fell, one by one, until the general stood in the same plain garments as his lower ranks.

"You begin training today," he barked, "and you'll probably bloody up those red garments—should blend in. You. You." Flinging a massive finger in two meaningful directions, he instructed, "Up."

Two men with olive skin—brothers by the looks of them—rose up quickly. They tried to conceal their nerves, but Remaine could see the fear on their faces as clearly as he could see the horizon-line behind them.

High General Sir Vector Cottley strode up to them and placed a hand on the shoulder of the first. "Have you ever struck a man?"

The recruit shook his head.

"And you?" asked the general to the other, who also shook his head, identically.

"We'll be fixing that. A Royal Guardian earns his weapons. Shields, then swords. Spears last. But you're born with your first weapon. Your fists. You don't have to earn those. Just prove you know how to use them."

Then the general stepped backward like a man who had started a fire and wanted to watch it burn. "When you're ready."

The two boys blinked in shock, first at the general, then at one another.

For a moment nothing happened. The watchful crowd pushed away from them like water from a drop of oil, but the brothers—Remaine was sure they were brothers now—looked wildly lost.

"No?" said the general, his thin tunic flapping in the breeze. A crazed look flashed in his eyes and with the speed of a tiger, he sunk his hand into the belly of the first boy with primal force.

A strained exhale escaped the boy's lips as he stumbled backward. His brother watched on, conflicted. Coughing and gasping for air, the first looked desperately at the general.

"Don't look at me, boy," said the general. "It was *he* who struck you. Now strike back!"

A torturous look of desperation connected the brothers for a split second before it was broken with a nod of unspoken agreement. The first ran at the second and a brawl erupted aboard the slick deck of *The Emerald Egg*.

The fighting felt endless. Remaine struggled to keep his composure as blood began to spill from noses and mouths and cheeks. The shouts between the brothers became more hysterical under the dome of watchful silence that surrounded them.

"Again!" shouted Cottley, shoving the first boy into the second, staining his hand with crimson blood. But the push was too quick, and the boy's head lolled back. He fell on his face landing in a pool of red, knocked out, his limbs splayed.

"Enough," the general said, irritated. "Sit." Sprawled out on the deck, the boy didn't move until his brother helped drag him back to his place. They nursed their wounds with their garments, the color of valor absorbing the color of defeat.

The morning passed with a series of fights, all like the first, and with each one, Remaine Plink feared he might lose consciousness at the sight of the violence. It was sloppy, brutal, inexperienced, yet one by one, the boys were thrown deeper into aggression at the bark of High General Cottley. At some point, when the sun had climbed to its highest point and the shouts of the fighting men had grown endlessly rhythmic, it was Remaine's turn.

"You!" shouted the general, pointing, his gaze a wildfire and his finger like a felled tree in its path.

Remaine felt the color drain from his face.

"Up, boy."

Remaine stood like an animal destined for sacrifice. When he was fully upright, Cottley looked him up and down. "A twig for snapping," he chuckled. "Let's see…"

The general scanned the remaining recruits, as he had with every boy prior, hunting for the best match. But for the first time, he found a hand raised near the starboard side.

The general smiled at Tarquin Pellatrim. "Ah," he said. "It's been a few years since I've seen a home-grown rivalry. Could it have been a girl you were both after? You lads are awfully young for love, aren't you?" Cottley looked at Remaine. "Family rivalry? Money? Doesn't matter. Up with you both!"

A ring in his ear was all he could hear at first, but the crashing waves against the ship broke through and suddenly Remaine found himself face to face with Tarquin Pellatrim, or rather, face to collarbone.

For one, brief moment, Remaine asked himself if he had ever fought someone before—if there was anything, even the smallest shrapnel of advantageous strategy he could draw on. The countless victories he and Igniro had had over the Berylbones in the stories in his mind did not count. The answer was no and that is precisely why Remaine Plink was knocked to the deck under the blow of Tarquin's first swing.

His head buzzed and his cheeks burst into flames. Beneath the burn, deeper into the grain of his bone, a pressure like a thousand heavily booted soldiers began to weigh down on him. He was ashamed to find himself already fighting back tears.

"Up!" the general shouted at Remaine for the second time, this shout infused with a bit of dark delight. Two enormous paws gripped

Remaine's armpits, throwing him back onto his feet. The general's boot collided with his lower back, and he was falling forward into Tarquin's second punch. "Again!"

The sheer, crushing force of Tarquin's fist making its violent contact with his face felt worse with the second punch. It was worse than any pressure he had felt during even the deepest of his dives and his ears pulsed painfully with blood. Perhaps it was his mind's desperate attempt to place the pain in a category, likening it to the collapsing embrace below the waves, that allowed Remaine to recall a miniscule fragment of useful information to help him through.

"Breath deep, Remaine," a nameless Plink said, the voice coming from some far corner of Remaine's mind. Who was it? His grampa, perhaps? "Three deep breaths, then hold the third."

In the bloody fog, his face on the deck, Remaine managed to pull himself to his hands and knees. Tarquin Pellatrim's legs were before him then—they were all he could see. On his third deep breath, he held it and lunged.

But he was too slow, and Tarquin's heavy foot slammed into his rib cage. Remaine heard a crack and screamed out, the act of which sent a sequential sharp buzz right up to the base of his skull.

"Stop it!" A voice rang out amid the sea of blinding white light and red-hot pain.

Remaine was barely aware of Estin standing over him. "He's had enough, General. He's... had enough."

"Where's your head, Merchant?" asked Cottley, with quiet fascination. "Questioning the high general's wisdom?"

"No."

"*No?*"

"No, High General, Sir," Estin corrected himself, lowering his head. "I just—he's not—he's had enough, sir."

Then the general surprised Remaine. He looked down at him as if to give Estin's words genuine consideration. His scarred face solidified like water in the coldest winter and all hope of guessing his next was lost.

"Perhaps," he said, his gaze chilling Remaine's blood. "But where he lacks the fortitude, you will make up for it, Merchant."

It was Estin's turn to freeze.

"Sword Merchant wishes to duel with his High General in the boy's place." At this, Cottley flipped Remaine over onto his back with a swift scoop of his boot. Estin's dark eyes darted quickly, drinking in every detail of his superior's movements.

Remaine scrambled backwards out of the way, wincing with each move. The general, however, looked casual and relaxed, ready to play like a cat with a mouse. He flashed Estin an evil grin then took his stance and stood perfectly motionless. It was understood by all, and not least of whom, Estin, that Cottley did not intend to move. He would let Estin strike first.

Remaine was horrified to see Estin glance down at him with a strange look of comfort in his eyes before launching himself at the general.

Unlike the earlier spars, this one was marked by graceful technique, its violence quick and precise, each maneuver executed with elegance. The two almost moved in agreement with one another, each flinging limbs into places where the opponent had just stepped away. For nearly a full minute they fought as if in a dance, then without warning, the general's wild-fire eyes heated with intensity, and he began to move at a speed Estin was unprepared for.

His leg swept Estin's feet out from under him with a crack like a whip. Estin fell to the deck in a cascade of black braids. The general hurled a kick into Estin's side. A painful gasp escaped Estin's lips. Remaine's own ribs burned at the sight.

Estin rose to his feet under the watchful gaze of the general, and after one deep breath, the fighting continued. This time it was short-lived. Cottley brought Estin down with another heavy blow.

Remaine's chest tightened with sympathetic pain once more as

Estin moaned beneath another kick. Then whirling like lightning, Estin moved. He struck the legs of the general out from underneath him. General Cottley toppled to the deck like a demolished tower, shaking the planks beneath him. Estin leapt to his feet. He spit, wiped his mouth, then raised his fists in defense. The general rose slowly, thoughtfully, bitterly. He stood like a monster exiled to the depths, now rearing its snout to the sunlight for the first time in a hundred years.

The general charged at his opponent, but Estin had anticipated the general's move. With a swift turn, Estin followed the dodge with a blow to Cottley's cheek. A gasp issued from the recruits at the sight of blood in the general's spit.

Then an expression grew from the uninhabitable hardness of the general's face that made Remaine wonder how long it had been since the high general Sir Vector Cottley had been challenged. And Estin, as much as his dark skin would allow, had gone pale.

"Forgive me, General," panted Estin, each of his words like spurts of water shooting out from behind a faulty dam. "I didn't intend to—"

"Silence that pathetic tongue of yours, you bottom-feeding sea scum," hissed Cottley.

The general prepared to lunge, lowering himself into a hunch like a mountain trying to crouch. He lunged but did not collide with Estin.

An invisible wall stopped the general and his fist pounded against it in midair.

Estin, having fully prepared himself for the blow, flinched and sucked in air, only to find the general's fist frozen mid-strike, just inches from his face, unable to come any closer.

Whatever stopped the general's fist also turned his face purple. Then it gripped his arm with invisible force, and his legs for that matter, and scooted him back across the deck as if he were one of the king's statues being rolled back onto a cart.

"Sir Vector Cottley," came a lyrical voice.

Everyone turned to see the prince, on the quarterdeck above, his enormous eagle perched on his shoulder. Beside him stood Lyme Stretcher, peering down at them all like an old dragon, and behind them, stood Captain Rawthorne, as well as the large redheaded man. It was not clear how long they had all been there, watching; all eyes had been toward the bow, and some still were, mesmerized by the frozen giant of a general.

"Thank you for the lesson," said the prince. "I think we ought to pause for lunch."

The general was suddenly released from the invisible grip upon him. The wildfire in his eyes blazed all the brighter as he bowed his head before the prince. Estin followed suit.

The general fumbled for his vial and stormed off, releasing into it a wispy string of the Old Cold.

CHAPTER 8

THE SURPRISING SKETCH OF REMAINE PLINK

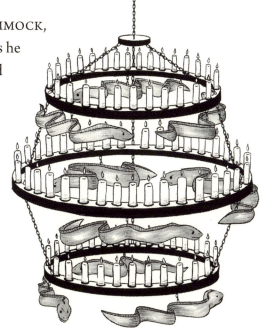

LATER, SWINGING IN HIS HAMMOCK, nursing his wounds as quietly as he could, Remaine was summoned to the prince's cabin.

The journey up from belowdecks was a wincingly painful one. Abovedeck, a few of the other recruits lay sprawled out in a line and several older guards tended to their wounds. Supervising, Estin stood above them all in the same place the prince had stood earlier. Remaine could feel Estin's gaze as he approached the prince's cabin. He hadn't asked Estin to do that for him. Had Estin got into trouble for stepping in? Was Estin mad or disappointed with him? Probably. The thought made him feel all squirmy, so he moved faster toward the cabin door. Remaine lifted the metal clasp of the door knocker, a molded silver head of a harpy eagle, and dropped it lightly to give the door a metallic knock.

Lyme Stretcher said nothing as he opened the door. With a long, tendril-like arm, he motioned for Remaine to step inside.

It was an experience to step inside the cabin and Remaine wondered, once again, at the logistical possibility of a ship this size. The room was domed, somehow, and the ceiling was painted with a familiar scene of wrestling warriors, wearing red, vying for victory over the blue Berylbone giants struggling within their grip.

The circular room was multi-level. On the upper-most level, an enormous, canopied bed was situated like a castle on a hill. At the far end of the room, on the lowest level, rather than a back wall, a broad window of diamond-shaped panes shone brilliantly. The space was filled with an oval table made of jet-black wood and matching glossy chairs. The table itself was mostly covered with loose scrolls and flattened parchment that, by the looks of them, were maps and charts. The whole area was lit by a golden chandelier, carved in the shape of a school of dozens of long, slender eels swimming in a circle.

The prince sat at the far end of the table. The sunset glow streamed in through the expansive grid of windows behind him, saturating the room in an egg-yolk yellow, silhouetting the prince and the high general, who sat next to him like a pet rhinoceros. The light gave the prince a divine air, but for the general, it gave his eyes an animal-like night-vision glow. His predatory gaze narrowed in on Remaine.

"Ah!" smiled the prince, raising a glass to him. "Welcome."

"Sit here, please," said Stretcher, guiding Remaine to the seat most opposite the prince and the general. Nearly twenty feet of table separated them.

Smoothly, Lyme Stretcher glided past Remaine, his long robes snaking behind him. Stretcher slid into the seat at the prince's right hand, and the three men, all at once, directed their gazes down to the table in front of them.

Remaine watched as Stretcher sighed, then gave a disinterested flick of his long finger at a wooden metronome off to his right. The arm of the metronome heaved and began to click in rhythm. With another sigh, Stretcher and the general each pushed several marble figurines across a game board that lay before them. Remaine did not recognize the game. Then Stretcher stopped the metronome and coiled his arms around his chest like two pet boas. He flashed the general a smirk. Sir Vector Cottley slammed a fist on the table. He grunted, apparently conceding defeat. The prince laughed.

"He is clever, isn't he?" said the prince.

This clearly irritated the general.

"The Hollowfiend is always on the hunt," said the prince, raising his glass to Stretcher, then he turned back to Remaine. "Hello, Remaine Plink," he said, turning his chair just slightly to align with Remaine. "How are you feeling?"

Remaine winced and hoped it looked like a smile.

The prince saw through the attempt. "I'm going to guess you've never been hit like that."

Although Silome had made an artform of swatting Remaine down like an annoying fly at the slightest provocation, her slaps were nothing like today's punishment. He shook his head.

"You're not alone there," said the prince. "These first few days at sea are, by design, the first few days of trials for my recruits." The prince reached over the table to grab a tray of goodies, all a powdery beige color. "Here, have a pastry."

Remaine's mouth was watering before he even took a bite. The flaky, creamy puff did not disappoint. He was so delighted by the sudden jolt of sweetness that he did not notice the snowfall of powdered sugar on his lap.

The prince moved to the chair closest to Remaine. He leaned back in a lordly way, bringing his left boot up over his right knee. He rubbed his shortly cropped hair, then brought his hand down around his chin thoughtfully. "My boy, I must be frank. I admire your courage to come here, and I extended the opportunity for you to stay sincerely—but I am not sure you're fit for the job of Royal Guardian."

His words felt like one of Tarquin's punches. Remaine stared at the prince, mouth half-full of pastry. He chewed rather slowly, looking around the room, noticing that the general and Lyme Stretcher had set up for a new game, bored by the exchange between the prince and Remaine.

"You're making me go home? N–no, you can't!" Remaine's mind began to race with the compounding shame that would go with his return.

"You will address your prince formally, boy," said Stretcher, without looking up from his game.

"Sorry," gulped Remaine, bowing his head slightly. His cheeks blushed red. "Your Enchanted, p–please. Unless I'm wounded in battle or something," he thought of Duke Hegs and the way Windluff had celebrated him when he had returned from battle. "If you send me home, it will only prove to everyone h–how worthless I am."

"Send Merchant home with him, my prince" the general grumbled over his shoulder.

The prince acknowledged the comment only by shifting his eyes. Then his gaze returned to Remaine and he raised his eyebrows with pity. "I have some sway, you know, over public opinion. I'll inform Hegs of your bravery. I do admire your bravery in coming, Remaine." He sipped from his cup and popped one of the pastries into his mouth without dropping a single flake of sugar. "We'll arrive at Kipswitch sometime tomorrow morning. From there we'll head to Parva on Weatherlee for another valor stop, then it's on to the Briskman Courses and the East Emeralds after that…"

A map on the table drew the eyes of both of them as the prince spoke, and he dragged it between them so that Remaine could get a closer look. Remaine was mostly familiar with all the locations the prince had described. He understood.

The prince continued, "Kipswitch is a transitory island, as I'm sure you know. A junction port. There will be ships heading to Moorington and Windluff. It's the best place to get you on the right course. I'm willing to help secure your passage on a ship that will take you back home."

The whole thing put a pang in Remaine's stomach. His eyes burned. It didn't even matter if the prince somehow provided Remaine societal pardon—cast him in some contrived courageous light. His family would know the truth. Silome would know.

The prince leaned back in his chair again.

"I will not lie to you, Remaine. From here, the work only gets harder."

Remaine looked up at him, wide-eyed, and suddenly the day flashed before him lucidly. He could feel Tarquin's savage punches hit his memory square between the eyes.

"It is my job to call forth valor and bravery everywhere I go in the Cracklemore Isles. We need all the men we can get in the East. Not to mention the growing threat of the Sand Pirates in the north. The Ravillions have many spineless enemies slinking around in the caverns of Cracklemore, and I am not interested in discouraging anyone from fighting for our cause. But," the prince paused and nodded slowly, with sympathy, "I must be honest about what I see."

Remaine shrank beneath these words. The prince sounded Plinkish.

At that moment, a knock came at the door.

"Your Enchanted," came the muffled voice of the captain on the other side. "The Singer Vulcutta has returned."

"Yes, thank you, Rawthorne!" the prince replied. "Send her in."

Remaine turned in his chair to see the double doors open. A whirl of silvery feathers filled the space as the harpy eagle announced her return. She flew to the prince at once, nearly knocking Remaine over in the process. Remaine flinched a bit. His chest still hurt from where she had stepped on him.

"Good girl, Vulcutta," said the prince, stroking the enormous, dragon-like head of the bird.

Vulcutta clicked her beak.

"Ah," said the prince. "Not now, probably. I'll receive the message later, thank you." The prince winked at Remaine. "She's carrying words from Hubert Hegs, I'm sure."

The Singer let out a high-pitched squeal. Her wings expanded like a canopy.

"Mmm!" said the prince, hopping to his feet. "Forgive me, darling. You must be hungry! A moment, Remaine."

Then the prince outstretched his hand and with a *click*, detached one of the golden eels from the chandelier, jostling the rest of the clinking eels in the process. The prince held the metallic creature out and stroked its smooth surface along its back. Suddenly, a living eel, black and slimy, wriggled in his hands, shedding off its golden armor that fell to the table with a clatter, then dissolved in whisps of yellow smoke, leaving only a small golden pebble.

Remaine scooted back in his chair at the sight of the slithering eel, snapping its huge jaws, gaping frantically, searching for water.

"It's all right," laughed the prince. "These are Vulcutta's favorite. They're native only to Chantyholm." He tossed the writhing black eel into the air where it met its violent end in Vulcutta's sharp beak. She swallowed the eel in one gulp. "I always preserve some in Aureate Shells to bring with us." He grabbed two more, freeing them from their golden encasements, and tossed them to Vulcutta, who shrieked with delight.

The prince sat again, "I'm sorry, where was I? Oh. Right." He leaned forward. "Do you understand, Remaine, why I do not think the path of Royal Guardian is the best for you?"

Of course, beneath all Remaine's hopes of proving himself and bringing something of worth to the Plink name, there was an aching curiosity, stirring down deep, to unravel the biggest mystery of all. *What was wrong with him?* Why had he missed the Great Charming? If anyone knew who Remaine Plink truly was, *and* what to do with him, it would be the prince. But how could he ask him? He looked at the harpy eagle, flexing its feathery neck as it finished off the extra eels. The golden chandelier still shone above, now in what seemed to Remaine a truly magical sort of light.

"How do you do that?" Remaine asked, instead of asking his more important question.

The prince tilted his head, curiously. "The eel?"

Remaine nodded.

"Surely you've seen charms before," said the prince, masking a small little laugh.

"Only a few," Remaine confessed.

"I suppose Aureate Shells are rarer," said the prince. "Most effective preservation charm—there's nothing they can't keep fresh."

"Can anyone do that?" asked Remaine.

"It's not that simple, no."

"You have to be a wizard?"

The prince chuckled. "What do you know of that?"

"Well, I know you're an Enchanter," said Remaine, "and the king is, too."

"*His High Enchanted*," snapped Stretcher. The high general grunted his agreement.

"Sorry," said Remaine. "I only mean… I know your family is special."

The prince smiled again. "Indeed."

"But the rest of it," Remaine said, nodding towards Lyme Stretcher. They both looked at the rusty old lantern resting on the table which Stretcher used as part of his magical performance during the Tour of Valor. Stretcher saw Remaine eye the lantern and a venomous look of protection flashed in his eyes. "Are you an Enchanter?" he asked Stretcher.

"Members of the king's court are not Enchanters, proper." said the prince. "The grand high pinion, Lord Doromund Venerack, is the magical advisor to my father, as Lyme Stretcher is to me. Beneath them are the rest of the court, all gifted in some way. But *Enchanter* is a title reserved for powerful bloodlines whose skills go beyond that of magical specialists. Unfortunately, the Ravillions are the last of that old strength. You can thank the Berylbone invaders and the Old Cold, for that."

The muscles in Prince Xeitas' jaw hardened at his mention of the source of the Old Cold, but then he relaxed and glanced in Stretcher's direction. "Lyme Stretcher and his fellow courtiers are what we call Charmers. Traces of the magical order exist in the rare few today. It's a requirement for the king's court. If they pay attention and train, they can master a few, specialist charms."

"And the rest of us," Remaine said, trying not to expose himself. "We get the Great Charming, and…"

"Yes," said the prince. "The vast majority of Cracklemore is made up of a more fragile constitution, I'm afraid. Again, you can thank our Berylbone friends for that. The Great Charming bestows an enchantment strong enough to keep the Old Cold at bay and provide you with a normal enough life. But the magic's contribution wanes after that, unfortunately. The Old Cold is relentless."

"What happens to people who don't get the Great Charming?" The question came out of Remaine's mouth before he had time to stop it.

The high general and Stretcher simultaneously snorted—it was the only thing they did in the same way.

The prince's brow furrowed briefly, and Remaine felt his body go numb. Did he just reveal his most shameful secret? Then the prince smiled and said in a light manner, "That's an interesting question. I've never heard of that. Have you?"

"Well… no…" said Remaine, thinking quickly. "But Frostblood seems bad. Is it possible for it to spread and make people unable to be Charmed?"

The prince looked pityingly upon Remaine. "Ah," he said. "I see. I imagine you have your father in mind? That was quite the display last night."

Remaine swallowed and gave a quick nod. The memory of the Tour of Valor, and his father's painful public display of Frostblood was now seared into everyone's memories. Though the prince had excused himself, it was clear the whole world knew of the unfortunate unraveling of Philo Plink. Still, Remaine was thankful to have dodged any suspicion.

"Such a paradise, Pylon Crag."

The prince's words were rich with sarcasm as he pointed to the easternmost edge of the map of the Cracklemore Isles where a single island, lumped in with the group known as the East Emeralds, sat ominously alone, bordered by swirls of lines that signified a perpetual wind. Remaine recognized Pylon Crag.

"With every Berylbone that breaks through the veil," said the prince, "so does their poison. It's the poor people of Cracklemore who must carry the ensuing Frostblood. I'm sorry your father has suffered."

Remaine felt himself lingering on his father now. In truth he felt quite mad about it. For so long it had all been kept from him, and he had learned to keep his questions to himself. He was feeling bolder now, and the prince seemed to be in no hurry. Remaine gathered his courage and ventured, "So that's what happened to him? My mother never told me. She always told me he had gotten sick on a fishing trip."

"I expect it was for the best," the prince said. "It's bad form to speak of the Old Cold and Frostblood so openly. We ought not give it dignity."

Remaine nodded.

"But yes," said the prince, nudging Remaine's chair with his boot. The prince raised his eyebrows encouragingly in Remaine's direction. "Your father, I imagine, met a Berylbone or encountered a strong dose of their curse somewhere at sea, and his life was never the same. And that's probably why none of your family ever heard the story. One usually doesn't encounter something like that and come away alive, let alone with clear memories."

Remaine tried to picture the scene, and he was quite good at that.

He saw his father, scurrying back beneath the terror of the icy-faced, marauding, humanoid specter at sea known as a Berylbone, barely escaping with his life.

"Either way, Remaine, I can assure you, the Great Charming still lives in your father and carries him through even the worst of his nights. He'll find true respite in Colony Gardens. I wonder why he has not already left?"

Remaine did not like thinking about that, but truthfully, he did not know why his mother had not spoken more about the relief he would find. Surely, she wanted him to find relief too. "I dunno," murmured Remaine.

"In any case, peace will find him."

"No Old Cold there," said Remaine.

"No," smiled the prince. "It's one of the strongest magical gifts left by the Old Enchanters. Colony Gardens is small, and it cannot hold all of Cracklemore, but it can accommodate the elderly and the sickest of its citizens—they can live out their years in peace, yes."

Silence grew between them, and it lasted for quite a while before the prince broke it.

"Which is why I think, Remaine, if you're honest, you don't truly desire to come with me. This path is fraught with challenges better suited for the likes of... well... the Pellatrim brutes." He winked at Remaine and gave a chuckle. "Or your friend, Estin Merchant." The prince's eyes flashed at the name, and the general looked uncomfortable. "Estin's showing great promise. But I think for you, a young Plink, whose family probably misses him, I think your journey is better suited for the beaches of Windluff."

It took him a while to do so, but Remaine found himself nodding. His shoulders drooped, and his head hung low. He saw the powdered sugar on his red tunic and brushed it off bashfully.

"Come with me, Remaine."

The prince stood up and took his goblet with him. At the far end of his chamber, a vast, mahogany wall was lined with portraits. From the left, stoic men in their prime with strange, decorated robes, all unmistakably Ravillion, gave way to men of similar appearance further on down the row until at last, on the far right, a portrait hung in the exact likeness of Xietas Ravillion. Remaine marveled at the precision of the artist's work. His family had never had the coin for him to experiment with paint (not that they would be overly excited at the idea, anyway), but he had always dreamed of it.

"Not my best side, I'm afraid," said Xietas. Remaine disagreed. Each portrait was painted to increase the perfection of an already perfect bloodline. Remaine couldn't spot a flaw if he tried. Neither in the painted image nor in the living subject. "Do you know who these men are, Remaine?"

A cursory glance told him the facts, obvious enough. "The Ravillion line?"

"Certainly," said the prince. "I assume you notice some are missing?"

Of course, he had noticed. Only some Ravillions were present. And no women. Even King Ignis was missing.

"That's because these men held the office of Chosen Winged Warrior, Remaine." He paused. "Each Ravillion inherits a seed of the ancient magic, and I'm of the Warrior's Charm. As are these before me."

As he said this, a similarity materialized in the faces. It was as if all of them were Xietas himself in another lifetime, or another generation. All with the same eyes. All with the same jaw and shoulders. All warriors.

"It is my job, Remaine, to find the men best suited to guard Cracklemore from the threats that beat incessantly on our shores. Men like my uncle before me, and his uncle before him, and his father before him, and so on."

Remaine fixed his gaze on the portraits as the prince spoke.

"So, though you will head home tomorrow morning, I trust you'll understand it is only because I have a duty to fulfill. An inheritance to steward."

The prince's words were not cruel. In fact, they were calm and clear. Remaine bowed his head sheepishly.

"But I can assure you," said Xietas, kneeling to Remaine's level and placing a hand on his shoulder, "every one of these warriors would be proud of the valor you've shown aboard this vessel. Everyone from Lamire, to Igniro… all of them down to me."

At the mention of his name, Remaine looked up, scanning the wall. "Igniro?"

"Yes, second from the left."

Remaine studied the portrait, the regal, well-groomed ancestor of the prince, posing in stately red robes. Remaine couldn't help but smirk.

"Something amusing?" asked the prince, lifting his goblet to his lips. Cottley and Stretcher perked up.

"Oh… uh… no, no. No, Your Enchanted. It's just…" Remaine was aware all the eyes in the room, including the beady, black, wide-awake eyes of the harpy eagle, were fixed on him. "Uh… never mind."

"I insist," said the prince with a casual wave of his hand. He took another drink.

"I… well… I guess I always imagined him differently. I always thought Igniro was more…" he stopped. He meant no offense, but he feared some might come.

"More what?" the prince asked.

Remaine searched for the right word, then finally said with trepidation, "Wild?"

"Wild?" said the prince beneath raised eyebrows.

"Or… brave?"

"*Brave?*"

"Uh…" Remaine stammered, "not that all these aren't—only just—" he was starting to panic, and he noticed a wicked smirk begin to grow on Lyme Stretcher's face. He knew he needed to choose his next words carefully and with absolute precision. Then it occurred to him: maybe he would not say anything at all. Maybe he would show them.

He hurried back to the table. An ink pot with a silver feathered quill sat near the edge of the map. "May I?"

"By all means," laughed the prince, draining his goblet, and leaning in with interest.

Remaine began to effortlessly sketch the image he had scratched out countless times, every line memorized. The familiar feeling took him as he did so—the hair on his arm raised, the leap of something in his gut—he was back on his perch in his cave. Remaine lost himself and all sense of time in the process. He scribbled until Igniro Ravillion the Great Mariner came into focus on the parchment.

"There," said Remaine happily, stepping back. "I think he would have carried his trident like this, and I do think it was a trident, not a sword—and I think salt would have made his hair… well," he motioned to the gnarled braids, "wild. And I think he would have worn his garment in the Luffy way, like this, and—"

Then Remaine stopped, because he was suddenly aware of how quiet the prince's stateroom had become. It was like all the noises had hidden under the rug or been gobbled up by Vulcutta. Remaine looked up. He found all three men studying him, eyes shiny and focused; he suddenly turned as red as the wine on the table yet he was not even sure as to why.

Had Remaine Plink been a bit older, he would have noticed the three men exchanging lightning-fast side-glances with one another—the sort of exchanges only adults can do when they wish to communicate secrets. But mostly Remaine saw the prince, returning his gaze to the image, drinking in the drawing, even as he lifted his goblet to his lips to drink some more, only to smile when he found he had already emptied it.

"That's quite the mind you have, Remaine," he said. "It's as if you see a whole world we cannot."

"That's what my family says," Remaine blushed. "They always tell me that I need to come back to our world. They think that's what's wrong with me—why I—" he stopped abruptly, his words nearly choking him. He had almost spilled his most humiliating secret.

"Why you what?"

"Why I… can't keep up with them." Remaine said quickly. And he knew, once more, he had sold the lie, because really it was no lie at all. "They're so much better than me, and I'm always behind. Grampa says it's because I'm living too much in my mind." As he said this, his own gaze dropped back down to his drawing.

"You know, Remaine," said the prince, descending to one knee and looking Remaine in the eyes. "I think I've changed my mind."

Remaine blinked at the prince. His dark eyes were like an eternal night sky. "We'd all do better to admit when we're wrong and today, I'm afraid I have wronged you fearsomely. I do hope you'll forgive me for judging you too quickly, especially since Vulcutta, here, already displayed her real liking for you. I'd be foolish to second guess her wisdom. I do want you on board, Remaine Plink."

Remaine did not know what to say.

The prince smiled. "I see something in you, Remaine. I am sorry your family does not see it. I'll tell you what—stick close to me, and I'll make a warrior out of you yet. Just like your Igniro."

A mountain of pride, or maybe joy, or maybe both, began to grow inside Remaine's belly, taking the form of a toothy grin that stretched across his whole face. "Yes, sir! Uh—Your Enchanted, sir! I will!" He winced as his rib gave a painful stab, but he didn't care. Still, the prince noticed.

"Wonderful," said the prince. "Now it's late and you have wounds to tend to. Off to bed."

And with that, Remaine was out the door.

Had he lingered outside, for just a moment longer, he might have overheard the conversation that followed his departure.

"Your Enchanted?" asked Lyme Stretcher, his voice a slick whisper.

"Fate has lavished her favor upon us tonight, my friends," said

Prince Xietas. "I think a slight detour is in order, to see some old friends. Inform Captain Rawthorne. We head north to Broken Bottle."

The high general shifted uncomfortably in his boots and rubbed the scars on his cheek. They all knew what island lay in the heart of Broken Bottle.

"I assure you, Cottley," the prince said with a smile. "They won't bite."

CHAPTER 9

THE MONKEYWOOD WITCHES

AT THE PRINCE'S REQUEST, Remaine stayed very close to him over the next two days—so close, in fact, that very quickly there arose among some of the men a jeering opinion that the prince had acquired a new pet in Remaine Plink.

During the first day following their change of course to Broken Bottle, Prince Xietas made a point to sit and listen to Remaine often, eager to learn about his adventures with Igniro. The prince's laughter and rapt attention garnered strange looks from all as Xietas toted Remaine around. But they were subtle looks, so he remained ignorant of it, until the prince's favor meant Remaine got to skip yet

another round of deckhand duties. That's when Remaine finally heard the grumbling—and he heard it first from Tarquin Pellatrim.

"Isn't it past your bedtime, Baby Plink? Papa prince going to tuck you in?"

Tarquin and Torrin were working under the command of the large, redheaded privateer first mate, and the three of them were wrapping a huge line in a tidy coil. A few strides away, the prince was speaking with the captain and so heard nothing.

"Careful, lad," warned the first mate in his sing-song voice. He eyed Tarquin with flaming eyes as hot as his hair. "You are dancing mighty close to disrespecting your prince."

Torrin elbowed his little brother in support of the large man, but not without shooting a disgusted scowl at Remaine.

That was the first time it occurred to Remaine he was amassing animosity. His cheeks flushed pink. Earlier he had seen the redheaded man whispering with Estin, the two of them surreptitiously glancing over at Remaine. Now it was making sense. He returned to the prince's side.

"Just keep us on the east side of the current, Captain," said the prince. His arms were folded across his broad chest, his jaw tight. The two of them looked out over the dark waters. "I know what I saw. The water went... pale."

"Of course, my prince," said Captain Rawthorne. "If it's out there, we'll spot it." He stood in a casual sort of way, fiddling a gold ring around his thumb. His blue Steller's jay hopped lightly on his shoulder, peering down at the fat, gray cat who looked lazily up at him, tail swishing. Then the captain said, "To speak with full candor, my prince, I'm much more concerned about Broken Bottle."

"Come now, Rawthorne. The rocks should prove an entertaining challenge for a captain of your caliber."

"I appreciate the compliment, Your Enchanted, but I wasn't referring to the rocks. It's what hides among them. I fear we approach pirate waters."

The prince gave a chuckle and clapped Rawthorne on the shoulder. "Hardly. I've never encountered threats in Broken Bottle. At least not of that kind. Few are bold enough to risk sneaky schemes in such risky conditions."

"With respect, my prince, we can never be too cautious. Are you certain you wish to go ahead? Instead, we could organize a rendezvous and—"

"I appreciate your concern, Rawthorne," interrupted the prince. "Always looking out for me—that's why I hired you. I trust you'll keep us all alive, eh?"

"Aye, sir," said Rawthorne, bowing his head. But even as the prince's gaze fell back to the waves, Captain Rawthorne's gaze lingered on the face of Prince Xietas, his muddy eyes calculating something. Then the privateer captain looked down, noticing Remaine for the first time.

"We have not formally met, young sailor. Name's Diggory Rawthorne," the captain extended a hand.

Remaine shook it. "Remaine Plink."

"And what do you wager, Master Plink?" asked the captain.

"Me?"

The prince looked down as well. "Yes, Remaine. A treasure trove of insight. A true Windluffian, you'll know all about dangers at sea—about the Pearlback."

"The Pearlback?" said Remaine. His mind flooded with rapid images—so many he did not know which one to choose. He pictured the statue in city square, near the Palace of Pools. Igniro (the wrong, foppish version), stood atop a slain sea monster, its neck speared right through with a long javelin. Remaine's version, drawn in the Butterfin Caves, was better, bigger. Either way though, Pearlbacks were long dead. Everybody knew that.

Yet, Remaine couldn't help but ask, "You think there's a Pearlback out there?"

"Probably not, Remaine," said the prince, sucking in some air through tight lips. He squinted his eyes shut and pressed the lids with a thumb and a forefinger. "The Pearlback has been all but lost to legend. Perhaps I'm just tired. I think I'll shut my eyes for a couple hours. Remaine, you should retire and do the same. Captain, alert the both of us when we come to Monkeywood."

Of course, Remaine did not sleep a bit after that, not with thoughts of a real Pearlback out there. And there was also the pestering problem of Tarquin, probably somewhere with the other recruits, laughing at Remaine's expense.

An hour later, maybe more, Remaine was summoned again.

Broken Bottle, a half-submerged range of jagged, rocky peaks stretching along the horizon for leagues, brought with it a moonlit fog that licked about the bow of the ship.

Remaine didn't envy Captain Rawthorne who, to focus, had demanded silence aboard *The Emerald Egg*, cautiously guided the colossal vessel into and through the craggy spikes.

Remaine shivered at the taffrail. Something besides the damp fog and the night air brought on the chill. Prince Xietas stood next to him carrying on a whispered conversation with the high general Vector Cottley. Remaine could not understand them, but he knew he wasn't meant to, so instead he observed the scene around them. For the next hour, they passed by towers of rocks, mineral behemoths materializing as silently as they disappeared. The deepening fog that nearly hid the rocks of Broken Bottle muffled the voices of the wide-eyed men, who scurried back and forth on the deck, careful to help guide the ship safely through the maze. Eventually, at the prince's orders this time, members of the crew began pulling on ropes in unison to lower a small, artisan lifeboat, elaborately carved and part of a collection all clearly belonging to *The Emerald Egg*. The little lifeboat alone was worth more than the entire Plink home.

The air of Broken Bottle tingled with the unknown, each craggy spire hiding its own mystery. As they rounded the next rock face there was a break in the fog, and in the distance, there was a lagoon and a mountain island with thick, lush foliage black as midnight. The ominous island, however, was a mere background to the water of the lagoon.

In all his life at sea, Remaine had never seen anything like the lagoon and he gasped at the sight. The water was luminescent, a swirling mixture of light combining an acid green with a glowing yellow and an incandescent blue brighter than any natural blue in the world. Remaine stood on the tips of his toes and leaned over the taffrail.

"Here we are, Plink," said the prince, with a friendly hand toward the suspended boat. "You first."

"Sir?"

"I told you to stick with me, didn't I?" he smiled. "Go ahead."

Remaine climbed aboard the vessel and the prince followed.

"Your Enchanted," came the slick voice of Lyme Stretcher. He raised a long, thin eyebrow. "Vulcutta?"

Prince Xietas looked to his left shoulder where his regal Singer perched like a gargoyle. "Ah. Of course," he smiled, "Old Stretcher's right. You'll be most unwelcome here, my lady. Off to bed."

The prince slid his arm under Vulcutta's talons and passed her from his wrist up to Stretcher's.

"Secure my quarters, please, Stretcher. Quickly. I wish to leave now."

The pinion bowed and disappeared with the Singer.

"Your Enchanted," called Captain Rawthorne. His face illuminated with the strange light reflected from the colorful waters. "I'd feel much better if you allowed one of mine to accompany you—even if just to stay with the boat—Chince?"

"Good man, Rawthorne!" returned the prince. "Send him on over!"

In addition to Lyme Stretcher who slithered aboard after delivering the Singer to the prince's stateroom, they made room for the large, redheaded man named Levo Chince. The high general came next. The monstrous size of the general had not yet become normal to Remaine, and his weight at the back of the lifeboat caused the front end to pop up dangerously high. The boat seemed to nearly sink once it was lowered down. When all aboard had settled, the high general began to row the vessel away from *The Emerald Egg* and into the lagoon.

There are certain things a boy simply cannot resist when he is twelve, and one of those things is to dip a hand into magically glowing water as it rushes by. Prince Xietas was smiling, so Remaine felt free to cup his hand and sink it all the way into the water. He brought a handful up close to his face.

"Oh!" said Remaine. "They're minnows! *They're* glowing."

"Old witches' guard dogs," muttered the high general, eyeing the water suspiciously.

"Manners, Cottley," said Lyme Stretcher, who was also looking with suspicion at the water.

The prince leaned in a bit closer to Remaine to gaze down at the bioluminescent current. "They light up when guests are coming," he said. "You can never surprise our friends."

"Who are your friends?" asked Remaine.

But the prince didn't answer. Instead, he cupped his hand in the water with Remaine, and together they watched a hundred micro, fluorescent minnows darting around. "Tell me, Remaine Plink," he spoke softly, and though the others were near, Remaine knew that the prince meant for his words to be private. They were closing in on the island, nearing the shore. "Have you ever wondered if you might be destined for… a purpose? A fantastic purpose?"

Remaine blinked. Suddenly he did not notice the minnows slipping from his fingers. It was as if Igniro the Great Mariner were talking to him.

"Remaine, I think we were meant to be friends." The prince clapped a strong hand on Remaine's back. "Stay close to me now, and…" He paused once more. "Only speak if asked a direct question. You understand?"

The tide helped to push the boat ashore. Gentle, glowing wavelets crashed along the beach. The prince hopped out first, his boots squishing into the sand. "Right," he said. "Mr. Chince, you stay here. Cottley, Stretcher, Plink, you're with me."

Remaine followed clumsily as the high general rocked the boat behind him. Once they were all ashore, Remaine turned to see Levo Chince, staring severely at him from the boat. Behind Chince, at the far end of the lagoon, past the reef, Remaine spotted *The Emerald Egg* silently awaiting their return in the eerie, greenish light.

The path through the jungle, like the water of the lagoon, was dotted with the illumination of creeping insects, all of whom scurried out of their way and scuttled beneath ferns as they passed. Despite the time of night, the air was hot and stiflingly humid, an oppressive heat worsened by their uphill climb along the faint trail. At several points Remaine wanted to stop, to catch his breath. Where his rib had cracked a little, the breaths were painful and increasingly more so as they climbed. But the haggard breathing of the high general behind him kept him motivated to keep moving. At one point they came to a particularly dark patch, and Stretcher took the lead with his lantern, the path suddenly exploding with fresh light. By the time they reached a sort of clearing, Remaine's damp tunic clung to his chest.

The rocky cliff onto which the trail opened overlooked the lagoon. Tall palms arched high above them, acting as a sort of shelter over the structure built onto the rocky platform that they saw before them. It was an old house nestled into the rock partly made of stone, partly covered with woven fronds, and partly held up by the cliff wall itself. Its windows twinkled from a firelight within.

Remaine stopped to take in the scene, but the high general gruffly prodded him forward. He scurried to catch up to the prince, and together, the four of them approached the old door of the home. The prince knocked, but no answer came.

It was in the silence of their waiting that Remaine felt, more than heard, a sound—a faint rumble, low and hardly audible, something deep, as if it rose from under his feet or emanated from within his chest. He turned to his left, and in doing so came face to face with two enormous, green eyes in the darkness. Remaine yelped and stumbled sideways into the prince, who caught him.

"Steady," said the prince. "Steady."

The eyes belonged to a black panther, who would have disappeared into the night entirely except for the ominous green glow. The panther's mouth hung open, hungrily. The rumbling came from deep within its throat. It was larger than any big cat Remaine had ever seen, and its presence startled even the high general who stood at a very safe distance. Then from the woods behind the panther strode three, shadowy figures.

They were all different, one thick of neck and arm and leg, one quite short and close to the ground, and one tall and thin with a pale braid down to her ankles, all females. All of them had mesmerizing faces with large, knowing eyes painted with all sorts of markings in white and black paint to match the paint in their oily hair. Most jarring to Remaine was the sight of their skin. Even in the faint moonlight and the muted light of the fire that glowed from within the home, their skin had an undeniable greenish hue.

Their presence, in addition to the panther, was enough to send a shiver down his spine. Remaine watched wide-eyed as other creatures scurried about their ankles or hung from the tree canopy overhead. Another panther arrived and flanked them, along with two enormous serpents who slithered from the tree line over to the base of the house. Several monkeys clung to the figures, and a small army of frogs croaked about their feet. All of them bore the same, peculiar green eyes as the panther, along with the same green-tinged skin of the women.

"Your Enchanted," said the largest of the women in a low, musical voice. She clutched at her earthy skirt and bent down on one knee. The other two followed. "Please pardon the menagerie." She rose and glanced at Remaine. He felt silly for his display of terror a moment ago.

"Not at all. The boy was just taken off guard. Would you happen to have a moment to spare for us this evening, Wesha?"

The other two women also straightened, and the large one named Wesha smiled with big, tattooed lips. "We live to spare a lifetime of moments to the Winged Throne." Then her voice took on a less musical tone. "Speaking of wings… The harpy remains away? You remember our family doesn't play well with birds." A monkey hollered its agreement and the panther licked its lips.

"Of course," replied the prince.

The women led the way to the house. The inside of their home had the burning smell of animal urine and sour milk. Remaine gagged. His mother would have died.

Nearly every corner housed little beds of different shapes and sizes, some suspended in the air, some tucked into open cupboards, and all manner of creatures lounged lazily upon them. He could hardly take in all the different animals peering down or out or up at him, their eyes alight with a deep, fiery, intrinsic emerald glow. Wesha and the other two women offered them chairs at an uneven table made entirely of stone that seemed to grow right out of the ground. The three women busied themselves at the far end of the room, in another stony area that Remaine took to be the kitchen. Before long, Wesha brought each of them a mug of something hot. The prince drank first, followed by Lyme Stretcher and Vector Cottley, so Remaine followed. It tasted like nothing more than water and mint.

"The sea smells different tonight, my prince," said Wesha, refilling his cup. "The waves warn us. So… we go to see. And we see you. And we smell something in the air. On the water. Something is… strange."

At this, Wesha eyed Remaine as she took her own seat. A monkey dropped from the ceiling and landed on her shoulders, making the high general jump.

"Ha!" laughed Wesha wickedly, "I see claws and teeth still haunt you, Vector?" The general shifted in his chair and Remaine saw him stroke a scar on his neck, but Wesha had already turned her attention back to the prince. "Tell me, how are things progressing in the Pass?"

"Very well," said the prince, sipping his drink. "From what I hear, nearly complete. Doromund Venerack will oversee the transfer to Chantyholm. I look forward to seeing them there."

"Bah," scoffed Wesha. "Doromund Venerack. What the king sees in him, I'll never understand. I'll expect a summoning to come clean up Venerack's mess. Ah well. Never mind. But, how can I serve *you* this evening, my prince?"

"Wesha, I'd like to introduce you to a new recruit, and a friend of mine, Remaine Plink, of Windluff."

"A Luffy boy?" sung Wesha, taking a sip from her cup. Then she added with stronger inflection and raised eyebrows, "And a new recruit, you say?" Remaine felt her take in his small frame. She smiled and sipped again.

"Vulcutta found him worthy," said the prince.

Wesha laughed. "As if the eagle ever says no."

The prince shifted. "The boy shows courage," he paused, then he said more slowly, "and potential."

The room was silent for a moment, and one of the enormous panthers strode silkily from one bed to another, his massive eyes lingering on Remaine as he passed.

"There are many peaks in this world to climb. Tell me—which do you see the boy ascending?"

"Just… the one," said the prince. Suddenly Remaine felt he was not in the room at all, or that everything they said was not meant for his ears. Prince Xietas rummaged in his robes and removed a small scroll. Unrolling it on the table, he swiped a quill from a messy nearby inkpot. "Do you mind?"

"Not at all," said Wesha, waving a large, green hand. She leaned back, intrigued.

"Remaine," said the prince, "I want you to draw, here, the very same thing you drew for me aboard our ship. Can you do that?"

Remaine could hardly believe his ears. Whoever these women were, whatever it was they were doing here, could it be true they all saw *potential* in him? So far from the world back home that had held no room for his gift, here his talent was prized?

Eagerly, Remaine took the quill and began to sketch out the scene. In his mind's eye he could already see everything before he ever even touched the parchment. He drew the dynamic movement of the ocean-sprayed Mariner, the grip of his trident, the ragged fit of his garments, the shadow of the Pearlback beneath the water. As always, he was unaware of passing time, nor did he notice Wesha set her tea down and lean forward, eyes wide as she watched. When he was done, Remaine looked up to find a thousand watchful eyes, most of them a glowing, acid green, staring at him. The orange coals of the fire were nearly dead.

"*Visions of a time long felled...*" muttered Wesha.

"Long what?" asked Remaine, rather abruptly.

"Prophecies are fickle, my prince," said the other woman, whose white braid was so long it nearly touched her ankles.

"There's only one prophecy that matters, Mora," said the prince. "And *it's* not fickle."

Wesha stood to her feet. "Mora misspoke. *Interpretations* are fickle." She strode to a cabinet and cracked it open. "You wish to test him, then?" she asked over his shoulder.

Xietas didn't respond at first. He glanced down at Remaine, gave him a quick smile, then replied, "Yes. Any information you're able to provide about his identity—his nature—it can't hurt."

"My nature?"

"Yes, Remaine," the prince said. "I don't think either of us know who, exactly, you really are."

Remaine furrowed his brow, confused.

"Yes," said Wesha. "Who are you, boy?" She widened her eyes slightly, and Remaine felt she could see more of him in that moment. She continued, "Of course, we saw you coming, my prince, we knew we'd be brewing something… but…" she looked at Remaine with shiny eyes, "I did not anticipate this."

The other two women busied themselves in a corner, the smaller one grubbing around below while the taller ferreted about in the cupboards above. They produced large, purple flowers from a hemp bag and tossed them into a big bowl. They began grinding the petals to a powder. Meanwhile, Wesha removed several other items from behind a corner curtain, and in just a few minutes' time another cup was placed before Remaine, this one filled with a greenish, smoky liquid.

"Remaine," said the prince. "There are only good things in store for you if you will simply trust me." He acknowledged the women with his hand. "I trust them, and you can, too. I want you to drink this. Do you understand? No harm will befall you."

"W–what is it?"

"There's a prophecy," said the prince, "about one whose mind is saturated with the visions of ancient days… *days long felled.*"

"Visions?"

The prince nodded and motioned towards the piece of parchment.

"You mean… that's real?" asked Remaine. His head felt light. "What else does the prophecy say?"

The prince looked at Wesha, then back at Remaine, thoughtfully. "It's… long, and broken up—much of it has been lost, or forgotten, but the line I speak of says, '*Unless the one whose breath is held with visions of a time long felled—*"

"—Breath is held?" gulped Remaine. "What does that mean?"

The prince smiled. "I told you. It's a way of saying someone whose mind is swept up in visions."

Remaine's heart was beating fast. Could this be what was wrong with him—why he was immune to the Great Charming?

"Remaine?"

"What?" startled Remaine. He had been staring off.

"Remaine, you can trust me. Drink, please."

Remaine looked at the prince and could not deny he had a true friend in him. He drank the liquid.

It slid down his throat like a warm soup, thick, but more like air than liquid. It tasted like rain and flowers, and then it tasted like black smoke.

As Remaine finished his drink, the three women all came to the table to sit across from him, and had it just been the seven of them, they might have all sat comfortably. But it was not just the seven of them, for every creature in the home had now gathered at the table too, and a scene began to unfold, a scene so odd that Remaine felt his own jaw dropping lower each second.

Every animal began to press in around the next, linking tails and arms and feet and toes. The two panthers stood in between the three women, paws resting on the women's legs, eyes fixed on Remaine, while monkeys hung from the ceiling, linking their swinging appendages. Then the women shut their eyes tightly, and without warning, they began to chant. The song was a harmonic, hypnotic round, their voices linked as seamlessly as the animals around them.

After a few moments of this, Remaine realized he was unable to close his mouth. A painful tightness gripped his throat and jaw, and as if unlocked by a key, his mouth was ajar, wide open and stuck that way. He began to panic. Now his mouth was opening wider—it was beginning to hurt. Tears blurred his vision as the women continued to sing, louder and louder. Remaine grabbed his legs and gripped tightly, then he gripped the prince's arm and cried out.

Suddenly it stopped. All of it. His mouth clamped shut, and the women fell silent, giving great big heaving gasps.

Remaine sat back in his chair rubbing his jaw, terribly confused. But that confusion was nothing compared to the feeling that followed, when Wesha stood and said through heavy breathing.

"A waste of time!" she panted. "Why do you bring a child? He is not of testing age!"

The prince stared dumbfounded at them. He peered down at Remaine, perplexed.

"How old are you?" he asked.

Next to Wesha the panthers were growling.

The smallest of the other two women spoke breathlessly, "Has he been Charmed or not!"

The prince's face twisted. "Did you not say you were twelve years of age?"

Remaine stammered. "I… I am…"

"How is this possible?" asked Lyme Stretcher, who had scooted his chair away from Remaine by a couple inches.

"What is this corruption?" asked Mora, disgusted.

"A vile perversion," said the smaller one. Both the prince and Wesha were staring at Remaine, analyzing his every move.

"I SAY WE TOSS HIM!" barked the general.

"*No!*" pleaded Remaine. "Please!" And then he spilled his great confession. He revealed his abnormality. He admitted that the Great Charming had passed him by, had left him empty. He found himself holding up his vial, and with tears streaming down his face, he pled with them to believe him as he recounted the night the Great Charming had completely skipped over him. Finally, with desperation, he looked directly at the prince and added, "You said '*the one who held his breath*'!"

"What did you say?" breathed Wesha.

Remaine glanced around, his skin prickling. "*The one whose… whose breath is… held*? The prophecy?"

"That's not what that means, boy!" hissed Wesha. Her panther bared its teeth.

"Interpretations are fickle," whispered the prince to himself, his gaze a world away.

Wesha stood to speak, but she never got the chance, for the door burst open. Levo was panting.

"Pirates, my prince! Pirates!" he shouted. "The bloody ship is under attack!"

The high general exploded to his feet first, followed by the prince. Within seconds, everyone was outside, standing at the edge of the cliff overlooking the lagoon. Shouts echoed across the ethereal water, and another ship, practically a toy in comparison to the great *Emerald Egg*, could be seen in its prismatic glow.

"Levo, keep the boy beside you and stay back," said the prince, already moving towards the trail. "I want him preserved at all costs. Cottley!"

But Cottley needed no invitation, he was already at the prince's side and Stretcher was right behind them, holding his lantern aloft. The three of them disappeared into the lush jungle.

"Come on, lad," said Levo, following a pace behind. "Stick with me." Remaine glanced over his shoulder at the three women. By the looks of it, they would be close behind as well.

CHAPTER 10

HARBOR'S HAND

WHEN REMAINE AND LEVO REACHED THE BEACH, they found the prince standing next to Stretcher at the water's edge. A hint of smoke filled their nostrils, and the jungle was alive with howling monkeys. In addition to the glow of the lagoon, now frantically swirling with color, there was a new illumination in the water. *The Emerald Egg* was alight with flames, licking the stern through the shattered glass windows of the prince's private chambers.

"YOU DIDN'T BEACH THE BOAT!" shrieked the grand pinion at Levo. He flung a long, bone-thin arm towards the lagoon, pointing at the artisanal lifeboat that Levo had left unattended, now bobbing freely in the water. The high general waded into the water, waist-deep, making his way to the boat. The prince was frozen, his face towards his burning ship as Cottley struggled to get the lifeboat back to the beach.

"M-my prince," stammered Levo, "m-my prince forgive me, I came straight to you—to warn you!"

"*Silence!*" ordered the prince.

From their position, they could hear shouts and more cannon explosions echoing across the water. Within a minute, the blossoming orange flower of fire in the prince's chambers began to shrink, but not before another one, a much larger one, began to grow on a smaller ship farther out in the lagoon.

The high general bellowed indistinguishable curses in the direction of the flaming vessel. He was still dragging the small boat back to the beach.

The three women arrived on the beach along with their entourage of accompanying beasts.

One large serpent slithered in between Remaine and Levo.

"BLAST IT TO HELL!" shouted Levo, nearly climbing up onto Remaine's shoulders to get himself away from the lime green viper. Remaine feared he might be crushed, but Levo collected himself.

Remaine did not fully appreciate how helpfully illuminating the lagoon minnows had been until, at that very moment, the water went suddenly dark. As if sucked from the lagoon by an invisible current, the minnows fled, leaving an eerie blackness. The only light left came from the small pirate ship on the horizon, fiercely ablaze.

The monkeys stopped howling.

"What's this?" asked Levo.

"Where did they go?!" barked the high general, slapping the black water in a display of either terror or fury.

But no one answered. A tickling sensation crept over the back of Remaine's neck. He turned to find both Wesha and the prince staring at him. The other two women matched their scrutiny, along with a hundred wide-eyed animals.

"You bring a curse to our home," breathed Wesha.

Then they heard it. A laborious moan, deep beneath them. The sound, muffled only a little by the waves, reverberated around the lagoon, rising up like a banshee's scream, putting every hair on end. It was like the cry of a whale, but that was akin to saying the growl of Wesha's panther was like the purr of a kitten. This was deeper, louder, bigger. Much bigger.

"Demon of the deep…" breathed the prince. He stepped forward, his eyes wide.

Out beyond the reef, a monster surfaced.

Remaine was sure he was staring at the beast's body; it was larger than any whale he had ever seen. But as it rose, with huge waterfalls pouring down its scales, milky white and awash with the yellow light of fire, Remaine gawked in disbelief. He realized he was only seeing the head and neck of the creature, partly veiled in swirls of fog. The rest of its body remained concealed beneath the waves.

Another scream, as if the sea itself was crying out, erupted from the throat of the monster. Wesha and the other two women wailed, pressing their hands to their ears.

The prince yanked a spear from General Cottley's hand. Remaine stared in wide-eyed disbelief. Did the prince intend to throw it? The distance was impossibly far, and besides, what was a spear to something of that size? But the prince moved with purpose, and within seconds he was standing at very edge of the water. His eyes darted between the monster and the spear.

The prince began to hum a quiet little melody and the spear in his hand began to glow. Then he threw the spear. It shot through the air like a flaming arrow. A single heartbeat later, Remaine saw the eye of the Pearlback, a black, pond-sized disc, squeeze shut in pain. A third wail erupted from deep within the creature's belly. The earth shook beneath them. A wake of water rose and retreated as the creature's massive body shifted beneath the surface.

The dragon head of the Pearlback stretched up into the low hanging layer of cloud-like fog. Silence sucked up the world, at least until Remaine heard the screams of men out on the prince's ship.

"No!" breathed Levo.

Screaming once more, this time in clear agony, the Pearlback brought its enormous chin down upon the floating bonfire of the pirate vessel, drowning it beneath the waves and sending a wall of water rushing into the lagoon and a plume of seawater into the sky.

Grabbing the back of his tunic, Levo jerked Remaine back up onto the beach, as the wall of black water hit the shore. From their vantage point they saw *The Emerald Egg* lifted and tossed against a rocky spire of Broken Bottle. They heard the crunch, but the ship remained afloat.

"Steady, Lad," breathed Levo, his large hand shaking violently.

Silence followed. The water settled; the stillness of night fell like a blanket. The Pearlback had disappeared beneath the waves.

It was Wesha who spoke first and her words were flat and lifeless.

"I want this disenchanted abnormality off my island. Prophecy or no—do *not* return with him."

The prince reacted swiftly. He grabbed Wesha's wrist violently. Wesha's sultry, composed face twisted in pain.

"Do *not* forget whom you serve, witch. You order me not." Remaine had not known the prince for long, but evidently something deep inside him had been stirred.

Wesha's silence broiled beneath his gaze, but she kept her mouth shut.

Soon they were climbing into the lifeboat. With extravagant protest, the high general exclaimed, "Not with that demon out there!"

"Out there, *my prince!*" snarled the grand pinion.

"Shut it, *Stretcher!*" Cottley barked back.

"We move now—while it nurses its wounds, Cottley!" declared the prince, silencing them both. And as if on cue, the glow of minnows began to light the water once more, reassuring them of the Pearlback's absence. "Move."

When they arrived back at *The Emerald Egg*, Captain Rawthorne extended his hand to hoist Remaine up. The captain's coat sleeves were mostly gone and what remained of them was black and singed. His arms were blackened as well, the flesh blistering and wet with blood.

The prince noticed the wound and spoke first. "Explain, Rawthorne."

Most of the men were still pale. The Pellatrim brothers looked positively dumbfounded and Captain Rawthorne looked troubled. He shoved his sword back into its scabbard with a click and wiped his brow.

"My prince—"

"TWICE, you've failed in your duties, *Captain!*" snapped Lyme Stretcher, flinging a long, bony finger at Rawthorne with a swish of his garments. "And *you!*" he screeched, his gaze whipped back in Levo's direction. "*You* let the boat drift out. We've hired IDIOTS!"

"Captain nearly died trying to stop 'em!" bellowed Levo Chince. "Look at 'im!"

It was true Captain Rawthorne had transformed from the stoic, quiet figure with pets in the corner to a bedraggled sailor, drenched in sweat and blood and utterly short of breath.

The prince spoke again, quietly, his eyes shining with focus. "Rawthorne tried to warn me," he said. "What happened?"

"My prince." Rawthorne bowed and began again "They were small—nearly impossible to spot. Manned by two, three men is all. I smelled the smoke before I saw it... coming from your chambers." Captain Rawthorne gave the prince a moment to digest, then said, "but the doors were locked. I tried to get in—" he held up his arms, singed and bloody, "Merchant helped me—we broke in eventually, but by then the stateroom was aflame, the windows shattered, then—"

"I saw the ship first!" interrupted Tarquin Pellatrim, stepping forward. He was all too pleased at the potential accolades that might come from such a contribution. But the prince was not in a rewarding spirit. He hardly blinked in Tarquin's direction. This made Tarquin pouty. He stepped back.

"He did," said Rawthorne, nodding in Tarquin's direction. "From there we all worked to take care of the flames. These two lads readied the guns," he motioned to the Pellatrim brothers. "We were armed and firing within a minute."

"And the pirates?" asked the prince.

"They would have made it back to their vessel by the time we opened fire, my prince."

"You're suggesting they're all—"

"Dead, sir. Yes. They'd have to be. They all… sank… and…" Captain Rawthorne looked as if he was going to be sick.

The prince took a step forward. "And?" he asked, sharply.

"And…" Rawthorne swallowed. "Everything they stole sank with them."

Suddenly thrown off, Prince Xietas' eyes darted and blinked, his jaw muscles flexed. Then he was marching across the deck to the doors of his chamber, followed closely by everyone else, anxious and curious.

The broken lock dangled from where Estin and Captain Rawthorne had finally breached it. The prince threw open the door. Remaine could see the charred interior. The smell of smoke was still thick, even as the open air rushed in.

Prince Xietas Ravillion whirled around. In a flash he had Captain Rawthorne pinned against the wall to the left of the doors, his forearm on Rawthorne's throat. The captain did not fight, his neck and eyes bulged beneath the force.

"I'm sorry, my prince," wheezed the captain.

"*Vulcutta!*" spat the prince. "You let them take her!"

"They… were… ." His voice strained as he gasped for air, "they were gone by… the… time…"

The prince slowly released Rawthorne, his face fraught with frustration.

"I'm—I'm sorry, my prince," the captain panted, rubbing at his throat.

"Test his story, Your Enchanted!" demanded Stretcher, still furious. Nobody moved as Stretcher disappeared into the previously opulent chambers of Prince Xietas, now just a blackened hollow. He returned a moment later, panicked.

"The Hoaxbite too, my prince," said Stretcher. "Gone." He coughed nastily and glared at Captain Rawthorne.

"Your Enchanted," said Rawthorne, bowing. "I cannot possibly understand the value of all they took. I can only beg forgiveness."

The prince allowed the words to settle between them. With each passing second, the prince regained his stoic composure, his breath steadying.

Into the silence, Rawthorne added, "However, I did find this."

He held up a silver object, tarnished with black charred marks. At first Remaine thought it was some sort of dish, but as Rawthorne turned it over in his hand, Remaine noted three holes in object. The silver was carved in the clear likeness of a snarling tiger. It was a mask.

The prince took the mask. "Sand Pirates? This far south of the Cracked Desert?" He looked to Rawthorne, who shook his head, mirroring the prince's confusion.

The prince glanced around the ship and out to the sea and up to the night sky like he was trying to piece together a puzzle.

Captain Rawthorne spoke again. "We cannot sail to the East Emeralds like this, my prince. I suggest we chart a course to Ravillion Bay. If it be your wish, I shall retire from service there."

The prince glanced at the mask, then again into his chambers, singed and sooty. "What of the damage to the ship from the hit on the rocks?"

"We have a few leaks in the galley, my prince," said one of the men of Estin's rank. Sweat was pouring down his forehead. "But she'll sail."

The prince gave a curt nod. "I'll require your chambers then, Captain," said the prince. "Get us moving. Tonight. And send your Singer to Parva. They'll need to postpone their plans for the Tour. After that, send word to Duchess Chipping. Inform her of our situation and our arrival. Oh… and should you have any instincts about what lies ahead… or below… don't hesitate. Follow them this time."

Though he tried to disguise it, the prince looked out over the black sea in worry. "I want us out of these cursed waters."

Somewhere out there, the Pearlback was lurking, and the thought of the monster slithered down Remaine's spine like a cold snake.

Had it not been for the terrors of the night before, the following day might have passed as a tranquil, even peaceful sort of day at sea. Piles of sunlit clouds softly smashed together in an otherwise perfectly blue sky. All the winds were warm and favorable, and to top it all off, a bountiful catch of fish presented itself around noon. *The Emerald Egg* had left Broken Bottle behind some time in the middle of the night, and by sun's rise the northernmost edge of the Pearl Sea was also far behind them. By nightfall next, at the prince's request, they had sailed into the shallower waters along the Weatherlee coast, always keeping the sheer wall of the mainland's western cliffs in view.

But in truth it was not a peaceful day. Even the dazzling white light that sparkled and danced on the waves was a mask, a mirage hiding the dark thing that lurked beneath, the monster that could surface again at any moment. *Demon of the Deep*, the prince had called him.

Really, it was all Remaine could think about. When he had awoken that morning, his stomach gave its great, heaving growl again, and to Remaine, it sounded just like the Pearlback. He had also dreamt of a white mountain rising up out of the sea, and at its peak, he had seen Igniro the Great Mariner.

"I've never seen anything *like* it," he said, mouth full of apple. He slurped the juicy pulp off the apple's core and wiped his lips with the back of his hand. "Well, not *truly*. I *have* seen it a thousand times in my mind."

The prince, who was less enthused to engage in conversation about the Pearlback up to this point, looked over to Remaine with a flash of curiosity.

"I can't wait to tell Silome about this. Though she probably won't believe me. She never really does. But I'll tell her anyway." Remaine took another bite of his apple. "I think I always knew it'd be that big. The statue in city center is way too small. The proportions are all wrong."

They were sitting in Captain Rawthorne's cabin. The cabin was much smaller than the prince's, but it was still bigger than any chamber belowdecks. Prince Xietas, staring at Remaine, leaned back in his chair, kicking his boots up onto the small table.

"Amazing," he said.

"What?" asked Remaine, wiping his chin.

"You've anticipated the beast? You knew its size?"

Remaine rolled an apple seed around in his mouth. He pictured his favorite stories—the ones where he and Igniro bravely defended the entire world from the monstrous Pearlback. "I guess so," he said.

"And your family," prodded the prince, "they never gave your thoughts any credence?"

Remain wiped his chin. "They're just stories I make up. Right?"

"Perhaps," said Xietas, leaning back. "But do I understand you correctly, Remaine? You *see* things..."

He was right of course. That was exactly the way it was. It was stronger than just imagining; when he'd lose himself on adventures with Igniro, Remaine felt like it was really happening. He pictured his perch in the butterfin caves, and the way Silome had somehow managed to brush it off as unimportant, even in her compliments of it. She didn't understand what it was like to be swept away.

Remaine nodded to the prince.

Xietas leaned forward, dropping his boots from the table and replacing them with his elbows and forearms. "I'll say this plainly, Remaine, so you have no need to wonder or doubt. The things discarded as meaningless by your family—these pictures in your mind, this adventure in your spirit that drove you to me—this... *gift* of yours? I want you to know, *I* think it to be one of the most important things about you. You are of incalculable value, Remaine Plink. Just as you are."

This gave Remaine a feeling like worms in his belly. He suddenly felt hot in the cheek and squirmy in his chair. No one in his family had ever strung three words together that expressed half as much pride as the prince expressed now.

A gentle smile painted the prince's face, and Remaine felt, profoundly, that something exciting lay ahead in his future.

Still, at all this talk of gifts, Remaine remembered, almost all at once, his encounter with the green women on Monkeywood. The prince had called Wesha a witch. What did they do to him? In all the excitement of the Pearlback, he had not had the chance to stop and think much about the alarming scene that had happened inside their island hut.

"Excuse me, Your Enchanted," said Remaine, having the grace to set the rest of his apple down, yet too embarrassed to say thank you for the prince's profession of support. "Did the Pearlback come because of me, like Wesha said?"

The prince's eyes blazed with focus, then shifted away to contemplate Remaine's question. "I'm not sure."

"You say I'm gifted," said Remaine. "But they called me…" he remembered, with a sour feeling in his stomach, her exact words: "they called me a disenchanted abnormality." He swung his sandaled feet from the edge of the large chair he was perched in. He was no longer hungry for the apple, and he left it half-eaten on the table.

"Their sight is limited," the prince said, resolved in tone. "The Winged Throne flies higher—we have a broader view. You can trust that."

Then he stood and strode to the round window. The bottom half was a simple, stained-glass seascape, and the top perfectly clear. The light shone in, washing the prince in shades of blue and yellow. "I have many questions myself, Remaine. For now, let's assume the best about you, rather than the worst. Yes?"

Remaine smiled. His appetite returned. He swiped the apple up again, taking another big bite.

First Mate Levo Chince was, for the most part, always eating. Or drinking. It was not a mystery as to how the redheaded man had grown to such sizeable proportions. And most of the time, Levo was chuckling, too. It was constant, his quiet little chuckling. Remaine marveled that Levo could find so many funny things in the world. With every coil of the rope, with every pull at the jib, with every mop of the deck, or, and especially, with every swig of his wine, Levo Chince chuckled.

Remaine was doubly surprised then, when Levo discovered him peering over the balustrade at the damage done by the Pearlback. The sudden appearance of the man over his shoulder made Remaine jump, but equally as alarming to Remaine was Levo's uncharacteristically serious face.

"Mad times," he said, as he took a bite of pickle with a soft crunch. "Most in the world thought it a myth, or at least long dead—the Pearlback—and now I seen it twice."

"Twice?" asked Remaine.

"I knew I saw it in Windluff. From your big cliff. I knew I saw it. The water was paler, and the paleness shifted, and..." his eyes widened, then he blinked, and a smile returned to his face. Then he chuckled. "Pickle?"

At dawn on their fourth day of travel, the ship changed its heading one hundred and eighty degrees after having rounded the Lion's Point, and it headed south into Ravillion Bay. The city was still a few leagues off, but as the sun rose in the east, the city's towers glittered before them—a vast, sparkling jewel, dwarfing the size of Windluff ten times over, and Ravillion Bay itself was dwarfed by the peaks of the mountains rising behind it. The mountains encircled the city like a dragon guarding treasure—Remaine stared hard at them, trying to digest their size—never had he seen mountains as mountainous as these, and he could not at all fathom why they were named, merely, the Hollian *Hills*.

As they drew near to the city, Remaine, upon invitation, took a shift in the crow's nest with Estin Merchant.

"If Silome ever challenges your strength again," Estin told Remaine, as they both stared at the mountains looming before them. "Tell her you survived a Pearlback attack, *and* a Sand Pirate attack."

Remaine shivered. It was strange how the Pearlback could do that to him, simultaneously frighten and intrigue him. It was only the hundredth time he had imagined its pearly white back barely visible beneath the water, but something about his perch in the crow's nest gave him a clearer picture.

"Estin." Remaine paused. "I never really thanked you for sticking up for me during training."

Estin leaned on his elbows on the edge of the nest. "Couldn't help it," he said.

"Did you get in trouble?"

"No. Well, at least not by the prince. The general doesn't like me much."

"You scared him!" Remaine said quietly, giggling.

Estin tried to join in his laughter, but his face became serious again. "I made him mad, you mean."

Remaine stopped. "Well, I know I made *you* mad by coming here... sorry about that..." Estin turned to look at him, and Remaine felt a stab of desire to prove something to Estin, so he added, "but the prince sees promise in me. I won't let you down, or him, or my family. I promise. Even Wesha. I'll show her."

"Who?"

"Wesha—the witch we went to see."

"Who was she?" Estin turned to face him now, intrigued. "The prince has taken interest in you, Remaine. Why? Why did he take you to see witches?"

"I'll let you know when I figure it out," said Remaine, honestly.

"Listen, Remaine," said Estin, "Whatever happens, please just—" he struggled for words. "Don't forget who you are. And—" he glanced around, then he said more quietly, "try to stay calm."

Remaine was about to ask what Estin meant by that when a shout came from below.

"Plink!"

Remaine peered down from the nest to see Lyme Stretcher, who motioned to him with a long arm.

"See you," Remaine said to Estin, then scurried down from the Crow's Nest.

"His Enchanted will see you at the bow." reported Lyme Stretcher. The man had changed clothes and now wore a hooded robe. His vulture-like face was concealed in part. Remaine turned and saw the back of the prince, there at the bow of the ship, standing like a carved figurehead. He thanked Stretcher and approached the prince reverently.

The city grew before them as they sailed closer. Everything about the world around him was tall and conical. The pointed towers of the city stretched sky high, imitations of the white mountain peaks behind them. The forest of pines all around were of a similar dramatic form, encircling the Hollian Hills—even the clouds above appeared menacingly large.

"We will not be in Ravillion Bay for long," the prince said, turning to Remaine. "While the crew regroups, and we formulate a plan of travel, I may ask you to accompany me on… an errand, or two. It's occurring to me that you might have keen insight on an old riddle we've been working on for some time—a riddle we found in the mountains." The prince shook his head. "I see you have questions, Remaine. I'm sure you have lots of questions. And no doubt you'll have even more. In time we'll address every last one of them. Trust me. I am with you—I promise to help you. But for now, stay close and be patient." He folded his arms around his chest.

The ship glided closer to the city's harbor, and Remaine drank in the sight of the massive sprawl of docks and piers. It was the only part of this city that reminded him of home.

There was a different shape which struck him, though. Out of the water, in the middle of the bay, sticking up out of the sloshing blue waves, was an enormous white hand carved out of marble.

The prince must have seen him eyeing the colossal appendage.

"Harbor's Hand," said Prince Xietas. "A relic from an ancient time."

The marble hand entranced Remaine and a tickling sensation ran down his back at the sight of it. It reminded him of Mariner's Cliff. He could picture the hand's huge arm which must lay beneath the surface of the water, and he could imagine the rest of the titanic figure the whole thing must be attached to, sunk deep below the waves. It was a sad figure, and the statue, when it was upright, Remaine knew, must have made people cry.

"Oy!" came a shout from midship. Remaine turned along with the prince to see Levo waving towards the passing shoreline where a silver stream, bordered by green foliage, was pouring out into the bay. Even at their fair distance, Remaine saw the unmistakable form of a large, pale-golden cat lapping up water. "A good omen for our arrival!" cried Levo, and the others cheered.

"Ah," the prince said quietly to himself, gazing out at the distant cat. It reminded Remaine of Wesha's panthers, but it was much larger. "A bay lion."

The cat raised her head and with enormous topaz eyes, watched the ship as it passed.

"They're celebrated in Ravillion Bay—an echo of the city's sigil," said the prince. "Bay lions are benign descendants of an evil, ancient monster that used to terrorize these lands. The Hollowfiend. Now extinct."

The prince scanned the coastline, then returned his gaze south to the approaching city. Then Remaine noticed Xietas Ravillion's cloak anew: its spouting collar made of a silvery, moon-spun mane and its silver-pelted edging made of a shimmering band of fur.

"The Hollowfiend." Remaine repeated reverently.

The prince smiled. "I suppose we're fascinated by things that terrorize us."

Remaine's mind returned, once again, to the Pearlback.

"We'll be arriving shortly," the prince said. "Gather your things. When we arrive, I want you to—"

"—stay close," said Remaine.

"My prince," said Captain Rawthorne. He had approached quietly and now stood directly behind them. "We should head to your quarters to discuss our plans for disembarkation at Lichenbluff Castle—Duchess Chipping will be waiting. Perhaps Pinion Stretcher and the high general wish to join as well?"

"Yes," nodded the prince. "Very good, Rawthorne."

Then the prince patted Remaine on the head and, with a swirl of his dark cape, strode away across the deck, disappearing through the double doors into the captain's quarters. Captain Rawthorne trailed behind, then turned back to look at Remaine.

"Care to give the men a hand, Plink?" he asked, pointing to a bolt rope lying loosely on the deck. "Needs wrapping up before we come into port. And when you're finished, would you mind clearing this cargo out of the way. I want a clean deck."

Remaine agreed, familiar with the rigging. And the stack of barrels and crates wouldn't be too much of a problem. The captain trotted off to meet with the prince and his men.

Harbor's Hand loomed above them, casting a dark shadow over the ship as they passed by. Remaine marveled at the sight, then, remembering his duties, began to wrap the line, muttering the little song his grampa had taught him when he was younger. "Loop below and twist it back. Loop below and twist it back." He could hear Deeno Plink saying, "I'd like to see a knot try to worm its way into *that*, Remaine!" He smiled at the memory.

But the smile was short-lived.

He had hardly blinked when it happened. Two arms wrapped around him—they were very thin but very strong. From behind he could hear steady, muffled breathing.

It was the knife to his throat that he was aware of most of all.

Whoever had him in their grasp was backing towards the railing and Remaine was stumbling along in tow. Before him several men climbed the masts, busily securing the rigging, completely oblivious to Remaine's predicament. Remaine's heart began to pound. Should he cry out? Should he make noise? This person had clearly been hiding in the cargo, waiting to pounce.

He decided to risk it. "Help!" he called, instantly regretting it. The blade pressed down his throat. He began to panic, his breath fluttering.

His cry for help had worked, though, and heads began to turn. At first, the sight of Remaine with a knife to his throat was met with nothing but confusion. It took what seemed a lifetime for any one of the crew to understand what was happening. Then one by one, it dawned on them: Remaine Plink was being held hostage. Calm, but severe orders were barked across the deck. That's when Remaine saw, out of the corner of his eye, another pirate on board. He was slight, mostly covered up with pale garments, and his face was hidden behind the metallic mask of the snarling tiger.

"Merchant," said Levo Chince carefully. His hands were up, palms out, as if to signal peace to Remaine's captor. "Go get the captain and the prince, now."

Remaine gagged from the increasing pressure on his neck as Estin slid down from his post, scurrying quickly across the deck.

"Stay still, lad," Levo said. The orange man spoke to Remaine, but his gaze was fixed on Remaine's captor. Levo looked more bear-like than ever. His shoulders were forward, his knees slightly bent. Levo slowly drew his sword. Remaine's head began to spin. A cold sweat broke out across his forehead.

"All right, kitty cats. Why don't you tell us what you want?" asked

Levo. The question received a few looks from the other men, but Levo's voice was steady, confident. He stepped forward. "Let the boy go."

Remaine felt his captor's grip tighten. He felt himself being pulled toward the ship's glossy taffrail. His throat stung with the pressure of the blade.

"Where's the prince?!" barked someone.

Remaine was pressed against the railing now.

"Steady, men," said Levo. "Merchant went to get him."

Finally, Prince Xietas appeared, followed immediately by Captain Rawthorne, Lyme Stretcher, and General Cottley, all trailed by Estin whose face was ghostly pale. The prince's face, on the other hand, was aflame with anger at the sight of Remaine and his captor. But any action the prince was about to take was halted. Levo was already in motion.

The prince's arrival was just the distraction that he needed. Levo Chince was on Remaine and the pirate in three sudden steps, so quickly Remaine nearly missed it. But he couldn't have missed it, because suddenly Levo was all he could see, and his loud cry was all he could hear.

Then Remaine Plink felt something. He had never felt the sensation before, but what else could it be? What else could a blade, right across your throat feel like?

His captor sliced quickly, like a hot knife through butter. Remaine saw Levo stagger back in shock. The second pirate seized *his* moment. He lunged at Levo. Levo dodged the jab, but not without first getting his shoulder sliced open. Levo cried out in pain. Remaine's vision blurred and then his eyes rolled back.

Suddenly, he felt himself yanked backwards—and before he could catch himself—off and over the railing of the ship. His vision darkened, but before he hit the water, he saw the two masked pirates, stabbed through their bellies by an outraged Levo, tumble off the railing towards him. Remaine hit the water, and the pirates hit him. Harbor's Hand towered above them, as if waving goodbye. All turned to black.

CHAPTER 11

THE BIRD CAGE AND THE BIRD LADY

REMAINE KNEW HE MUST BE DEAD when he felt the plush comfort of the bed beneath him. Never had he felt anything so soft when he was alive.

He wiggled his toes and his fingers. Then, an awareness of the rest of his body began to dawn. The soreness of his muscles, the pain in his ribs—and his *throat!*—the excruciating burn across his neck, they confirmed to him he was still very much alive.

His eyes flew open. Of course, he was alive! The mad pirate might have thrown him overboard, but the prince would have saved him!

With a thudding pulse pounding in his ears, Remaine observed his surroundings. The resplendent bed was just the beginning.

As with *The Emerald Egg*, the Ravillions had spared no expense in the décor and comforts of whatever lodging he now found himself.

The room was huge, the ceiling towered. An orange fire blazed in a marble fireplace at the foot of his bed. The rest of the chamber seemed to grow out of the fireplace, sprawling out from the stone structure with glossy dark woods and velvety rich carpets. Hanging on the wall was a tapestry that matched the blankets on the bed, each a deep indigo with swirls of silver and gold embroidery. Three tall windows to his right, like pillars of crystal stretched from floor to ceiling, allowing a muted gray light to fill the corners of the room where the dancing firelight did not reach. He forced himself, despite the pain, to his elbows and squinted to see out the windows.

An enormous, formal garden sprawled outside. Geometric hedges of velvety green enclosed informal explosions of hot-colored flowerbeds, now fading in the change of seasons. Yellows and purples, reds and blues, they all melded together like a dusty painting, set within the strong frame of pristine, maze-like borders. Beyond the gardens, the hillside rolled downward with the lane, and below that, glittering in a moon-shape arch along the waterline, was the city of Ravillion Bay.

His vision began to spin. Remain put a clammy hand to his forehead. He looked down at his chest and found he was in a long dressing gown. Vision still whirling, he looked over and saw a large chair by the fire, clothing draped over its back.

The prince would want to know he was awake and Remaine wanted to hear about what had happened. He forced himself up from the bed and wobbled over to the chair. The clothes were most certainly not his own. There was a long green shirt with formal buttons. Remaine had never worn anything like it. Black pants with elaborate pleating were draped over the chair's arm and on the floor sat new boots and stockings. A wool cape with silk lining hung over the chair's other arm. As a dockdweller from Windluff, not only would he have no need for clothes like these, but he never could have afforded them. He held up the heavily buttoned tunic. Frankly, he did not understand them.

Pain brought his hand to his throat where he felt a straight, scabbed-over line running the entire width of his neck. One moment he was on the deck, and the next there was blood, and then he was falling, and then all he could see was Levo, with his bloody shoulder, peering down as two pirates fell in the water on top of him. That was everything he could remember.

Feeling like he might tip over with dizziness, Remaine steadied himself on the back of the chair and called for help. He needed help.

Once, when he was very young, Remaine had lost his voice screaming for help. He had gotten lost deep in the Butterfin Caves. His screams, the salt water, and perhaps his panic, had dried his throat out completely. For two days he had been stripped bare of all but the weakest of whispers.

This was not like that. When Remaine opened his mouth to call out for help, absolutely *nothing* escaped. He stopped, brought his hand to his throat, and tried once more. Not a sound. Nothing.

He did hear something, however, from outside the door—faint and far away. He was sure it was music coming from a stringed instrument of some kind.

Remaine stumbled to the door and pushed it open. A cathedral-like hall lay on the other side. Other than the faint strains of music, the hallway was silent as a tomb. He stumbled out to the banister that lined the edge of the passageway. Remaine felt like an intruder. He moved unsteadily, but reverently, along the gallery towards the music, his vision still whirling.

All at once a swift, blurry figure with white gloves bowled him over. He fell back on his elbows.

"Oh, my boy!" shouted the man.

Remaine winced, keeping his eyes shut for fear of vomiting.

"Tsk, Tsk, Tsk," said the man, helping him to his feet. Remaine did not know who helped him, what he looked like, or anything about him. He didn't care. He needed to lie back down.

"Up too early I'm afraid," said the man. "I imagine you are feeling like you might lose your dinner!" He chuckled, coming around Remaine to help him back to the room. "Of course, that's to be expected. Not to worry, not to worry. Come with me. Yes. There you are. Right through here. Mm-hmm. Yes, now back into bed you go—that's it."

Remaine climbed in and let his head sink into the deep pillow. He peeked out at his helper—a pink-cheeked, bespectacled man.

"Hard to know how each will handle it," the man continued, smoothing out the blankets. "Some just slumber on through, not waking for a few days, and others? Well, others are a bit more fitful."

Remaine closed his eyes again, trying to nod his head in understanding.

"That's it. You rest. I'll tell the master."

Not far from the docks of Ravillion Bay, the viscount scrutinized the road from a balcony wreathed in grapevines. The man's patience, like the fruitless vines, withered. With irritation he recounted his annoying morning. It had begun with the arrival of yet another person to further complicate things.

The viscount was called Belwin. He stood straight-backed—high, like his sharp cheekbones and bristly, like his peppered hair. He had straight, terse lips. In fact, everything about the man was sharp-lined and straight-edged, like the immaculate high-collared coat he wore fully buttoned-up to keep out the chill.

Although, when it slid its icy fingers around his throat, Belwin had to admit, he rather liked the cold. It kept things rigid, and therefore, orderly. With warmth came leisure, the lazy soulmate of slovenly slothfulness. The only warmth Belwin needed was found in a porcelain cup full of dark, bitter tea that he raised to his lips with delicate precision. Belwin's ears pricked at the quiet voice coming from the opening of the double doors behind him.

"Your carriage is ready for you, my lord." The butler was nearly the same age as Belwin, yet the two could not have been more different. Where Belwin was rectangular, sharp, and cool, the man was pleasantly round, rosy, and cheerful. For good reason, the butler, Mr. Maxwell Jollidore, had come to be known, simply, as Jolly.

"Good," said Belwin. He turned around to face Jolly and found him standing with two cloaks, each draped over an arm.

"The maroon or the black, my lord?" asked Jolly, lifting each arm in turn. "The red is richly in tune with the season," the butler beamed. As his hands were preoccupied with the cloaks, he adjusted his spectacles with a scrunch of his nose. "And of course, the black is eternally dapper."

Belwin eyed the cloaks, each made of heavy velvet. The choice was clear enough. "Black," said Belwin. "I'd like to blend in today, Jolly. Thank you."

Jolly gave a curt nod and dressed his master with swift, efficient hands. Belwin noticed Jolly's twitching mouth.

"Yes, Jolly, what is it?"

"Oh, of course all is well," Jolly said quickly, "but the boy did wake up for a minute."

Belwin's jaw tightened.

"I saw him back into his bed though, my lord. I imagine he'll drift off for some time now."

Belwin grunted, pulled the hood of the cloak up over his head and headed out to the gallery that looked down on the great hall. He strode crisply down the main staircase to the front doors. Trotting ahead, Jolly opened the front doors gallantly for him.

His carriage, black and spacious, was, as usual, waiting for him just outside the manor, the very spot where the other carriage had pulled up earlier this morning.

Of course, when the carriage had arrived, Belwin's curiosity to see the boy got the better of him. He cracked his neck now, even as he had done earlier when the masked figures had stepped out from their carriage.

The snarling tiger masks were silly, in Belwin's opinion. Almost as ridiculous as the two cousins who wore them. Still, if stunts were going to be pulled, even without his knowledge, he was glad they were concealed. Belwin had kept his distance as the two figures hauled out the limp body of a scrawny boy, still wet and gray as granite. The morning sun had been white and it had washed all color from the boy's skin.

"Were you followed?" Belwin asked flatly.

"Relax, Rawthorne," said Quill, the taller of the two. Her voice strained slightly beneath the weight of the lifeless boy.

"We were like shadows, lord viscount!" the shorter one, Gill, had added.

Then Jolly had rushed out to meet them and had ushered them inside. He bowed to the viscount before closing the door, sealing the limp boy and the masked duo inside his home.

That was his morning.

Presently, Belwin stood alone in the crisp, autumn air. It was a minor relief but a relief nonetheless that he did not have to deal with the issue now, assuming the boy had drifted off to sleep again. *Later,* he told himself. *Later.*

For now, his own carriage whisked him away from the manor, down the hill and through the shining streets of Ravillion Bay. Belwin was too caught up in his thoughts to notice. He sat in the carriage, stewing under the low and controlled heat of poignantly focused anger. For years he had worked hard to keep the Rawthorne name pristine and totally free of all suspicion. And somehow, with one grand, sloppy voyage, Belwin could see an unsightly water stain forming.

As per Belwin's instructions, the driver took him to the back entrance of the Royal Aviary. The glass dome arched high, rising above most of the surrounding citadels. A wind had picked up and Belwin tightened his cloak around his already buttoned-up neck before stepping out.

He was glad to have chosen the black cloak. A crowd of similar dark hoods bustled about him and Belwin passed by them with ease, disappearing through the aviary's archway.

Willow used to admire the bird paradise more than any other thing in the city, and if it weren't for her, Belwin would have never stepped inside. To his late wife, the Royal Aviary was beautiful, enchanting, vast. For Belwin, it was oppressively hot and thick with an ungodly stench. Still, he thought of Willow now as he rushed beneath the arch into the vaulted glass dome. A wonderous world of greenery and waterfalls and birds of every kind sparkled before him, like an oasis of summer in a city well on its way to winter.

With intention, Belwin stepped up the stone stairs, past the large cages that housed the Singers-in-training, and on through a grove of palms where a squatty cottage stood on the bank of a pebbly brook, its dilapidated roof peppered with bird feces and the birds that had dropped them. It was a living rainbow, but it smelled like living death. He knocked on the door, regretfully undoing the top button of his collar with a grunt. He needed some air already. The sooner he left this humid place the better.

The sight of his younger brother at the door's opening threatened his inner calm almost instantly. He bit his tongue and walked into the old house.

Not until the door is closed, thought Belwin.

It was Diggory Rawthorne's face, always curious and light, that most enraged him. Diggory's face was tanned and weathered—perhaps that was the secret to his luminescence. He simply let the sun bake the glow into him.

"Are there any Singers present?" asked Belwin. He kept his voice a careful whisper as he scanned the room. It was a worn-out place with objects strewn about so haphazardly it was unclear which things were treasure and which things were trifles.

"I needn't tell you again, silly lord," said another voice, full, and rich, and rhythmic. The large woman emerged from behind a beaded curtain, bedecked in multi-colored robes, and multi-colored birds. The Singers perched on her arms and head like mooching travelers. "My children will not betray us under my command."

"Of course," said Belwin, straightening even more. "Still. You'll understand."

The large woman gazed critically at Belwin, her eyes shining beneath a furrowed brow covered in unique tattoo markings. Her name was Pua. "Away, my jewels. The ornery one doesn't trust you."

The birds ascended from her and flapped about the room in a storm of brightly colored feathers. For a brief moment, there was a tropical hurricane of screeching and flapping. Then, at last, the room fell silent. Even his little brother's blue Steller's jay had gone. Belwin straightened his already creaseless vest and smoothed his hair. "Thank you," he said, then scowled at Diggory.

"I'm glad you got my note," Diggory said first and Belwin could have slapped the casual tone right out of him.

"I did," said Belwin, "and your burdensome little present too, now lying soaking wet on silk sheets in the bay view room, I'd imagine."

"Surely Jolly saw to a change of clothes for the boy," Diggory said, sincerely.

But Belwin kept his gaze hot enough to melt his little brother down until Diggory added sheepishly, "I confess the boy's situation surprised me as well, Belwin."

"Is that all that surprised you, brother?" scoffed Belwin.

Pua strolled across the room, humming to herself, and poured them both a cup of hot tea. The heat inside the aviary was particularly suffocating today and Belwin had begun to sweat. He refused the cup.

Forcing himself to sit on the only clear corner of the wooden chair next to him, he kept his words pumped with venom. "You're a fool, little brother."

Diggory Rawthorne looked genuinely hurt by the words.

"You act surprised!" said Belwin, annoyed. "You've barely had a few years of sailing under your title, under the auspices of the royal family, and in one, boyish voyage you throw it all away. You planned an attack on a Ravillion vessel, without so much as a day to think critically about the implications!"

"There was no time," said Diggory calmly, rubbing his forehead. "I had to act. When the prince rerouted us to Broken Bottle, I knew we were going to Monkeywood. I knew V—" Diggory lowered his voice. "I knew *she* wouldn't be allowed on the island."

Pua gave an irritated hum and swatted a big hand with displeasure. "Monkeys and cats, still treated like kings and queens by my cursed cousins."

Belwin's gaze bore a hole into his little brother. "Are you certain everything we've worked for isn't now compromised because you wanted to play pirate?"

"I have the prince's trust."

"A reckless and arrogant assumption," spat Belwin.

"Belwin." A quiet voice from the far end of the room interrupted.

Belwin couldn't help but close his eyes and smirk beneath the sound. Of course, his father was here to defend his youngest, yet again.

Belwin felt embarrassed he hadn't seen Terveo Rawthorne before, but as he turned to find him hidden in the shadows like an old owl concealed by the woods, he allowed himself the mistake. The bone-thin man was barely visible.

"You approve of all of it, then?" asked Belwin, flattening out his tone. He did not want any of them to think he had been surprised by his father's presence, and frankly, his question was rhetorical.

Turning his back to his father, Belwin walked over to gaze out the window. The stream of warm water that ran through the Aviary trickled along lazily inside the bird sanctuary. A few yellow canaries hopped through the branches of a dark-leaved tree on the other side. Belwin spoke slowly and with finality.

"Timing is everything, father, have we not agreed on that?"

"Of course."

"Then anything which compromises our position, prematurely, is a mistake."

Diggory spoke. "We have not been compromised, Bel—"

"Are we *certain*?" hissed Belwin, whirling around.

There was a pause.

"Belwin," said his father in the patronizing tone that always drove Belwin mad. The former viscount looked tired. "We are still too naïve to the mysteries behind the Ravillions—behind their power. That much we have *also* agreed on."

"Yes, I know. And that's why you sent Uncle Dasko into the desert and that's why you applaud Diggory's little charade. To *learn* more. And yet somehow, in all this *not-so-subtle* research, Diggory here has managed to attract the attention of every Isle in Cracklemore."

Belwin's words boiled and he let them simmer in the room before adding, "Eventually we'll need to move with real purpose, father, and every minute we waste seeking answers or playing foolish games at sea, risks exposure. Especially since you, Diggory," he glared at his little brother, "were *sloppy*. And rash."

Diggory said nothing. Beside him sat a leather satchel. A fat gray cat popped its head out, giving a yawn.

Pua gave a heaving gasp and clutched a meaty hand over her heart. "You dare bring him into my home?"

Diggory smiled and pulled the fat gray cat into his lap. "Oh Pua, I thought you loved animals."

"Pua loves all animals," she said, "but Pua treasures the Singer most of all. Birds, Rawthorne. Cats. Eat. Birds."

"Barrow wouldn't dream of eating your birds," said Diggory. "He and Staunch are the best of friends." At the mention of the jay's name, the cat looked around. Diggory pressed his own nose against Barrow's and whistled a little tune which the cat seemed to like.

Belwin rolled his eyes and pinned Diggory again with a question. "Well, go on, then. Explain yourself. What happened?"

"As soon as we turned north, away from Kipswitch," said Diggory, scratching the cat's chin, "I sent Staunch to Lemon Lake. If Monkeywood lay ahead, then we needed to be ready, and we needed someone to blame the whole thing on. I knew Quill and Gill would be all too eager. I told them to ready *Dusty* and to head to Broken Bottle."

Belwin raised his eyebrows. "You thought *Dusty* could outrun *The Emerald Egg* if something went wrong, did you?"

"It was never going to outrun the prince. It just needed to sink in front of him."

Terveo Rawthorne spoke again, his voice as dry as a desert wind. "I'm sure Quill and Gill were devastated to participate in a pyrotechnic stunt."

Diggory smiled. "Like I said, all too eager. We had been waiting for a reason to use that piece of driftwood anyway. This was the perfect opportunity. When the prince went ashore, Quill and Gill were right on cue in *Dusty*. I sneaked into the prince's chambers, got Vul—her— to set fire to the room and got out."

"How did you get in?" asked Belwin.

Diggory raised his eyebrows and tapped the metal hilt of his sword, carved in the shape of a figurine; the answer was obvious and Belwin felt foolish for asking.

"Also found this in there," said Diggory, burying a hand in his bag. He produced a small wooden box and tossed it to Belwin.

"What's this?" Belwin asked, opening it up. A small, white shape, like a pointed egg, lay inside.

"The prince called it a Hoaxbite," said Diggory.

Belwin shut the box. "And the prince's crew? You're confident none of them witnessed your escapades?"

"We were in enchanted waters. The witches' minnows were putting on a show in the lagoon. No one noticed me entering. No one noticed *Dusty* approaching. Or at least not till Quill and Gill let her canon loose. By then, the fire was raging in the prince's cabin and it looked as if pirates had truly attacked. Levo and I played our part. He rushed to retrieve the prince. I ordered the prince's men to put some holes in *Dusty*. No one thought twice. No one questioned my orders. Everyone—prince and all—watched as *Dusty* burst into flames and sank, her 'sand pirate crew' drowning with her. No enemies to interrogate."

"And Quill and Gill?" asked Belwin.

"Already stowed away aboard *The Emerald Egg*. Plenty of places to hide until we came to Ravillion Bay."

Belwin picked carefully through his little brother's charade. If he had executed it all with the precision he claimed, then the Rawthornes might indeed still be in the clear, except...

"But things got sloppy." Belwin said. "The boy."

A slight, defeated exhale came from Diggory. "I confess, the Plink boy's capture complicated things. But Silome contacted me the morning after Monkeywood. She had gotten word of her brother's whereabouts. She begged me to help him."

Belwin pictured the young Plink girl. Ever since he had known her, she had been like a steady migraine. He would never forget the way she had cornered him in Windluff—a thirteen-year-old girl jabbing her finger into his sternum—knowing things she never should have known. Now he had to deal with another Plink.

Diggory continued, "Quill and Gill were still inflated with excitement from Broken Bottle, so when I told them about Remaine, they didn't hesitate. We planned it out carefully. The Merchant boy was all too eager to help. He and I stalled the prince at just the right time—we knew we would have to wait until Harbor's Hand. And Levo knew he'd have to lose a little blood to make it all convincing. He didn't want me showing him up, anyway." Diggory held up his scabbed forearms.

Belwin bit his tongue at the mention of Estin Merchant. He never should have gotten involved. But that was minor compared to the scene this Plink boy was causing.

"Fool!" said Belwin. "The whole city is awash with gossip already about the prince's scene in the bay—about how he demanded an immediate search in the water. They say he was crazed, zealous. They're saying he went mad after the boy fell over—they are wondering who the kid is to him? Or did you not consider this? Of course, you didn't. *Sloppy.*"

Diggory's face reddened. "Y–yes," he admitted. "I knew the prince had taken a liking to the boy, but when Remaine fell overboard, the prince..." Diggory's eyes were wide as he recalled the scene, "I did not realize the extent. He began charming the waters with Lyme Stretcher, lifting out great heaps, trying to pull up the boy. He did everything he could, but Quill and Gill had taken the boy too deep—all the way to the hideout in Harbor's Hand. The prince sent me into the waters to search and Levo too, even with his split-open shoulder, as well as half the crew. I feigned the search, doing my best to keep the others from exploring Harbor's Hand too closely."

Belwin felt his blood grow even hotter. His brother had gotten too confident, too bold.

"Yes, but Belwin has a point. Why *does* the prince want the Plink boy?" asked Terveo Rawthorne. "Who is he to the prince?"

"I don't know," Diggory admitted. "There's something about him the prince is interested in, though. And I can't help but feel it's all... strangely... coincidental."

"How do you mean, Diggory?" wheezed their father.

"I dunno—our connection with Silome to begin with—then the luck of having Merchant on board to help—and speaking of Merchant... the prince favors him, too, and he shows... *remarkable* talent. We're fortunate to have an unexpected ally in him, even if Silome never should have roped him in. And then… of course… the chances of our paths crossing in time to save Remaine… it all just feels—"

"—like it was never the plan," finished Belwin. He sucked his teeth and scowled.

Then Pua gave a great, heaving laugh. "You Rawthornes and your plans. Diggory's closer than you think. I've been trying to tell you. The deeper forces of the world will never let you plan every second, no matter how hard you try. Ships find their way to fate's islands when their time comes whether you want them to or not. The Plinks, this Merchant boy, the prince… and the favor you've found with him, *Captain* Rawthorne… secret destinies are at work." She paused, eyes shining, then added, "Broken Bottle began to stir after that night. Birds flying overhead saw. They came to me. I know of what fate brings forth. I know of what emerged from the depths in those waters."

Belwin noticed his little brother's tanned face had gone pale. It was a small consolation, to see his brother's leisurely disposition crumbling beneath the gravity of Pua's words, if not his own. Diggory swallowed and spoke. "Yes. I—we—none of us expected it. At Monkeywood. Beyond the reef."

Belwin's narrow eyes widened.

Terveo sat up. "It's true then…" he whispered.

"The sightings," Diggory's mouth formed a straight line. "Yes. I have no doubt they've all been true. It's not dead at all. Just… hidden. But now surfacing—and just as big as the legends tell. *Bigger*." Diggory's eyes glazed over and he added, thoughtfully, "I've never seen the prince so terrified."

Before too long, all their gazes had shifted to Pua, and Terveo asked, "What do you make of this?"

Pua fiddled thoughtfully with a strand of thick beads that hung around her wide neck. "My sisters and I never ventured to Monkeywood—the Animal Charmers there practice ways forbidden to us—cursing themselves with green poison…" She paused before adding in a breathy tone. "I do know of beasts and… *baubles,* as you say, but of the *ancient* creatures and the boy's role in all this, there is still much mystery."

At the mention of the ancient creatures, Pua turned to the corner of the room where a domed object sat inconspicuously in the corner, barely visible in a sea of other clutter. The dome was draped with a dark sheet, but the shape was unmistakable.

Belwin's mouth dried out. He struggled to swallow. "So…" he said, and it was as if nothing else mattered for a brief moment. "After all of it? You were… successful, then?"

Diggory nodded. His cat jumped back into his leather satchel.

Belwin felt his heart skip a beat.

"*Into mortal seas the seat immortal shakes…*" sang Pua, walking towards the object. She placed a trembling hand on the fabric, then closed her eyes to inhale deeply, before pulling the fabric into her fingers and whisking away the cover.

The cage itself was ordinary in every way, and by the looks of it, had seen many hard journeys. But within the bars, the iconic, silvery mass of Prince Xietas Ravillion's Singer, the harpy eagle, Vulcutta, sat hunched, her beak buried in her back. At the sight of them, she turned her face to the room, releasing a piercing shriek and opening her massive wingspan, feathers bursting through the slats of the cage.

Pua hastily threw the cover back on the cage, hiding the prince's Singer, her movements a blur. "Leave her with me," she said breathlessly. "Black of heart she may be, but ancient are her gifts," Pua's voice dropped lower. "Precious is her mind." She turned to face them. "We'll have the prophecy soon enough."

"The prophecy," breathed Belwin. He wasn't sure if he had said it audibly.

Terveo gave a grim nod and placed a hand on his eldest's shoulder.

"We have to know more before we strike. We have to know what shakes the Winged throne."

Belwin swallowed hard and gave a simple nod, never taking his eyes off the covered cage.

"I must go track down Dasko," his father continued, drawing his hood. "I'll be back within a fortnight. And Pua—"

The large woman looked up at the old man.

"Were your Singers able to ascertain anything else—anything from your cousins in Broken Bottle?"

"They were only able to eavesdrop a little—birds are not welcome on Monkeywood. But yes. They heard mention of a curse," she said. "Of a boy who holds his breath."

Small, almost nonexistent smiles appeared briefly on all their faces. Terveo stared evenly at her. "Thank you, friend, for your help."

Pua bowed her large head.

Out of habit, and despite the heat, Viscount Belwin Rawthorne tightened his cloak and fastened his buttons once more, right up to his jaw, and left the scene, leaving the bird cage in the care of the bird lady.

CHAPTER 12

RAWTHORNE MANOR

The next time Remaine woke up, he heard the music again. The room in which he slept was the same. How long had it been since the pink-cheeked servant had tucked him back in?

He felt leagues better than the first time, so he sat up, gingerly, hoping the spinning was gone. When his vision stayed clear, he approached the door with more confidence. Remaine pushed it open and walked out onto the vast hall. Finding the prince in a place this huge was going to be a challenge. He would start with the music.

A flickering orange light went with the music, and all of it flooded the hallway from a tall door left ajar at the far end of the hall. But as

Remaine drew near, the music stopped abruptly. It was replaced by muffled voices. He approached the door tiptoeing softly, then peeked inside.

An enormous fire framed by a stone mantelpiece carved in the likeness of two sitting lions dominated one whole wall of the room. Washed in the flickering light hunched a woman—a very old woman judging by her stooped form pressing firmly down upon a cane. But far from feeble or weak, this woman, Remaine knew instantly, was nobility. Against the firelight, her face was indistinct, but her silhouette was one wreathed in furs and silks; her hair was piled high in ringlets encased in a pearled netting and her jewel-adorned neck sparkled and flashed.

"I'll not wait all day!" she snapped, pounding her cane on the stone floor near the flames. "And please, Jollidore, more heat. I'll not ask again."

Remaine recognized Jollidore. His large, circular spectacles slipped forward, and his cheeks blushed deep as he bowed low.

The man called Jolly moved to stoke the fire with his white gloved hands, but at the sight of the logs, and his gloves, he hesitated.

The woman tightened her furs around her neck, catching her jewels in the process. "Oh, for goodness' sake," she said, tugging at her necklace. It was difficult to see who moved them, but without question, three logs fell from a pile into the flames.

"In my day it was a respectable job to do such things," said the woman. "Now we just use tricks."

Remaine was still puzzling over the scene when two more figures strode into view—a girl, followed by a young woman, the latter plain in every way, and dressed in an apron. The aproned woman ushered the girl in front of the fire, posing her like a doll before the bejeweled old lady.

"Hmm," said the old woman critically. "Give us a turn now, my love."

The girl twirled, fanning out her crimson gown. "Better," said the woman. "How like your mother you look. Good. Though it's still too loose there in the back. Wynnie, pinch it here, see? Yes. Good. You can have it done by tonight, then?"

Wynnie, the aproned woman, gave a slight bow in the direction of the old woman. "Very well, Lady Solace."

"And can you move easily, Serae?" asked the old woman.

The girl swished around, and with a smile leaned forward, lifting a leg high up behind her as gracefully as a bird. She grinned.

"Good. Now with music once more. Wynnie, take it from the second movement, just before the transfer."

Wynnie disappeared from Remaine's view to a far corner of the room. He heard some shuffling, then the music began again—a stringed melody that made Remaine feel as though a light rain was falling in his chest. The young girl named Serae began to dance.

Remaine leaned in closer. It was one movement too much. The door fell in at his pressure. It swung inward and banged loudly against the wall, leaving Remaine frozen in place like a thief caught red-handed.

"I'm sorry!" was what he wanted to say, but he found he still could not speak. So, instead, he gawked like a bottom feeder, as every eye in the room turned to him. The gaze of the young girl, her huge brown eyes wide as an awestruck deer's, was particularly intense. Then she smiled brightly and gave Remaine a little wave. The other two women simply stared.

"He wakes!" burst the rosy-cheeked man. His jet-black hair was combed smoothly atop a round head and his smile ran ear to ear. "You've stumbled upon the wrong room!" He laughed and bobbed over to Remaine quickly, throwing an arm around his shoulder and turning him back towards the hall. He shut the door on the women and ushered Remaine to the grand, curving staircase.

"You'll have to forgive my absence, young sir, I *did* have every intention of being *right there* when you woke up—it became a sort of game for me, checking in on you frequently, trying to time it. I would pop in—Awake? Nope! Then, again, a few minutes later—awake? Nope! Of course," Jolly leaned in close now, and his words continued to tumble out fast, yet lower in volume, as if he were telling Remaine a secret joke. "I promise I never forsook my other responsibilities despite how often I popped in!"

Remaine could barely keep up with Jolly. He moved his feet as fast as he moved his tongue.

"—but of course, it's an impossible thing to time—BUT I TRIED!—still, it looks like I just missed you, and oh, you must have felt awfully confused! When you woke up the first time—I almost caught you that time—and oh, now, the second time, I am sorry, and—oh—"

At this, Jolly stopped dead in his tracks and blinked with his huge, magnified eyes. His wide smile turned into a frown. "I see you haven't dressed yet—did you not see the garments I put out?"

Remaine looked down at himself, then back up at Jolly, who beamed once more.

"We better turn straight around and get you dressed before we see the master."

Remaine definitely agreed with Jolly. It would be embarrassing to meet the prince like this. Back in his room, Jolly stripped off his nightgown and swiftly dressed him in the strange, formal clothing that was still draped on the chair. With eyes as big and wide as a bug's, just inches from Remaine, Jolly did up all the odd buttons, talking the entire time.

"I began to wonder if you *would* wake up again, you were sleeping so long, but of course you *would* wake up, the gruggleblades only bring sleep, of course only if you're careful—*yowch!* If you got stabbed, they'd be like any other blade I'm sure—but you didn't, of course! So, it's off to sleep you go," Jolly made quick, fake snoring sounds, then he added, "and boy did it knock *you* out."

Remaine felt confused. Jolly paid him no mind. The servant chuckled and shook his head.

"There. A dashing fit, sir, if I do say so myself. You make a proper nobleman!"

Remaine looked down, shifting uncomfortably in the strange fabric.

"Right!" said Jolly. "Back downstairs. Follow me."

Jolly bobbed ahead, his black shadow bouncing along behind him, matching his dark servants' livery and his slick, black hair. As Jolly led the way back to the gallery, down the wide staircase, Remaine felt the close surveillance of the gigantic portraits which lined the walls. Then they came to a set of magnificent double doors.

"The master's right inside," said Jolly.

Remaine gulped. The prince would be happy to see him up and well, wouldn't he? He suddenly remembered the stowaway pirates. The prince was probably furious at them! Then another thought occurred to Remaine—what if *he* had done something wrong? What if *he* had somehow invited the capture by standing where he shouldn't have! Surely, he should have stayed by the prince's side—then he wouldn't have gotten into that mess!

Before Remaine had a chance to calm his thoughts, Jolly knocked once then opened the wide doors.

Yet another grand room swallowed Remaine whole, this one was made almost entirely of glass. It was a dining room and Remaine winced as shafts of bright white light from the garden world outside flooded the space, sparkling off the hanging chandeliers and gleaming off the long, shining table lined with high backed chairs of black velvet. It was a regal sight. But Prince Xietas was nowhere to be found.

Instead, a man with neatly cropped peppery hair sat at the far end of the table, his eyes fixed on the pages of a book. He did not look up at Remaine's arrival.

"Do sit, boy," said the man. "Pour him some coffee, Jolly."

Jolly gave a quick, enthusiastic bow, then reached for a silver pot. Remaine stood awkwardly, eyes darting from the man, to Jolly, then back to the man.

Jolly pulled out a chair with one hand and offered a delicate teacup to Remaine with his other. Dazed and confused, Remaine took the cup and sat down.

Remaine made another attempt to speak, but remembered he was mute. The panic swelling in his chest rapidly increased. As if he could sense Remaine's distress, the man looked up at him from his book with an obligatory glance. It lasted for less than a second, at which point the man looked back to his book and returned to his reading. Then he spoke, his eyes still fixed on the page.

"My name is Belwin Rawthorne, viscount, and you are in what we call, uninspiringly, Rawthorne Manor. For now, you will stay here. You may not leave."

Remaine gripped the hot cup, clinging to its warmth for comfort. At the sound of the man's name, Remaine furrowed his brow. Belwin took notice.

"Yes. Rawthorne. You've already met my younger brother, Diggory."

Remaine blinked. The man proceeded as if it were grunt work to do so.

"I will not accept you as my project. I am your host and I will keep my home open to you. But not my time. You have much to learn, and upon the return of your voice, I'm sure you'll find that task much easier. For now, you will keep to your chamber as much as possible and stay clear of the front hall and the wandering eyes of visitors. And under no circumstances are you to go outside."

From behind the glass window, there was the sound of bees as they buzzed in the extravagant gardens.

Finally, the man looked up from his book. "Jolly will assist you in finding food at present since you have missed lunch. Oh, and—" he snapped his fingers towards Jolly who was already halfway out the door. Somehow Jolly seemed to know exactly what the snap signified, because a moment later he returned with a bird cage, in which sat a seagull.

The bird was at once familiar. It reminded Remaine of home, of Chicken, though this seagull was notably younger and smoother. Although the bird was silent, Remaine could hear seagull cries in his head. He could feel the slosh of waves against docks. He could smell the sea. For some reason, the memories formed a lump in his throat.

Jolly opened the birdcage, making every effort to respect the bird. The seagull looked calculatingly at Jolly's hand then, with more curiosity, turned its small head in Remaine's direction. At the sight of him, the bird hopped from the cage, and walked with webbed feet until it was within touching distance.

"Your sister left you a brief note," said the viscount with disinterest.

Remaine nearly choked on his coffee as the Singer from Windluff straightened up and opened its beak. *Silome?*

"Hey little brother," came the voice of Silome Plink. "I'm sorry for the stupid bird. You'll have a hundred questions, and I can't answer any of them in this way, but I wanted you to know you're safe where you are. These people aren't bad. They're filthy rich—it'll make you sick—but they're good ones. They'll explain everything…"

Her voice paused for a minute. Remaine could hear ambient screeches and he realized that Silome had been in the Aviary at Brineymore Round when she made this message.

"Anyway," continued Silome, "stay where you are. Stay away from the Clawfoot. They'll explain. I'll send more word when I can, but for now you need to understand you're only in danger if you venture outside. Clawfoot's not to be trusted. And don't try to contact me, or anyone else. As far as our family knows, you're dead. You got that? You're safe. But you're dead. So just… *stay dead*, alright? I'll send another bird when I can."

There is a strange moment that always follows a Singer's message, where the creature becomes birdlike once more—completely unaffected, as if it had not delivered any message, while its words still reverberate in the air. The sight of the seagull hopping back into the cage to be whisked away was impossible to reconcile with the message he had received. He wanted to question the bird. He wanted to squeeze more answers from it. He wanted to scream at Silome somewhere *inside* it. But the bird was just a bird again.

Remaine blinked up at Belwin, who was rising to his feet.

"When the prince informed Duke Hubert Hegs of your surprise arrival aboard his ship," said Belwin, with a tone that sounded almost like boredom, "the duke informed your mother. Silome was present for that conversation. Fate seemed to favor you both, for Silome had an ally aboard *The Emerald Egg*. She wasted no time in contacting Diggory to arrange for your capture, Remaine, and if it were up to me, that risky little maneuver never would have happened. But since it has, I strongly urge you not to waste her efforts. Notice she did not mention your name, or ours, and Clawfoot is the name we've given to the prince. Your sister knows better than to reference anyone directly."

Belwin drummed his fingers on the book that he had closed and set down on the table. "Now, I suggest you return to your room and go to sleep again. From what we can tell, sleep seems to be the best way to recover from the gruggleblade poison which, at present, is still coursing through your neck. Until you sleep it off, you'll remain without a voice, and, in the meantime, I refuse to engage in trying to interpret any charades you might wish to perform to express your inquiries… though you might find Jolly here more willing to play."

Jolly grinned and waved a gloved hand.

Belwin strode over to another set of doors, but before he left, turned to say, "Meals are at seven-thirty, twelve, and six. Sharp. Do not come late. You will go hungry. Also," he adjusted his high collar, "if there are other guests, you will eat in your room, unless directed otherwise. Jolly, am I missing anything?"

Jolly opened his mouth to respond but Belwin was quick to add, "Oh, right. We serve tea between two and three. Speaking of which, Jolly, is my daughter still upstairs?"

"Yes, Master Belwin," Jolly said, pointing a gloved finger, "she is still practicing with Lady Solace, I believe. And getting fitted by the governess."

Belwin gave a curt nod. "Please invite them to take their tea with me in the library."

Belwin disappeared through the doors leaving a rather icy wake behind him.

"Not to worry, young sir," said Jolly, carrying a tray of food as he took Remaine back to his room. "The viscount is like that. Busy, busy, busy. All the Rawthorne masters are." Jolly laughed.

They arrived at the room Remaine was to call his for the time being.

"As the master said, you just need a little more sleep and you'll be feeling better in no time."

Jolly set the tray down on a small desk near the fireplace. He bounced over to the windows and began to draw the long curtains.

"Lovely view of the garden," said Jolly, releasing the mass of fabric from its braided loop. "You'll see Mr. Wooling down there from time to time. And over there," he pointed with his white-gloved finger, "are the vineyards—that's Master Belwin's favorite spot. He's quite the viticulture expert you know. And then, right over there, by that pergola, there—" he stopped with a chuckle, covering his mouth. "Oh, pardon me! That's nothing."

Remaine was too tired to pursue Jolly's comment. There was a metallic clicking sound as Jolly yanked on the right curtain. The ring had gotten stuck and would not slide. Jolly yanked some more. *Click, click, click.* It would not budge.

Jolly sighed at the problematic curtain. Then he put both his hands inside his coat pockets and gave a rather loud clearing-of-the-throat sound.

Remaine gawked. There was no mistaking it. The curtain slid into place on its own.

Remaine suddenly remembered the fire logs in the room with the young girl earlier.

Jolly turned, winked, and held a finger to his lips as if he had just set up a monumental prank. "Oh," he giggled, tapping his forehead.

"I suppose there's no real danger in you blabbing away just yet." Then he gave him another big smile and patted him on the head. "Very good. Well, if you find you need something, just ring for me there," he continued, pointing to a golden cord hanging near the head of the bed. "One of us will come. There used to be more of us, but, of course, anymore we've had to keep our numbers few—easier to protect secrets, you see? Anyway, it will probably be me! Which, of course, will be my pleasure. But Miss Canny might show as well. Either way, you'll be well taken care of, I swear." He leaned forward and whispered behind the back of his hand, "Though none of the others are as punctual as me!"

With that, Jolly left, shutting the door on his way out and leaving Remaine all alone in the room. He eyed the curtain critically and looked back at the door where Jolly had just been standing. His head hurt and so did his throat. Confusion sloshed around in his mind like muddy water. He sat on the bed and took a deep breath. Where was he? Who were these people? And where was the prince?! Why did gruggleblade sound so familiar? And then there was *Silome...*

It was enough to drive him mad.

But he was tired and despite Silome's words and all the questions they inspired, Remaine tipped over onto the plush bed. It would have to wait until he had more sleep. The fire crackled at the end of the room, his food turned cold, and Remaine fell back asleep.

CHAPTER 13

THE HOLLOWFIEND'S HUNT

IF IT WASN'T FOR JOLLY, Remaine would have missed breakfast the following morning.

"Of course," said the butler, dressing Remaine once more and tugging at the wrinkles in his uncomfortable new garments. "I would have sneakily procured you a morsel, Master Plink, had you slept in, not to worry, but still, we best do as Master Belwin says. There. Crisp as toast!"

Remaine looked down at himself, rubbing the sleep out of his eyes. He missed his fisherman's toga, and his feet felt cramped, crammed into the shiny shoes. He managed to smile weakly and tried to say thank you. A froggy, crackling whisper scratched somewhere in the back of his throat before fizzling into silence.

"Now don't you worry my boy," Jolly encouraged, dusting both of Remaine's spotless shoulders. "A day or two more is all, and you'll be a hummin' and a hollerin'. Now! I have my own duties in the dining hall. You'll excuse me, of course. You know the way. I'll see you down there!"

Jolly closed the door with white-gloved precision, and Remaine heard him humming to himself as he trotted away.

Breakfast was extravagant. Jolly was omnipresent, lifting silver domes off dishes, pouring hot drinks, or cold ones, each in its own different glass, and pushing chairs in or pulling them out for those around the table.

Including himself, Remaine counted a small crowd of five. They were seated so far apart from one another Remaine might have assumed them strangers. But there was no mistaking the family resemblance between Belwin, sitting in his place at the head of the table, and the young girl, sitting at the middle of the table to his left. As for the old woman, sitting opposite the girl, Remaine could identify some sort of connection between her and the young girl. Bearing no family resemblance at all was the plainly dressed woman who sat closest to the girl's left, almost invisible in comparison to the other three.

When he first entered the dining room and sat down, Remaine felt himself blush beneath the stares. Not a word of greeting was uttered, and yet the silence seemed as loud as cannon fire. Then Jolly poured him a drink, unveiled a hot dish of buttered toast alongside something yellow and green that he did not recognize, and set down a juicy piece of fruit that resembled a peach. His stomach growled. Fortunately, when he looked up to see if anyone noticed, he found all the stares had been retracted. The other four had returned to their breakfasts and were eating in silence. All but one. The young girl shyly flashed him a smile and gave him another small wave from the side of the table while keeping her hand in her lap.

Remaine smiled back at her. She blinked her enormous brown eyes, then picked up her fork and knife.

"Father," she said, her voice soft and timid, as she set the cutlery back down. "Would you mind introducing our guest?"

"Hmm?" said Belwin, humming into the teacup he held to his mouth. In his other hand, he held the book—the same one as he held the day before. "Oh. Right."

Pulling the teacup away from his lips, but keeping it close, he said in monotone, "Serae, Wynnie, Lady Solace, this is Remaine Plink. You all know his elder sister, Silome."

The three of them dipped their chins, their smiles spanning a gradient from Lady Solace's meager grimace to the plain woman's polite smile to Serae's wide, enthusiastic grin.

"Remaine, this is my daughter, Serae, and her governess, Wynnie Canny. And this is Lady Remurra Depps, the mother of my late wife. She is a Solace by title. You'll address her as such."

Remaine dipped his own chin and tried to smile as Belwin Rawthorne introduced each of them, but he could not deny the slippery nerves worming around in his gut as the viscount spoke. There was something about this house, these people, and the viscount, especially, that made Remaine feel like he couldn't breathe. The only other time he had felt this kind of tension was his night at the Tour when he had served the prince the bad butterfin before all the Windluffian nobility.

"What do you think of Ravillion Bay so far, Remaine?" Serae asked brightly, turning toward him. Even at such a young age, her posture was perfect and she held herself like a young lady.

Suddenly self-conscious of his slouch, Remaine straightened up, and opened his mouth to speak, then remembered he couldn't, and just shook his head.

"Oh, I forgot," said Serae sweetly. "So sorry. We've really mastered the gruggleblade, haven't we?" She forced a small chuckle, but her father eyed her severely. Apparently, such things were inappropriate to discuss at the table. "Sorry, father."

"Jolly, please pass our compliments on to Rosy," said Belwin flatly, successfully changing the subject. "Breakfast is delicious."

Truthfully, Remaine was glad he still did not have a voice. How would he have answered that question anyway? What he thought, so far, was that he was in a strange house, he had been kidnapped by pirates, and everyone around him, including his sister, was convinced that the prince—the one person who showed any real concern for Remaine—was not to be trusted. But the food was good.

Remaine took another bite.

They ate in silence for a few more minutes before Lady Solace spoke. "Your father has departed, I presume, Belwin?"

Belwin looked up from his book and gave her his full attention.

"Indeed," he said. "Before dawn."

"Must be a relief for him," said Lady Solace through pursed lips, "to know sunshine and warmth await him in his travels." At this, she adjusted her fur collar. It was the first time Remaine noticed the dramatic collar, but now that he had, he did not know how he had not noticed it. The orange and red collar was as thick as a tree trunk, and wrapped itself around Lady Solace's neck, framing her beaded hair and painted face like a gigantic caterpillar curled up on her shoulders.

"It crushes the soul to know the frost is already upon us," she continued, ignoring the blazingly beautiful garden outside the window as if it had done her wrong. "Summer hardly raises her golden head before autumn breaks her neck with vindictive prematurity. And even then, one can hardly pray for a mild day of autumn before the chill of winter blows in, pilfering any remaining scraps of joy with its icy claw. A few pleasant days, then the snow dampens life as we know it, abandoning us to slowly freeze to death for months on end."

Lady Solace dabbed at the corner of her mouth.

Belwin inhaled slowly, blinked, and said, in an apathetic drone. "Would you like a few more logs added to the fire, Lady Solace?"

"I see someone has not lost the decency to ask!" she retorted. She shot Jolly a stabbing look.

Blushing, Jolly sprang into action. Within a few minutes, the fire was crackling wildly behind Lady Solace, who sat stiffly, but more contentedly.

After breakfast was eaten, Remaine made the mistake of trying to leave the room before everyone else, at which point he was scolded for a lack of manners by Lady Solace, and instructed, with great irritation, by Belwin, to stand and wait, allowing the ladies to exit first. Following the etiquette lesson, Jolly led Remaine back upstairs where he relished the opportunity to collapse on the bed once again—it *was* a comfortable bed. He conceded to himself that both the food and the bed at Rawthorne manor were good.

He had hardly been awake for two hours and yet he felt exhausted. Jolly promised to return shortly to check on him. Then Remaine was alone, again. Staring at the ceiling, he found himself wondering how many of his days would look like this: suffocating hosts and luxurious isolation.

He sat up to take another look around the room. Surely there was something with which he might distract himself. At the far end of the room, the fireplace flickered and the two chairs facing it were inviting enough. He walked over to one of the chairs and sat in it. He found he enjoyed the chair as much as the bed. A few books were stacked on a low table nearby, but Remaine could not read, so he didn't bother picking them up. He noticed another door and got up to open it. It was a closet, empty save for a few articles of clothing depressingly like the ones he wore now. He closed the door and wandered over to the window.

The gardens lay before him, and Remaine spotted a man moving through them. The man wore olive green and tan clothing, caked in dirt. A wide-brimmed hat and scarf hid his face entirely, but by the looks of his bent posture, Remaine guessed he was not a young man.

The man leaned over an evergreen shrub and gave one of its branches a precise snip with his sheers.

Remaine's gaze reached out beyond the Rawthorne gardens, down the hill, and out to the shining waters of Ravillion Bay and to the cityscape that kissed her shores. The spires of the city stretched out like a carpet of spikes, but one spire in particular drew his eye. The spire belonged to a narrow castle crowned in turrets and conical towers that was perched on the edge of a small cliff that overlooked the bay.

Suddenly, Remaine *knew* the prince was there, in that castle, and his head began to pound. A boiling, bubbling feeling of frustration started in his gut and questions began to flood his head. *What did Silome mean the prince could not be trusted?*

There was a knock at the door. Remaine hurried across the room and opened it.

Expecting to see Jolly, he was already looking upward, but seeing nothing there his gaze immediately traveled downward. At his own eye-level, Remaine saw the smiling face of Serae Rawthorne.

"Uh, hello again," she said, grabbing a thick dark braid of hair that hung over her shoulder. Although her long dress completely covered her feet, Remaine could see her shifting her weight from foot to foot. "I was wondering if you might want to come, uh, play a game?"

Even if he could have spoken, Remaine did not know what he would have said.

She must have noticed the confusion on his face. "I don't have lessons for another hour. Wynnie usually lets me read or go outside. And Grandmother likes to be alone till lunch. And Father is already gone. So—" she looked around like a nervous animal suddenly afraid it had wandered into the wrong meadow. "I mean, I'm sorry," she added hastily, "you're probably tired. Goodbye."

The young girl turned to go, but Remaine poked his head into the hall, his movement catching her attention. Her eyes enlarged with excitement. Remaine shrugged his shoulder, signaling to her he was both interested and not much good for conversation.

"Oh, don't worry!" she said, rushing to grab his hand. "You don't need to talk for the game. You just play. I'll teach you."

Serae led him down the opposite end of the gallery, then turned right down another long hallway. They passed portraits, marble busts on plinths, and little alcoves that held huge candelabras. Enormous, rectangular windows punctuated the hallways too, letting in great squares of light onto the carpeted floors. As the house unfolded before Remaine, he could not help but stare with an opened jaw. The entire Plink home could fit inside *that* one room, or *that* one... or *this* hall, or even that alcove over *there*.

They came at last to a set of glossy double doors. Serae heaved them open. They entered a cozy room with tall-backed armchairs and a few small tables surrounded by floor-to-ceiling bookshelves on every wall.

"This is our library," Serae said, waltzing in.

It wasn't until Remaine was fully inside, standing in the middle of the chairs, that he realized the room itself was a balcony, overlooking an even grander space with more seating and more floor-to-ceiling bookshelves. Light poured in from the tallest windows he had ever seen. Remaine gawked as he turned around and around. Then he saw Serae, on her knees before a low table, opening up a wooden box.

"Here," she said, motioning for him to sit.

He kneeled opposite her, still taking in the room, but Serae didn't seem to notice his awe and wonder. She was too excited about the contents of the wooden box.

"I *never* get to play," she said, unable to hide the wide smile on her face. "Well, that's not true. Sometimes Wynnie likes to play, but she has other responsibilities too—she's my governess *and* our housekeeper for the time being, so she's usually too busy. The other girls in the company don't care much for games, so I can't *really* play with them, and besides, we're *always* practicing. And Father doesn't like games at all. Neither does Grandmother. Oh! *Please* don't mention anything to my grandmother. She *especially* hates this game." She bit back her excited smile as she lifted game pieces from the wooden box. "Well, I guess I do play a fair amount. Mostly with Uncle Diggory. He's the best at it. He beats me every time. One time he tried to let me win but I knew what he was doing and told him he wasn't allowed."

It only took her a minute to set up the game, and as soon as she did, the sight of it sparked familiarity in Remaine's memory. It was the same game Lyme Stretcher and the high general had been playing in the prince's cabin aboard *The Emerald Egg*. For some reason this gave Remaine a sense of excitement and he leaned forward eagerly.

"Prepare yourself," said Serae, lifting her eyebrows in a flash of drama, "for the Hollowfiend's Hunt!" She smiled, then added quickly, "Don't worry, it's not scary, and it's easy to learn." Then she launched into a zealous explanation of the game.

"This is the Hollowfiend," she said, pointing to a wooden pyramid-like object carved in the likeness of a vicious lion. The lion's mouth was open and two small red jewels served as the lion's eyes.

"Now. The Hollowfiend dwells in the Hollian Hills just outside Ravillion Bay. Some say they've seen its red eyes, but others call them liars, because if you *see* its red eyes, you *die*!" she giggled again. "Anyway, the Hollowfiend never sleeps. He's *always* on the hunt. He's... always... *moving!*"

At this, Serae unhooked a little metallic rod tucked neatly into the lion's mane. It had a weight attached to it. She gave it a push, and the metal rod fell forward with a *click* sound, before swinging the opposite direction with a *clock*. *Click, clock, click, clock.*

"This is your first time, so we'll start slow," said Serae, adjusting the weight on the metal rod. Then she turned to the board laid out before them. It was a board of obsidian black and pearl white squares, and it had been set up with two rows of figurines at opposite ends facing one another.

"Here are my citizens," said Serae, "and here are yours. Our task is simple: get to the other side of the city without getting caught by the Hollowfiend."

Remaine furrowed his brow. He desperately wished he could speak. Serae took notice and eagerly continued. "It goes like this. We take turns moving pieces, one square each. We can't move pieces through occupied squares. First person to get all their pieces to the opposite side wins. BUT—" she raised her eyebrows again, making her gigantic eyes appear even larger. "Here's the catch. We *have* to move to the rhythm, alternating turns, moving all our pieces, one square per turn. If you break the rhythm when it's your turn, the Hollowfiend *eats* your citizen."

Remaine stared down at the figurines, each uniquely carved to resemble a different kind of citizen. He saw a chairman with feathered epaulettes carved on his shoulders. He saw a young child carved in a running position. There was also a mother carrying an infant, a man with a hammer, another young man with a cow, and a sailor with a fishnet. Serae's side of the board had figurines with similar iterations.

"First person to get all their pieces across the board ends the game, but it's the person with the most left—with the most who survived the Hollowfiend—who wins. Ready?"

Remaine looked around the board anxiously. The *click-clocking* of the Hollowfiend metronome pulsed in his ears. He swallowed drily.

Serae moved first, right on the beat. *Click.*

Remaine hesitated. *Clock.*

"Dead!" said Serae, snatching one of his pieces and tossing it below the snarling lion. "Ready?"

Remaine readjusted his position. Serae moved smoothly with the *click*, and this time he advanced a piece of his own right on time with the *clock*. Back and forth they shifted pieces. *Click, clock, click, clock.* Remaine hesitated again after Serae moved a piece that blocked him in.

"Dead!" she giggled again, swiping up another piece.

Much to Remaine's surprise, and delight, this was how the morning passed at Rawthorne Manor. Remaine did not win a single game, but Serae was altogether pleasant about her winnings and Remaine found himself enjoying her company. By the time she had won her twentieth game in a row, Remaine smiled at the sudden realization that he might have made a new friend.

The doors to the library's balcony burst open and Wynnie Canny rushed in.

"Serae!" she huffed, blowing a loose strand of hair out of her face. "You're late!"

Serae's eyes widened with surprise as they found the clock on the top shelf of the closest bookcase. She popped up. "I'm sorry, Wynnie," she said, "I was teaching Remaine how to play."

Wynnie hurried over to them both, hands on her hips. Remaine guessed her to be a few years older than Silome. She looked down at Serae's dress, now bunched and badly wrinkled about the knees.

"Oh Serae," she said, squatting to work out the creases with her hands. She had a worried, paranoid sort of way of moving around, fussing with Serae's dress. "You could at least fan out your silks before you sit." She fiddled with the dress for another minute. Serae smiled and rolled her eyes in Remaine's direction. Then Wynnie stood.

"Who won?" she asked.

Serae grinned and gave a little curtsy.

"You're learning from the best, boy," said Wynnie, conceding a small smile in Remaine's direction. "Serae. Come along. Two more days of practice, before—"

"Don't say it!" said Serae, sucking in air and closing her eyes. "I can't bear to think of it. I'll get too nervous." She let the air out slowly while pressing her hands down her sides.

"Well, if you practice, you won't be nervous," said Wynnie, tugging Serae's arm. "Come. Lady Solace wishes to observe you in an hour from now. We'll see you later on, Remaine."

Serae gave Remaine one of her friendly little waves as they shut the double doors behind them. Remaine sat alone in the library. He realized, then, that the metronome was still going. He stopped it and slowly put the game pieces back into the wooden box as best as he could. Then he sat there, drumming his fingers on the table, looking around the room. Two tightly spiraled staircases, one at each end of the balcony, wound down to the bottom level of the library. He chose the one to the left, descended, then walked over to the enormous windows. The center window turned out to be a door. He clicked the handle and pushed.

He was standing on the south side of the house. Despite the sun's direct blanket of light on his face, he was hit with a rush of very cold air swirling in around him. Remaine stared in awe at the high, snow-capped mountain rising above him.

He stepped outside and took a deep breath, looking around.

"Shut that door, boy!" snapped a voice from behind.

Remaine obeyed reflexively. He stepped back into the library and quickly shut the door. He turned to see Lady Solace, standing at the library's entrance, both hands upon her ivory cane. Her face, still wreathed in fluffy orange fur, was stone cold and focused. "Besides the fact you've been strictly prohibited from stepping foot outside, you also commit the more severe crime of letting in the cold."

Remaine did not know how to apologize, so he just nodded and allowed his head to hang a bit lower in hopes of showing respect.

"Though, I don't blame you for wanting to get out," she continued, moving towards him. A circle of high-backed chairs lay between them. Lady Solace took the one nearest her. "One can only handle so much confinement..."

She gazed out the window to the mountains. Remaine felt frozen in place. "Wynnie is a good girl," she sighed, "She sees to it I'm well-disguised when I go out. But there's only so much a mask and make-up can do to hide my age."

Lady Solace gave a cynical chuckle and placed a bony hand on her cheek. Now that she mentioned it, Remaine had taken notice of her age. It was rare to see someone so advanced in years as Lady Solace was still residing in the West. Why had she not yet relocated to Colony Gardens?

"Well don't just stand there, boy," she said, acknowledging Remaine once more with a surly expression. She held her chin up. "Sit and read to me or leave me be."

Remaine looked around for a moment, even though he already knew which of the two options to choose. He gave another awkward bow and left the library.

He did not see anyone else for the rest of the day. That is, except Jolly, who arrived at his room with spectacular punctuality to inform him that lunch was ready. When Remaine arrived downstairs there were no others present, so he ate quietly and quickly, feeling uncomfortable every time his glass was refilled for him.

A few hours later, Remaine took tea in his room. He liked the taste of it well enough. The tea was richer and creamier than anything he had ever had on the docks back home. And thanks to Jolly's tutelage, it was sweeter, too. It was during tea that he met Rosy, the cook who had come along with Jolly so that she could introduce herself to Remaine. She was a roundish woman with a body like a wedding cake, kind eyes inset in bags of skin like folds of bread, and black hair piled up like a stack of buns on her head. She was "the lady with the ladle" as she said. It felt weird to have someone cook for him and clean up after him, but Remaine smiled and shook her hand.

For much of the afternoon, Remaine found himself thinking of nothing else but the Hollowfiend's Hunt. The ticking of a clock near the stairs got him thinking about it again and he half-heartedly wandered the halls hoping to stumble upon Serae and hoping she would want to play again. But then he passed by a familiar set of closed doors, heard the strains of music and Serae's voice along with Lady Solace's and he knew she was busy. He wandered on, hoping he could remember his way back to the library. He took a few wrong turns, but eventually he found the right set of double doors. He went into the library, pulled out the Hollowfiend's Hunt, and began to practice.

This consumed the greater part of an hour, but the Hollowfiend's Hunt just wasn't the sort of game one could practice very effectively alone, so he gave up and wandered back to his room, still hoping to bump into Serae. Unfortunately, this was not the case, and it was not until dinner later that evening that Remaine finally got the chance to see Serae again. Jolly helped him dress in a smooth gray jacket with lots of brass buttons and Remaine headed to dinner, hoping to talk to Serae about the Hollowfiend's Hunt.

Jolly ushered Remaine to the back of the chair he had sat in earlier that morning; he stood like everyone else, waiting. Then, once everyone had arrived, they all took their seats at the same time. Another painful period of silence passed. The food arrived and they clinked their silverware and poked at their plates.

The silence broke, though, when Belwin took a swallow of his dark red liquid and then spoke. "Serae, how were rehearsals today?"

Serae bobbed her head, elegantly slicing a piece of meat in two. "Good, I think," she said. She held her fork in an unusual way, and at the sight of it, Remaine looked at his own hand and adjusted his grip to match. He straightened his back, too.

"*Very* good, my lord," said Wynnie, smiling. She wiped her hands on the napkin spread out on her lap. "I think Serae would fit the part beautifully."

"Of course, she would," said Lady Solace, jutting her chin upward. "She'll get the part. I have no doubt. She's got Vashing blood in her. Dancers—as light as feathers—every last one of my sisters. And me. And my daughter."

Belwin sucked his teeth and swirled his glass of wine.

"And your grandfather, too, you know. The Depps were graceful creatures—the men like deer, the women like cats—that's what drew me to him."

"Yes, Grandmother," said Serae. Her voice was respectful, but Remaine thought he saw her flash him the smallest eye roll. "So you've told me."

The door burst open abruptly and Remaine could not hide the surprise on his face at the sight of the man who strode through.

Captain Diggory Rawthorne stepped in. He looked tired but managed a smile. His blue, mohawked bird clung tightly to his shoulder and his fat cat trotted along behind. Remaine had completely forgotten he was related to Belwin and Serae.

"Sorry I'm late, everyone," he said. "No that's all right, Jolly, I can do it." Diggory pulled a chair back and sat down. "It's been madness at Lichenbluff."

Remaine could not tell if Lady Solace's pinched face of displeasure was due to the presence of Captain Rawthorne or due to the presence of his two animals. She kept a fierce eye on all three of them.

"I imagine it has," said Belwin, downing the last of his goblet. He brought the glass down on the table a bit harder than necessary.

Jolly brought a covered dish to Diggory and removed the silver dome. He poured a glass of wine with careful hands, smiling with pride the whole time.

"Good man, Jolly," said Diggory, raising the glass to his lips. He stopped halfway. "Oh hello, Remaine. It's good to see you conscious."

Remaine's face burned as red as Jolly's. Diggory smiled encouragingly and continued, "I do apologize for the surprise in the bay. You can thank your sister for it. And Levo Chince. And a couple others, I suppose, but really it was at Silome's request. I'm sure you've been all caught up." He said this last bit as if it were a question, glancing over at Belwin, who did not change expressions in the slightest. "Or maybe not..." said Diggory. "You did tell the boy, Belwin, yes?"

"You know, in fact, I did, Diggory," said Belwin. "The boy knows it was his sister's aim to get him off *The Emerald Egg*, though I doubt he is aware of what, exactly, that stunt cost. Tell me, what is all the madness at Lichenbluff about?"

Diggory took a bite of potatoes, and thoughtfully chewed for a moment. "The prince wants to stay in Ravillion Bay for a while longer."

Belwin shot daggers in Diggory's direction. Diggory seemed to intentionally ignore his brother.

"When do you sail next?" Belwin asked.

"Not sure," said Diggory. "Since he is staying for a bit, the prince has decided to hold an impromptu Tour of Valor here."

Belwin was less than enthused. "What? When?"

"In two days," said Diggory. "It'll be announced tomorrow morning."

Belwin closed his eyes and rubbed his temples. "I suppose the prince doesn't care that the Brumaloss is only a month away—to suddenly spring another celebration on us like this... the chairmen will be at each other's throats trying to get preparations ready."

"He seems determined," said Diggory. He took a bit of his food and passed it down to his cat, whispering, "Here you are, Barrow."

"I can't imagine Duchess Chipping is thrilled."

"Of course, she's not—but this is her prince, not another chairman."

Belwin was rubbing holes into his temples. "If it's not the Brumaloss, it's the Tour; if it's not the Tour, it's the work in the pass—"

"Mirror Pass?" asked Diggory.

"Yes, Diggory. Still fixated on the pass, I see."

"Mirror Pass still warrants that much discussion among the chairmen? Belwin, come on. One year of construction is nothing. Two years is understandable. But it's been years of work up there. It's worth a look, don't you think? Something could be—"

"Enough," droned Belwin. "Not now."

A beat of silence followed.

"Well, I can't imagine what the chairmen have to fuss about," said Lady Solace, "Really. What civilized person bemoans a grand night out, let alone *two*! And in two months' time! Not to mention two of a caliber such as the *Tour* and the Brumaloss." She sipped her wine. In the light of the chandelier above, her diamonds glittered with celestial brilliance. "When I was young, I was the sovereign of a grand night out. If I could still attend, I would. I don't care how wicked the prince is. At least he has the decency to throw a good party."

"Yes, Lady Solace," said Belwin with a deep sigh, his eyes half-closed. "When you arrive as a guest, I'm sure it *would* be wonderful, but when you're in charge of logistics… we've already been informed that this year's Brumaloss will be special. As many dukes and duchesses of Cracklemore who can make it have been invited. On me falls the burden to see they're taken care of and satisfied while here."

For a while, the conversation wore on in this manner and most of it went over Remaine's head. What he was able to gather, however, was that Belwin held an official position within the city, though it was unclear as to exactly what role he played. On the other hand, Diggory appeared almost oblivious to Belwin's world and found excuses to make quiet jokes in Serae's direction. She would giggle, he would make a face, and Belwin would make a mean face directed at the two of them. They ate in silence until Lady Solace found something to complain about. Eventually, dinner gave way to dessert. It was a pie of some kind and because Diggory strongly insisted, everyone, Jolly and Rosy included, sat together and enjoyed some. Lady Solace did not approve of this last part, nor did she approve of the part when, suspended delicately from his own lips, Diggory fed his blue jay a piece of crust.

After dessert, Serae left with Wynnie and Lady Solace, so Remaine did not get a chance to talk with her about the Hollowfiend's Hunt. Jolly escorted him back to his room where he again retired with no complaint. A few minutes passed. The sweet of dessert still lingered in his mouth. He was desperately thirsty. He looked at the braided, golden rope hanging near the bed and decided he did not want to bother Jolly. He opened his door and tiptoed out to help himself to water.

He heard whispers.

"I've been there all day, Belwin, I assure you, it's the same as before.

No one suspects a thing." Diggory's voice hissed from below the balustrade and the sound made Remaine instinctively get low. He crawled to the edge to get a closer look. Belwin was inches from Diggory at the far end of the hall.

"It doesn't matter, Diggory!" hissed Belwin. "You know as well as I do that the prince couldn't care less about the Tour! He has decided to stay in the city because of the boy."

"He won't find him, Belwin. Each day that passes confirms the boy's death."

"It's not *the Plink boy* I'm worried about, Diggory." Belwin's jaw was clenched, and his eyes wide. "He's *in my house!* With *my* daughter. With *my* family."

"They're my family too."

"Yes, and you sure don't mind putting them all at risk!" Belwin snapped.

"Look, Belwin, I'm sorry. This is not going according to plan, I'll admit, but we can't change it. They can work whatever enchantment they want in those waters—there's *no body* to find. It's all going to work out."

"It had better, Diggory," said Belwin.

The viscount turned on his heel and stormed off. Diggory hung his head. His cat purred and wound around his legs, but Diggory ignored the affection. Eventually he too turned and walked away.

Breathing hard, Remaine slowly and silently backed into his room. His heart pounded in the same sort of way it did when Silome caught him relaxing on his secret perch. He went over to the window and stared down at the glimmering city. A pointy, cliffside castle caught his eye—Lichenbluff Castle. That was where Diggory had been. That was where preparations were being made for the Tour of Valor in two days' time. And now he knew two more very important things. Prince Xietas was in Lichenbluff Castle. And Prince Xietas was looking for him.

CHAPTER 14

LICHENBLUFF CASTLE

OVER THE NEXT TWO DAYS, Remaine followed every rule. Frankly, he did not like how much attention he had garnered since leaving home, so it was to his own benefit to keep his head down. He was stuck at Rawthorne Manor, that much was certain, and if he had to be here, he wanted to lie low until there was something worth poking his head up for.

As it turned out, there was something, but before he could poke his head up he kept himself occupied by sticking to Jolly's schedule and keeping quiet during mealtimes, all of which was painfully boring. Remaine could not understand why he had to change his clothes for different meals, nor did he understand why anyone cared who sat or stood and who entered or left first or last, from any given room. All of the rules made his head foggy.

Of great interest to him, however, were the morning times right after breakfast, when he would meet up with Serae to play the Hollowfiend's Hunt. By day three, even though Serae had bumped the speed up by four clicks, Remaine had won three games. Truthfully, he had only won two—on the third, he broke a few rules; Serae quickly scolded him for that. The taste of victory was more savory than he'd imagined, but it quickly turned bitter when Serae overturned his win.

When he did win fairly, though, he thought of Silome. She was always winning at things. No wonder she felt so superior. How different life must be for someone who lives every day in a state of victory. Even the sharp pain in his ribs dissipated when he was winning.

His voice was slowly scraping back to life, and he managed to ask Serae through labored wheezes about Silome. "You know my sister, then?"

"Uh huh," she said, setting up the board. "Well, sort of. She only comes during the summers, and usually only for a couple of days. I'm often with the company during that time, practicing, so I don't see her too much. She kind of scared me at first."

Remaine laughed. Serae laughed too.

"But then I thought she was amazing. She began sword practice with Levo two years ago, and she picked it up fast."

Surprise, surprise, thought Remaine.

"And then she helped create the gruggleblade, and everyone loved her for that."

Remaine was surprised to hear this. And there it was again… the gruggleblade.

"Oh, right, I guess you wouldn't know. Everyone in our… um…" she thought for a second, "house, I guess, is sworn to strict secrecy." Remaine noticed she had begun to fiddle with a tiny jewel that hung on a delicate chain around her neck while she spoke. Then she dropped her voice to a tiny whisper and brought a hand up to block any imaginary listeners, "Father told me not to tell you about anything we're up to in case you tattle, but I think we're friends enough."

She smiled. He smiled too.

"Anyway," she said, her gaze returning to the board. "Silome brought along a plant called gruggleroot from a friend back home—at least that's what she told us—some sort of weed from your ocean that makes you sleep."

Gruggleroot! That's why it sounded familiar. Remaine knew at once what Serae was talking about. Silome had been stealing gruggle-root from Cressa Merchant's stores.

"My great uncle worked with it for a while, mixing the stuff with some other stuff, I'm not sure. My great uncle Dasko is a real genius. Eventually he and grandfather made the gruggleblade. Seals you up and puts you to sleep as fast as it opens your skin."

Who *were* these people? He recalled the few times he had been a witness to strange things in the manor. During his first day awake he had seen the log toss itself into the fire and the curtain move itself when Jolly couldn't do it. Since then, he had seen two more odd moments. Only yesterday morning, when he was looking out his window at the gardener—he couldn't remember his name—he thought he saw the plants *move* in a strange way. And just last night, after dinner, when Remaine passed a room he'd never seen before that had a huge desk and more books, he saw Belwin scribbling on some kind of paper. Just as he peeked inside, a book jumped from the shelf into Belwin's hand.

"Are you..." he wheezed, trying to find the right words. Serae blinked at him like a sweet, innocent deer. He tried again. "Are you *enchanters*?"

There was a mischievous smirk which flashed on her face for barely a heartbeat before disappearing. "Now I *really* can't talk about that. Father would be very upset."

Then Serae shrugged, as if what she said was as normal as porridge, then she added, "Ready? No rule breaking this time." She reached over and tipped the metronome into motion.

Besides the little mistake with the Hollowfiend's Hunt, breaking the rules was as difficult for Remaine as keeping them was for his sister. He was unable to count the times he had shaken with fear as he watched her sneak out of the family home to discover some sort of trouble with Estin and others down on the Docks.

And yet there he was, later that night, for the second time in his practically grown-up life, climbing out of a window in secret. Remaine hardly recognized himself.

It was a frigid climb down, the vines and lattice work were cold to the touch. The sun had only just set but the temperature had plummeted and, like Lady Solace, he bit down on the sharp air with clenched teeth. A wind had picked up too, threatening to send Remaine tumbling into the topiary below, but he held on with stiffened fingers and descended slowly. But not too slowly. He would not miss his ride.

Harnessed to a sleek black horse who scuffed at the gravel and snorted, releasing a plume of steamy breath from his nostrils, the carriage was there. Remaine peered out from the shadowy coverage of a shrub manicured in the shape of a perfect sphere. Flanked by lit sconces, the door was ajar. Over the past two days, he had determined this would be the scene and when he found everything right where it should be, he breathed a sigh of relief.

The carriage sat empty, awaiting the arrival of its passengers. The driver, whom Remaine recognized at once to be Mr. Levo Chince, stood with his back to the carriage at the front door of the manor. Oblivious to his carriage, Levo shifted, hands clasped behind his back, trying to keep warm as he awaited his passengers.

As Remaine approached the horse as stealthily as possible, the gravel crunched under his feet. He froze at the sound of his own footsteps and winced, glancing back at the driver. Levo Chince had not seemed to notice. Remaine stepped forward again. From his cloak, like a party trick, Remaine produced an apple he had swiped from the kitchens. He raised his eyebrows dramatically, trying to exude kindness as he extended the apple to the horse—a disingenuous offering. Much to Remaine's relief, the horse gave no care as to his motives, and instead gave a happy stomp. The horse munched on the treat as Remaine positioned himself behind the carriage, out of the direct view of anyone in Rawthorne Manor. He heard voices and dropped himself low to the ground.

As he struggled to thread his body through the carriage's framed underside, Remaine cursed his sister. *She has always made stuff like this look easy.*

His sister. He cursed her one more time. It was not that he did not trust her. He trusted Silome with his life. Even as he recalled her words from the Singer earlier, he knew for certain she believed what she had said. Still, there was too much unaccounted for. Silome did not know *everything*—she had never spoken with the prince like he had. She did not know Xietas Ravillion like Remaine knew him. Remaine had resolved to himself that he needed more answers, and he knew he would not find all of them inside Rawthorne Manor.

Having wormed himself into an unpleasant position under the carriage's frame, he froze and held his breath. Several bundled figures hastened from the house and climbed into the carriage. Remaine watched their feet get closer and then disappear as they stepped up. The door to the carriage closed with a click, and the driver swung himself atop. With the sudden snap of tightening reins the carriage lurched forward and Remaine along with it.

He saw nothing of the passing city. In addition to his limited view beneath the carriage, Remaine's entire body, from his fingers to his toes and even to his eyes, froze solid as the carriage journeyed through Ravillion Bay. He could hear well enough. They had gone through a town square of some kind, had passed a fountain, Remaine guessed, then they had come to a bridge, that much he deduced with confidence. The sudden slowing of the carriage along with the surrounding foot traffic and excitable voices told him they had arrived.

The sounds also told Remaine there were crowds. *Good*, he thought. He was banking on crowds. He adjusted his numb body as best he could and prepared himself. Enough commotion should hide the sudden appearance of a boy in the middle of the street. The carriage halted, he was just about to drop off from the frame, but the sound of approaching footfall stopped him. A short, muffled conversation ensued. Remaine could not catch all the details.

Then the carriage lurched forward and picked up speed once more, leaving the crowds behind. Remaine choked back a silent "No! Wait!" He grimaced and repositioned. He had lost his chance.

Everything about his body had gone painfully rigid. He hung his head down to try to get a better view of things. An upside-down world passed by. They had left the crowds behind and were now rapidly traveling down a curved stone road. On one side, an open cliff face with the waters of Ravillion Bay lapping below, and on the other side, the backside to Lichenbluff Castle.

Mr. Levo Chince pulled back on the reins and called out to the horse. The carriage stopped. A panic overtook Remaine as he realized this was the destination. If he dropped now, he would surely be spotted. With shaky hands, he readjusted, knowing it might be his only chance. The drivers' boots landed on the ground. There was an opening *click*, then two more pairs of shoes. The latter hurried away from the carriage and down a stone corridor toward two large doors that opened to a flood of yellow light and an explosion of red costumes. Remaine hung like a spider, afraid to move, trying to think fast.

He was not quick enough. The carriage lurched forward again. Remaine clung with unstable hands as it followed the road further down the backside of the castle. With his weight unsupported by anything more that his frozen fingers and with his whole body stiff and frigid, Remaine witnessed with horror as his icy grip, like the scraping of a mollusk from the side of ship, finally gave loose. He fell to the ground like a frozen corpse, but not before his cloak snagged on the metal frame.

He was thankful he could not feel his frozen body at that moment, as the carriage dragged him across the cobblestone drive. Then with a loud *SHHHHEEEEKT*, his cloak tore. Remaine lay, crumpled in the dark in the middle of the cliffside drive at the foot of Lichenbluff Castle.

Then the pain hit him. He would have cried out loud if he had a voice. He swore silently all the more, realizing exactly where he was. In front of the back entrances—the dungeon accesses. Locked, to be sure.

With great effort, Remaine rose. Limping into the shadows, he sought cover, pressing himself against the castle walls. He crouched into the shadows and watched as two more carriages dropped off their passengers and sped off in the same direction as the carriage he had stowed away on.

The road, Remaine concluded, must wind itself back up to the front of the castle where he could see the crowds filing in for the Tour. He thought quickly, peering out, as if to find his answer. Afraid he would meet carriages head on if he backtracked, Remaine turned left and began to scurry along the shadowed walls like a dungeon rat.

He was just thinking to himself that all he needed to do was find a way into the castle when he nearly ran into a door as it swung open directly in front him. An explosion of sound and light erupted from the open archway, and several figures in aprons carrying big pots filled with steaming liquid came through. Others followed carrying carts of food scraps. Remaine froze in the shadows, holding his breath as they began tossing the garbage into big barrels.

"I want it closed up afterwards, Peely!" said a large man, tossing a wet carcass into the barrel and then wiping greasy hands on the belly of his apron. "Or we'll have a rat problem like last time."

The door to the kitchen was big and heavy, and it swung just slowly enough that Remaine was able to move out of instinct. Without thinking, he darted into the kitchen and headed for the first piece of cover he could find—a wall of white aprons and a shelf with a thousand folded rags.

Around him, the kitchen made for kings hummed like a beehive. There must have been a hundred people inside, chopping at long, thick tables, throwing things into big copper pots, or stoking one of the five enormous fireplaces along the opposite wall.

Crowds. Remaine took a quick, calming breath and disappeared.

He had an apron on before those from outside had come back in, and by the time they had, Remaine was in the thick of the steam which spewed in plumes periodically from any one of the pots bubbling throughout the room.

There is an art to blending in—not one Remaine had mastered by any means, but one in which he was naturally skillful to the degree which any sort of boy who is altogether plain, and forgettable, with no real talent, and with no becoming or distinguishable physical traits of any kind, and certainly with no height or strength to call his own might be. And, advantageously, (Remaine whispered words of thanks to the Plinks back home) he knew his way around a kitchen.

No one questioned his presence. Remaine moved with purpose, as one does in a kitchen. He never lingered, yet he didn't rush. On occasion he would pause to let someone in a greater hurry pass by, and at one point he was handed a pot of a creamy red sauce and told to take it to another table, which he did without hesitating. In a stroke of forethought, he even dipped his hand in a bag of flour and tossed a bit onto his face; a feeble disguise, but satisfactory nonetheless. Finally, he made his way to the far end of the room where there, in the midst of the sea of busy, unfamiliar faces, he noticed another door leading to what looked like a very large corridor that stood ajar. Unfamiliar faces, Remaine thought, except one.

"I should think the Crush, tonight," said Belwin Rawthorne curtly. Unlike the three women he was talking to, the viscount had no apron and wore instead a red, high-collared velvet vest, a black jacket with red buttons, and boots with silver buckles. His shoulders fanned out with the fancy red epaulettes of the chairman.

Remaine slipped out of the way, keeping his head down. He turned his back to Belwin and busied himself near a long line of dried herbs hanging from a rack. Out of the corner of his eye, he watched as one of the women handed Belwin a glass. He sipped with a hawk-like focus.

"Yes," he said. "Good age. The prince enjoys a Crush." He pointed to a bottle of a clear, foggy liquid. "Gloves!" he said, as the woman reached for the bottle with her bare hands. "Here I'll do it. And the pinion…" Belwin scanned the wall, then selected another, darker bottle. "Give this to him."

The three women bowed and, after having put their gloves on, received the two bottles like midwives cradling newborns. "Very good. They'll be seated in the balcony any moment now." With those words, Belwin disappeared into the corridor. The three women spent a moment arranging the bottles carefully on a splendid cart, then they, too, exited the kitchen, turning right.

Remaine thanked the Enchanters. They may have forgotten to Charm him, but tonight he had found some fortune. The wine would be his guide. He just needed to go *with* them. He needed a reason to go with them. He needed a lie.

Grabbing the first bottle of wine he saw, he sped out of the kitchen and turned right, glancing over his shoulder to look behind him. Ahead of him, Belwin was nowhere to be seen. There was no sign of the women, either.

Running, he came to a small flight of stairs. At the top of the stairs, he noticed long carpets covering the floors and elegant tapestries lining the walls. He also heard the muffled sound of voices. He followed his ears and was soon trailing the women pushing the cart.

"Excuse me!" he shouted, or at least he tried to shout, remembering, once more, he had no voice. Something like a raspy gargoyle cry broke free from his mouth.

One of the women turned around. Seeing the concerned look on his face and the bottle of wine in his hands, she stopped the others.

"Who are you?" she asked. The woman was tall and fair, and she had a face like a bird.

Remaine motioned to his mouth and throat and shook his head.

"You can't speak?" she chirped.

He shook his head again. Then, seeing the confusion on their faces, and knowing there was no other choice available to him, he gave his best attempt to charade a lie. He held up the bottle of wine in one hand and motioned back over his shoulder with the other hand.

"That wine?" asked the woman in the middle. She was less birdy. Then Remaine wheezed the name "Rawthorne" as a final hope to sell the story.

"Rawthorne? He wants *that* one?" said the birdy one. "Curses, cat pee, and Harbor's Hand slap me!"

The woman yanked the bottle out of Remaine's hand and turned on her heel. She marched back to rejoin the other two women, exchanging hushed complaints at such a rate that not one of them noticed Remaine trailing along behind.

Eventually their corridor collided with another, then forked out once more, but not before Remaine passed the entrance to another busy chamber, this one much more colorful than the kitchen of white-clad cooks.

A red sea of costumed men and women with black-lined eyes and powdered faces milled about in a vast room that had a wooden floor and an entire wall made only of curtains. The lighting was low, their voices hushed. It appeared to Remaine that the ways in which Ravillion Bay chose to celebrate the Tour were much grander than Windluff's.

Remaine kept moving. If that was the stage entrance for the Tour's performers, then surely he was getting close to the prince. The hallways now were populated with elegant men and women in fancy red dress. Remaine kept moving and kept his head down.

He finally came to a quieter hallway leading up to the balcony. When he rounded the next corner, he expected to find the women again, but he did not. Only their cart was there, sitting at the foot of a flight of stairs, and next to the cart stood four tall members of the royal guard.

When he had left Rawthorne Manor earlier that night, Remaine

Plink had felt a hunger for answers he knew would be left unsatisfied unless he spoke with the prince himself. And deep down, he knew the prince was the only one who appreciated his gifts. And by all accounts, he knew if he simply revealed to the guard who he was—the boy the prince was looking for—they would happily escort him to the prince. But for some reason, at the sight of the guards, before they had a chance to get a good look at his face, Remaine bowed his head. He could hear the voice of his sister telling him to stay hidden. He could not do both for long, but for now, the conflict raged on in him.

"You with the girls?" said one of the men.

Another stroke of luck. Remaine nodded, bowing his whole body slightly forward, hoping the lack of eye contact might appear as a sign of reverence. He was thankful for the flour on his face, too.

"Get, then."

Remaine scampered up the stairs without looking back, his heart pounding in his chest. He came to a stone archway, draped with red curtains. Pulling back the fabric just slightly with a steady hand, he peeked inside.

The expansive balcony, complete with several sofas and a dining table, was populated by a host of figures.

Along with Prince Xietas, who stood at the balcony's edge, Remaine could see Estin Merchant, as well as six or so other guards. The newest recruits from Windluff hovered together around the dining table at the far end of the balcony. They picked at clusters of grapes, cheeses, and bread sprawled out in colorful displays. Tarquin Pellatrim lounged lazily in one of the chairs by the table. No matter what the truth was, Remaine knew he'd always be unwelcome around Tarquin. He paused, chewing his lip and continuing to observe the scene. He saw Lyme Stretcher standing next to the prince and the two of them were talking to the three women Remaine had followed out of the kitchen.

But all this notwithstanding, Remaine saw, climbing into the balcony from a separate flight of stairs that led up from the audience,

Belwin Rawthorne. Remaine flushed with panic. He had very nearly revealed himself. He watched as Belwin approached, followed by a woman Remaine did not recognize, though by the looks of her regalia, Remaine knew she must be of high importance in Ravillion Bay.

The two of them bowed to the prince. "Your Enchanted," said Belwin.

"Viscount Rawthorne," said the prince. "Duchess Chipping."

Belwin smiled curtly and the regal woman gave a nod. Then Belwin took note of the wine bottles and the women holding them, the women whom Remaine had followed. His eyes grew wide.

"No, no, give me that," said Belwin, taking one of the bottles of wine away from one of the women. "Forgive me, Lord Stretcher. I don't know why they brought this bottle."

"But..." said the woman to whom Remaine had given the bottle.

"Enough," said Belwin, silencing her. "Please serve them their drinks, now." He motioned towards the original bottles.

The women, clearly confused and disgruntled, began to pour the prince and his royal advisor their drinks.

Duchess Chipping spoke. "I'm sorry to hear nothing has come of your search for the boy, my prince."

The prince sighed. "I've sent Cottley for the boy's sister."

"His sister, my prince?"

"Yes. For his entire family, in fact."

The duchess pursed her lips, intrigued. "You're interested in more than just him, then?"

"Perhaps," said the prince. "There might be something in the bloodline."

Remaine furrowed his brow as he listened. As far as he knew, there was absolutely *nothing* extraordinary about the Plink bloodline. Had he lived his entire life in the docks of Windluff with neither coin nor prestige to his family name, only to find out now that the Plinks were of royal interest? His stomach turned at the thought of the prince taking interest in Silome.

"Very good," said Duchess Chipping. "Well, I do hope the ceremony pleases you tonight, and your upcoming travels are... eventless."

"I think I'll stay here, actually," said the prince, his tone flat. "The Brumaloss is just around the corner."

The duchess raised her eyebrows. "Goodness, His High Enchanted mentioned this would be a special year—that's why he's sending half the king's court—it will be our absolute honor to host you as well, my prince."

Duchess Chipping bowed her head low, careful not to spill her drink. Then she asked, "Do you know which members of the court will be joining us? The king gave no specifics, but I'd like to see all preparations are made well before they arrive."

The prince's gaze was distant. "Hmm? Ah. My apologies, Duchess. My mind is elsewhere—on the Plink boy again, I'm afraid. You asked about the court? Yes. Courtier Venerack will be attending, I know for certain—he has work to do in Mirror Pass. I do not know who else my father is sending."

"Very good, Your Enchanted."

Remaine felt his body yanked backwards. A large hand covered his mouth.

The big red bear, Levo Chince, threw him against the wall. Eyes aflame, he held a finger the width of a broomstick to his lips. "Shh."

With Levo in the silent hallway stood Captain Diggory Rawthorne, whose muddy eyes held the sharpest and severest gaze that Remaine had ever seen. Diggory shook his head slightly at Remaine, as if in warning, but said nothing. Levo pulled Remaine further back to the shadows of the wall as Diggory strolled casually through the curtain. Remaine caught a glimpse of Tarquin Pellatrim when the curtain swung open.

Did Tarquin see him too?

"Got lost," chuckled Diggory with boisterous levity. "Lived here my whole life and this place is still a maze to me."

Remaine's breathing quickened beneath the fiery pressure of Levo's grip, but he did not fight him.

"Thank you," Remaine heard Diggory say. There was a clink of glasses. "Ah, a Crush. Good choice, brother."

There was another muffled exchange about grapes.

Then Remaine was moving, down the stairs, Levo's hand at his back.

"Don't say a word," Levo breathed down his neck. Remaine didn't bother to gesture to him that he was still unable to speak.

Levo prodded Remaine through the halls of the Lichenbluff Castle like a shepherd with a runaway sheep, and Remaine, unsure of what else to do, complied.

Levo led him outside, down another flight of steps, out past several stationed guards who stood, indifferent to their presence, ultimately bringing Remaine to a waiting carriage. Levo shoved Remaine into the carriage, making Remaine feel even more like a sheep on its way to be slaughtered.

The carriage heaved violently as Levo clambered on top.

"You're a slippery little Luffy fish, I'll give you that, laddie," said Levo, peering inside, his head hanging upside down. "Your sister teach you that?"

The carriage heaved again as Levo adjusted himself on the seat.

"You slipped me eye once before, and I'm still sore from what it cost me." He rubbed his shoulder. Remaine winced at the memory of his own blood spraying Levo, followed by Levo's blood spraying him. "I'll be filleted if I let it happen again. Here."

Levo smiled, tossing a wad of fabric into the carriage. It landed right on Remaine's lap. It was the cloak that had caught and torn when Remaine fell from the carriage. Holding it up, Remaine could see the ragged tear at the bottom. With the snap of reigns, they were off, and Remaine slumped back into the seat of that carriage with no fruit to show for his sneaking out and breaking the Rawthorne rules.

CHAPTER 15

MR. LECKY WOOLING AND THE GARDEN CHEST

REMAINE DID NOT STEP ONE TOE out of the line the next day, nor the day after that, nor any day the following week.

When Levo Chince had brought him back to Rawthorne Manor following his little escapade, Remaine was told by Jolly to take a bath (he was still somewhat covered in flour from the Lichenbluff kitchens), after which he was given a cup of hot tea and offered a cozy spot by the enormous hearth in the upstairs lounge. There he waited, in the warm calm, preparing for the icy storm that Levo warned him would inevitably come. It blew in moments later: the reprimand of Belwin Rawthorne.

The storm, accompanied by red Tour fireworks exploding outside, began with a *bang!* as the double doors to the room were thrown open. A copper bust atop a shiny mahogany plinth wobbled precariously as Belwin's boots stormed into the room. Remaine noticed Serae at the doorway, peeking in from outside, biting her lip.

"Fool!" was the first thing Belwin spat out upon seeing the wide-eyed Remaine sitting on the rug. "Did you lose your senses entirely? Did your mind somehow drown when you fell off that ship—or perhaps you just left it behind in Windluff? Were we not clear? *Was I not clear?* Do you realize what could have happened if you had been discovered—what would have become of us? Of me? Of my daughter? My home? Our name? Our lives?"

Remaine endured the blast like a sloop in a maelstrom. His skin flushed hot and cold so fast he hardly knew which was which.

"Oy, Belwin," said Levo calmly from the far corner. In a chair entirely too small for him, he bent forward and rested his forearms on his knees. "He's just a lad—"

"Chince." Belwin held up a hand. His lips formed a tight line. "Quiet. It is to your great fortune, Plink, you cannot speak. I'd have you defend yourself, only so I could relish the opportunity to shred any defense you might build."

In the middle of Belwin's reprimand, Diggory entered the room and behind him, Remaine noticed, Serae disappeared entirely as Wynnie yanked her away.

"You may continue to stay here because you would be abandoned to death outside these walls, feckless and naive as you are," continued Belwin coldly. "But I want you to *disappear*. If I am aware of your presence in the least bit, then you are not hiding well enough." Diggory cleared his throat as if to speak. "No, Diggory. I do not care. I will see the boy removed. Am I clear?"

Remaine could only nod. He wanted to cry, and later, when he was lying in his bed, he did.

The following day he stayed in his room. Jolly had the grace not to ask him to join everyone downstairs and brought his meals to him instead. At one point Jolly offered to usher Remaine to the kitchens so that Rosy could make him something comforting, but he declined.

The next day went much the same way, and Remaine felt the worst he had in a long time. After spending another frustrating day alone in his room, his feelings of despair were only compounded by the arrival of another Singer from Windluff, whom Jolly brought into Remaine's room before turning down his bedsheets for the night.

"A message for you, Master Plink." Jolly set the bird down on the table near the fireplace. It was a plain, gray thing, with a pale blue head.

After fiddling with the bedding, Jolly let himself out, saying as the door was closing, "The window latch is just there, Master Plink, for sending the bird off when you've finished. The Rawthorne lords have asked me to remind you to refrain from sending any sort of reply. Nighty-night!"

The door closed. From his seat on the windowsill, Remaine stared at the bird. He did not give it much critical thought, but the general impression he felt at the prospect of hearing from his sister was less-than-thrilling. He had not had a good day and he did not feel in the mood. Remaine nodded at the bird, inviting it to speak.

"It's me again," came Silome's voice from the bird's open beak. "I hope you're surviving up there. You're probably being forced to eat dinner in stupid shirts with neck buttons that choke the life out of you." Remaine felt like he could hear her eyes rolling through the mouth of the bird. "Anyway. Things here are... weird. The great, golden pumpkin keeps rolling by—you know who I mean—acts like he cares about us—yesterday he showed up at our house—thought the whole thing might capsize—says he's concerned about our family—keeps saying the East is calling for them. Fat chance he cares at all. The whole thing has Mom acting... different. She seems worried. Don't tell anyone but—sorry if any of you are listening—but I think I'm gonna break the rules and tell Mom about everything. I know I'll be in trouble, but I can't just stand by and watch her fall apart about her son's... change of fate. Anyway. There's something about Heg—I mean the great golden pumpkin—sorry—that's got me kinda worried, too. Mom's not telling me everything, I know it. All right, that's all for now. Keep your head down. Don't do anything stupid. Don't leave."

Remaine unlatched the window and let the bird out. He was too tired to give the message too much thought. As far as he was concerned, it did not provide him with any answers. At the moment, he felt indifferent as to whether his family even knew of his whereabouts or not. The Plinks were horizons and worlds away. He went to bed stewing on Silome's last words—the orders to keep his head down and not do anything stupid.

The next day, however, things improved slightly. For starters, his ribs had healed almost entirely, and he was able to let out a big, pain-free, sigh of relief that Belwin was out of the house. Since Belwin was gone, Remaine decided to follow Jolly's invitation to come out of his room and take his lunch in the dining hall. Serae was there. Her smile brightened things. In addition, he found the mere act of stepping out of his room to be surprisingly helpful for lifting his spirits.

The doors to the hall burst open to the large figure of Levo Chince. He tossed something white at Remaine.

"Take that shirt off, lad. Throw this one on." Then he swiped some toast from the table and gave it a generous spread of butter.

Remaine unraveled a plain white tunic, loose and airy. He shivered at the sight of it, and looked longingly down at what he was currently wearing. It was getting colder outside, and the temperature inside felt little better. Remaine had on three layers and was all buttoned up to his chin. The white tunic did not look nearly as warm.

"Why?" asked Remaine. It was the first time he had spoken in days, and he was as surprised as anyone to hear a gravely volume emanate from his throat.

"Do I hear the lion's roar coming back? HA! Great!" Levo beamed and clapped Remaine on the back. "Serae, bring him to the long hall after this, eh?" He took a huge, crispy bite of his toast and left the room with a strut.

"Good to see you out and about," said Serae, moments later, as they were walking briskly down a long hallway, Remaine at her heels. "And good to hear your voice."

Serae's long brown hair hung straight down her back today. Remaine thought to himself that it was pretty.

"Yeah," said Remaine, rubbing at his throat.

"Don't let Levo scare you," said Serae as they arrived at yet another set of large doors. "Just give him a big hug and he'll melt like wax in fire." She turned to Remaine and smiled encouragingly.

Remaine found himself for the greater part of the morning in a room he had never been in, this one on the main floor, at the back of the manor. It was a long room, somewhat like the dining hall, but it held no table, no rug, no chairs. There were musical instruments at the far end of the room, and where the walls were not covered in mirrored glass or lined with tall windows, there hung more ornately framed portraits. Three chandeliers hung heavily from the high ceiling, and on the opposite wall, were two dozen swords of various shapes and sizes, hanging two-by-two, in neat X-shapes.

"Ladies and gentlemen," Levo roared, his voice echoing in the vast space. He wiped the smeared butter from his red beard with the back of his hand. "Our little warrior!"

"Warrior?" Remaine's voice was little more than a scratch.

"The Rawthornes and I was talkin'," said Levo, forcing a burp back down, "about what would be best for you, laddie. And being the bold beast I am, I'll speak the truth… you don't stand much of a chance out there."

Remaine blushed and felt a familiar shrinking feeling in his gut, like the one he got so often back home.

"What do you mean?"

"You're sneaky enough, but sometimes even sneaky rats get caught," said Levo. "And then what?"

Remaine stared at him.

"I saw you aboard the *Egg*—that was… difficult to watch. And you were about as difficult to subdue and haul away from Lichenbluff as a sleeping kitten."

Remaine curled his toes up tight beneath the pitiful gaze of Levo Chince. And yet, despite his words, somehow Remaine knew the mostly good-hearted Levo meant no ill will.

"I'm here to help you out a bit," continued Levo, as if to confirm Remaine's silent thoughts. "Show you how to… uh…" Levo shoved his hands in his pockets and searched for the right words. "Well, you know… just make you not so easy to grab from behind and get stuck in a choke hold!" He burst out laughing.

"You're going to teach me how to fight?"

"Oy, you're a long way from that, lad," said Levo. "I can teach you how to hold a sword. But mostly I think I need to get you thinking about how to stay standing on your feet. How about that?"

Levo dragged Remaine into the center of the room and positioned him firmly by the shoulders. "Spread your legs a bit, lad—hell, no wonder you're so floppy." Then he stepped back to examine him. Remaine blushed at the scrutiny, anxious to hear Levo's verdict.

Levo said nothing, to Remaine at least, but to himself, he began to mutter. Stroking his big red beard, as if combing it for secret information about Remaine, he began to circle his student. Remaine gulped, wondering what on earth Levo was contemplating.

Then, without the slightest warning, Remaine fell forward onto his face. A place between his shoulder blades, roughly the size of Levo's hand, throbbed.

"All right, sorry about that, laddie! Up you go. Quick!"

Levo picked up Remaine, who felt more than ever like a limp kitten, and placed him back on his feet. Remaine rubbed his nose and cheek where they had collided with the floor. "What was that for?" he wheezed.

"Trying to see where you carry all your weight. You favor your left foot—it stepped forward first—and then you're clearly right-handed. You also flop."

"I flop?"

"Aye, you flop. I've never seen anything like it and I don't know how else to say it. You're a flopper—you wobble like an uncooked steak. Or bread dough. Or—"

"I get it." Remaine interrupted. Then he thought of something. "Or like a fish. I've been swimming all my life."

"HA! Aye, lad! Aye!" Levo clapped Remaine on the back again and chuckled. "Of course, you have. Explains everything. So, let's work with that, eh? I think I'd be as dumb as a dirty dog to train you on anything but a rapier. I'm afraid you're not sturdy enough for the long sword, and the scimitar needs less flop and more… flow… hmmm… a cutlass might be fine enough, but you're extra slippery and doubly scrawny, so I think you'll do well with something lighter. The rapier it is."

Levo monologued about blades for several minutes. Most of it fell on deaf ears for Remaine. Eventually the redheaded giant walked over to the small library of blades hanging decoratively at the end of the room. Levo hummed and hawed, pausing for a minute to knock distractedly on the glass window next to him. "Oy!" he laughed, knocking again. "Oy! Mr. Wooling!"

Remaine peered out the window to see the same old man he had watched so many times from his room: bum in the air, nose in the dirt. All at once the man straightened up and returned Levo's wave with a grin. Covered in soil and sweat, he returned to his work.

"Mr. Lecky Wooling," smiled Levo. "Head Gardener. Now. Let's see, lad. Ah!"

Levo grabbed a weapon and returned to Remaine, thrusting a skinny little sword into his hand. The blade was simple and clean, and the handle, too, was minimal in design.

"This here's your knuckle guard, see?" Levo pointed to the small, smooth shield that covered his hand. "When I was younger, they made me feel nice and cozy, but now I've got fingers fat as a baby's thighs—this little shield makes me feel trapped."

Training with Levo, Remaine found, was about as easy as waltzing with a bear, only, the bear was the one who could waltz, while Remaine was repeatedly trampled underfoot. Every move felt foreign to Remaine, and even when he felt like he might instinctively know what to do, Levo was quick to slap his leg with the flat part of his own blade and bark, "No. Again." On more than one occasion, Remaine was at a total loss as to what Levo was asking of him. Remaine found that for all the passion Levo had, he sometimes lacked a clear way of explaining anything. "Do not slide and wiggle, laddie. Plant and thrust. If you intend to strike, you must kiss the strike—picture a pretty lass."

At lunch time, Jolly delivered a tray piled high with ham and cheese sandwiches and a crystal bottle filled with a deep red liquid.

"Rawthorne wine?" asked Remaine, remembering how zealous Belwin had been at the Tour of Valor about his precious drinks.

"Oh, heavens no!" exclaimed Jolly. "Rawthorne sweet juice, my boy." He tapped a finger to the side of his nose. "A true diamond in the Rawthorne collection, I think." Smiling again, he filled up their goblets.

Jolly joined them for lunch. They munched their sandwiches in silence for a bit, then Remaine finally asked, "What are you both doing here?"

It felt good to finally ask some questions, as strained as the delivery might be. Levo and Jolly paused and looked at him, blinking curiously.

"Uh, I mean… how did you come to be here? To know the Rawthornes and… everything."

"My mother," began Jolly grandly, clearing his throat, "was nurse to the former viscount, Terveo Rawthorne, and his brother Dasko—then their governess after that, you see." He dabbed his mouth with a laced napkin then rose to his full height, as if preparing to recite a poem. "And so, of course, the Rawthornes have always been family to ours and ours to them. It is an honor to serve in their home." Jolly sat down and picked up his sandwich again.

"I was just a stray, lad," said Levo through a mouthful of food. He swallowed noisily and laughed. "And Diggy Rawthorne has a soft spot for strays."

"Diggory brought you in?"

"Met him at port when the royals began looking for privateers. I'm a good sailor, and I know my way around a blade, but Diggy—he's a rare type—deft as a dancer—picks up anything with a sharp edge and schools you with it within the hour. Lovely singing voice as well. Greatest friend I ever had. Treats me like a brother, even if his own brother isn't too fond of me." He chuckled once more then said, with head hanging low. "Had faith in me when others didn't."

"Does Belwin like anyone at first?" asked Remaine.

"No." Jolly and Levo replied simultaneously.

"Why?"

Jolly adjusted his glasses and cleared his throat again, pretending he hadn't heard Remaine's question. Levo shifted uncomfortably.

"Did something happen?" asked Remaine.

Levo eyed him, looked away, then eyed him again. "His wife and mother, uh—"

Jolly's face crinkled in sadness. He held a hand to heart at the mention of the late Rawthorne women.

"They died years back, and uh... Belwin hasn't been the same since."

"What happened?"

Coincidentally, at that moment, the door slipped open to reveal a new arrival: a fat gray cat, who massaged his neck on the edge of the door as he entered. He gave a little *mip* sound, then trotted towards them. Just behind the cat was Diggory Rawthorne, his blue jay as usual, perched on his left shoulder. In addition, he had a snow-white dove seated on his right shoulder.

"Like I said," Levo mumbled, tipping his head toward Diggory but rolling his eyes pointedly at Remaine. "He's a soft spot for strays." Levo whispered, "Don't mention that last bit—about the Rawthorne ladies—to Diggory, all right?"

Remaine furrowed his brow. Jolly headed out the door, pulling it softly closed behind him.

"So," said Diggory, hands in his pocket. "How are we coming along?"

Remaine's shoulders dropped. He would not be the one to divulge the pitiful truth.

"The lad's a natural!" Levo beamed, winking at Remaine.

Diggory strode toward them and noticed Remaine's rapier leaning against the wall. Using his own sword, he flicked the blade up into the air, catching the guard with his free hand, as graceful as the white dove.

Diggory smiled. "Good choice, Remaine."

"I didn't choose it," said Remaine, shrugging his shoulders.

"Indeed," said Diggory. "Still. I'm partial." He held up his own blade, a similarly-sized blade whose silver handle, Remaine noticed, was ornately carved in the shape of some sort of figurine. "Come. Let's see if you share your sister's proclivity for swordplay."

Remaine swallowed hard, aware in one painful moment, because that's all it took, he had gone both sweaty and pale. There was a presence about Diggory, (about all the Rawthornes, really) and that presence entered the room with him and hung over Remaine in an undeniable feeling of pressure. And now, at the mention of her name, Silome, too, was in the room. He could sense her spirit, standing next to him, dwarfing him yet again.

"I don't… uh… I don't really know what I'm doing," stammered Remaine.

"Well, then that's Levo's fault," smirked Diggory.

"Give him one of your wiggle slides, lad!" laughed Levo.

Embarrassed, Remaine held his sword out and faced Diggory with all the focus he could muster. Diggory ran his blade down Remaine's and crossed one foot over the other. He struck, then, like a pouncing lion, and Remaine stumbled backwards, just managing to steady himself.

"Easy, easy," said Diggory. "Again. Try again."

After squaring up, Diggory repeated the same move exactly as he had before and, to Remaine's great shame, it produced the same result. Remaine stumbled backwards once again.

"Take a breath, Remaine, and pay attention to *me*. Our bodies give our opponents warning as to our intent before our blades ever move."

They squared up. Diggory struck again, and this time, Remaine did notice, as if by some miracle, Diggory's right shoulder and knee bend and lean just a microsecond before his blade moved in. It was enough for Remaine to get his blade in a generally helpful region. There was a metallic *SHING* as Remaine's sword awkwardly met Diggory's. Remaine fell back once more, but (and he couldn't help but give a small smile), he had exhibited a bit more purpose in his own movements.

"Eyy," Levo egged from the side, his smile as broad as his shoulders. "I like it, Wiggles! There's the Plink grit!"

"How did Silome find this place?" asked Remaine hoarsely, holding his sword up again. It was strange how the tiniest success drew him back for more.

Diggory circled him, then pointed his sword down at Remaine's feet in an invitation for him to do the same. "Cross left. Good. Her story is her own to tell, Remaine. And cross right."

"But it's my story too," said Remaine, and much to his own surprise, and to Diggory's as well, as he said it, he lunged forward just as Levo had taught him.

Diggory parried the move with an elegant flick of the wrist, but his muddy eyes widened, and a smile broadened beneath them.

"Indeed!"

Diggory advanced with casual speed, allowing Remaine to parry. Normally Remaine hated pity moves, but he was tired of stumbling, so he played along. There was another satisfying cross of metal. He dropped his blade to his side.

"But why all the secrets? Who *are* you? Why do you hate the prince so much?"

There they were, all his questions, bubbling up. Perhaps it was the return of his voice, or maybe it was the sword practice—some sort of outlet for all the frustration—but he felt his confidence growing.

"Everything we do must be a secret, Remaine," replied Diggory, dropping his blade as well. "Silome knows that too."

"But *she* gets to know, doesn't she? What's so special about her?" Then he remembered his night at Lichenbluff, and what the prince had said. "And what does the prince see in Silome anyway? In my family?"

Diggory gave him another smile and sighed. He looked up at the ceiling, then out the window where Mr. Lecky Wooling was still rummaging around in the flower bed, rear end in the air. Diggory squinted his eyes and grabbed the brow of his nose, clearly deep in thought.

"I cannot speak to the prince's interest in your family, Remaine. I have my thoughts, but I think I must exercise patience with those." He rubbed his head. "But your sister—she is not *more* special, Remaine. She has no advantage over you or anyone else in that way. Silome was… she was just much older than you when your father's accident happened. And that event shattered her world… and opened her up to a new one."

The mention of his father made his skin tingle, and a knot tightened in his gut like neglected rigging.

"Remaine," said Diggory, noticing the concern, "so much of this story is not mine to tell. But…" he looked over at Levo, who nodded. "Silome understood, more than you, I think, that something very dark had *happened* to your father. Did your family ever discuss the destination of your father's voyage?"

Remaine shrugged. "Destination? It was a fishing voyage. Somewhere east of Moorington."

"Why would he need to go that far east to fish, Remaine?"

Remaine blinked at him, and the familiar feeling of smallness returned.

"Why fate befell him this way—we are not permitted to know such things—your father was one of the sailors chosen to witness the Lock of Pylon Crag." Diggory spoke slowly, respectfully, paying attention to Remaine's reactions as he did. "Most consider that ceremony a once-in-a-lifetime opportunity. Perhaps once-in-a-bloodline. Silome remembers it being a time of great celebration when your father won a spot aboard."

Remaine knew what Diggory was talking about. He knew about the great enchantment performed on Pylon Crag. That island marked the edge of Cracklemore, home of—he looked at Diggory as if to confirm—"The first crack in Cracklemore..." Remaine said out loud, searching Diggory's face. "Where the Berylbones break through?"

Diggory affirmed with a tired sort of nod. "We're not sure, Remaine, but yes. That is what our histories tell us. Until the Ravillions perform the Locking ceremony to make strong the borders for the next seven years, Pylon Crag is where the Berylbones break through."

Remaine watched Diggory's face twitch with some hidden, ambiguous musing as he said all of this, but frankly he did not care what Diggory was thinking about it all. His thoughts were with his father.

"And that's where he went?"

"Yes," said Diggory. "Your father was chosen. Like so many others. But unlike them, and for reasons we still do not know, it was your father who paid a heavy price. He returned a mess, shrieking of Berylbones and curses. When your mother took him to the healers, Silome tagged along—not that your mother knew she had tagged along."

This did not surprise Remaine.

"But it wasn't just your father who suffered." Diggory was weighted by the heaviness of his own words. "Like I said—we cannot understand the ways of fate. Belwin, too, was affected."

Remaine's head spun with this news. "Belwin went to Pylon Crag too?"

Diggory nodded.

"But you said *affected*. Was Belwin attacked by Berylbones, too?"

From what Remaine could tell, Belwin Rawthorne was a picture of health. Poised. Collected. To a fault. Dispassionate. Stable as a statue. There was no way he, too, had Frostblood.

"In her secret visits to your father," continued Diggory, "Silome bore witness to something. Something we had been keeping a secret."

"You didn't know she was there?"

Diggory shook his head. "You Plinks have a gift for stealth."

Remaine pictured Silome crouching, hiding under her father's bed in some healers' center.

"Belwin lay in a bed near your father, and Silome heard us say that we had found—" he hesitated again. "We had found a cure for Belwin."

Another feeling swelled in Remaine's gut, and it made his eyes start to sting. He blinked the moisture away and continued to listen intently.

"It was enough for Silome." Diggory stated. "She dedicated her life to finding us after that." He paused for a moment, then added, "We were on the next ship home before she had the chance to interrogate us, but when Belwin showed up on the docks of Windluff, for business, years later, and happened to run into Silome, she recognized him immediately. And it was then that she began to threaten him with extortion.

This did not surprise Remaine at all, but Levo laughed. Diggory chuckled too.

"She threatened to tell everyone about what she had seen if Belwin did not invite her to his home. Of course, he protested. She was quick, though. Fiercest thirteen-year-old he had ever met. By the end of the day, she had convinced Belwin to take her back to Ravillion Bay for a 'summertime opportunity' of some kind—she made it all into a slick story to trick your parents, and your parents believed her."

"League of Young Traders," mumbled Remaine.

"League of Young Traders?" Diggory asked, raising his eyebrow. "That's what she ended up calling it?"

Levo laughed. "She's got a silver tongue, that one, but she is about as imaginative as a cowpie."

"We've been seeing Silome annually ever since," Diggory said.

He put his hand on Remaine's shoulder. A few, unbound strands of loose hair hung in dark pieces around Diggory's face. Remaine could see the weathered lines on his forehead and the dark circles under his eyes. The muddy pools shone with a friendliness, a kindness, as if Remaine was another one of Diggory's animals.

"It's not because she's special, Remaine. It's because she sought it out. Stick around and we'll show you what we know. I promise."

The swordplay resumed after that, with talk of little else except the techniques involved. First, Levo and Diggory would show the moves, then Remaine would take one of their places to mimic the lesson. After a few sweat-drenched hours, Remaine was thankful to see Jolly return. He brought a message.

"Evening, masters," said Jolly, bowing. "I wanted to inform you all—Lord Terveo Rawthorne has returned from Lemon Lake and supper will be ready within the hour. I've drawn your bath, Mr. Plink," he paused. It was the first time Remaine had seen Jolly speak without some sort of smile on his face, "and, uh, we'll be in the library for the Beguiling."

Jolly closed the door quietly leaving Remaine, Levo, and Diggory alone again in the long hall. There was a beat of silence.

"The Beguiling?" Remaine asked.

Diggory slid his sword into his sheath and rubbed his eyes. Barrow the cat, who had been lounging in a strip of sunlight from one of the tall windows, sensed the shifting of events and scampered over to him, swishing his tail.

"Aye," said Levo, wiping the sweat off of his forehead. He downed the remaining sweet liquid left in his goblet. "You'll not hear it called anything else by us, laddie."

At the dinner table, Remaine pulled at his collar with a finger, suddenly desperate for air. He still had not gotten used to the stately, restricting dining attire of Ravillion Bay. He inhaled deeply and cracked his neck, trying to do so quietly as the others around the table clinked their silverware and sipped their wine in sophisticated silence.

Seated across from him, Levo caught Remaine's eye. With two, meaty fingers, he too discreetly undid a button of his formal dinner coat. He shot Remaine a wink. Then he shoved what appeared to be an entire dinner roll into his mouth in one bite.

"I thought the witch would be joining us, Belwin," said Lady Solace. She sat in her usual place, off Belwin's right hand at the far end of the table. Her beaded shawl glittered in the flickering candlelight as she raised a glass of dark red wine to pursed lips.

"Pua, is her name, my dear lady. I hardly think 'witch' a helpful term." The voice came from a new member of the family seated opposite Lady Solace. He was very old and his skinny neck shot out of his forest green, high-collared robes like a tree sapling in the grass. He looked very much like Belwin, but unlike the salt-and-pepper of Belwin's hair, Terveo Rawthorne's hair was entirely white.

"She'll be along for coffee," said Belwin. He took a modest and precise bite of food from the end of his fork.

"And how are we doing down there, Mr. Plink?" asked Terveo Rawthorne. His words were crisp and curt.

"Fine," was all Remaine managed to reply, leaning forward to acknowledge the man.

"Good," said Terveo. "My sons have informed me not all has been fine, though?"

Remaine swallowed. He hoped his cheeks weren't showing as much heat as they were feeling.

Terveo looked up from his plate to stare down the table directly at Remaine. "I trust we can trust you, now?"

Remaine nodded. He busied himself with his food as soon as Terveo Rawthorne looked away.

Belwin took a sip of his wine.

"More, my lord?"

"No. Thank you, Jolly. Not tonight."

Diggory raised his glass. "I'll take some more, Jolly, thank you."

Jolly bowed his rosy head and walked the length of the table. He bent formally as he poured another glass for Diggory.

"This one is good, Belwin. A Mountainside?"

"Mm Hmm," confirmed Belwin. "Three seasons past. Perfect age for an elevation variety."

Levo winked at Remaine, turning his mouth down in a dramatic, pompous frown, poking fun at the silly wine talk. Remaine smiled back and took a sip of his water.

"Were you able to rendezvous with Uncle Dasko, then, father?" asked Diggory.

"You know, Jolly, I'll take some as well," said Terveo. "Yes, Diggory, I did meet with Dasko."

"Any luck on his end?"

"A little, yes." Terveo sipped thoughtfully, staring at the wall. "At first, nothing. He's been staying with the Lavender Sisters, so naturally Quill and Gill show up on occasion—Broken Bottle was the most fun they've had in years—anyway, not two days before I arrived, Dasko did say he stumbled upon a most interesting lead. I think he's on to something. And he's very interested to hear from Pua."

"As are we all," said Belwin. "Shall we?"

An out of the way chair in the corner of the library beckoned to Remaine, and as no one else showed interest in it, he sat in silence and sipped a cup of bitter coffee from a delicate little cup. It seemed the Rawthornes were always drinking something, and it varied according to the time of day. Remaine had noticed it was a custom of the Rawthornes to have coffee every evening after dinner, presumably in one of their four sitting rooms, though mostly at these times Remaine had been escorted to bed. Tonight, however, he was invited to join, though Belwin hardly seemed enthusiastic about it.

On their way to the library, Remaine had seen Terveo pat his eldest son on the back and say, "The boy is harmless, Belwin. And it's best he knows sooner than later. The more he knows, the less likely he is to try anything again."

Another woman joined them in the library and the sight of her made Remaine's head spin with fright.

She was a large woman with an even larger voice. Although her skin lacked the greenish hue of the strange women from Monkeywood, her tattoo markings made Remaine think she was somehow connected, in some way, to the witches. The thought of Monkeywood made his breathing grow shallow. She was accompanied by what at first appeared to be a high, rainbow collar around her neck. Only when the rainbow shifted and squawked was it clear it was not a collar at all. It was a row of ten or so small, multicolored parrots, standing wing-to-wing along the woman's shoulder line, twitching their heads in observation.

"I apologize for my tardiness," said the woman.

"Evening, Pua," said Terveo, passing her a small cup of coffee.

It was a large room and there was a good distance between the woman the rest of the family members, and Remaine. Pua noticed him right away, though, and traversed the distance with a bold, heavy stride. "And here he is," she said, her eyes glittering in the firelight. "The prince's pet."

Remaine held her gaze, though he did not understand her tone. Was she mocking him?

"Any progress, Pua?" Terveo asked, strolling over to the fire with his cup and saucer in hand. He stood next to Belwin; the father and son duo made a formidable pair together. Their stoicism bathed in the fiery light which made them both look rather frightening.

"Perhaps," said Pua, turning away from Remaine to face the

Rawthornes. "I'm trying a new charm tonight while she sleeps. It occurred to me this morning—it might be the one. I'll send word soon if it works."

Jolly coughed, politely, and bowed. "My lords and ladies. It begins."

It had happened so gradually Remaine had not noticed at all, but now, as if by magic, the room was awash in an odd, purplish tint. A thick mist pressed itself against the tall glass doors which looked out onto the garden, and all at once it dawned on him: it had been one month, a full rotation of the moon, since the Great Charming had passed him by. His mind raced with all that had happened since he had left Windluff. Only one month? It felt more like a year.

Remaine shifted uneasily in his seat. What were they all doing here, now? All the Rawthornes gathered in the same room, so close to one another, as the Great Charming came. He thought of his mother's insistence upon privacy, yet here they were, casually close and indifferently social. Diggory flashed him a quick smile.

Jolly made his way over to the glass doors then turned and asked politely, "Ready?"

No one spoke as Jolly opened the doors. The room, which had gone eerily silent, was suddenly filled with the susurration of light, tinkling rain.

A warm, humid wind swirled into the room; its movement visible due to the purple mist which clung to it. Like steam from a kettle, the Great Charming filled the room, softly, silently, but entirely. It washed over everyone inside.

Remaine's gaze circled around the room as he tensely gripped the arms of his chairs. But his mother's words echoed in his mind and he looked away as each person inhaled the warmth of the Charming, shutting their eyes tightly in the process.

That's when he saw her. She plopped right down next to him on her knees. She startled him but did not seem to notice his surprise. Serae smoothed her dress and then pushed a chunk of loose hair out of her eyes with her left hand.

"Don't you wish you could experience it just one time," whispered Serae longingly. "Just to know what it feels like? I know I do."

You have no idea, thought Remaine. "When do you turn twelve?" he asked her.

"I'm thirteen," said Serae.

Her words echoed in his head. He stared at her, blinking, thinking, mouth open.

"You—you're not Charmed?"

Serae looked up at him, quizzically, but her look quickly softened with understanding. "No."

Remaine closed his mouth. He did not know how to respond to Serae. Her gaze went back to her family members, and Remaine's did too.

"But… how come… ?"

"Why doesn't it work on us?" asked Serae. She looked up at him, blinking her gigantic brown eyes. She smiled. Then, as simply and as easily as she might say 'I'm tired and I wish to go to bed' she told him: "Because we drank the special tea."

He coughed.

"Silome made it for you, right? Before the storm came?"

Still in shock, Remaine thought back to the Great Charming from a month ago. It had been a while since he had willfully tried to recall that horrible day. Everything about it made him sick to his stomach. But there it was, right there in the middle of his memory. There was Silome, offering him a sip of the tea she had brewed before the storm came. He looked down at Serae, his mouth slightly ajar, his face wrinkled in confusion.

"Silome's tea? *That's* why I'm not charmed?"

Serae nodded, then leaned forward to whisper behind her hand. "Beguiled."

"Beguiled?" repeated Remaine.

"It's *like* a charm," she whispered, hands resting in her lap. "That's what Grandfather says, and Pua, and Great Uncle Dasko…" She shrugged. "It's a bewitchment." She shrugged. "A… beguiling."

Then came the great exhale. Blue wisps of the Old Cold left the lips of the grown-ups, funneled into their vials.

"So, what's *that*, then?" Remaine asked. If the Great Charming was all bad, then how did they explain the cold?

"Well, it's…" Serae stammered, her eyes wide with fascination. The room held a ubiquitous sobriety, like at a funeral. They both eyed the blue liquid sparkling around the room in small glass bottles. Serae, having paused, started once more, "*that's*… the *real* Charming."

Suddenly, the open doorway that led out onto the veranda and to the garden beyond was darkened by a shadowy figure with a wide-brimmed hat who emerged out of the mist. He walked with a blocky, deliberate, bow-legged gait, made all the clunkier by the heavy object he held in his arms. Coming more steadily into focus, the man entered the room. He was carrying a wooden chest. Its frame had bands of silver flowers decorating its sides.

"Evening my lords and ladies," said the man, who Remaine recognized as the Head Gardener, Mr. Lecky Wooling. He smiled, but it was a somber sort of smile, as if beneath it lay news of tragedy. Mr. Wooling opened the chest. Remaine's breath caught in his throat.

A swirling blue light illuminated the gardener's face, highlighting the dirt and bits of yard debris stuck in his hair and on his collar. The glass behind him glittered with the reflection of the blue light, and even the high ceiling seemed to ripple and shift with the color.

Then Serae whispered so quietly he barely heard her. "That's why we hold on to what we can. Mr. Wooling looks after it. The rest goes into vials… then to the Palace of Pools like everyone else—you know, to blend in."

It felt as if the curtain had finally been pulled back—not with any sort of clarity—but with a sense of horrible shock. Whatever all this was, or whatever it was he believed this might be, it became clear to Remaine in that moment: the world was much bigger and much darker than he had ever imagined. He had never been allowed inside Windluff's Palace of Pools, but it was as normal as an afternoon nap to see people going in and out all the time. It was there that people poured out the Old Cold into the fountains, washing it away forever. Everyone did it. But here? Here the Rawthornes were hoarding it—stockpiling it.

He watched closely as each member of the Rawthorne family, followed by Levo, then Jolly, then Pua, approached Mr. Lecky Wooling, stepping into the blue light. They greeted him, exchanging somber smiles, then one by one they poured their small fraction of blue, misty breath into the chest. When they were done, the head gardener shut the chest, nodded curtly to them, then disappeared back into the garden.

CHAPTER 16

BAUBLERS AND CHARMERS

ALL TRACES OF WARM, MISTY WEATHER had dissipated by morning. In fact, when Remaine woke to the sight of snowfall outside his window, it was hard to believe the Great Charming had come at all.

Snow was rare in Windluff. Remaine held a collection of two or three memories where he had briefly enjoyed a short-lived blanket of the stuff. This morning he threw off his own blankets and ran to the window. He grinned. The snow on the ground was spotty and sparse, but the falling flakes were big and dramatic, each one vying for his attention as they drifted down.

Like a magic trick, the flakes melted as soon as they hit the gardens below. He did not know how long he had been standing there, shivering, watching, wishing the flakes would stay, when a knock came at the door. He whirled around.

The door opened and Jolly peered in. "Master Plink, good morning! I trust you've seen outside! Of course, you have. There you are at the window. First snow of the season!" Then he was in the room, rubbing his hands together, helping Remaine dress, gabbing the whole time.

"The first snow marks a holiday for us here in Ravillion Bay. You'll see. I suppose this will be your *first* First Snow!" he chuckled. "It's a pesky holiday—you can never plan on it because who knows when the first snow will fall—Master Belwin doesn't care much for it because of how difficult it is to plan for—" he lowered his voice to a whisper and added with a wink, "but I do relish it! You go to bed. No snow. You wake up. SURPRISE! First Snow! Unless of course the first snow falls during dinner—then you either scramble to celebrate that night, or you save it for the next morning." Another chuckle bubbled out of Jolly. "Of course, either way is joyous. Yes, turn here for me, would you? Good, good. A late dinner party or an early special breakfast! Arms up! Thank you. And back down. Good. Anyway, difficult to choose—the late dinner party or early breakfast!" He clapped and shook his head. He was positively glowing with excitement. "Time to feast and celebrate! But oh, not to worry, you won't be expected to give a gift."

"A gift?" Remaine mumbled, fiddling with his collar. He had gotten used to the buttons and he busied his own fingers around his neck, leaving Jolly to stand back and beam with pride at Remaine's progress.

"Oh, not to worry!" said Jolly. "Of *course*, you won't be expected to give one."

When he got to the dining hall for breakfast, Remaine found Serae even more excited than Jolly. She leapt up from her chair when he walked in.

"Have you seen?!" she burst out elatedly.

Her joy was contagious, and Remaine found himself laughing, though he was not sure why.

He took the seat nearest her and buttered his toast as she spoke.

"Wynnie said I didn't need to rehearse today. Good thing, too, my feet ache! Grandmother didn't like it much. She hates the snow."

She munched away at something crumbly which fell onto the front of her dress in light flakes and looked very much like the snow that was falling outside. She made a half-effort to brush it off. Then, probably because both Wynnie and Lady Solace were not present, she continued speaking with her mouth uncharacteristically full of food, "After this, do you want to play?"

It had been a few days since Remaine had played the Hollowfiend's Hunt. Serae had been so busy with rehearsing and he had been all but banished to his room. If this is what First Snow meant—a free morning to play the Hollowfiend's Hunt—he could see why Serae was so happy. He beamed at her. The two of them finished their breakfast in a hurry and made their way to the library.

They had hardly made it to the stairs when Wynnie stopped them.

"Serae!" she shouted, catching up. Wynnie frowned at the sight of Serae's crumb-ridden dress and dropped to one knee, brushing the crumbs away and smoothing the folds in the fine fabric. "Oh Serae," she fretted, her voice warbly with concern as if Serae had lit the dress on fire. "I'm begging you—*begging* you. This is Parvan velvet, you can't just—"

She sighed and stood, straightening her own apron. "Anyway, you're wanted in your father's study."

Remaine looked at Serae, unable to hide his disappointment. Serae's face drooped as well. "Now?"

"Yes," said Wynnie. "Both of you, actually."

"Both of us?" Remaine asked.

"What does father want with both of us?" asked Serae.

"Your grandfather, actually," Wynnie replied.

Remaine and Serae walked down several more hallways lined with long windows through which they could see the sparkle of snow still falling.

"Hopefully it won't take long," said Serae.

"Yeah."

When they opened the door, they found Terveo Rawthorne seated at Belwin's giant desk, peering closely at an open book as if he were studying an insect that might be crawling across the page. Remaine recalled that only a few days back he had seen a book float through the air a few feet above where Terveo's head was now.

"Ah, there's my granddaughter," said Terveo, straightening up.

The old man held himself stiffly, much like Belwin. He did not project the same icy aura as Serae's father, but there was no denying the relational resemblance.

"Hello, Grandfather," said Serae, giving him a slight curtsy. "You wished to see me?"

"I did, yes," responded the man, giving a gentlemanly nod. "Well, truthfully, it was your friend here I wished to see. But since you are indeed friends, or so I've heard, I thought he might feel more comfortable if you joined him for a while this morning."

Questioning expressions wrinkled both their faces. Terveo smiled wryly. "Oh, don't look so tortured, young lady," he said.

"Sorry," mumbled Serae. "It's just that it's First Snow, and Wynnie and Father gave me a free day, and we were just hoping to play, and—"

He cut her off with a simple flattening of his brow, then motioned for them to both sit opposite him at the desk.

Remaine and Serae sank into two large chairs. Their feet barely touched the ground. Then Terveo said, "Remaine, I am sure you have a long list of questions. We asked you to be patient while you've been here, and we've all agreed it best to refrain in answering them until we know more about what your future holds."

An uneasy feeling began to churn in Remaine's gut as Terveo spoke. As awful as the isolation had been, the perk of the last few days was that he had become practically invisible. Now he felt the spotlight returning.

"With each passing day, your disappearance crystallizes in the mind of the prince and his focus shifts away from you. Your family thinks you are dead—all except your sister. This is also good. Now, to keep things going this way, all we need is for *you* to trust *us*." He paused for a moment, staring Remaine down. "And I suspect you'd like some questions answered before you do that. Am I right?"

Remaine stared back. As much as he had wanted to play with Serae, the sudden offer of answers to his questions made him nod. He was glad, too, that Serae was at his side.

"Very good." Terveo leaned back and laced his fingers together. "Remaine, I'm sure you've probably noticed a few oddities here and there since your arrival, haven't you?" Terveo smirked, knowingly.

Remaine wasn't sure what the acceptable answer would be to Terveo's question. When he did not reply, Terveo paused. He straightened up. "How about we ring for tea?"

Having just come from breakfast, Remaine thought the request a bit excessive. Besides, weren't the Rawthornes strict about their refreshment schedule? Still, Terveo rang for tea. They filled the time with light and vague conversation about sleeping arrangements, food, and the like and within a few minutes, Jolly appeared with the tea tray, rosy-cheeked and delighted.

"Thank you, Jolly," said Terveo. But when Jolly made a move to serve the three of them, Terveo held up his hand to stop him. Jolly slowly backed away as Terveo removed, from the inside pocket of his green jacket, a silver spoon. He moved the spoon towards the sugar bowl, but not before the sugar in the bowl moved towards him.

There was something about seeing it happen directly in front of him, so openly, that made Remaine's skin prickle, and his mouth fall open.

A small pile of brown sugar crystals seemed to come alive. The crystals levitated from the bowl, climbing over one another in their efforts to form a rough, spherical shape. A few dropped to the table, but for the most part, the crystals stayed close together as they floated from the sugar bowl to hover over Terveo's cup of tea. Then they plopped into the cup with a small, brown splash.

Terveo looked at Remaine. Remaine looked at Serae. Serae looked back, eyes wide. Then, with a small, close-lipped hum, Terveo gave his spoon a flick in the direction of the cream pitcher. At this, the cream, too, poured *upward* from the pitcher, flowing in a perfectly curved arc over the tray and into the teacup like a rainbow. Terveo smirked with satisfaction and stirred his cup with the silver spoon. As he sipped, he raised his eyebrows at them.

Remaine stared at the objects on the tray for a moment longer. Then he spoke. "Y–yes," he said with a lingering rasp in his throat. "I've seen the… oddities."

"Though not too odd, I should think," said Terveo. He took another sip. "You've seen a charm or two before."

It was not a question, rather it was an invitation. He waited patiently for Remaine to respond.

"Yes," he said. "I saw Pinion Stretcher's charms at the Tour of Valor. And the prince—he stopped the high general from fighting somehow—and he threw a spear half a mile—and then the witches, on Monkeywood—"

"Yes," said Terveo. "But tell me, Remaine, *besides* the prince and his servants, have you seen anyone else perform things like that?"

Remaine scrunched his brow. Of course, he had seen a few oddities at the house, from Jolly and Belwin but somehow, he knew Terveo did not have those in mind. So, he shook his head, and said, "The prince told me the Ravillions are the last of the Enchanters, and he said Charmers were rare, and everyone else was too affected by the Old Cold to harness the Great Charming."

Terveo considered Remaine's words, taking another sip of tea. "Bit of a letdown, don't you think?"

Remaine blinked.

"The Great *Charming*," continued Terveo. "Breathe it in and you become *Enchanted!*" Another wry smile.

Remaine looked down at the desk, as if he might more clearly see the memories in his mind—memories of his family, other Windluffians, everyone in the whole world for all he knew—all speaking the same way about the Great Charming. It *was* the moment of enchantment. That's why Silome was so good at catching butterfin. He looked back up at Terveo.

"The Great Charming," continued Terveo. "Without question, the single most dazzling, and powerful charm any of us have ever witnessed, unfathomably vast, reaching all of Cracklemore within hours…" he slowed his words and eyed Remaine carefully, "and yet, despite its grandeur and cosmic scope… it *barely* manages to stave off the Old Cold for *most*."

Terveo let Remaine think on this for barely a second before continuing.

"Haven't you ever wondered what a life enchanted might look like, Remaine?"

Another beat. Remaine had never actually imagined a *real* life beyond his family. Adventures and stories—those were endless. But a real life enchanted? For all twelve years of his existence, Remaine's life enchanted just meant being able to keep up with Silome—being able to make his whole family proud—or at least make them not so embarrassed by him.

"Personally, I think 'enchanted' too strong a word," said Terveo, "for what *we* all get out of it, at least. It is either the greatest let-down, or, perhaps," Terveo opened his hands, as if posing a question, "it is indeed as grand as they say, but grand in other ways. Perhaps 'enchanted' isn't too *strong* a word—perhaps it's just the wrong word entirely."

There was a slyness to Terveo Rawthorne's delivery as if he delighted in baiting Remaine, in pulling him in. It was working.

"The Great *Beguiling*," he said. "That's what we've come to call it. And it is, to be sure, the single most dazzling and potent charm the world has ever known. But what if its strength lay elsewhere, Remaine? What if it was never intended to stave off an ancient illness?" His eyes were on fire as he looked intently at Remaine. "What if it were not a charm of protection at all, but a spell of deception." He leaned forward, and for the first time, offered both Serae and Remaine a smile that appeared to be of genuine affection, even relief or gratitude. "And you two are immune."

Remaine crossed his feet, glancing sideways at Serae. "My sister's tea?"

Terveo leaned back. "Your sister's tea."

Terveo signaled Jolly and the tray was removed. In its place, Jolly put down a glass pitcher of clear water. Terveo dug around inside the neck of his robes once more, producing a pendant that hung on a long chain around his neck. With a small click, the pendant opened. A warm, golden glow shone from within.

Terveo gave the pendant a small tap and an oblong stone fell out of it and into his hand. The stone was the source of the yellow light. When it fell, it threw dancing shadows around the room. Terveo dropped the stone into the water. They watched it fizzle and pop as it sank.

"We know maddeningly little about the Cat's Candle," said Terveo, sinking back into his chair.

They all stared at the bubbles in the pitcher.

The yellow haze from the stone deepened the lines on Terveo's face. His gaze remained fixed on the water as he added, "Besides discovering Barrow's love of scooting it across the floor with his paws—hence its name, Cat's Candle—we also discovered, almost by accident (you'll come to find out that nearly everything we've discovered to date has been by accident) the Cat's Candle is able to produce a tea that has healing properties of some kind."

Another puzzle. Terveo let Remaine think for a moment, then continued. "The royal family would have us believe all charms, as rare as they might be, are sourced in the Great Charming. But we have come to find the exact opposite to be the case."

"The… Cat's Candle?" Remaine asked.

Terveo's eyes sparkled.

Remaine pictured the garden chest of Mr. Lecky Wooling—how it had glowed bright blue when he had opened it and he recalled what Serae said last night. He risked the question. "And the Old Cold?"

"Indeed. But again, let us hone our language and get our terms straight," said Terveo firmly. He removed yet a third object from the depths of his robes—his own vial, aglow with its soft blue haze. "The Old Cold, you say. Have you ever actually felt it, Remaine?"

Remaine thought for a moment, then shrugged, shaking his head.

"Turns out," continued Terveo, "you're not alone there. Most have not. And the ones who have felt it think as critically about the sensation as those who haven't. Here, hold out your hand."

Though he was almost certain all would be well, Remaine trembled as he held out his hand. Terveo uncorked the vial, and let the blue, airy liquid spill into Remaine's palm. He felt nothing.

"Cold?" asked Terveo.

Remaine studied his cupped hand, then looked up at Terveo's face. He shook his head.

"Odd, isn't it?" asked Terveo. He helped Remaine transfer the blue vapor back into his vial and sat back down. "Now I don't mean to judge. It was not until my boys were grown men that I even *thought* about it—that I even thought to question it. And it wasn't without prompting and help from outside. It is, after all, the Great Beguiling."

Terveo's words weighed heavily upon Remaine's shoulders, sinking him deeper into his oversized chair.

"The Old Cold, you call it. But as you can see—there's nothing cold about it. It's my very breath. It's my very *life*, my boy."

His words swirled in Remaine's mind like the blue misty haze had in his hands just moments ago.

"People say," Remaine began slowly, choosing his words carefully. "People say they *feel it*. People say it's freezing when the cold leaves them."

"Ah," said Terveo. "A crucial piece of the lie. Following the arrival of the Great Charming, people feel the very real sensation of being chilled to the bone immediately. The chill takes them *as they exhale,* but perhaps we might hypothesize another reason for that sensation of cold as they breathe out. Who's to say the chill isn't brought on by the intake of something foreign entering the body just as something else inside the body slips out?" He gave his vial a shake. "What if the chill comes from the *inhaling* of a foreign bewitchment?"

"But... the storm *is* warm," said Remaine. Of this he was certain.

"Of course, it is," said Terveo. "It must be warm and inviting at first if it's to be readily received."

There was a moment of silence as Remaine processed Terveo's hypothesis. On the desk between them, the pitcher of golden water continued to fizz.

"So... what then?" asked Remaine. "We..." It was a struggle, to be sure, trying to articulate the ridiculous, trying to reorient his thoughts in this new direction. It was like trying to tie a knot with too short a rope. The words felt awkward and clunky, but he tried anyway. "We drank this tea. So we aren't chilled by the storm. We still have the blue *stuff* in us?"

"We think so, yes," said Terveo. "That *blue stuff*. The purest magic in the world. The first and *real* Great Charming."

A silence hung between them for a moment, then Remaine asked. "Why don't you all just drink the tea, then?"

Terveo let out a chuckle and pressed a hand to his forehead. "Oh, my boy. Believe me. We've made ourselves sick with the stuff." He closed his eyes and leaned his head back, releasing a heavy sigh. "Truthfully, we're not entirely sure what the Cat's Candle even is. And the most we've discovered is that it brews a tea that holds off the Beguiling for those who have yet to experience it."

"Who else?" Remaine asked.

"No one else," said Terveo. "Just you two. Serae was the first."

Serae gave a small smile, then said, "Well, sort of. Father, actually—"

"Well yes," Terveo conceded. "Your father was the first beneficiary of the tea, there's no doubt about that. But he was well past the age of twelve and had long before been Beguiled."

Remaine remembered what Diggory had said the day before about how Belwin and Philo Plink had both been affected on the same voyage. "That's how Belwin recovered from Frostblood? Why doesn't Silome just give some to my dad?" asked Remaine.

"I see someone has not honored the code of secrecy. You know of Belwin's past?"

Remaine blushed. "N–not really—I guess I picked up on a little—"

Terveo sighed again, then added. "Yes, the tea seemed to work something in Belwin, something that we've been completely unable to reproduce in others like him. We can only make guesses as to why it only worked once. To tell you the truth, my brother and I have nearly gone mad trying to figure it out. We think it's because with Belwin we caught it soon enough, though even that comes with broken logic. For now, the whole thing…" he sighed, smiled, then kept going, "the whole thing lies buried in caverns of mysteries, I'm afraid. For some reason that we cannot explain, the tea began a healing for Belwin. I can tell you that your sister has tried the tea many times, in secret, with your father, Remaine. I'm very sorry."

Remaine looked down at his feet.

Terveo added in a lighter tone, "But a little over a year ago, when our very own Serae dodged the Beguiling, Silome found new hope. You. She sent us word the day after you escaped the storm."

Remaine remembered how Silome had sent off a Singer in the Brineymore Round the day after the Great Charming missed him. His head spun with questions, not least of which was the most obvious: What was Frostblood, then, if it wasn't a clogging of the Old Cold in the body? And there were more questions, too. If everyone was Beguiled and *that* was the source of Frostblood, then why wasn't everyone sick? And why did the tea work only on Belwin? Another question popped into his mind, and he asked it out loud: "So you all can... *do* stuff? You just drink this tea, and you can charm stuff around?"

"Bauble," whispered Jolly from the corner. He had been standing still as a statue, practically invisible this whole time as Terveo was speaking, but as Remaine turned to look at him, he found the butler right there, bright red and smiling. Terveo looked amused.

"What?" asked Remaine.

"We *bauble*," said Jolly, fighting a chuckle. "Well—" he began, looking to Terveo as if to ask for permission.

Terveo nodded.

"Well, of course, they're hardly *charms*, you see, at least not in the proper sense. As Lord Rawthorne pointed out, of course, correct terminology is a noble endeavor—so we're not really Charmers. Charmers are of higher caliber in power and skill. Isn't that right, Master Rawthorne?"

"Yes, you are correct, Jolly. We are not Charmers."

"We're something else. We're what we call..." he hesitated, finally giving in to his giggle, then said, "Baublers. A term coined by some of ours for, uh... what *we* do."

Remaine looked back at Terveo who held his chin in his bony fingers, still amused. There was a trace of smugness in his gaze. Serae seemed pleased by the conversation. With another nod of permission from Terveo, it was her turn to speak.

"What he means is, proper charms require something special—a whole bunch of magic—which none of us really have. Right, Grandfather?"

Another nod from Terveo.

She continued. "So, we need help from... baubles." She smiled and shrugged.

At this, Terveo slid his silver spoon across the table. Remaine grabbed it and held it up to examine it. It was, in every way, a simple, silver spoon with an elegant, swirling design on the handle.

"With a little help from a few friends," resumed Terveo, "we discovered how to harness magic outside of us—how to bottle it up into objects—into baubles, we call them. Of course, even the best Charmers do the same—you've seen the royal advisor's lantern, I assume. But their capabilities far exceed ours.

"Vessels to hold the magic seem to be a rule in wielding magic if you are not of the Ravillion caliber—of the Enchanter class. The true histories are difficult to sort through, Remaine, but this is what we've gathered in our research." Terveo spoke slowly, seemingly more to himself than to Remaine. "Anyway," he said, nodding to his spoon. "The spoon was an accident. It was the instrument I was using at the time of the experiment. But the trick worked. We made a bauble. Two, in fact—a pair of spoons. My brother, Dasko, was with me. He has the other."

Confused entirely, Remaine looked over to Serae. She was fiddling with her necklace, and she held up the small jewel with a shy smile. Jolly, with his hands in his pocket, winked at Remaine as he removed something sparkly and small—a brooch, perhaps.

"Baublings may not be proper Charms," said Jolly, "but they are quite *charming!*" Jolly didn't even bother to try to stifle the giggle on this one. "Of course, that's what *I* like to say."

"Yes," said Terveo with a good-natured eye roll. "That is what Jolly likes to say."

Jolly joyfully continued. "I think it's delightful the sorts of things we can do! Things like closing the door." He clasped his hands together with enraptured happiness. "Or I can scoot a chair from one side of the room to the other, for example."

"Magic of… convenience," said Terveo.

"*Most* convenient! Sugar in the tea!" said Jolly proudly.

"Yes, thank you, Jolly," said Terveo. "Simple little *baublings*, as we like to call them, baublings of comfort and ease, but—" he paused for a half a second, "—but we're quite limited, you see." His tone became more serious. He stood, strode over to the window. Remaine noticed that the snow had stopped falling. In its place was a vast, gray sky.

"Our abilities barely reach the length of a room before they fizzle out," said Terveo. "There is still so much we don't know. And much of what we do know, we know imperfectly. We've stumbled and tripped and fallen into information. We seem to be scraping together bits and fragments of a lost world, a forgotten history. We're novice and naïve in every way. At least we Rawthornes are. Along the way, however, we've collected true allies who have helped us. You've met Pua. Her kind have the gift of Animal Charming—they are able to harness the source of power that exists within beasts. And Mr. Wooling, of course—he has gifts of his own. But the rest of us are quite bound."

"So, what sort of magic is in your... spoon?" asked Remaine. "Tea?"

Terveo chuckled, then looked right at him. "No," he said. "The tea was good for Belwin; the tea was good for you two. After that—not much more. No. Our baubles are imbued with this," he shook his vial, sloshing around the blue vapors.

"Turns out," he continued, "to let the real charm of life leave you is, unfortunately, a snap. But to get it back, to retake the life charm—the deepest part of yourself—to restore your very breath—*that* is much trickier."

"You can't just swallow it back down?" Remaine asked.

"I wish it were that simple," said Terveo. "But the effects of the Great Beguiling are more pervasive than that. The Ravillion enchantment is strong, and we are weak. To reclaim the real Great Charming, we must fight hard for it."

He held aloft his spoon and smiled.

The doors behind Remaine flew open. Jolly stepped aside as Levo sauntered in, buttoning up his cloak. Diggory and his accompanying pets, followed along with Belwin, whose outstretched arm served as the perch for a black and yellow canary.

On seeing the bird, Terveo straightened, and his face hardened like stone. "Yes?"

Belwin said nothing, but he flicked the bird from his wrist. It flew gracefully to the table, nibbled at something in its own neck, then delivered its message.

Remaine recognized the speaker. Her voice was rich and deep; something about its cadence entranced him.

"I've got it. Come today," the voice paused, then added "and bring the fish."

The bird waited for a nod of confirmation from Terveo. Terveo stood and opened the nearest window. The bird flew away.

The room fell quiet for a moment. Belwin spoke with a tone as frosty as the icy air flooding the room from the open window. "It's foolish to take the boy out right now."

Terveo scratched his chin. "Jolly, find Wynnie for us, would you?"

Levo walked over to the window. "There's a thick fog today. No one will notice Wiggles."

"I'm not worried about a person," clipped Belwin.

Remaine furrowed his brow. Apparently, he was the 'fish' Pua had mentioned.

"How certain are we that she's still in the Bay?" asked Terveo, squinting at the gray clouds. "Has she been spotted recently?"

"She was seen at the Point again yesterday," said Belwin tersely. "She's here."

"All will be well, Belwin," said Terveo with finality. He looked at Diggory, who had picked up his fat cat and was cradling him like a baby, scratching his upturned belly. "Best leave the animals here, Diggory."

Diggory set the creature down. His paws hit the floor with a soft plop. In tune with his master's will, Staunch hopped off Diggory's shoulder.

Jolly returned, accompanied by Wynnie Canny.

"Ah, yes, Wynnie. Please see that Remaine is properly concealed as soon as possible. We'll meet you outside."

Wynnie stood at the door and gave Terveo a quick bow. Suddenly Remaine found himself whisked away upstairs. Serae was also in tow. Wynnie took them both to a room unfamiliar to Remaine, down a hallway he had not yet explored. Remaine could tell it was Wynnie's room.

The room was neat and orderly, but it was not, by any stretch of the imagination, a plain or tame sort of room. Great swaths of bright fabric were hung on racks or folded in gradient piles according to hue. Needles poked out of the arms of upholstered chairs and the plump middles of scattered pincushions like little soldiers in neat rows; spools of yarn and thread and ribbon jutted out from the dowels of a massive wooden coat rack like ripe fruit hanging from a tree.

Wynnie tugged Remaine all the way to the back of the room. She pushed a chair out of the way to reveal a wall covered by a painted ivy mural. She pushed on the wall. It opened to reveal another small room. Remaine gasped at what he saw.

There were faces staring at him. Hundreds of faces.

CHAPTER 17

VULCUTTA'S SONG

THE FACES PEERED AT HIM. They had horrifying black holes where the eyes should be. Holes that hung in long ovals. The strange, fleshy material wobbled and swayed as Wynnie hurried by them. The masks were limp and lifeless, yet somehow Remaine felt they were all watching him. The room smelled of perfume and old wood and something else—something so strong that it made him wrinkle his nose.

"What is all this?" Remaine asked.

"Wynnie worked with the Ravillion Bay entertainers before she became my governess," said Serae, picking up the closest mask. She put it on, then spoke through the mouth's opening. "She's a lovely cellist!"

"Serae!" hissed Wynnie. "Put that back!"

Serae obeyed, but not before sticking her tongue out of the mouth hole.

Wynnie rummaged about for a few minutes. Eventually she found a mask with a skin color similar to Remaine's. This one had an odd protrusion of a nose and twice the number of freckles.

"Here," she said, ushering the two of them out of the dimly lit mask room and back into the bright light of the bedroom. She sat Remaine down in a chair and got to work at once, adhering the mask to Remaine's face. He felt something warm and sticky on his skin. It smelled awful at first, but after it cooled, the smell diminished. As the mask began to meld and mold to his face, Wynnie spoke to him.

"This will hold all day," she said, pressing her hands firmly across his eyelids. "Blink for me. Thank you. Raise your eyebrows. Thank you. Your body temperature will slowly help it attach to your skin. Too much, though, and it melts. Whatever you do, don't stand near any fireplaces."

With every blink, Remaine felt more at home in the new layer of skin. Wynnie dusted him with a strange powder then brought him over to a mirror hanging on the wall. Remaine almost jumped at the strange sight before him. Somewhere in the odd reflection, he recognized himself, but even that fragment of familiarity faded away as Wynnie secured a dark wig on the top of his head.

"There!" she said with pride.

Serae giggled. Remaine giggled too.

"Last thing," said Wynnie as she threw a dark cloak around him. "I want all of this back in pristine condition, you hear?"

"Head down," said Belwin Rawthorne. It was the second time Belwin had barked that order at Remaine since they had left the manor. The first time was as soon as Remaine walked out the front doors into the crisp morning air, which he could hardly feel through his mask and cloak. The second time was at this moment, as Belwin ushered him out of the carriage.

It had been a silent ride. Remaine sat next to Diggory. Across from him sat Belwin. Next to the viscount sat Lord Terveo who, quite distractingly, also wore a convincing mask that unwound his age by at least thirty years. Above them, in the driver's seat, sat Levo. The only sounds on the trip came from Levo as he sang a chanty and snapped the reins.

The curtains of the carriage remained shut as they journeyed into the city. A thick fog had fallen over the city. The chill froze all communication, and only when he stepped out of the carriage, falling alongside Levo, did Remaine brave a question.

"Who is *she*?" asked Remaine.

"Hmm?" They were in the city, making their way to an enormous glass-domed building the likes of which Remaine had never seen before. It came into focus through the fog as they walked, like an enormous island steadily seen from the bow of an approaching ship, darkly, ominously.

"She," said Remaine. "Belwin said *she* was spotted yesterday."

"Oh," said Levo. He glanced up at the Rawthornes a few steps ahead of them, perhaps for permission to answer the question. He lowered his voice and said, "The king's macaw. The beady-eyed gargoyle," snickered Levo. "Mother of all Singers."

They arrived at the door to the glass dome and entered. Remaine gasped at the tropical world inside. In stark contrast to the white world of Ravillion Bay outside, here color flashed like fireworks. The sounds of running water and bird's songs flooded his ears, bringing life to the thick muffle of chilled silence outside in Ravillion Bay.

Levo sped ahead to a large archway and posted himself up casually. He nodded to the Rawthornes as they passed.

"Be back shortly, Levo," said Terveo.

"I'll keep you covered," chuckled Levo, peeling an orange he had drawn from his pocket.

As they journeyed deeper into the aviary, Terveo slowed his pace to walk next to Remaine. As they passed a loud waterfall, he said, "We have come to believe there are traces of an ancient magic—relics of an ancient world—still present today, Remaine. The Cat's Candle, for one. The old figures—you saw Harbor's Hand when you came in—some of the old castles—Lichenbluff for one. And the Singer, most famously, carries within itself a relic—a magic—from an age long ago."

Right on cue, a flock of bright purple birds exploded from a nearby tree and soared up to a rocky perch high above them.

"They carry messages," mused Remaine. He had never questioned the Singer's ability.

"Yes," said Terveo. "Some are stronger with the gift than others."

Remaine thought of Chicken and smiled.

"They're also smarter than other birds. They are resilient, and they carry an obsession, an instinct to find the recipient of their songs at all costs. But they do not hatch this way. They require charms, and the steady hand of a Charmer, to bring to life this ancient magic."

"Pua?"

"Yes, Remaine. She's powerfully skilled in the ways of charming the Singer, befriending them, inviting them to pass their gifts down to their offspring. But there is one Singer far beyond her influence, far beyond her ability to befriend and charm. You are wearing a mask because we must hide you from—"

"—the king's macaw?" asked Remaine.

Terveo looked down at him. "Yes, one Singer we must be wary of—the Mother Singer. The king's feathered lieutenant herself is, we think, a *living* relic of another time. Again, it is difficult to know which histories we can trust—but she appears in all of them. She is fiercely loyal to none but King Ignis, although it seems she is running errands for the prince as well. She has been spotted patrolling Ravillion Bay since your arrival." He paused for a second and eyed Remaine critically. "I do not know who the prince thinks you are, Remaine—but you seem to be of the utmost importance to him. So please—"

"—keep your head down!" snapped Belwin.

Remaine felt the Rawthorne's were asking him to rearrange everything he knew—it was like asking someone to live their life upside down. Some changes were easier than others—but this piece about the prince... it just didn't fit. Somehow, he knew the Rawthornes were wrong about him. Still, the king's old macaw was frightening, to say the least, and that fear alone was enough to lower his head.

They climbed over a few bridges, under several vast canopies of lush greenery, alongside a cliff face, until they came to an old, dilapidated house, frosted in a thick layer of bird droppings.

At Belwin's knock, the door swung open. After seeing the outside of the house, the inside of Pua's house was exactly what one might expect. Remaine hated to think what his mother would say if she were here, but he did his best to keep a pleasant smile on his face when Pua offered him a seat amidst the clutter and a chipped cup of something warm to drink. Then, her large round buttocks in the air as she worked, Pua began to hum and busied herself in a few cupboards below the counter.

Besides the ruckus coming from Pua's shuffling in the cupboards, all was silent. The audience of perched onlookers, feathered and all-knowing, seemed to emanate their own critical thoughts in an almost audible sort of way.

No one said a word for a minute. Diggory began to whistle a little tune that the birds took great pleasure in. The Rawthornes sipped their tea politely. Remaine attempted to do the same, but the permeating smell of bird poop, tea aside, was enough to make him gag. He pictured his mother with such clarity. He knew the precise strategy she would be formulating if she were here; he knew exactly which corner of the house she would attack first.

Without taking her eyes off her task, Pua sung back over her shoulder. "Have you told the little fish about the prophecy, or no?"

Belwin fidgeted, but Terveo said lightly, "No, Pua, we have sought to slowly acclimate him to the beleaguered pot of truth, rather than put him in to boil all at once."

"I see," said Pua, straightening upright, apparently having found what she was searching for. She busied herself a bit longer before turning around rhythmically, as if she was the figure in an oversized music box.

"You've met my cousins, little fish."

He stared at her. He did not like thinking about the Monkeywood witches.

"Don't worry, little fish," she laughed. "I'm not like them. Old and corrupt are their ways, but more ancient are mine—you're safe here."

Her words fell out through a smirk that made Remaine's stomach twist a little. He took a breath, then sipped the unpleasant liquid she had given him. She turned to the others. "What fate awaits our little pet after this?"

Remaine shuddered. It was one thing to be called little fish, but now to be called their pet—and to hear them discuss his fate…

But the others were unphased. Belwin answered flatly: "Death."

Remaine choked on Pua's broth. "You're going to *kill* me?" he blurted out.

Diggory burst into laughter. "Not you, Remaine."

Pua ate up the confusion like a delicious meal. "You haven't told the boy about *her*, either?" She shook her head. "The Rawthornes and their secrets…"

Pua disappeared for only a moment then reappeared holding a veiled dome. They heard a clicking sound from underneath the fabric. Pua removed the sheet with a flick of her big wrist, revealing an enormous bird the color of dusky smoke.

"Vulcutta…" breathed Remaine. "I thought she—"

Diggory shook his head.

The bird blinked slowly and opened her beak even more slowly. A black tongue rolled out, then disappeared as the beak clicked shut again.

Terveo rose to his feet and took a deep breath, his lips a firm line. "So quiet," he whispered.

"Resilient to many of my charms," Pua said, "but eventually I found the right one to lull her…" she hummed a series of notes and the bird blinked slowly once more.

"And what song does *she* sing, Pua?" asked Terveo hoarsely.

Pua's face hardened. She did not respond. Instead, she looked at Remaine once more. "You've seen the Harbor's Hand, little fish?"

The abrupt change of direction in the conversation felt like a splash of cold water, yanking Remaine and the others away from the tense scene of the prince's most prized possession held prisoner.

"Y–yes…"

"And what did you see?"

The Rawthornes seemed puzzled by her query, but Remaine knew what she was asking. He looked deep into her eyes, desperate to know her intentions behind the question.

"You mean…" he muttered, "What do I imagine beneath the water?"

"Uh huh," she encouraged. "What do *you know* sits beneath the waters of the Bay at this very moment? Something precious few know for certain."

If Remaine were not so focused on Pua, he would have noticed the Rawthornes slowly putting their drinks down and leaning in.

But Remaine's eyes were elsewhere. His gaze had disappeared into his mind, back to his perch in the Butterfin Caves. The Great Mariner, etched into the wall, was as clear as day. And next to the mariner he saw a new figure being sketched into existence. He saw every stroke, every detail. A man more regal and less wild, an appearance refined like pure gold. The man stood with an outstretched hand waving upward to a loved one far away. That hand was the same hand that Remaine saw sticking out of the water in Ravillion Bay.

He blinked, and suddenly the room came into focus again—he saw Pua's fiery gaze on him, and the Rawthornes staring, and Pua's birds twitching their heads around to get a better view of him.

"I imagine the prince took you to Monkeywood, only *after* he found out about your ability to see things," Pua said smugly.

Remaine remembered that he had sketched Igniro for the prince, in his cabin. Pua was right.

"What is this, Pua?" asked Terveo. The old man's brow furrowed so intensely it made the strange texture of his mask crinkle in odd ways. "What ability? See things? What things?"

Pua ignored him. "And they had you drink something, little fish?"

Remaine remembered it all too well. He gulped and nodded.

She let out a great, heaving laugh. Then she paused, sighed, and laughed again. Remaine twisted in his seat. The Rawthornes appeared uncomfortable as well.

Pua said, "And you gave them nothing."

Remaine stared at her.

"They tried to take a bit of your breath, little fish," she laughed. "But it didn't work, because you drank your sister's tea."

Remaine remembered how his mouth had been pulled open on the island, how he had thought his jaw might break.

"They were after the Old Co—" he stopped and glanced over at Terveo. "My breath?"

Pua's eyes shone.

"They didn't know I hadn't received the Great Charming, though," said Remaine. "Why didn't they just ask me to breathe it out?"

"It's not the same," said Pua. "When it's extracted, by force, it lends itself to the thief who takes it. Coupled with their corrupt charms, your breath would… reveal… all of you to them. If you possessed a secret, an ancient destiny… they could discover it."

"What secret?" asked Remaine. "What destiny?" He looked around the room and felt a surge of heat in his face. "Who *am* I?"

His question fell at precisely the same moment that all three Rawthorne men asked, "Who is he?"

Terveo cleared his throat. "Pua, please, be clear now."

Pua held out a large hand to Remaine. "Tell them what you see."

Remaine shrank back beneath their gazes. He did not know exactly where to begin, but eventually he found the words to describe the Butterfin Caves, his perch, Igniro, and Harbor's Hand. As he spoke, Terveo barely blinked. Belwin, too, was sharply focused, weighing every word as if he were waiting to catch Remaine in a lie. Diggory appeared stunned as well, his gaze darting all over Remaine. Rubbing his jaw, he sat back, deep in thought.

"There is a prophecy, little fish," said Pua, "first sung centuries ago by the Mother Singer. Only she carries it in its entirety, that much we know for certain. Pieces of the prophecy were heard and sung by Singers afterwards but lost are most of the pieces. The prophecy exists in fragments heard and collected and forgotten by different audiences at different times, all centuries apart." She paused, placing her hand on the cage. "Vulcutta's song is short, but she carries the most I've ever heard of the prophecy. It speaks of one to come—one who sees—one who will be key in the permanency of the Ravillion rule."

Then the large woman began to hum a lilting melody.

Vulcutta's beak clicked open. She stopped blinking. Her wings fanned out.

The haunting air of Vulcutta's voice all but lifted every one of them from their seats, raising the hairs on the backs of their necks. It was equal parts masculine and feminine, at once deep and lovely, both melodic and rhythmic, and every word shot through the room with command, holding every creature in its grip.

Into mortal seas
the seat eternal shakes
and scepter breaks
Unless
the one whose breath is held
with visions of a time long felled
that he might see
from mortal seat immortal seas
and lend his sight, that it might seam the crack in throne,
the tear in scepter
grown anew to last forever...

The final words tumbled from the exhausted bird in a decrescendo of spurts and choking. Pua, expecting the bird's distress, held her hand up. She picked her own song back up, humming to Vulcutta, lulling her back into sleep.

But the other birds in the room were restless now, and so was the harpy eagle. Even though its eyes closed beneath Pua's song, Remaine couldn't help but feel the bird was yet more agitated than before.

Terveo was about to speak, in fact he took a step towards Remaine, but he was stopped by a loud BANG! and a sudden flash of light that exploded throughout the room. It came from the locket hanging around Terveo's neck.

Pua fell, hitting the floor with a heavy thud. Vulcutta's cage tumbled from the tabletop, crashing to the ground, rolling across the room. Remaine tumbled backwards, banging his head violently on a rickety chair and landing clumsily on his hands and knees. Groans came from all around the room.

Terveo gripped both Diggory and Belwin as they all struggled to get their feet back under them.

"Are you all right?" Diggory asked his father. Terveo clutched the Cat's Candle around his neck, nodding. But his face betrayed a look of fear.

"Explain this!" hissed Belwin, fighting to smooth his disheveled robes. "What happened?"

Pua, still lying on her side on the floor, breathed heavily and said between strained breaths, "I… I don't know… the harpy's song—the prophecy… and the stone… the light stone you carry…" She pointed her thick finger at Terveo. "Ancient Relics. Connected somehow. Related…" She trailed off, looking around the room.

The birds had erupted in panic. It was a miracle the Rawthornes could hear each other speak with all the noise. Pua's pets hopped from one perch to another, flapping their wings maniacally, pecking at each other's backs with crazed looks in their beady eyes.

"But why now..." Pua said breathlessly. "Unless..." She rose to her feet and much to his disliking, fixed her eyes on Remaine. "Unless the one of whom the prophecy speaks stands right here before us and the ancient things resound together. My cousins on Monkeywood were fools. The prophecy was right before them—the one who held his breath—but they never imagined it could mean exactly that—they only saw in him a curse. Yet here he sits before us."

Remaine gulped. "But... Serae holds her breath too!"

"That may be," said Pua, "but only you hold your breath with visions of a time long felled..."

There was a shriek from the corner and a metallic clang.

On its side, door ajar, Vulcutta's cage lay empty.

Pua gripped at her heart and gave a great, heaving gasp. "The eagle!"

The sound of shattering glass came from the kitchen. The tail of the monstrous Singer could be seen whooshing out the window.

Before Remaine could blink, Diggory leapt over upturned clutter as graceful as a deer. Then, out the door in pursuit of the bird, he too disappeared. Belwin ran right behind him, issuing a stream of curses as he went.

A look of horror plastered itself to Pua's face like one of Wynnie's masks. "The bird, Lord Rawthorne," she breathed heavily, "she knows too much. She must not go back to the prince."

The former viscount, suddenly betraying his advanced age in every way despite his own mask, steeled his gaze and beckoned for Remaine. "Come."

Along with the vast population of birds living within the aviary, the heated sanctuary also warmed a small army of citizens; scattered visitors milled about by waterfalls or sat on rocks, dictating messages to public Singers or receiving messages from far-off acquaintances. Every one of them proved to be an obstacle to chasing the prince's eagle.

The predicament was clear enough as the Rawthornes did their best to keep the bird in their sight without signaling, in an overly dramatic way, exactly what it was they were up to. The Singer alone was enough to garner attention. But now, besides her distinctive presence attracting attention, everywhere Vulcutta flew, she flapped awkwardly, flinging herself with great effort, sending out a rainbow of colorful birds in her wake.

Terveo and Remaine came to a bridge just as crowds of people were crossing from the opposite direction. Remaine was not sure how it happened, but somehow Terveo pulled ahead in the commotion. Remaine fell behind. The crowds passed. Remaine could not see Terveo. In a bit of a panic, he began to run. He followed a trail, rounding an enormous rock, and ran headlong into two royal guards. He tumbled backward.

From the ground, Remaine stared up at them.

"Hey, watch it," barked Torrin Pellatrim, dusting off his cloak as if Remaine had defiled it.

"Don't I know you?" asked Tarquin Pellatrim, eyeing Remaine closely.

Disgusted, Torrin and Tarquin studied Remaine's masked face.

Remaine shook his head, quickly got to his feet, and ran off. His heart was pounding in his chest. He did not dare to look back.

Vulcutta was tiring. The gangly bird flew lethargically from tree to tree, getting nearer to the entrance with each leap, slowly pulling away from her pursuers. Then, at the entrance to the Aviary, the bird mustered enough strength to soar out, gusting past a small crowd of startled onlookers who were oblivious to the chaos and the chase.

Remaine found the rest of his party. Terveo, Diggory, and Belwin Rawthorne were standing, breathing heavily, just outside the entrance of the aviary. Diggory sucked in a great gulp of air and coughed it right back out. He had one hand on his hip and the other was shading his eyes from the white glare of a winter's sun. The sun had broken through the fog and the bay was sparkling.

"I don't see her," he huffed, squinting towards Lichenbluff Castle.

Belwin cursed again, pacing beside his little brother.

"There!" shouted a voice, and Remaine turned to see Levo, fifty feet away, searching the sky in the opposite direction. He was pointing south, towards the mountains. "She's not going to Lichenbluff."

"Mirror Pass," wheezed Terveo.

"Of course," Diggory said quietly. "She's headed to the Pass." He looked desperately at Belwin. "Didn't you say the king's court was coming to oversee work in the Pass? They're probably here now—the prince is with them."

"Levo," said Belwin. "The carriage."

They sped away at suicidal speed, climbing through the southern hills of the city. Tucked between Terveo and Diggory, Remaine hugged his knees to his chest as the men pressed their faces to the windows, trying to keep their eyes on Vulcutta.

Then they were into the mountains. The carriage raced along the cliffside roads as the bird darted in and out of view, miraculously maintaining the lead despite its charm-bound fatigue.

At first the road was smooth and wide and they flew along steadily. But then the steep road began to curve and switch back. As the horses slowed on a nearly vertical climb, the bird vanished from view.

"No!" shouted Belwin.

Remaine's teeth were chattering. His seat in the carriage was facing backwards this time, but he too craned his head to see if he could help in finding the bird.

Diggory was the first to spot something. "There! Stop! LEVO STOP!"

The Rawthorne brothers leapt from the carriage and shot into the tree line before the carriage had fully stopped. Levo was on their heels. Terveo poked his head out of the open door, shielding his eyes from the blinding snow with a bony hand. When Remaine attempted to join the men, Terveo held him back with the other hand. "No, no, my boy. You stay hidden."

Remaine shrank back into the carriage and waited in silence.

The Hollian Hills were about the only thing on land that could make Remaine feel as small as the ocean made him feel. The pines, tall and sharp, had somehow managed to cling to the sheer cliff faces with zealous roots. A murderously cold wind blew through the trees as if the mountains themselves were whistling through their teeth. He listened for a bird cry, but none came.

Levo returned to the carriage. He poked his orange lion's head inside, breathing like a birthing mother.

"They have her, m'lord," he heaved. "They've baubled a few branches around her—Belwin's keeping her beak shut—she's getting stronger."

Terveo's jaw flexed. "Thank you, Levo."

Terveo climbed out of the carriage. "We're too close to the work happening in the pass. The place will be peppered with the king's men, and it's only a matter of time before some of them come this way."

"M'lord?" said Levo.

"Get the boy home. Get the carriage out of these mountains."

Levo's face twisted with concern. "Please, Master Terveo, I'll help the brothers—"

"I'm not dead yet, Levo. Take the boy." Terveo buttoned up his cloak, then said almost to himself, "I think it's time the Rawthornes stand together."

Levo looked up at the mountainside and pointed out a faint trail in the snow. "They're just over that ridge."

Terveo ground his teeth for a moment. "Get the boy back inside, Levo. No exceptions."

"When should I return?"

"Wait for the cover of night. I want to be free of any Singer's gaze. We'll hike back down to the canyon's entrance. Meet us there."

Unfortunately for Terveo Rawthorne, he would not be free of any unwanted gaze. Up on the cliff, head tucked into her shoulders to keep out the cold, a prehistoric-looking bird was watching. Her belly was yellow like egg yolk, her talons gnarled like ancient roots, and her turquoise back, wiry with haggard feathers, was like an old moth-eaten blanket.

The king's macaw watched closely as an old man disappeared into the woods of Mirror Pass. A large, red-haired man, more bear-like than human, shut the door of a carriage pulled by black horses and turned back towards the city.

There was something odd about the whole thing, the macaw thought, blinking her black eyes. She thoughtfully picked at the remnants of a dead mouse still clutched in her terrible talons. She had been looking for a boy for weeks. Was it a coincidence? Not five minutes after she heard the haunting cry of a lost sister, she smelled a boy?

She choked back the last of the mouse, clicked her beak, and eyed the retreating carriage. The smell of the boy had faded along with the carriage. It was worth following.

CHAPTER 18

VISITORS AND INVITATIONS

SNOW WAS FALLING AGAIN when they pulled into the drive at Rawthorne Manor. An angry gray sky hung overhead and a frigid wind brought the carriage door open with a snap.

"Hood up, laddie!" barked Levo, ushering Remaine out of the carriage.

Remaine obeyed. The two of them hurried through a heavy curtain of swirling white flakes up to the rectangle of yellow light spilling out through the open double doors.

It was the first time Rawthorne manor felt invitingly warm. Compared to the winds outside, Remaine decided he wouldn't complain about the home's inner temperature ever again. Standing in the open doorway, Serae greeted them with a smile that quickly turned into a frown at the sight of merely two.

"Where's Father? And Uncle Diggory? And Grandfather?"

"Let's get inside, lass," said Levo, nudging both Serae and Remaine inside.

Before too long, they were seated in one of the many parlors in the manor, this one primarily mint green in color with great, fluffy white pillows on the couches and curtains with copper fringe framing the windows. The sky was growing darker by the minute, and through the tall windows the snow outside shone golden from the firelight within. Jolly had delivered piping hot cups of tea into their cold hands within minutes. Remaine shivered as he cradled the small cup. He had spent most of the day shivering. His head hurt from all the shaking.

"Mirror Pass?" asked Serae, brow furrowed. She knelt on the rug near the fire, her skirts fanned out around her in a large circle. It was the fanciest dress he had seen on her. Her dark hair was tied up in braids with a white bow, and the necklace around her neck shone like a drop of fire. Remaine thought her especially pretty.

"Aye, lass," said Levo. "I couldn't stay—your grandfather wouldn't let me—and it was urgent they catch the bird."

"Vulcutta," whispered Jolly, clasping his white gloves together. His fingers came to a point which pressed against closed lips.

Lady Solace, who had been sitting as regal as a lioness off to the side, scoffed, "Mirror Pass? All the gold in Chantyholm couldn't tempt me to pursue a wild goose chase into Mirror Pass. Not in this storm."

Wynnie had also joined them. She was picking at Remaine's mask, slowly peeling it away. "What's up there besides the rebuilding of the bridge, Mr. Chince?" she asked.

Levo shook his head. "Not sure. Diggory thinks there's more than just bridge repair happening in the Pass—something fishy. Something royal." He grunted. "Master Belwin disagrees—thinks Diggory and Master Terveo are finding demons under every rock."

"Indubitably," said Lady Solace, lips pursed.

"But *why* do they need the Singer?" asked Serae. "Is this about the prophecy?"

"Shh, lass," Levo shifted uncomfortably. "Aye. It is."

"I thought Father didn't care about that," said Serae. "He said great

Uncle Dasko and Grandfather get funny about that sort of thing, but it doesn't actually matter."

"Perhaps," said Levo. "Or… perhaps it matters more than anything else. Not one of us in this here room is the one to decide, though, that much I know."

Wynnie helped Remaine with the last tug of his wig, then she put an arm around Serae. "Don't fret, little miss, there's still a feast to be had." She lifted Serae's chin. "None of the Rawthorne lords would want us to skip First Snow."

Serae perked up a bit. "You said they'll return late tonight?"

Levo smiled and winked at Serae. It was enough to reassure her. "Wynnie's right. Let's proceed with dinner." She looked at Remaine and beamed. "And presents! I'll stay up late and wait for Father, though he'd hardly mind—he doesn't care much for First Snow anyway—but we can celebrate some more once they're back!"

As he had never celebrated First Snow before, this all sounded fine to Remaine. More than fine, really. Something about the sight of Serae disappointed by her father's absence, and the mention of the prophecy, all of it, in truth, made Remaine's stomach go all twisty with guilt. In one way or another, all of this was his fault. They were risking everything to hide him. Serae was celebrating First Snow without her father, uncle, and grandfather because they were too busy chasing down a bird, now lost because of him—a bird that was singing prophecies *about* him.

Remaine stood to his feet. "Can I… uh…" he stammered, not exactly sure what to say now that everyone was looking at him, "Can I… help with something?" The only place he could think of where he could possibly be of any help came to mind. He threw his idea into the air. "Can I help… make dinner… maybe? I'm not too bad in a kitchen."

Jolly's cheeks ripened like apples in the fall. "You wish to help prepare the First Snow Feast?"

Remaine could not tell if he had crossed an invisible boundary in household etiquette, so he added quickly, "I just thought I could pull my weight around here—just for one night?"

Serae was up on her feet too. "What fun! Can I help too! I've never helped cook!"

Lady Solace nearly fell off her chair. "Young *lady!*" she huffed. "Compose yourself and grasp a sense of propriety. You most certainly will *not* be helping in the kitchens."

"With all due respect, my lady," said Jolly with a bashful bow, "and with propriety in mind, it's my duty to take lady Serae's wishes into first account."

The flames in Lady Solace's eyes erupted at this, but her lips sealed shut like a gate of cold granite.

"I'll escort you both downstairs, of course, if that is what you'd like," said Jolly.

"Not in that dress!" fussed Wynnie, scurrying behind Serae.

Serae all but skipped out of the room. Wynnie was close behind her and had Remaine in tow. Levo chuckled. Lady Solace clutched her jewels.

Rosy was already hard at work preparing dinner when they burst through the doors. Jolly quickly explained the situation to her, and Remaine described a little about the sorts of things he had learned to cook back home. Mostly it had to do with preparing fish, which wasn't the same as tonight's lamb on a bed of potatoes—so, he offered to help with the soup. Making soup couldn't be all that different from making sauce. Serae tagged along happily and waited for Remaine to make the first move. Rosy leaned over them apprehensively, wooden spoon in hand—her ample form like tiers of cake about to topple, the tops of her wrists resting on her hips.

"M'lady," she huffed to Serae, "Tsk. Tsk. I'll say outright and upfront I don't know what this will be like and I don't approve. If it should be as sour as green raspberries—it won't be because I didn't try to stop it!"

"It's all right, Rosy," said Serae, patting her arm. "Remaine's a cook."

Rosy muttered something under her breath, then returned to the potatoes. Still pink with embarrassment that the young lady of the house was, by her own request, *working* in the kitchens, Jolly bowed as he backed out of the kitchen and returned upstairs. Serae grabbed two spoons from a nearby drawer and handed one to Remaine.

"What do we do first?" she gleefully beamed. Remaine's stomach gave a flutter of excitement—he was happy knowing he had not completely spoiled the night. He snatched the spoon, dunked it into the simmering liquid before them, blew on it a few times, then took a sip, smacking his lips.

"What do you think?" asked Serae, eyeing him as she did the same.

"It's pretty good," said Remaine. "But I have some ideas."

The onions came first—that addition was easy enough. Remaine got Serae started chopping. She wept as she did so, which split Remaine's sides with laughter—Serae had never chopped an onion before. Remaine fiddled with the garlic for a while, then tossed some into the pot. After that, they spent the better part of an hour dipping their fingers into different spices then tasting them to see which ones would work best for the soup. Rosy tried to ignore them, but curiosity got the best of her, and she often tipped her upturned nose in their direction to take some peeks.

By the time Jolly returned Remaine and Serae had sipped nearly a full bowl of soup each, and both agreed it tasted much better than before. Rosy's barely hidden smirk told Remaine she agreed with them.

"Now, you two, time for your transformation—of course, I'm sure Rosy will miss you down here—but you better get dressed before Lady Solace runs away into the night." He winked at them, dusted them off, and sent them upstairs.

After Remaine had dressed, he returned to the dining hall and found himself oddly happy about dinner. It was a welcome contrast compared to the stuffy prison it had often felt like since his arrival.

Somehow, despite the strange day he had experienced, he had enjoyed his evening thus far. Pua's house and Vulcutta had all faded from his mind when he arrived in the dining hall. His mood heightened all the more when he saw Serae hurrying towards him, hands behind her back. Unable to control her own excitement, she produced a beautifully wrapped box with a silver ribbon.

She beamed. "For you."

"Me?"

"We give gifts on First Snow," said Serae. "Usually just small things—sometimes just things lying around if we don't have time to go out and get something when the first flakes fall. Sometimes people plan ahead, though. I did on this one."

"Y–you—" Remaine stammered, "you *planned* a gift for me?"

She grinned. "I had Uncle Diggory help me."

Remaine's stomach gave a little flutter at this. His cheeks flushed.

"Go on," she urged.

"Now?"

"*Yes!*"

Remaine glanced around the room. Jolly was fussing with final details. Levo was chatting to Wynnie outside the room and Lady Solace was barking something from the top of the stairs. Remaine pulled the ribbon and tore off the paper. The box was a small, perfect cube and it fit squarely in his hands. He removed the lid, peeled back the layers of silk inside, and found, nestled at the bottom, a small figurine.

The shape of the figurine was unique but its purpose was instantly recognizable. At the sight of it, a grin spread across his face so wide it almost hurt. Serae brought both her hands to her own smiling mouth too.

"Do you like it?"

It was a personalized game piece for the Hollowfiend's Hunt. It was a little wooden figure carved in the shape of a fisherman from Windluff. The Luffy fisherman wore a traditional toga, tossed over one shoulder, and in his hand, he held an old-fashioned trident. He looked nothing like Remaine, not with his strong frame, long, pulled back hair, and intense brow, yet Remaine felt an instant connection to the piece. He held it delicately, then tightly.

"I'm all set to leave tomorrow night, you know," said Serae. "So, you owe me some games after dinner. *And* tomorrow. As many as we can get."

"Leave?" asked Remaine.

"Oh, not far," Serae smiled. "Just to Lichenbluff Castle. All the performers stay the whole week before the Brumaloss. We rehearse until our legs break." She sighed. "But it's all right. Wynnie will be with me. And it'll give you some time to practice."

She smirked.

Remaine looked down at his present again, slowly turning it over. "I don't—" he began. "Uh—thank you, Serae."

"He better watch out," said Serae, "that trident will do him no good against the Hollowfiend." She made a tick-tock sound by clicking her tongue.

Then, at that exact moment, as if the click of her tongue was loud enough to echo out in the main hall, there came a knock at the front doors.

"They made it back!" Serae announced. They both made for the door.

Levo stopped them. "Easy, lass," he said quietly. "That wasn't the plan. I'm to pick them up later tonight. Remaine, back over there, lad." Levo raised his giant arm and pointed to an alcove in the hall that offered a small place in which Remaine could conceal himself.

There was a quick exchange of looks around the hall. Levo kept his steps quiet as he approached a window, trying to see out before anyone opened the door, to no avail. Lady Solace retreated swiftly back upstairs. Then it was Jolly, Wynnie, Serae, and Levo, there at the front doors. They whispered together, then all departed except for Jolly, who opened the door with rehearsed formality.

"Ah," said Jolly, as happily as ever. "Good evening and happy First Snow to you, my good servants. How can I help you?"

Jolly held the double doors mostly closed, but after a few muffled words, one of the doors was pushed wide open and Remaine caught a glimpse of the visitor. His stomach jumped into his throat.

The Pellatrim brothers stood on the threshold, shoulder to shoulder. They were hunched beneath the snowfall, leaning forward, as if they might run Jolly over. At the sight of them, Remaine pressed his back tightly against the wall. Had they spotted him? Had they recognized him at the aviary? Then he remembered that split second, like a flash of lightning, the night he had snuck out to Lichenbluff Castle—had he caught Tarquin's eye after all?

"I'm afraid you're mistaken, gentlemen—" Remaine heard Jolly say. Then, "W–wait! You can't just barge in!"

Remaine spun around. It was difficult to stay concealed, but he was quick enough to slip back into the dining hall just before the brothers stepped fully into his line of sight. Once inside the dining hall, he risked another peek into the hall.

Both brothers were prowling the open space like well-groomed wolves. Torrin, big and dumb, looked especially canine in his movements. Behind him, Tarquin tripped over the rug which suddenly bunched itself into a small mound. He fell onto his face.

Jolly's eyes were extra wide behind his spectacles and his cheeks were extra red. His gloved hand, Remaine noticed, was fiddling with something in his coat pocket.

Remaine darted to the other end of the room where another set of doors awaited. He pushed them open, just as he heard the gruff barks of Tarquin arguing with Torrin as the elder helped the younger up. They bickered as they approached the dining hall, just as Remaine was leaving it.

Once in the next room, Remaine ran headlong into someone and nearly shouted out loud with surprise.

"Shh! Lad! Shh!" whispered Levo. "This way. Quick."

Levo ushered him hastily through two more candlelit rooms connected by different doors that spared him from going back through the main hall.

Jolly's voice was loud outside the room as they hurried through. "My boy, I'm sorry, but you have no right to—"

"Quiet, *servant!*" spat Tarquin. The sound of his voice made Remaine bite his tongue. He could hear Tarquin push Jolly against the door. "The royal guard has *every* right."

"Go through there," mouthed Levo, pointing to yet another set of doors. As Remaine scurried off, Levo turned the opposite way, in the direction of Jolly's voice. Remaine could hear Levo burst into the main hall.

"Evening, lad," Levo said lightly, "Good to see you again. What brings you here?"

Muffled voices.

Remaine snaked his way through the dark room. His nose recognized the distinct smell of books before his eyes adjusted.

The carpet kept his footsteps silent as he made his way through the lower level of the library. He crouched down next to a bookshelf and hugged his knees. His heart was pounding in his ears. His mouth was dry. The heavy silence hanging in the room made him feel as if he couldn't catch his breath.

He heard a door open, then a whisper.

"Remaine!" Serae hissed.

Her voice was coming from the balcony level where they played the Hollowfiend's Hunt.

"Down here!" he whispered back, relieved to have someone else in the dark room with him.

"Remaine!" she whispered, flying down the spiral staircase. "They're moving—room to room. The big one won't talk, but the little one thinks you're hiding here! Who are they?"

"Friends from home," muttered Remaine, dropping his forehead to his knees.

There was a loud bang at the door. Serae's face froze and her eyes focused. It took a few seconds for Remaine to realize what she had done. Giving the small pendant which hung on a chain around her neck a small twist, Serae had locked the library doors from a fair distance away.

"Quickly," she said, crossing to the glass doors to the gardens. She pulled the door open and pushed him out. "Run around the back. Meet me in the kitchens!"

Then Serae shut the door behind him and began lighting the candles in the room. He watched through the window as she grabbed a book, tucked it under her arm, took a deep breath, and then, with a casual air, she opened the door.

"Hiding in here, eh?" said Tarquin, pushing Serae aside.

"Why yes," said Serae. "I often do hide in here. Best place for quiet reading, which you rudely interrupted."

Tarquin scoffed as he began to search the library.

"Serae!" yelled Wynnie. Both Tarquin and Serae turned around to find the governess, on the library's balcony, beckoning for Serae. "Let the king's man do what he came to do. We have nothing to hide. Now come up here and clean up for dinner."

Serae, already in pristine, formal attire, obviously did not need to get ready at all. Wynnie tugged at her skirts, uncomfortably. Serae shot a glance at the glass door and made her eyes extra wide, signaling for Remaine to get moving. Then she walked away, heeding Wynnie's call. Tarquin turned around and continued his search.

Remaine was about to make a move for the kitchens when he heard, through the glass, Tarquin's booming voice again.

"I know you're here, Plink," he said, peering around a bookshelf. "I saw you that night at the castle."

Remaine felt his body begin to tremble violently. The snow was dumping, his fingers were numb, yet he could not bring himself to move.

"And then today," Tarquin continued. "Today, Torrin was convinced the ugly kid in the aviary looked like you. Maybe it was you. Maybe it wasn't." He darted around another corner, kicking over a bookshelf that came crashing down with a loud thump. "Either way, it was enough for me. I saw the Rawthorne Lord, too—saw him that night at the castle—and saw him again at the aviary. What are the chances of that, huh? So, we figured we'd come on over to his house." Then he laughed. "But unfortunately for you—we are not here to bring you back. That's right, Mommy Prince doesn't even know we're here. I didn't tell him I saw you that night—didn't send word to him about today, either."

Remaine's heart was pounding so hard he feared he might tip over.

"I don't know why he's so obsessed with finding you, or why Estin Merchant is so obsessed with protecting you, but I'm…" He paused, his eyes slowly moving over towards the window. "I'm obsessed with ending you, Plink, and ending the obsessions. The prince never needs to know."

Before they locked eyes, Remaine was running, as fast as his frozen feet could go, through the snow. He did not think about where he was headed. He blew past snow-covered hedges, scraping his arm on a thorny bush. He slipped several times on icy cobblestone paths. Then he found himself springing beneath a snow-frosted grove of trees.

In the middle of the Rawthorne gardens, a moving shape, jagged and shadowy, swooped down. The flash of color flew right at him, knocking him back onto his elbows. It wasn't until he was down on the ground that he fully comprehended which bird he was looking at.

The king's macaw, gold and turquoise, with eternal black pools for eyes, and talons like knives, flapped her massive wings as she clung to the branch nearest Remaine. Her gaze kept him frozen in place. Every flap of her wings felt as if she controlled the icy winds. He dared not breathe at the sight of her.

She wasted no time. The bird extended her wings as if to fly, then cracked open her ancient beak. The king's Singer released her message.

"Remaine," issued the voice of Prince Xietas, "I believe you are still alive. If this message finds you safe and well, please know I am searching for you. I am certain by now you have been fed more lies about me than I could possibly hope to dispel in a single message. I am also certain there is a part of you, deep down, that knows they're not true. I trust you know me better than your captors. You know there's more. When this message finds you, please, send my father's Singer back to me with confirmation you are well—that you will meet me. Time is not on our side, Remaine. Meet me at the fountain in Mosaic Square, the night following your reception of this message. I will move all the Isles of Cracklemore to meet you. I promise, I'll explain, but you must trust me, Remaine. Tell no one. And trust me."

CHAPTER 19

THE CRACK IN TIME

REMAINE WAS NUMB FROM HEAD TO TOE when Serae, Rosy, and Wynnie whisked him inside and plopped him down near the kitchen fire. Serae and Wynnie had to leave to feign a normal dinner upstairs, but Rosy sat next to him, rubbing his shoulders to get him warm. Wrapped in a blanket, he ate his dinner in the kitchen.

He had finished eating and had almost nodded off to sleep when everyone barged back into the kitchen. This surprised Rosy so much

she spilled her tea. Then, the sight of Lady Solace in the kitchens, perhaps for the first time ever, made Rosy drop her cup entirely.

"They're gone," said Levo, his red beard and hair particularly wild tonight. By the looks of him, he had just run his fingers through both, tugging a little too hard at the ends.

Remaine sat up. "They know."

"I should say so!" said Lady Solace, shouldering past Levo. She looked like a mad old goose ready to honk. "You *foolish* creature. Master Belwin was right in every way about you."

"Grandmother…"

"Hush, Serae. Wynnie, escort my granddaughter to bed this instant. Jolly—see to the boy's disappearance upstairs as well. Mr. Chince, waste not another minute in retrieving the Rawthornes."

Lady Solace's demands were quickly carried out. Remaine followed Jolly upstairs, trailing behind like a reprimanded puppy. His head was pounding and his stomach would not settle—not with the knowledge of him ruining First Snow—and not with the prince's message ringing in his ears.

The whole of tonight made Remaine feel stupid from top to bottom. He could hear Lady Solace's voice. *You foolish creature!* Remaine did feel foolish. He felt foolish for having been spotted in Lichenbluff by two brutes bent on killing him, but he also felt foolish for having thought, even for a moment, that something as simple as First Snow might be reason to celebrate, when the reality surrounding all of this was that he still sat kidnapped in a house with people who were only telling him bits and pieces of what he knew. The prince's voice sounded in his ears again.

I promise, I'll explain, but you must trust me, Remaine. Tell no one. And trust me.

What if the prince *and* the Rawthornes were both misunderstanding one another?

Jolly made a few feeble attempts to cheer Remaine up as he helped prepare his room for sleep, but Remaine did not take to any of them. Jolly, however, was persistent in his efforts and he continued to ramble on about how we all make mistakes, about how we just need to make the best of things afterwards, and about how there's always a way to make things better. His repetitive use of the word "make" inspired a new joke about "making" the bed, which he debuted as he turned down the covers. It maddened Remaine how lighthearted the man was, even after a night like tonight.

Suddenly, Remaine had an idea.

"Jolly," he said. The man stood up straight, relishing the interaction already.

"Master Plink?"

"Jolly, do you think you would be willing to help me make it better?"

Jolly's eyes widened with joy.

"I probably shouldn't leave my room tomorrow," said Remaine, "but what about tomorrow evening? When things are quiet, would you be willing to take me into town—I would like to maybe purchase a gift for the Rawthornes."

Jolly twiddled his gloved thumbs as he chewed on Remaine's request. His bug-like eyes darted around the room in calculation. "I don't know, Master Plink, there are other ways—"

"It won't take long, Jolly—just one quick stop."

Jolly adjusted his glasses thoughtfully.

When they were in the carriage the following night, regret began to settle in for Remaine. Hoodwinking Jolly sent painful stabs of guilt right through him. The poor butler had done nothing to deserve it and he would probably get a scolding from Belwin later. Remaine could see it clearly: Jolly, beet red beneath the flame of Belwin's gaze, nodding anxiously, nervously smoothing his hair, wringing his gloved fingers together.

Still, the further into town the carriage ventured, the happier Jolly became at the bustling commerce.

They passed a shop window where bright leather shoes bedecked with heavy silver buckles glimmered. It was the sort of thing Jolly would be jolly for, so Remaine told himself that one day he'd return and buy Jolly a pair of shoes, no matter how much gold they cost.

Remaine also tried to convince himself that his rendezvous with the prince would be so quick that Jolly might even enjoy himself in a shop or two while Remaine disappeared for a few minutes. Jolly did not suspect a thing when Remaine asked him how to find Mosaic Square from where they were going. Jolly was more than happy to explain.

"Ah," he said, cleaning his lenses, beaming. "Mosaic Square—gorgeous, gorgeous, *gorgeous*. It's just up *that* way," he said, pointing out the window to his left. "Right near the fountain. Of course, it's busy this time of night—all the hot drinks are served there—the late Willow Rawthorne did love a hot drink on the Mosaic. Even Master Belwin, too, would smile when they had the chance to enjoy a night together near the fountain."

"What time did the Rawthornes return last night?" Remaine asked. He had sat pathetically in his room all day, drifting in and out of naps, and he had not thought much about them all till now.

"I'm afraid they have not returned," said Jolly. A look of grave concern etched deeply into his face as he continued to look out the window.

"They're still out there?" Remaine asked, horrified at the frigid thought.

Jolly's face drooped with concern. "Mr. Chince looked for them all night."

Remaine gave a hard swallow as the carriage bounced along. A gentle snow fell outside, much calmer than the night before, and a bundled populous hurried about in the glow of the warmly lit streets.

"Did he find anything? Say anything?" asked Remaine.

"No information, no," said Jolly. "But he did tell me, just before I came upstairs to get you—he suspects the Rawthorne masters found something in Mirror Pass—Master Diggory was right about the pass—something strange is happening up there. When I asked Levo what he thought, he said Diggory hadn't given him any details. Then I told him we'd be back shortly and that was that."

Remaine's heart stopped. "You told him *we* would be back shortly?"

Jolly looked puzzled. "Oh yes. But not to worry, Master Plink," said Jolly, tapping his nose. "Mr. Chince loves a good gift, and a good surprise, as much as anyone. He wished us well."

Remaine felt nauseous as they came to stop. They climbed out of the carriage and began their trek into the markets.

As it turned out, sneaking away from Jolly was even easier than hitching a ride with him. It did not surprise Remaine in the slightest that the man knew everyone in the square and by their first names, too. With each person he would turn red, shuffle his feet, and laugh humbly as they exchanged pleasantries. Jolly remembered the names of every niece, nephew, and pet. At one point Jolly collected a large basket of baked goods from a man named "Thatcher," whom Jolly called "Oats." It was just as Oats was showing Jolly a wart on his elbow, evidently discussed in a previous conversation between the two of them—that Remaine was able to take advantage of the distraction and slip away into the crowd behind them.

Darkness thickened. Remaine hurried along the row of shops as quickly as he could without drawing attention to himself. Hood drawn, he peered ahead and saw a large, ornate fountain, currently not in use. What he assumed to be Mosaic Square glittered just north of the fountain—an expansive courtyard of glittering tiles, mostly shades of silver and white, taking the shape of a fierce lion in the snow, baring its teeth—the Hollowfiend.

Elegant, fur-bundled shoppers surrounded Remaine. Most of them clutched mugs of something warm while some sat at little tables playing the Hollowfiend's Hunt. Each game bore unique little figurines and different colored tiles. Remaine cautiously slowed to a walk, tempted to watch the game, yet forcing himself to keep looking for the prince.

"He lives." A sly voice slithered out from behind him. Remaine did not need to turn around to know that Lyme Stretcher was waiting for him. But turn he did and there, cloaked in a deep red robe lined with black fur, was the prince's grand pinion. Remaine swallowed and gave a guilty smile.

"Come with me, Plink."

Stretcher led him away from the Mosaic Square and within seconds they were walking down an alleyway; dirty snow piled up against the brick walls and the occasional rat dodged them. They emerged onto another busy road where a carriage awaited them. Stretcher motioned Remaine inside.

"Oh—" said Remaine, with a bit of panic. "I can't leave, I—"

"Get. In."

Remaine felt the heat in Stretcher's stare.

By the time they were moving, Remaine knew for certain he would be sick with regret. Somewhere in the market Jolly was probably already frantically searching for him. What had he done? Remaine hardly recognized himself—was he some kind of wild orphan, suddenly allergic to rules, abandoning those trying to help him…

Lyme Stretcher side-eyed him menacingly as they sped through the streets of Ravillion Bay and out of the city. He asked him nothing, though Remaine felt he was somehow mining all the information he needed with his sharp eyes.

"Where are we going?" Remaine finally asked, as the pointed rooflines gave way to the pointed treetops. They were climbing, now, and the road had suddenly gotten much bumpier.

"To a place feared by all who live here." Stretcher replied with relish.

The carriage came to a stop. Stretcher uncoiled his long fingers and motioned towards the door, saying with his oily voice, "You'll find him at the entrance."

Remaine climbed out of the carriage. The frigid air whistled around him.

The sun was setting. He stood in the shadow of a mountain whose peak was lost in huge purple clouds with orange bellies. Pine trees towered around him like sentinels of the mountain and only the faintest trail lay before him leading through their midst. The wind gave a long howl and Remaine shivered. He felt strongly, despite the carriage's departure, like he was being watched.

Not far from Remaine the same, chilly wind disturbed snow-laden branches, sending a gentle dusting of flakes down onto Belwin's nose. He brushed them aside, unphased. His brother and father were beside him. The three of them crouched behind a boulder, and peered out at the scene below.

"Two companies on the east side," murmured Diggory, counting quickly and silently.

"And one on the north," added Terveo.

"And another at the entrance…" Belwin's voice trailed off. He was annoyed. Annoyed, primarily, because his brother and father had been right; something else *was* happening in Mirror Pass. The reconstruction of the bridge did not require the simultaneous construction of a fortress and certainly not one as massive as the one that stood before them now—an impressive hybrid of raw, mountain rock smashed together with the calculated construction of the shiny orange and blue reefstone and timber around it. And then there was the small battalion of guards. Cloaked with heavy whites and grays, they nearly disappeared into the frosty blanket of snow.

Besides all of this, Belwin was further annoyed at their circumstances. Yesterday they had managed to bauble the blasted eagle out of that tree. Belwin was the one to end her life—they had no other choice. They had gotten as much of the prophecy from her that she carried. They knew she would have found the prince before too long. It had to be done. Diggory buried her near the pile of huge boulders where they had found shelter for the night. The Cat's Candle had supplied enough light to help them find supplies for a fire and two snow rabbits for dinner. From there they hunkered down and weathered the storm.

Unfortunately, their efforts to return down the mountain had been blocked by the king's men—small hordes of them either heading up or down from Mirror Pass. At one point they watched the prince himself depart from the fortress and head back into the city. He had been in a hurry.

Belwin looked over his shoulder, back near the line of trees where they had spent the night, then his gaze returned to the fortress. For months, suspicious of all the activity in the mountains, Diggory had been talking about Mirror Pass. But Belwin and Diggory had both inspected the bridge's repairs, and Belwin had concluded there was no reason to question a multi-year project and probe it further. Yet here they were. Forced to hike in through a different route they had discovered much more than bridge repair.

Ultimately, his annoyance outweighed his concern. "I admit defeat," declared Belwin, straightening up. He had to duck his head from the low hanging branch that had concealed them from above. He pointed to the fortified structure. "Fixing the bridge is an obvious cover up for building that. But we're still short any helpful answer, so before we're discovered, I suggest we move on."

It was clear Diggory wasn't interested in moving. He sat mumbling to himself, perched like a panther on the side of the rock. Terveo turned slowly towards his eldest, then to Diggory, then back to his position behind the rock.

"You're both mad." Belwin pronounced in disbelief.

Silence.

"Father. You cannot wish death so zealously upon yourself. Upon us!" Belwin's chest ached for Serae and the possibility of orphaning her. For some reason this made him ache for Willow, too, and his blood pumped hotly.

Diggory turned to him. "Belwin. You see the same as us—there's something going on in there. We'd be mad not to investigate more thoroughly."

Belwin felt something almost like relief at the look of concern on their father's face. Terveo, frail and hunched, eyed the fortress carefully. "More armor than I'd have liked to have seen, Diggory."

"Thank you," said Belwin, turning to face the path through the trees which had led them here. They had been watching the guards long enough to learn their rotational patterns. With the right timing and a bit of luck they had a decent chance of sneaking back down unnoticed.

"What do you propose, son?"

"We leave," Belwin responded without hesitation. But his father had not addressed his eldest.

"The rotation is straight forward," Diggory said. "Look, that company is right on schedule. I say back door."

Belwin could not believe his ears. "Suicide," he breathed.

"If we watch each other's backs, it doesn't have to be." Diggory's voice was unruffled, strategic, and Belwin hated him all the more for it.

With every step down the hill, darting from tree to tree, Belwin was kicking himself for agreeing to come along on this little outing. Still, beneath the wildfire in his chest that raged against the idiocy of his father and brother, there was a steadfast loyalty that kept him on their heels, risking his life. He told himself he would kill them both if this turned out to be a waste of time.

The Rawthornes approached the east end of the fortress and stopped in the shadow of the trees, calculating their next move. The guards were on rotation, dotting the perimeter in small, mobile companies; a closer look revealed each obvious entrance was host to at least six, permanently stationed men. Belwin felt triumphant.

"There. Even if we slip past the first wave, we're not getting inside unnoticed."

"Shh," Diggory said, thinking once more. A light snow began to fall steadily and aside from the occasional shouts from the men and the intermittent howl of the mountain winds, all else was silent—until a whinny came from out of sight, behind them, deeper in the forest. It was followed by another, then several more.

The men spun around to face the dark interior of the woods. Belwin ground his teeth on another curse for Diggory. The sounds of horses were close. They would be exposed at any minute. Diggory, playing to his strengths, leapt silently from their position. He motioned for them to follow. Like a cat he scampered up a nearby tree, extending his hand for Belwin and Terveo to follow.

"Diggory!" hissed Belwin, motioning toward their father. Terveo, too, shared a wide-eyed fear at the prospect of getting up the tree.

"Diggory," Terveo breathed, "I… don't think I can…"

"Belwin," Diggory snapped. "You first. We'll pull him up together."

A few more snorts echoed through the woods. He had no choice. Belwin climbed quickly to a secure spot on a large branch, then bent over with Diggory, extending his hands to their father.

Like a helpless child, Terveo clung to them both. With one great strain, they pulled their father up onto a branch and into the cover of the evergreen. Barely a minute elapsed before a line of horses passed beneath them. The horses were led by a small crowd of workers bundled from head to toe in fur-lined cloaks. One horse turned into a few horses, which quickly became twenty horses, then thirty horses. The men corralled the horses together as they appeared from the trees and directed them out towards the east entrance.

"Look!" said Terveo, motioning back into the forest. Twice as many cows were being led from the canopy of the trees and into the massive back courtyard of the fortress.

"I think..." said Diggory, trailing off. He had perked up, alert, like an animal. "I think this is it."

"This is *what*?"

"This is it!" He pointed to the horses who were being herded into the fortress by the workers. "We'll go in with the cows."

Belwin was still formulating a rebuttal when Diggory jumped from the branch and landed on the snow below. Still speechless, Belwin followed. They helped their father down. With hoods up and faces covered as much as possible, the three Rawthornes fell in among the workers before any one of them had time to think through the purpose of all of these animals. The fortress opened its jaws and swallowed them up.

The insulation of the snow-covered trees muted the sound of Remaine's footsteps. He stepped silently along the path, continually looking back over his shoulder. The path rounded, then curved back once more, then opened into a wide, clear area of hard black stone. The stony clearing was backed by a cliff-face that rose high into the sky. Splitting the sheer rock wall before him was a single crack that widened near the bottom suggesting an entrance.

"Those who know of this place call it the Crack in Time." The voice came gently at Remaine's back. For a fraction of a moment, a sharp pang struck his gut. He could almost hear his sister's voice of warning in his head. But it was fleeting, and he turned to face Prince Xietas Ravillion, bedecked in silver furs, his face as severe as the cliff itself. The prince lowered his lantern and smiled at Remaine. "The terrors of the past supposedly dwell inside."

Remaine's numb toes curled in his boots. He sidestepped nervously.

He had too many thoughts to count, yet in that moment he could not articulate even a single one.

"I have questions for you, Remaine Plink," said Prince Xietas. "Like, how did you survive? And how did you come to Belwin Rawthorne?" He took a step forward. His eyes shone. "Some of it took me no time at all to work out. I've had my suspicions about Levo Chince, but then when my father's Singer found you with the Rawthornes, I knew Captain Rawthorne to be the source of all this. I admit the Rawthornes' betrayal came as a shock, and Diggory's betrayal rather stung."

The prince drew close and lifted Remaine's chin, lightly touching the scar on his throat. "This was clever." He moved in front of Remaine now, a few steps towards the split in the rock so Remaine could see only his back looming above him. "I have more questions… but I think in asking them I will only do us a disservice if your new friends have planted any seeds of doubt about me—I would hate to cause you embarrassment. I would hate to force you to lie and perhaps further the gap of distrust between us."

The prince turned back to Remaine and placed his right hand heavily upon Remaine's shoulder. Then he said kindly, "I will not force you to tell me anything. I hope you coming here is a sign we might be friends again?"

Remaine blinked, his own head dizzy with confusion. He managed to nod.

"Good," said the prince. "Because we are going to need each other in there." He looked up at the craggy opening in the cliff, entirely black and ominous.

"What's in there?" asked Remaine. His voice was small compared to the prince's.

"As I said. Terrors of the past, Remaine." He smirked. "But I think, with you, we'll best them." He paused, then added. "I do not jest."

The prince strode forward. Remaine shivered in his shadow, though he felt a twinge of pride at the prince's words. The Crack in

Time seemed to grow larger as the prince drew nearer to it, his broad shoulders and heroic height seemed to shrink in the shadowed depths.

"Come along, Remaine," he called back. "All will be well."

Remaine ran after him like a frightened puppy, all pride vanishing. The only thing worse than going in was being left alone out in the cold.

The prince's lantern barely lit the black walls of the cavern at all. Groping for something to hold onto, Remaine stumbled in the darkness.

Then he tripped and banged his chin on the icy cold stone floor. As he fell, he knocked the lantern from the prince's hand. It shattered. Everything went black. Cold air met warm blood. A hand picked him up by the collar and pulled him back to his feet.

"Stay close," said the prince, apparently unconcerned by the total darkness. Remaine grimaced at the pain and shuffled along after Xietas, thankful his pink cheeks were concealed by the shadows.

As they rounded a bend in the tunnel the darkness lifted. From an imperceptible height above, narrow shafts of pink light pierced the cavern's walls, like arrows of sunset in an onslaught against the mountain. Remaine gasped at the chamber, suddenly reminded of the Butterfin Caves. He stood in a similar place now, though the cathedral-like cavern of the Crack in Time could have housed a dozen Butterfin Caves.

"Congratulations, Remaine," said the prince. "You've made it farther than most."

"D–doesn't seem so bad," said Remaine.

"Yes. It's been fortuitously silent thus far."

As if on cue, there came a sound from the black belly of the cavern. The sound was low to the ground and Remaine felt it in his feet and chest as much as he heard it with his ears. It was a deep, guttural vibration.

"Ah," said the prince. "There we are."

The deliberate calm with which the prince spoke was as alarming as the horrible sound. Remaine felt paralyzed, every hair stood on edge. His stomach turned to water.

"Do as I say, Remaine. We'll be all right."

Prince Xietas took another step forward. Remaine noticed he did so stealthily.

The place reeked of animals much like the royal aviary, but unlike the aviary, there was nothing beautiful to allay the stench. Belwin stood among livestock and men in a vast chamber dimly lit by torches. It was a humid place; it was just warm enough for the snow to melt, but not quite warm enough to make the water less icy and miserable to the touch. The cows and horses trod anxiously in the puddles that dotted the stone floor. Gruff voices shouted back and forth at the far end. They had come to a standstill.

All three Rawthornes bent their ears to try to discern the exchange, but the sea of beasts that lay between them made it impossible to decipher anyone's words.

Somewhere a whip cracked and the herd lurched forward. An enormous set of doors at the far end of the room opened. Within minutes, the Rawthornes were carried deeper into the belly of the fortress. And if the foul smell of animal dung and mud had not been so severe as to cause all three Rawthornes to lift their cloaks over their noses, they would have noticed as they ventured down the dank corridor, the undeniable dank of decay and the metallic tinge of blood.

With each step the ceiling dropped lower and lower until at last they came to a standstill once more in a wide, suffocatingly low chamber that branched off into several avenues.

Three figures at the far end of the chamber stood on a raised platform, surveying the herd. The two on each end, holding cloths to their noses, were cloaked and hooded. The one in the center, however, stood tall, his pointy black beard an arrowhead directing the beasts to his feet. His ears glittered with jewelry and his head was bald; the shiny, tight skin accentuated his most striking feature: green skin.

"Dapples, Vellamares, Opaques, *east wing!*" shouted the green man.

A few wranglers confirmed the breed of the herd with the guard before heading down the hall with a dozen or so horses.

"Is that..." whispered Terveo.

"The king's court," Belwin nodded, grimacing. "Part of it."

There was no denying Courtier Doromund Venerack, Master of Beasts. The flanking courtiers were too concealed to make out their identities.

"Be generous this week, men!" shouted Courtier Venerack. "Get their bellies nice and full before they set sail!"

The three Rawthornes turned to look at one another.

To Remaine's silent horror, the sound did not stay put. As the prince progressed deeper into the vast chamber, the guttural noises moved. They shifted from the left to dead ahead, then worst of all, to somewhere directly behind.

At one point, Remaine thought he might have seen something flashing in the darkness. When he turned to look, he saw only shadows. Even the shadows felt alive.

They came to another wall, rather like the enormous cliff face at the entrance. This one, however, was solid; it rose up, free of any brutal crack. The prince came within a stone's throw of the face of the wall, then motioned for Remaine to stop.

"What do you see, Remaine?"

Remaine did not know how to respond. He was staring at a gigantic rock wall—a dead end.

"I—uh..."

Another guttural growl from behind yanked Remaine's attention away.

"Don't just *look*," pressed the prince. "*See*. Tell me what you *see*."

But the sound returned. This time it was as close to him as his own breath. Remaine couldn't help himself. He turned around to see orb-like eyes advancing from the shadows toward him.

"*Diggory!*" hissed Belwin.

"I *know!*"

They were inching closer to inspection, and with every step they were also coming closer to the three, shadowy figures of the king's court. It was only a matter of minutes before they were found out.

It was Terveo who spoke next. "Come. Back this way." He motioned towards one of the corridors that lay behind them now, a long hallway completely void of light.

They did not question him. As inconspicuously as possible, they took steps upstream from the flowing herd, moving back up the tunnel until they were able to slip into the dark hallway.

"Further in," Diggory whispered.

With hands on the damp wall, they fumbled silently along the smaller corridor, but it wasn't long before Terveo tripped and collapsed into a puddle of murky water. A muffled heaving sound escaped his lips, echoing back down the corridor. They froze. Belwin ground his teeth, breathing sharply through his nose. They waited for a full agonizing minute. There was no movement from the main corridor.

"Diggory," Terveo whispered, rising to his feet. "I will not fare well like this." He rummaged in his robes and produced the small, metallic locket he wore around his neck. He gave it a twist and produced the golden crystal. It radiated a soft, yellow glow.

Belwin could bite his tongue no longer.

"Where is this all going?" he whispered. "We're beacons down here. Father, put that away. We turn around now and go ba—"

Belwin was cut off by another sound. It was difficult to say if they heard it first or felt it first. It reverberated deep in their chests and in the soles of their feet and throughout the corridor around them. It was the deep, guttural roll from some monstrous throat.

The sound cut through Belwin like a molten knife, stabbing his gut with a sharp pain of panic. All heat drained from his body. Every hair stood on end. The three Rawthornes slowly turned toward each other.

"That sounded like..." Belwin breathed.

Realization dawned.

Diggory and Terveo looked at one another knowingly. Only Belwin was just discovering it.

"This is why we've come?" accused Belwin, straightening up. The chill from the beast beyond suddenly disappeared from his body and was replaced with a growing flame of fury. The flame that lived deep in Belwin's soul; the flame that never truly burned out.

"How *dare* you..."

Diggory met his gaze, his eyebrows gently lifted in a guilty, sheepish expression.

It was all too much. Belwin lunged at his little brother, grabbing him by the collar with clenched fists. His cool, controlled demeanor cracked. Over a decade of rage steamed, boiled, and began to hiss out. He threw Diggory up against the cold wall of stone.

"Is it not enough, little *brother!*" spat Belwin, inches from Diggory's face.

"Belwin!" whispered Terveo, clawing at his eldest's shoulder, the golden light around his neck flashing. Belwin shrugged his father off. He pressed harder against Diggory. Frustratingly, Diggory showed no sign of resistance. Like a wet rag he folded beneath Belwin's grip. At least he had the grace to sustain eye-contact with Belwin's fiery glower.

"I thought it would have been enough for you, Diggory, to bear the guilt of their deaths. To be the one *responsible* for all the agony we've endured—to be the one responsible for my daughter's motherless future—so, tell me, *tell me... is* that not enough for you?"

Diggory's eyes shone with tears in the glimmer of the Cat's Candle. "Belwin..." he pleaded.

"No." Belwin said through gritted teeth. "No. You..." Belwin lifted one finger from his clenched fist, pressed it firmly against Diggory's collarbone, then dragged it up onto Diggory's scrappy chin. "*You don't get to save them, Diggory!*"

Belwin was surprised to feel the warmth of tears in his eyes, but it did not matter. He pressed on. "*You're the one who killed them.* You won't bring them back. And I swore I'd never follow you into your obsession with that bloody monster again, and like a *fool* I find myself here with you."

Belwin released his little brother. He took a step back. His gaze shot manically around the corridor. He couldn't stop himself now. "It all makes sense," he panted. "Your fixation on Mirror Pass ever since you found out about the bridge repair. Have you always known *why* this was being built?"

"No," confessed Diggory, sincerely. "I suspected something, but—"

"But ever since you got back, you've been more convinced. More certain. Why?" Belwin had no physical grip on Diggory, but he was careful to keep his little brother locked in his gaze. It worked. Diggory spoke quietly, his back still pressed against the wall.

"You're right," said Diggory. "I was more convinced. I—" he struggled to find the words. "And I've been trying to explore this on my own since the night we returned. But I never found an opening. It's been my aim, all along, to learn more... but I never intended for you to be here with me."

Diggory looked exhausted, as if his confession took all his energy. He added, pathetically, "I haven't been able to stop thinking about it... ever since I knew the prince had the plans."

Belwin furrowed his brow.

"Real plans. Not vague, chairman plans. Detailed charts. I knew the prince had the plans for Mirror Pass in his cabin, so I resolved to get them."

"At Broken Bottle?" asked Belwin, quickly putting the pieces together in his mind.

"Yes." Diggory said. "I intended to bauble my way in at Kipswitch to look them over, but when the prince redirected us to Broken Bottle, and I realized Vulcutta would be in there too, it all sort of came together. I would steal the plans and Vulcutta all in one go."

"This was never about the prophecy for you, was it?" Belwin scoffed. "It's always been your obsession with—"

"—the prophecy tipped the scales. You were right, Belwin, my choices were wild, risky—but I knew if I succeeded, it would be worth it."

"All we know is the boy is instrumental for some Ravillion power play. But the Ravillions are already in power! And the plans for the Pass? Tell me, what did you discover on the plans, Diggory?" hissed Belwin.

"They're *holding* something in here. So many different holding cells—unspecified contents—but holding cells. I thought—"

"I know what you thought."

For the first time in a long time, perhaps since the night he had lost them, Belwin found himself shaking uncontrollably. With an unsteady hand, he fumbled to secure his high collar, only then becoming aware of the tears which ran freely down his cheeks. Then he sank to the ground, hanging his head between his bunched-up knees. The feeling was foreign to him—beneath him—and yet there he sat. His sadness was palpable.

"Oh, my son," Terveo said, dropping beside Belwin, covering him in an embrace. "How grief still bites."

They sat silently for a moment. Belwin lifted his gaze.

"And what do you intend to do, Diggory? Slay the thing?"

Diggory blinked at him.

A wheezy laugh burst from Belwin. Then another. Then another.

"Of course not. Not Diggory. Diggory, whose best friend is a house cat. You looked away when I took Vulcutta's life. You'd never dream of slaying the monster that devoured our own mother, and…" the next words caught in his throat, but Belwin resolved to spit them out with venom. "Then finished off my wife afterwards."

"We don't know that, Belwin," said Diggory quietly.

"Don't. Don't you dare defend it. You play that stupid game with my daughter, teaching her to love the stories—to find them entertaining—to be unafraid of the Hollowfiend because it's all just fun. Fine, Diggory. I'll let *you* be the one to tell her it was her own Uncle Diggory who led her mother right into its jaws. Tell me the truth. What answers did you hope to find? That Willow and Merhanna Rawthorne are *not* dead? Were you hoping to find them on those plans in the prince's cabin?"

Just then they heard another throaty growl but this one was accompanied by heart-rending, high whinnies of a few horses. Then came the terrible sound of mangled mauling, followed by a few cheers and enthusiastic claps. The three Rawthornes listened in stunned silence.

Another growl echoed through the dark chamber. This one came from deeper down their own corridor. An identical growl, followed by an identical shriek of more horses. This time the mooing moan of a cow was thrown in. As soon as they looked over their shoulders, as if they might actually see the horror in the pitch-blackness, a third sound erupted from the opposite direction, followed by several more identical echoes from yet another direction.

They slowly turned to face one another and even Diggory's brow was furrowed with concern. And confusion. Belwin asked the question they were all thinking.

"How many are there?"

Diggory blinked. "Just…" He rose to his feet, closing his eyes and craning his neck, focusing on the sounds coming at them from all directions. Then, as if willing it to be true, he whispered. "Just one."

"*How* many holding cells did the plans detail, Diggory?" said Belwin, rising to his feet.

"He would require space if they had captured him—to roam—I figured—"

Despite his concern, Belwin couldn't help but savor the folly of his brother. "You thought the *multiple* holding cells were for keeping *one* beast quiet. Content. Locked up. No. Whatever's down here... it's not alone. That's why the king has Doromund Venerack overseeing this place. This is as monstrous as we all know it to be. You thought you'd come here and find a sweet old pet, captive, innocent, shivering, all alone. And maybe..." as painful as every word was to articulate, Belwin continued, knowing each word would be a knife to his naïve little brother's ears, "... maybe you'd even find our mother and Willow. And I also imagine in this little fantasy of yours, all of them would be here, ten years older, eager to see you, waiting to be rescued, and maybe *then* you might ease your guilt."

His words worked. Belwin watched as Diggory's face melted into a blank mask; his tragic wounds buried deep beneath. Belwin felt as though he had grabbed his brother's very soul and strangled it. In spite of himself, a knot formed in his gut at the sight of the sudden damage. He swallowed.

"Three more this way!" came a voice at the entrance of their own tunnel.

Terveo was already concealing the Cat's Candle when torches appeared in the distance along with the silhouettes of several guards and the shadowy blobs of three cows in tow.

"Come on," Diggory said, returning suddenly to a cat-like stance. He slid along the wall and slinked deeper into the darkness. The other two followed closely behind him, hoping to lengthen the distance between themselves and the voices behind them.

Leading them, Diggory held his father's right arm while Belwin held on to his father's left. It did not take long before Terveo insisted, once more, on light. The brothers agreed. The Cat's Candle illuminated their path again. Finally, they saw a break in the tunnel and hurried to the opening. Diggory was first to peer inside.

"No guards," he said. "Let's go."

They stepped into a rough, circular cavern with moist black walls that glittered with the yellow light of the Cat's Candle. Their eyes watered and their nostrils burned with a putrid, acidic smell that hung in the air. The room was empty except for the several stalagmite mounds as tall as the Rawthorne men that broke up the expanse of the floor. Straight ahead of them, yet another black tunnel split off from the chamber, and directly above its opening was a lattice grille made of reefstone, much like the open gate of a portcullis. To their right was another latticed grille although this one was closed sealing off its tunnel. Terveo held the Cat's Candle aloft and saw that the tunnel from which they emerged also bore the same gated structure. That gate was fortunately open.

"Sealable chambers." Terveo noted. "Security measures."

The deep rumbling sound came again, but this time its proximity was unnervingly close. All three of them turned to face the sealed chamber on the right.

Curiosity is a strange thing. Belwin remembered thinking so as he found himself, along with his father and brother, stepping towards the latticed gate in an attempt to catch a glimpse of the very thing whose growl had frozen their blood.

Time slowed as Terveo raised the Cat's Candle. It was not a tunnel at all. It was a small holding cell. And there at the back, the beast lifted its head at the foreign light and bore its fangs.

Though he did not realize it, Remaine's hands had found the cloak of Prince Xietas and he clung to it with a steely grip. The two eyes glinted. They were low to the ground but rising. Just along the edge of the huge black pupils, a thin, bright green iris was visible, glowing unnaturally in the shadows.

"Don't move," the prince whispered. "Not one move, Remaine."

Truthfully, Remaine could not have moved if he had wanted to. He felt as though all his blood had left his body entirely, leaving him without any heat at all, frozen in place. At last, the beast crept into the small ray of light, letting out another growl that rippled through the stone and straight into Remaine's bones.

To Remaine's horror, the mane-less form of a she-lion came fully into view. She was unlike any lioness Remaine had ever seen. The straw-colored fur was patchy and matted and, in some places, non-existent, as if she had fought for her life only moments ago. At the bottom of her enormous, blocky head, a wet mouth hung open and, like the pupils of her eyes, it shone like a bottomless black hole. Her gums and tongue, even most of her teeth, were black like crude oil; her maw dripped with saliva as she approached. As she neared the grate, controlled tremors reverberated in her throat.

"Hollowfiend," the prince whispered, his hand outstretched in front of Remaine. He took a step backwards, gently pressing Remaine to follow suit. Hollowfiend. Remaine could hear a faint tick-tock sound in his head at the mention of the name.

The prince held up his sword. At the sight of it, the lion's slimy grin widened and her tail flicked. The blade was enough to give her pause. She lowered herself slightly to the ground, eyeing the prince, keeping her distance.

"Remaine," Prince Xietas said steadily. "I will not let anything happen to you." The prince had placed himself between the lion and Remaine. "But I need you to do something for me now."

Remaine tore his gaze from the lion to glance at the prince.

"I need you to tell me what you see behind me—on the wall."

Remaine looked back over his shoulder at the veined wall of cold black stone.

"Nothing," Remaine whispered. "I don't see anything."

"Turn around and face the wall." The prince commanded Remaine firmly but quietly. "I will not let her touch us."

Remaine remembered the prince launching a spear at the Pearlback. If there was one person he felt safe with, it was Xietas Ravillion. Remaine swallowed the strange lump in his throat. He turned completely around to face the wall. He saw nothing, still, but he faced the wall, nonetheless.

"Relax, Remaine. Breathe. Tell me what you *see*."

Remaine took a deep breath. He kept his gaze on the wall.

There was a slight shift, or a hint of a shift. And then, something. Remaine blinked. Perhaps, there was something in his eye. But the longer he stared, the more he was convinced. He could not deny the strange form taking shape in front of him, or at least in his mind. It was just like the Great Mariner back home.

Where the veined wall towered above him, Remaine saw, as clear as a winter's sunrise, a cloaked figure. The figure was on one knee. He looked off over his shoulder and his face was furrowed in worry or pain. With an outstretched arm he was leaning on the wall.

The story began to unfold in Remaine's mind. The man had been running—this was his final stop. He had kept his most prized possession locked away—right here. Remaine's mind took off. Suddenly he saw the man aboard a ship, then he saw him beneath a tree. It was difficult to tell which things were part of the stories he made up and which things were...

The lioness snapped her teeth behind him and Remaine blinked—the image disappeared as quickly as it had come. The wall was bare again.

"Remaine?" urged the prince. "What do you see?"

"I... uh..." he stammered. "A man was here—I think. He had his hand on the wall."

"Show me."

Remaine looked back to the wall and could see it plainly, the exact position of the man's hand. "There." Remaine pointed to a dark smudge on the stone.

The prince looked over his shoulder, studying the spot Remaine indicated. "Come," he said, backing up towards the wall. "Show me exactly what he was doing."

As they moved back, the lioness advanced. Her grin widened to reveal her sharp teeth. Facing the beast, the prince kept his sword up as he stepped backwards with precision.

"Here." Remaine touched the wall. There didn't seem to be anything special about the spot.

"And how was his hand positioned?"

Remaine screwed up his brow. "Like this."

"And where was he standing?"

"He was kneeling. Here, like this." Remaine knelt.

"You're certain?"

Remaine nodded. At this point Remaine was as interested in the prince's questions as much as the prince was interested in what Remaine had seen.

"Thank you, Remaine. Now one last thing—I want you to take this sword."

"What?"

"Steady yourself," the prince commanded as he prepared to pass the weapon to Remaine. "She will not touch you. Take this blade and take up my spot. It is important you do not drop the blade. Do you understand?"

Before Remaine could protest, the prince was transitioning the heavy longsword from his own grip to Remaine's. The emerald-studded hilt was massive, the blade heavy. It pulled his arms down like an anchor. Remaine clutched the grip with trembling, sweat-drenched hands. The lioness flicked her tail, eyeing the blade, pacing back and forth. She did not advance.

There were two of them actually. Belwin's eyes, wide with terror, darted back and forth between them as each of them rose up to their full height. The she-lions were bigger than any he had seen before. Their bodies were more muscular. They had less fur. Their black mouths hung open, dripping with strings of saliva. The sounds which emanated from their throats were so engulfing they felt almost visible. The three Rawthornes did not move. Overcome, they stood transfixed by the shining eyes.

The shock wore off at the sight of torchlight approaching. Voices echoed down the chamber they had just traveled through.

"Quick!" said Diggory. "This w–"

BANG! The two lionesses, in perfect unison, launched themselves at the cage in an explosion of deafening roars.

"Oy!" came a voice from down the tunnel. "We're coming, you devils!"

But the lions would not be placated. As if driven by an instinct stronger than survival, the two beasts erupted in a fit of snarling, flinging themselves at the steely grate, baring their jagged teeth, and forcing their enormous paws through the holes in the mesh. One paw snatched ahold of Terveo's boot. He shouted, kicking his foot in terror.

Belwin's pulse quickened; the torches were visible. They were out of time. He looked at Diggory. The two of them grabbed their father, dragging him behind the nearest stalagmite, shielding themselves from the approaching men but not, much to their dismay, from the lions.

When the men came into the room with the cows, the lions paid their meal no attention. Green eyes fixed on the Rawthornes, they continued to claw one another, drawing blood with every swat of their paws, desperate to get out.

"Enchanters be good," breathed one man.

Pressed against the rock tower that concealed them, the Rawthornes held their breath.

"What's gotten into them?" asked another worker. "I've never seen them so..."

"Well, I ain't feedin' 'em like this."

"What do you mean 'you ain't?'"

"Look at 'em! We're as good as beef if we lift that gate!"

It was then that a chilling sound came from the cage, but it did not come from the lions. The sound was metallic and rocky. It ground in their ears like the crunch of breaking bones. Suddenly, there was a slight crack in the rock where the latticed grille met the cave wall. And where the crack had formed, the metal had slightly flared. It was enough. One lioness stepped back. She shook her head, flattened her ears, and threw herself at the grate.

"We've got to get out of here," hissed Belwin. He jabbed his thumb toward the last tunnel, black and vacant before them.

Diggory agreed with a sharp nod.

If they kept low to the ground, they might avoid detection.

Belwin went first. Amidst the moans of the cows and the roars of the lions, he managed to do so without being seen. Diggory followed. The two brothers motioned for their father to come next. He started to move.

At that exact moment, one of the men announced, "I don't believe it! They're gonna break through!"

"Seal it! Seal the room! Now!"

Before Terveo had time to run, a guard appeared at the entrance of the tunnel in which Diggory and Belwin crouched.

"Oy—'oo are you!"

They stared wide-eyed at each other for one second. The Rawthornes stayed still, hoping to keep the man's gaze fixed on them while their father made a move.

The guard lifted his hand. In one swift motion, he brought his hand down on a lever attached to the wall. The gate of the portcullis dropped with a clang, separating Belwin and Diggory from the guards, the monsters, and their father.

"Wait!" Diggory blurted out.

The man looked at them in confusion. "You're drunken fools. Do you not see what's happening?! Who are you?"

The noises in the cave were unbearable. The lions were covered in their own blood yet bore no signs of stopping their attack. The cows moaned with madness. The handful of guards that held on to them were shouting back and forth.

"Let's go!"

Terveo stood to his feet now. The man who had closed the gate on Belwin and Diggory turned to see their father.

"And 'oo are *you?!*" He shouted, grabbing Terveo by the collar. "And whaddya do to 'em!" He jabbed a thumb at the lions. "Come on! We're getting out of here."

He threw Terveo toward the tunnel, back in the direction they had come. Belwin and Diggory erupted in protest. Terveo looked over his shoulder at his sons as the guard dragged him away and then the last gate was shut. Diggory and Belwin were left in the darkness, separated from their father by a room with two wild-eyed lions and three doomed cows.

Prince Xietas disappeared behind Remaine, quietly moving along the base of the wall. Remaine faced the beast. He held the sword with shaking hands. He was certain it was the heaviest thing he had ever held. The prince began to mutter and then the muttering turned into a faint hum. A little melody, barely audible, floated up from behind him.

CRACK! The sound of stone ripping open blasted from behind.

Remaine fell to the floor. The lion shrank back into the shadows. The prince nearly fell on top of Remaine, but with a graceful side-step managed to avoid his huddled form.

When all was quiet, Remaine lifted his head. In a silvery shaft of moonlight, a billion dust particles swirled. Remaine coughed. Rising to his feet, he brushed the dust from his arms and knees. The sword lay on the ground. In a flush of panic, he snatched it up and held it out before himself, a wave of fear flooding through him.

"It's all right, Remaine," the prince said, taking the blade from him. "She ran off. Well done."

Remaine thought the prince was complimenting his stand against the lion, but the prince had his gaze fixed behind Remaine.

The wall, which had been a flat surface, now caved inward. It was as if a boulder had pummeled itself into bread dough, leaving behind a round, hollow hole, twice the height of the prince, and three times as deep. The spherical cave was shadowy, but as far as Remaine could tell it was empty.

Prince Xietas strode forward with confidence, rooting around for something in his thick furs. Within minutes, a yellow flame appeared on the end of a torch. Flooded with light, the small hollow revealed nothing but a dome of bare stone. Moving slowly, the prince examined every square inch of the space.

As the minutes passed, the prince's movements seemed to sharpen. The torch whirred back and forth as the prince combed over every crag, every indent, every millimeter of the cave.

"This can't be it," he said under his breath. "Where..." Then he stopped and looked at Remaine. "What do you see?"

"I don't see anything," Remaine answered truthfully.

It could have been the torch, but Remaine thought he saw something flash in the prince's eyes. The prince stepped up to Remaine, coming within inches of his face, then said calmly, "Remaine, there is much you have to learn about this cold, cruel world of ours. In time,

I hope to teach you. Your destiny was written long ago, and I will see it finds you. I promise to answer every question that comes to your mind, but first, you mustn't lie to me. What do you see?"

The prince was so adamant about his question that Remaine stepped back in earnest to take another look. He took a deep breath, yet even when he relaxed, in the way he did before when he saw the kneeling man, the cave was unchanged. It was what it was. An empty hollow in the rock. "I don't—I'm—I'm sorry."

"It's not here, Ravillion." A familiar voice boomed from the shadows behind them. Somewhere in the vast, black chamber, invisible to them, the heavily accented sing-song voice sounded again. "Laddie, it's time you come with me."

Levo stepped into the light, blade drawn. He advanced slowly; an orange bear trained to fence.

Remaine must have been in shock because he did not say anything. The prince stepped between Remaine and Levo.

"I wondered if you'd show up, Chince. I think you can lower your blade, my friend."

"I'll chew and spit out any niceties you serve me, Xietas. I've learned not to listen to any lies you breathe, nor those of your slithering string-bean friend outside… who's currently knocked out, by the way."

The prince side-stepped and motioned an invitation for Remaine to join him at his side. He asked in all sincerity, "Have I lied to you Remaine?"

"Don't confuse the boy, you snake. Every word you say is—"

"I'm not keeping the boy here against his will, Mr. Chince." The prince put a hand on Remaine's shoulder. "He's free to go with whomever he chooses. He knows well enough that with me there is the promise of truth and a future—there is honor and prosperity for his family. He knows he'll discover the truth about who he is. And with you—well, more lies about me, I'd wager."

"Enough!" Levo barked, lunging forward. His blade crossed with Xietas' in a ringing of steel. Remaine tumbled backwards.

Levo lunged, using his whole body, as if he were as likely to throw a punch as he were to fell his blade. The prince, on the other hand, let his blade do all the work as he parried each move with ease, his stoic face impossible to read.

"I won't fight you, Mr. Chince," Xietas said between blows. "I'm not your enemy. The boy knows it."

"Liar!" Levo shouted.

Remaine watched, terrified, as the two men collided. But the clang of metal was interrupted by another sound; it was the low, reverberating growl of the lioness emanating out of the shadows.

It happened so fast Remaine hardly had time to scream. In a single lunge from darkness, the beast pounced on Levo aiming to tear at his throat. Levo gave a yelp of surprise, lifting an arm to block the oily mouth, but he was thrown to the ground.

Levo let out a shriek of panic as the lion growled over her prey. Then in one horrifying motion, the lion sank her teeth into Levo's collar bone. His shriek was silenced.

It all happened in a blink. As if possessed by something, Remaine flung himself at the beast, letting out a scream for the monster to release Levo. The lioness roared with irritation. Her great paw swatted at Remaine. Her claws slashed his cloak. He felt the razor-sharp tips tear at his skin as the force of her strike launched him backwards. His head slammed back onto the cold stone. At once his vision blurred. Blood dripped down his chest in three long stripes of red. He blinked and shook his head. The monster returned to Levo and took another bite.

The prince cursed and plunged his sword into the belly of the lioness. She moaned and swatted at the blade, then tumbled backwards onto the stone floor. Licking at her belly, she collapsed to the ground.

Remaine crawled over to Levo. The prince fell to his knees beside them, one hand on Levo, one hand on Remaine. A pool of blood had already begun to form. Prince Xietas breathed heavily.

"He's alive!" Remaine said shrilly, clutching his own chest. It was warm and slick to the touch. "We have to get him out of here!"

Again, the prince muttered something under his breath, then hoisted Levo onto his shoulders. It was the first time Remaine had seen the prince look strained at all. With less effort, he heaved Remaine over his other shoulder. Then he ran back through the darkness, out into the open air, fleeing the Crack in Time.

Early the next morning, as the yellow dawn illuminated the fog that hung thickly about the entrance to the Crack in Time, two more weary men found themselves scrambling out of the very same cave. Belwin and Diggory Rawthorne shielded their eyes from the unbearable brightness of the morning light that oppressed them after their horrific night-long blind journey through the most treacherous caverns of Cracklemore.

CHAPTER 20

THE SECRETS OF THE RAWTHORNE FAMILY

WHEN REMAINE WOKE, it was to the scent of citrus and lavender. He squeezed his eyes shut and gave them a good rub before finally opening them up to take in his whereabouts. The ceiling of the room was domed and intricately painted to look like a dreamy, misty forest. He lay on a comfortable couch. He was snug under a heavy blanket next to a large marble hearth that blazed with a cozy fire. Above the hearth hung two formal portraits, side by side: one of Prince Xietas and one of King Ignis. In each portrait, perched on their shoulders were their loyal Singers.

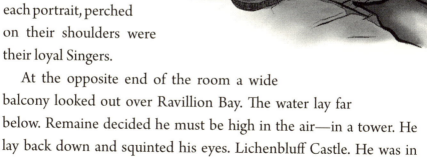

At the opposite end of the room a wide balcony looked out over Ravillion Bay. The water lay far below. Remaine decided he must be high in the air—in a tower. He lay back down and squinted his eyes. Lichenbluff Castle. He was in Lichenbluff Castle.

Gathering energy into his head and neck, propping himself up with his elbows, Remaine tried again to take a look around. More of the room came into focus.

In the middle of the room was a table. On the table, mostly covered in a blanket and with his head propped up by a pillow, lay the mountainous mass of Levo Chince. A stack of neatly folded white towels lay alongside him and a pot of something hot steamed at his feet. Beyond that, Remaine could see the arching, cobra-like frame of Lyme Stretcher bent over Levo's head scrutinizing the situation.

"Is he any better?" Remaine's voice cracked with exhaustion. The memory of the lion was creeping back into his head and Remaine shuddered at the recollection of her ripping into Levo Chince.

The grand pinion administered a small vial of clear liquid to the barely visible mouth hidden in the bushy red beard. Levo's brow furrowed. His body forced a cough, then it lay still once more. "He lost a lot of blood. You both did." Stretcher reported with indifference. He returned the vial to a cabinet. "Several healers were summoned in advance. They were ready for you both when you arrived. They stopped the bleeding, mostly, but he's been on the edge."

"Will he make it?"

"Perhaps," said Stretcher. "We will know soon whether or not he will survive."

"S–survive?" With great effort, Remaine pushed himself up to a sitting position. Everything hurt. His chin hurt from where he had smacked it against the floor, as did the back of his head. More than that, however, his chest stung beneath bandages.

The tall, arched doors of the chamber opened to reveal Prince Xietas. The prince flashed a smile at Remaine, then strode smoothly towards Levo. "Where are we?"

"No progress," said the advisor bluntly, wiping his hands on a towel. He straightened up and cracked his neck. "No regress."

"No regress is progress, Stretcher, have a little faith." The prince turned to Remaine. "You've been out for nearly eight days. No, no—stay put. Don't worry. I had Stretcher keep you asleep for most of it so you could heal painlessly. We've taken care of you the whole time—you'll be fine."

Remaine's stomach lurched. Everyone must be worried about him—he had disappeared, then he never came back. Surely Jolly was frantic after Remaine had abandoned him in town.

When he turned back, the prince was offering him a goblet of something warm. Remaine took the goblet and sipped the liquid—it tasted of cream and honey.

"We will do what we can for your friend, Remaine," said the prince, sitting next to Remaine's bed. "Though I imagine if he wakes up and finds himself healed under the care of a Ravillion, he'll mourn his survival with a great, theatrical display."

Remaine looked up at the prince, who winked down at him. Then the prince turned back to Levo and stared at him, or through him, his gaze a deep sea of questions and frustrations.

"I..." Remaine hesitated.

"Yes?"

Remaine had come to the prince with a purpose. He had to find out for himself.

"Levo thinks the Ravillions are..." began Remaine, hesitant to finish the thought in front of the prince.

"Evil?"

The word felt almost trite when Prince Xietas said it. Remaine nodded.

"Do *you*?" asked the prince.

Remaine hesitated again. He could hear his sister's voice in his head. For a moment he thought of Serae, and Diggory, and Jolly—he did trust them—but what if they were mistaken?

"I—I don't think so," said Remaine. "You seem nice enough to me."

The prince laughed. "Nice? I don't know if I've ever been called that. But I'll accept it." He took a sip from his own goblet, then leaned forward, resting his elbows on his knees. "And what do you think of the Rawthornes, Remaine?"

"They're nice too."

"Hmm," said the prince. "Well, you do know what this means for you, then?"

Remaine shook his head.

"Eventually you'll have to make a choice."

"A choice?"

"Yes. A choice. You cannot *honestly* carry on, Remaine Plink, thinking I am nice and thinking those who try to destroy me are nice as well. One of us is being quite wicked."

Remaine turned this dilemma over in his head. "Maybe you're both mistaken?" he offered.

"Mistaken?"

"Yes." Remaine sat up more. "Maybe you could talk to them? Maybe they just don't know who you really are?"

"And who exactly am I, do you think?"

Remaine paused again. He felt pressure to get it right, so he started on ground he knew to be solid. "I think you're Xietas Ravillion, Enchanted Prince of the Cracklemore Isles."

The prince smiled.

Remaine continued. "I think you're the Chosen Winged Warrior—the way you fought the Pearlback—and the Hollowfiend!"

The prince squinted, peering into Remaine's soul. "And am I trustworthy, Remaine?"

Remaine looked over at Levo, recalling the night in the cave. The prince had refused to fight him. When the lion had attacked, the prince had defended Levo. He had also saved both their lives when he could have taken only Remaine and left Levo for dead.

"Yes. I trust you, Y–Your Enchanted," said Remaine. And he meant it.

"I wish that was enough to convince your new friends, Remaine.

Unfortunately, I fear we have a battle ahead. As long as they believe the Ravillion line is…"

"Powerful," said Remaine. He suddenly felt a stab of guilt for talking about the Rawthornes so freely—it was true, they assumed the prince was of a darker, more sinister breed, but Remaine did not want them to get into trouble for it.

"They're not wrong about that, Remaine. We are of the ancient bloodlines. Ours is the kingdom, the charms, and the great task."

"The great task?"

"To bring peace to all of Cracklemore, Remaine. It was once a single land. But it began to crack, to crumble—the lightning came, the earthquakes, the Berylbones, the Old Cold. Our task is to fill the fissures of the earth. Only the Ravillions can do this."

"Then why do you want me?" asked Remaine. This caught the prince off guard, and Remaine pressed him with one more question, perhaps the question he was most eager to understand. "Who am I?"

The prince paused. "You are special, Remaine."

"The prophecy," said Remaine.

"You remember Wesha's words, then," said the prince.

Truthfully, Remaine was thinking of Vulcutta and her song before her escape into the mountains. Had she survived? For some reason, Remaine chose not to mention Vulcutta. If the prince knew of the eagle or if he didn't, would news of Pua enrage him? Remaine simply nodded.

"*Unless the one whose breath is held with visions of a time long felled that he might see—*"

"—See what?" Remaine swallowed, his mind racing. "Unless he does what?"

"*… from mortal seat immortal seas,*" replied the prince. "It means from your mortal position, you have the ability to see immortal realities, Remaine."

"Unless the one…" said Remaine. "Unless he—"

"*—lends his sight that it might seam the crack in throne, the tear in* scepter, grown again to last forever," said the prince. Then, almost as if decreeing it, he added. "We require your services to build the eternal dynasty of peace, Remaine. It cannot be done without you."

"You... you really believe it's me?"

"I do, yes."

"Because I don't breathe out the... Old Cold?"

"Yes, and your ability to see as well, of course."

Remaine wondered what the prince would think of Serae's immunity. But it was true... he could see things. "And you want me to help you fix the Cracklemore Isles?" he asked.

"Yes."

Remaine scrunched his face. "I don't know how to do that. I can only see old statues and stuff."

"For now, yes," said the prince. "But now we come to it, Remaine."

"To what?"

"Remember what I asked you, back on Monkeywood Island?"

Remaine recalled the moment in the rowboat, the water aglow with swirls of rainbow minnows. "You asked if I ever wondered if I had a destiny... a purpose."

"Yes, and I think we're meant to discover yours together. And when the world sees it—when your family sees it—they'll be proud."

Remaine's eyes stung. That *is* what he wanted, more than anything, yet here he was in Lichenbluff Castle. It was the one place he knew Silome would hate him for being in. He felt frustrated with her—like he would never please her. Maybe making his family proud was a fool's errand after all. Suddenly it felt like it had been years since he had even pictured their faces.

The prince extended his hand. He motioned for Remaine to join him, then strode out onto the balcony. His enormous collar of silver fur blew and ruffled in the wind. Wrapping the blanket around him, Remaine walked out to the balcony and approached his side. Together they looked down at the gray and white waves far below them.

Extending into the bay from the cliffside upon which Lichenbluff Castle was built, the private dock that moored two magnificent ships was directly below them. From their vantage point, the men who scurried about on their decks looked like little black termites.

"We've been in Ravillion Bay long enough," said Prince Xietas. "These vessels will set sail late tonight, after the Brumaloss. I want to extend to you, once more, an invitation to join us."

"To join the guard?" Remaine asked.

"No, I don't think so." The prince turned to look down at Remaine. "If the prophecy is to be believed, Remaine, then you have a role to play which neither of us fully understands. Your fate is…" he stopped, his eyes darting back and forth, up and down, studying every feature of Remaine's face. "Veiled, Remaine. For now, I want you to be my…" Again he paused, searching Remaine's face, searching for the right words to say. "My ward. My apprentice. I want you to tell me all your stories, Remaine. Take me on your adventures, so I can learn. Be my apprentice, and I'll be yours."

Remaine felt numb from head to toe, aware only of a slight tingling that shivered down his back, through his legs, and right into his boots. "I… uh… I don't know what to say."

"Say you'll go back in there, get some breakfast, and rest up a bit more." He winked. "We've been sustaining you, but you could use a piece of bread or two." The prince roughed up Remaine's hair, then said with a confident finality, "Tonight, you'll accompany me downstairs to the Brumaloss. You'll sit by my side as royalty. You'll be present with me among all the company I keep. Where I go, you'll go."

They came back inside, and Remaine, content for now, busied himself with breakfast. The prince left the room quietly.

On his way downstairs, the prince met someone he had not seen in weeks. The high general Sir Vector Cottley approached him at a jog. When he reached the prince, he fell to one knee like a crumbling fortress, his armor creaking the whole way down.

"My prince." Cottley's scarred face was beaded with sweat.

"Ah, General Cottley. It's been some time."

"Yes, my prince. I have done as you asked. They are here."

The prince ran a hand across his short hair. "I confess I had almost forgotten of your errand with all the excitement of this last week, Cottley."

The general stood. "Excitement, my prince?"

"We found the boy."

General Cottley's pale scars twitched and stretched as his face contorted in surprise. "Alive?"

"Very much so."

"Where?"

"Another time, Cottley. I fear the story is more complicated, and more sinister."

The general scowled, knowingly. "I, uh…" he paused and rubbed a hand across his own head. "I, uh, I took the liberty to separate the girl from the rest. She's mean, she is." His wide eyes glazed over as he replayed some traumatic memory. "She was madder than demons when I collected the family. Came at me fast and terrible. I put her in her place, but I didn't trust her to stay with the rest. She'd probably chew through the locks."

"Indeed?" chuckled the prince. "Very good. You may secure her upstairs—not in my chambers. Remaine is in there. You understand?"

The general nodded. "And the rest?"

"Keep the rest aboard. We leave tonight."

"Very good, my prince." The general held his forefinger up. "There is one more thing, my prince. The duke came too—the big one—for the Brumaloss. He has made a request to speak with you as well."

The prince sighed. "Very well."

High General Cottley bowed and left.

Atop its snowy hill and several miles away from the prince's suite in Lichenbluff Castle, Rawthorne Manor sat totally vacant save for two souls, both of whom were sneaking quietly out the back door.

The first one walked a bit bowlegged, leaving heavy prints in the snow, pausing on occasion to lift his lantern to more closely inspect a bit of foliage. He'd mutter something to himself then march on. The heavy footprint he left behind offered a path for the second one, much smaller in size, glad to avoid any excess snow in his shiny shoes. The cheerful man babbled with the bowlegged gardener as they made their way through the Rawthorne gardens.

"Just like the viscount said," Jolly chattered in a mostly quiet whisper, "not three hours passed before those guards showed up looking for him and master Diggory. Every day they've added another! Now they've got four new men stationed at the bottom of the hill with the other five, and one more up top near the grove."

"Shh," cautioned Mr. Lecky Wooling. "Not here, Jolly."

"Yes. Yes of course." Jolly made a motion of sealing his lips with his white-gloved fingers.

The two of them made their way down an avenue of giant topiaries shaped in the perfect likenesses of doves, made even more exact by their covering of snow. The path forked three ways around a large fountain, now completely frozen over; the men took the one which led to a clearing, circled by a thick hedge. A small stone gazebo sat at the edge. Once inside, they dusted snow off their shoulders then scanned the space for any unwanted onlookers. Jolly wrung his hands anxiously, breathing hot air into them. He felt satisfied they were alone, but Mr. Lecky Wooling was not yet convinced.

The gardener scowled and continued to patiently inspect every square inch of the enclosed space, his wide-brimmed hat exaggerating the dips and turns of his head. The massive hedge which ran around the formal seating area smelled of sweet pine, even under its dense blanket of snow. The snowy covering muffled all sound like giant, emerald earmuffs. Its depth and density pressed itself up against the gazebo so much it had nearly swallowed half of it.

When Mr. Lecky Wooling was satisfied they were alone, he approached the hedge where its growth was crawling slowly up the open side of the gazebo. From the pocket of his coat, he produced some hand-held shears and brushed them over the plant, murmuring quietly to himself. A lovely little tune thought Jolly.

Then the hedge moved. Ten or so branches curled back on themselves revealing a dark opening. With one final glance over their shoulders the gardener and the butler slipped inside leaving the hedge to close behind them.

Wooling held up the lantern. A small path, completely enclosed by the hedge, led them forward. When they came to a place where the dirt and rock beneath their feet changed, their steps produced a hollow sound. A smooth wooden trapdoor lay before them. Its brass handle twinkled in the yellow light.

Again, Wooling dug around in his oversized coat and produced a brass key that could only belong to the lock before them. He inserted the key and with a metallic click the lock opened. Wooling heaved the door upward, revealing stone steps into a black tunnel below. The butler and the gardener climbed down.

Belwin hunched over the stone table, his shoulders tensed and his palms flat upon the sprawling map. Water dripped from the cavern wall beside him, shining like a tiny trail of fire in the candlelight.

Diggory approached from behind. The mere presence of his little brother threatened to undo him, yet even as Belwin reviewed the schematics on the table he knew he would have to refrain from exploding. Several times this past week he had nearly lost all control—mostly when Diggory tried to offer help. Belwin had made it clear to Diggory the moment they left that dreadful cave that, as far as Belwin was concerned, Diggory had lost all authority within the Rawthorne home. All disaster seemed to find its source in his younger brother.

This aside, the viscount still needed Diggory for the day ahead. So, although his blood boiled, he would refrain from erupting. Besides, Diggory's voice was thick with guilt still, as it should be, and Belwin was in no rush to put an end to his suffering.

"Jolly's here," said Diggory.

"Mm hmm." Belwin gave the schematics a final look, his eyes lingered on a semi-circle of parallel lines attached to squares. Written above the geometric shapes in neat letters were the words: *North Cellar*.

Belwin turned and followed Diggory from the room if one could even call it that. The cave itself was really just one large, open space with a few off-shooting hollows, some more tucked in than others.

The Rawthornes emerged from the most concealed of the side hollows to find their butler and head gardener there by the deep, glassy pool of water that ate up three-quarters of the cave's floor.

"My lords," greeted Jolly, bowing slightly. Wooling nodded. "Good morning."

Belwin rubbed the bridge of his nose with his thumb and middle finger then ran his hands through his hair, aware suddenly, that the night had passed and the water in the hidden cave was no longer oily black but had begun to take on the slightest bit of color. Even a few skinny shafts of gray light pierced through tiny fissures in the rock overhead. It had been a week of living in this place—by far the longest Belwin had ever stayed down here. He had sent Rosy away with generous compensation and promised her the position would still be hers should calmer days return. Some, however, were too deep into this mess to release, like Jolly, Wooling, and Wynnie.

"I suppose it is morning," replied Belwin. "Any news?"

"Of Mr. Chince and the Plink boy, my lord, I'm afraid there's none." Jolly's face was uncharacteristically somber.

"And Pua? Were you able to meet with her?"

Jolly dipped his chin and wrung his white-gloved hands together. Then he looked up to the black ceiling of the cave as he tried to recall the necessary information. "Yes, my lord. I rendezvoused with her in town yesterday afternoon just where you said. She received your first message and still appeared unwell by the news of Mirror Pass. She told me your theories are almost certainly accurate. If the monsters' eyes shone green in the way you described, then something dark is indeed at work. Magical breeding, like Pua's work with Singers, but poisoned, corrupted, like the work on Monkeywood. Like the work of Doromund Venerack."

"Anything else?" asked Diggory.

"Nothing. Just to be careful."

"Did you tell her of our plan, Jolly?" asked Belwin.

"Oh yes. Of course. She is concerned, in her own way, but agreed we have no other choice."

Belwin folded his arms. He was hungry and tired but more than anything he wanted out of this place, he wanted to know what was happening out there under the sky, and he wanted to see Serae. "Have we had any other visitors in the past two days?"

"Just the same bunch. They repeatedly knock on the door and request to peek about the manor. I let them every time."

"Do they ask questions?"

"Always the same ones," said Jolly. "I give them the same answer.

You took a ship north and did not say when you'd be back. More of them come every day. And they're stationed about the hillside."

"Well, we mustn't keep you long, then," said Belwin.

Jolly gave the Rawthornes his most loyal smile. It was void of the usual cheer, but encouraging, nonetheless. "I'll return if there's any news."

Then he and Mr. Lecky Wooling disappeared into the dark tunnel which would after a long while take them back to the Rawthorne gardens.

Diggory sat on the cave floor near the water. He locked his hands around his crossed shins. Barrow, the fat gray cat, took immediate advantage of the situation and curled up into a little ball in the cavity between Diggory's chest and knees. Belwin, not out of any real interest to be closer to his brother, but rather out of sheer exhaustion, sat down next to Diggory. He folded his arms and stared down into the clear pool.

For a while, they sat there in silence, staring at the glassy surface.

"He always said this place was their greatest secret—said it held the seeds of hope," said Diggory.

Belwin did not reply. He did look around, though. A few miles away his father shivered in a subterranean cellar deep in the dungeons of Lichenbluff Castle, and yet, this was the place where his fingerprints could be found everywhere. All the maps and documents, the few old books with clues supposedly buried within their pages—this place housed a lifetime's worth of work that Terveo and his brother had put in hunting them all down, and they had managed to do it all in a little over a decade.

"Dasko and Terveo Rawthorne's greatest secret," Belwin repeated. "Or the greatest dead-end obsession for two mad brothers."

"Maybe that's what it takes," Diggory replied quietly.

"If they're the right obsessions," Belwin said.

When Diggory did not say anything more, Belwin stood. "For now, I see these past ten years as a waste of time. Our father and uncle have wasted energy. Wasted brilliance. Wasted talent. We've followed them, spending all our energies hunting for histories, doing our homework, looking for prophecies, and collecting the information, when we could have destroyed the royal family five times over by now."

Diggory stood so suddenly Belwin stepped back. Barrow dropped to the ground and with a flick of his tail, he followed Diggory as he strode over to a small alcove in which sat a single object—a small, locked chest with bands of beautifully carved silver flowers.

"Because of this, Belwin." Diggory picked up the chest and heaved it at his elder brother. Belwin caught it, enraged at the act, but too shocked to reply. This seemed to be Diggory's intention because he continued with zeal.

"*That* is the fruit of their labor. Their brilliance, their energy, their homework discovered the value of *life*—the *truth*." Diggory unsheathed his sword and stared at the hilt. The handmade silver hilt was bespoke—he had made it years ago, working his favorite figure of the Hollowfiend's Hunt into the handle as his own bauble. "Their research produced *this*."

Within seconds, the suffocating silence that hung in the air had snuffed out the small flame of Diggory's boldness. Throat swollen with guilt, Diggory ran his thumb across the silver figurine which had become his own bauble—a beautiful woman holding a child—a mother. He said, "*My* obsessions, however..." He approached Belwin, retrieved the chest, and returned it to the alcove. With his back turned to Belwin, he added, "for the rest of our lives lived out under the stars, Belwin, you have every right to see my obsessions for what they are. They are fruitless... *dead-end* obsessions."

Belwin wanted to storm off, but he felt his brother crumbling and he did not want to turn away.

"This *is* all my fault, Belwin," Diggory said, eyes full of tears. "I don't know why my mind—my memories—why they betray me. I remember the Hollowfiend. I remember seeing him. I felt like I could hear him. But he was different."

"Dreams," said Belwin. "You were having dreams, Diggory."

Tears fell onto the sword hilt. Diggory shrugged. "As *real* as memories," he said. "But I never should have told our mother. If I had known she and Willow would wind up in the forest, believing me like they did, curious to see him for themselves, I—"

A clacking sound echoed in one of the alcoves further down the cave. The sound was steady, growing closer. The warm glow of candlelight accompanied it. Unlike the sound, the light jounced unsteadily off the walls as it drew nearer, held by the tremulous hand of Lady Solace who stepped into view giving her cane a last loud clack.

The old woman appeared to have doubled in size, having dressed herself in five large overcoats. The enormous collar of the outermost layer arching even higher above her head than usual. She looked less like a lion with a mane and more like a brown peacock whose tail feathers were in full display. She held the candelabra aloft and eyed the Rawthorne brothers critically.

"Have I not made myself clear?" she scolded.

They both stared guiltily.

"Is it not enough that we must hear mention of that wretched beast in this city day and night? I will not hear of it from my daughter's husband."

Then she shot a wicked look at Diggory, continued. "And far be it from *you* to ever mention it again. Whatever dreams you might have had long ago," said Lady Solace firmly, "whatever imaginations of friendly monsters you entertained, and whatever silly legends this city believes, as if it were merely the subject of nursery rhymes—one thing is certain: the Hollowfiend *is not* a dream. It consumed my daughter *and then* it killed your mother, whom my daughter was foolish enough to blindly follow."

Belwin was in the habit of biting his tongue when Lady Solace spewed words of spite against her own mother, Lady Merhanna Rawthorne, for befriending his wife, Willow, when he had married her. He bit his tongue again. It was no one's fault but Lady Solace's that

Willow Depps, when she became Willow Rawthorne, found a true mother in Merhanna Rawthorne, having never found one in her own mother, this old, bejeweled crow who stood before them.

Lady Solace took one more step forward. "And you of all people should have internalized this by now, Diggory. It was you who came upon the scene—who found all that remained, the blood—" she inhaled sharply and clutched at her necklace. "Fools. I am surrounded by fools."

When Lady Solace realized that neither of the Rawthorne men intended to respond to her tirade she gave a firm nod of satisfaction. Holding her nose high she wobbled back to her own private corner.

"She's right," said Belwin to Diggory. "Their deaths are all that matter. And in the time that you've spent wishing it were otherwise, looking for more answers and reading books, wondering if other legends or myths might be important or even if your dreams were real," he lowered his voice, "Ignis and Xietas Ravillion have bred an army of Hollowfiends. And now they hold our father prisoner."

In truth, Belwin wished he *had* heeded Diggory's advice to explore Mirror Pass sooner. They would have discovered this scheme. They could have planned. But all that did not matter now.

The brothers did not speak again until they had to, an hour later, when Wooling arrived once more. This time he was accompanied by Wynnie Canny. She spoke sharply and in low whispers, in her paranoid way.

"Here are these," she said, handing Belwin a pile of neatly folded fabric. "They should get you in the door no problem." She also produced a box, handing it to Diggory. "As long as you also wear these. They're new faces. And here's the adhesive—less is more. Master Terveo is..." she paused and swallowed. "He's being held in the north cellar, second to last chamber, just as we thought."

Belwin noticed there was a terror in her eyes.

"You're certain?" Belwin asked.

"I am," she said. "I–I saw him."

Diggory and Belwin both shifted uneasily at this news. The tension that lay between the brothers, impaling each like a double-ended spear, disappeared, for just a moment, at news of their father.

"And?" asked Diggory.

"I managed to find him last night. Just after dinner—Serae was with the company, rehearsing—I managed to sneak away. I found him. He was so weak—" Wynnie's eyes watered and Belwin felt his blood chill at the sight. She had always been the type to fuss, but it was always in a vigorous, energizing sort of way. This wasn't just worry he saw in her eyes. This was dread. "He was trying to tell me something," Wynnie continued, the tears building in her eyes. "Or trying to get me to leave—that's when I heard them coming."

"Who?"

"I hid at the sound of their footsteps. Whether by good fortune or evil fate, I saw the whole thing."

"What whole thing, Wynnie?" Belwin kept his voice evenly tempered.

"I saw…" she closed her eyes and gathered her courage, inhaling sharply. "I saw the Master of Beasts—the green one." She opened her eyes wide looking back and forth between Belwin and Diggory, then her gaze focused on the empty space between them as she forced herself to recall the awful scene. "I saw him appear out of the shadows. Had I moved from my spot, I would have been spotted—would have run straight into him and…"

"And what?"

"And a–a monster, m'lord." Wynnie was a horror-stricken shell of herself. "It was like a…"

"A lion." Belwin finished the sentence so she would be spared the task. She looked up into his eyes with a strange mixture of terror and wonder on her face.

"Yes," she breathed. "But—but not like a bay lion. It was larger, patchy fur, half its flesh showing—those green eyes."

Belwin could see her measuring their reactions. It dawned on her slowly. They had already seen it. She asked what any citizen of Ravillion Bay would ask.

"A Hollowfiend? Truly?"

"Yes," said Belwin, not bothering to look at Diggory. "Tell us, Wynnie, tell us exactly what happened next."

Wynnie swallowed and, perhaps in the newfound knowledge that the others shared in her terror, she managed to regain some of her composure. "The man—the green one—he brought the monster *to* Master Terveo. Then the lion—it *bit* him—bit his leg, just here." Wynnie touched her calf. "Not to consume or even to tear at him. It was—" her eyes were frantically darting around as she searched for the right words, "it was calculated, slow. But Master Terveo screamed, and—" A shiver overtook Wynnie. She paused, then inhaled deeply and continued. "The beast master began to ask him how he escaped the Eastbound Ship to Colony Gardens all those years ago—to ask him how he had stayed hidden—why he had been in Mirror Pass—what he knew about Remaine Plink and then…"

"Then what? Wynnie…"

"I don't know." She shook her head, eyes wide. "S–somehow the lion drew answers out of Master Terveo. He fought the creature, but the way the answers came from his mouth, it was as if the monster had control of his mind or his tongue or something."

"Hoaxbite…" murmured Diggory.

"What?" asked Belwin.

Diggory whirled around to rummage about on a long table that was placed near the cave's wall. He shoved aside a few scrolls and found the small wooden box. He opened it up and removed an ivory object.

"This." He held it up. "When the prince interrogated Remaine and me aboard *The Emerald Egg* that night Remaine stowed away," Diggory's brow furrowed as he spoke, recounting the details. "He used this—a Hoaxbite. When he used it on me, I couldn't move. It was the first time I'd seen it—but now I know what it is. It's a lion's tooth."

Belwin's eyes narrowed.

"They're—" Diggory rubbed his jaw thoughtfully. "They're breeding Hollowfiends because Hollowfiends must be able to handle enchantment—they're infusing them with dark charms to harness an ability."

"That's why Venerack is involved," said Belwin. "Just like Singers. It takes special charms—it takes an Animal Charmer—to recognize the ability of the creature—to pass it along into their offspring."

"The way they attacked us through that cage," said Diggory. "It's like they *knew* we were no friend of their master… this must be part of their ability." Then he added, "Pua would rather die than have us compare the Singer, and her charms, to what's happening in the Pass."

A sickening knot formed in Belwin's stomach. "Wynnie, what did my father tell Venerack? What do the Ravillions know?"

"They know about you two."

"Surely they've deduced that by now, already," Belwin said. "Whatever inconspicuous future we had, it is dissolved. What of his escape from the Eastbound Ship?"

"Master Terveo did struggle against the monster—sputtering only one-word answers like 'lies' or 'life' or something like that. The king was frustrated with the master's resiliency. That's when he told the lion to bite harder—and the lion did. He asked about Remaine, then; he asked the master what he knew of the prophecy."

"What did he say?"

Wynnie's composure broke once more, and tears filled her eyes. "Between the screams, he told him—he said—'The prophecy is broken. The prophecy is veiled.'"

Belwin let out a long breath, one that he didn't realize he had been holding until it escaped between his tight lips.

Diggory looked at Belwin and nodding his head, gave him the

smallest of smiles. "Father's working his way around the Hollowfiend's poison. Answering truthfully, but cryptically."

"Clever Master Terveo," said Wynnie.

Belwin pinched his nose again. "There's only so much of avoiding the poison that he can do. Anything else? Did he tell them anything else?"

"No, m'lord," said Wynnie. "He fainted, then. I imagine when he wakes, they'll question him more. It's imperative—rescuing him."

"Thank you, Wynnie." Belwin took a deep breath and said a bit quieter. "Wynnie, tell me Serae is all right"

Wynnie smiled. "She is, m'lord. She's the most beautiful dancer on stage."

This had been the hardest part since their return home. Belwin came home and found Serae already gone to Lichenbluff for the week in preparation for the Brumaloss performance. The company always lodged there for the days leading up to the show. It pained him to leave her there, but if she was being watched, where else could he want her to be besides Lichenbluff? Belwin had made the decision to keep her there until the moment they made their move.

Belwin returned Wynnie's smile, realizing it had been some time since he had used those facial muscles. Then the young governess left. Belwin and Diggory were alone again with nothing but the secrets of the Rawthorne family and the raw materials for their foolhardy plan.

CHAPTER 21

THE BRUMALOSS

WITH ALL HER WINDOWS AGLOW, Lichenbluff Castle stood against the night sky like a prima donna, adorned, radiant, and all the more beautiful in the gentle snowfall.

The non-descript, black carriage crossed the bridge to the castle unnoticed, one of the hundreds caught up in the rattling excitement of the Brumaloss.

Belwin snipped at Diggory, who was peeking through a slit in the black curtain. Belwin knew Diggory risked nothing by stealing a glance at the spectacle, but somehow it made Belwin feel better if he could control every last detail—especially when it came to his little brother. Even if they were masked. He repeated once more, "We take no chances."

A little window slid open behind Diggory's head and the voice of Jolly tumbled in. "Approaching the bend, masters. Supply check." The Rawthorne brothers said nothing. Belwin gave Diggory a curt nod.

The carriage came to a halt. They held their breaths.

"Four crates of wine for tonight and three crates of goblets," said Jolly.

A deep voice responded to Jolly. Then came a click and the carriage door swung open, flooding the dark interior with light.

"And two handsome lads to serve it, of course," Jolly chuckled. If Belwin had not known him so well and if he was not so distracted by the mask that had transformed Jolly into a blonde, horse-faced man, Belwin would have believed the butler's fake airiness without question.

As expected, the two guards hardly blinked in Diggory and Belwin's direction. Even if they had, Wynnie's disguises would have kept the guards from staring. Earlier in the evening, when Belwin and Diggory had crept back through the Rawthorne gardens to rendezvous with Jolly at the bottom of the hill, the masks had alarmed poor Jolly. If the masks were good enough to fool their butler, the Rawthornes felt confident they would be good enough to get them inside.

Hiding behind their masks with false mustaches and their white server's aprons, the Rawthornes played their part assisting the guards in every way, opening the crates, and examining the bottles. Within a few minutes, the guards had waved them on. Diggory and Belwin sighed with relief.

"Next. The kitchens," Belwin said, almost to himself. Belwin would never admit to the Plink boy that the boy's little excursion to Lichenbluff a few weeks ago had inspired Belwin's first phase of tonight's plan: get inside the castle via the kitchens.

Jolly steered the horses down the curved road that hugged the back of the castle. This time it was Belwin who risked a peek through the curtains to see outside the opposite window. There, not too far below, in the waters of Ravillion Bay and safely secured in the private harbor below Lichenbluff Castle were the spiky masts of two enormous ships.

If all went well, Belwin and Diggory would be there shortly to meet Pua.

They came to a stop. Belwin and Diggory jumped out, each carrying a crate. Almost at once they were forced to play their parts as a large man from the kitchens spotted them in the open door, his silhouette like a bulky stack of lumpy boulders.

"That had better be the flour!"

"Sorry!" Belwin shouted. "Wine, I'm afraid. Pardon me."

Belwin and Diggory left no time for anyone to question anything. They plowed through the door, set the crates down, then returned to grab the last crates. "Care to give us a hand?" Diggory asked the large man on his way back to the carriage.

The man grumbled and helped them with the two crates. Diggory was careful to grab the final one himself—a longer, skinnier box that held a neatly displayed row of wine bottles inside. As they hustled back into the kitchen, Belwin looked back over his shoulder at Jolly and gave him a nod. Jolly returned it, then snapped the reins.

The kitchen was a circus of chaos in typical festival fashion. The long, vaulted chamber of cream-colored brick was crawling with people in white aprons, scrambling about like ants in an anthill, busying themselves in crowded rows along lengthy tables.

Belwin, Diggory, and the large, boulder-like man set the crates down against the wall. Before the man could even turn around, Belwin and Diggory disappeared into the sea of workers. They darted past enormous vats of boiling, peppery stew. The steam that rose from the pots clung a little too tightly to the gooey disguises adhered to their faces. Belwin pressed a hand to his brow and hurried past. Diggory did the same.

The doors leading out of the kitchen were in sight when a large bell above their heads began to ring. Everyone stopped what they were doing to look up. The Rawthornes followed suit. The large brass bell rang again at the hand of a small man in an even smaller little balcony overlooking the workstations.

"Two minutes to six!" he shouted. "Time to pour!"

Right on time Belwin thought. He could not help but smirk at the precision of his own timing. Unlike his father and little brother, he had planned tonight down to the last second.

Belwin and Diggory moved with the current, helping the closest servant with a cart, stacked carefully with goblets and wines. Belwin noticed a few of his own glittering items in the display and when no one was looking, he quickly arranged them properly, annoyed that he even had to. The servant whom they were assisting, a tall, pock-faced man with thick eyelashes, barked at them. "If you insist on being in the way I'll run you over!"

"My apologies," Belwin said lightly. "Allow me." With efficiency he helped the man in neatly organizing the final goblets. Then, with all the effort in the world to refrain from sounding smug, he said, "I believe it's the Crush, first, not the Bloom. Bloom comes at the same time as the meal."

The man, with beads of sweat on his forehead, frantically calculated Belwin's information. Without looking up, he nodded with gratitude. "Right. Um… right."

He pushed the cart past them and joined the line of others with similar displays. Belwin and Diggory did not ask permission. Coming alongside the man as if it was their job from the beginning, they joined the assembly line of wine servers. Then, with trembling hands, they quickly removed the contents from the bottom of the cart and swapped in the long skinny crate Diggory had been holding. They propped the lid open to display the neat row of bottles. They were both sweating in the kitchen heat.

"What are you doing?" asked one of the women, polishing a final glass and setting it on a tray on the upper shelf of the cart. "And what's all that?"

The Rawthornes stood. Belwin coughed and as he did, he clutched at his chest where, hidden behind his dress tunic, a small jewel hung on a chain around his neck. The bell on the balcony rang by itself.

"Part of the crew," said Belwin. Then he pointed below. "And part of the menu. You heard the bell—let's move." Belwin and Diggory exited the kitchens and turned right towards the party upstairs. As they moved down the hallway, Belwin allowed himself a peek over his shoulder in the direction of the dungeons.

Prince Xietas used a gold pendant to fasten the gray dress cloak around Remaine's neck. It was pressed with the Ravillion seal of the swirling R and macaw. Bent down on one knee, Xietas almost matched Remaine in height. The prince smoothed the shoulders of the cloak and brushed off an invisible speck of dust, then from the folds of his own cloak he produced a final gift for Remaine.

The dagger seemed too small for the prince, but in Remaine's hand it felt substantial. It was elegantly simple. Slender and silver with an emerald at the hilt that matched the stone on the prince's longsword.

"In case a beast creeps a little too close again," he smiled. Then he stood, let out a long breath, and placed his crown upon his head. The prince shimmered from head to toe in his decorated regalia, and Remaine was reminded once more of the Tour of Valor. The Tour felt like a lifetime ago, but Prince Xietas Ravillion looked just as commanding tonight.

"We're not going back there, are we?" asked Remaine.

"Where?"

"That cave," Remaine said, lifting the dagger. "You said in case one creeps too close."

"Ah," said the prince. "No. Of course not. But you never know what we might find on any night in Ravillion Bay." The prince winked.

Remaine shot him an anxious smile. The memory of the cave came back to Remaine fresh and vivid, it made him shiver. He asked, "What were you looking for in the cave? Levo said it wasn't there—and what was it that I saw? It was all so…" he shuddered, recalling the Hollowfiend again, "frightening."

The prince stepped closer and let his heavy hand fall on Remaine's shoulder. "In time, Remaine, I'll show you how to be brave."

The promise was tantalizing. Remaine's shoulders felt heavy with the weight of how often he had felt fear lately—with how much of a coward he had been. He wanted nothing more than to be brave.

"There will be plenty of time to talk later," said the prince. "Dukes and duchesses from all over Cracklemore will be at this year's Brumaloss. It should be a special one—lots of guests. Stay close to me, eh?"

As they moved to leave the chamber, Remaine turned one last time to look at Levo who was still asleep on the table.

"You're welcome to come and check on him as often as you'd like, Remaine," said Xietas. Remaine smiled again. He followed the prince down the stairs of the tower, through a long gallery hall, down several more flights of stairs, through yet another long hallway, until at last they came to the opulent staircase that, like a river, emptied them into the grand entrance of Lichenbluff Castle and a roiling sea of guests.

It did not surprise Remaine to find that all eyes were fixed on him as the two of them stepped into view. He figured it would be the case. But somehow, seeing the chairmen and the nobility all dressed up like the subjects of intricate and elaborate paintings eyeing him carefully, whispering to one another, made Remaine hesitate halfway down the steps. The prince paused. "Close to me, Remaine. Remember?"

He gulped and continued walking.

The castle was awash in the light from a sea of candle-lit chandeliers and hundreds of torches on silver sconces. The people of Ravillion Bay had spared no expense for their most prized celebration. Each guest was dressed in their best, wearing their finest pieces. One woman, Remaine thought, looked so much like a tropical Singer he thought she might open her mouth and deliver another's message.

Then he noticed that the small cluster of women gathered around her wore similar gowns and he figured it must be the latest fashion. The elaborately detailed gowns looked very uncomfortable, as if an entire flock of birds had made their homes on collars, on heads, and on hips.

They continued to walk and along the way the prince paused several times to speak with guests. Each time he began to walk again the crowd would part, people would bow to clear the way, and every last person would stare Remaine down from head to toe—some out of scrutiny, others out of curiosity.

The prince paused to speak to a tall woman wearing all black and Remaine heard him say, "Ah, yes, Duchess Chipping, this is my ward, Remaine Plink, of Windluff."

The woman clutched her chest, her eyes darting between Remaine and the prince. The black feathers that spiked out from the shoulders of her gown shook. She looked exactly like a crow.

"A week ago, I was in disbelief to hear you found him alive, your Enchanted," breathed the woman. "Yet here he is, in the flesh. I am happy for you." She eyed Remaine curiously, studying him like she was trying to understand a very complicated riddle. "Your ward, then?"

Xietas lowered his forehead toward the woman and smiled proudly, resting his hand on Remaine's shoulder.

Duchess Chipping turned to Remaine and bent herself slightly in a delicate curtsy, careful to hold steady the goblet of wine in her hand. "It's an honor to meet you, young Master Plink. You must have much promise to be taken on by the prince of the Cracklemore Isles."

Remaine smiled and his cheeks flushed red again.

This kind of exchange happened several times as they wound their way through the palatial entrance of the castle, down another vast hallway, and at last into the familiar auditorium Remaine had caught a glimpse of not too long ago. They arrived at the lower level, an enormous round room dotted with tables, all sumptuously adorned with silver and crystal. Candles lit the room, spotlighting the statues that occupied every alcove. They each depicted stately poses, not a one of them was chipped or damaged like the statues in Windluff. The whole place roared with excited chatter. Some took their seats at the tables early; others stood, mingling and sipping their drinks. As the prince and Remaine made their way into the melee, the crowds continued to part, and chins continued to dip in reverence.

Suddenly, a desperate cry cut through the noise.

"REMAINE!"

Before he had even completely spun around, Remaine found himself wrapped up in the arms of his mother.

"Remaine! Oh, my son!" The effusive emotional display of Fortis Plink garnered attention faster than the prince himself.

"Mom!" Remaine hugged her back. At the smell of her skin, his gut twisted with both homesickness and relief. He suddenly remembered the night he had snuck out of the Rawthorne Manor and, eavesdropping in this very room, had learned that the prince had sent for his family. He had forgotten about it entirely until now. Now here she was. But—he pulled back and looked at her—she was different.

Far from wearing her usual garb of toga and apron, ready to clean all of the Salt District's dirty laundry, Fortis Plink now sparkled like a noblewoman. His eyes grew wide at the sight.

"Ah, Miss Plink," said the prince.

Remaine stepped back from his mother's embrace just by a step, aware of the attention and aware of the prince behind him. He coughed a little in embarrassment.

"I cannot imagine the relief you must feel in finding the rumors are true—your son is alive."

Remaine watched his mother dip her head slowly to the prince, both as a bow and as an affirmation. When she lifted her face, he saw something in her eyes. He had seen it before—often when she had finished tending to his sick father. A mask of sorts, a façade to hide her fear.

"Miss Plink," the prince continued casually, unbothered by the watchful crowd. "You'll be proud to know I've named Remaine my ward. Your son brings great honor to the Plink family."

Fortis blinked down at Remaine; her mouth was slightly open. "O–oh, I see," she managed to say.

"Is that so?" came another voice from behind Fortis. It was a soft, sickly-sweet voice and it could only belong to one person.

Now that he rolled into view, Remaine did not know how he had not noticed him sooner. Hubert Hegs, Duke of Windluff, was dressed from head to toe in shiny, cream-colored silks. He was the spitting image, and shape, of a gigantic pearl.

"I can't imagine why you'd want the Plink boy as your ward," the duke said, chuckling. He pursed his lips and looked down at Remaine.

"Oh, I can," declared Jileanna Hegs. She appeared from behind her father. Remaine's mouth fell open at the sight. Never had he seen anything like it.

If Hubert Hegs was the pearl, then Jileanna was the poor oyster that had coughed him up. Surrounding her head, Jileanna's collar was an accordion of a thousand silvery folds of fabric. The same pleated design spanned her waist, and then circled each ankle, giving the overall impression of an awkward, open-mouthed oyster, freshly shucked. Her gloved hands were held hostage by an incredible stack of at least one hundred bracelets and her face was an over-saturated canvas of white and silver paint, with one garish blob of red in the middle, right where her mouth probably was.

Even the prince was taken aback at the sight of her.

"Prince Xietas would be a *fool* to not see something special in Remmy," Jileanna admonished.

Stunned, Remaine scratched the back of his head. The prince raised his eyebrows. Fortis shifted uncomfortably.

"Now, now, dearest Jilly, we must never say the words 'fool' and 'prince' in the same sentence."

Jileanna's eyelashes flapped so rapidly that Remaine thought he felt an actual breeze. "Forgive me, Your Enchanted."

"It's quite all right, Miss Hegs. Now, Remaine and I must find our seats—have you all found yours?"

"Indeed," cooed Hegs. With his new cane designed to match his attire—he motioned to a table in the middle of the large circular room. Hegs said, "My prince. Our arrangement still stands, then? For certain?"

Prince Xietas glanced down at Remaine, then back up at Hegs. "It does."

Before they separated, Fortis clutched her son by the arm.

"Remaine?" she said, her eyes darting back and forth between each of his. Her voice was strained. It seemed she wished to speak but had lost the ability.

Remaine felt small again like a little boy in trouble. "Mom, I'm sorry I ran away. I didn't mean to make you mad. But I promise everything's good now, all right?"

The prince put one hand on Fortis' shoulder and the other hand on Remaine's shoulder.

"You'll see your son again, Miss Plink. For now, though, be filled with pride." He smiled. And despite his mother's voiceless struggle to speak with her son, they separated without another word.

The prince led Remaine up yet another staircase that hugged an interior wall of the theater until, finally, they arrived at a large private balcony. The balcony was clear of guests save for Lyme Stretcher, the high general Sir Vector Cottley, and a few guards.

Remaine peered over the edge of the balcony and watched as his mother took her seat next to Duke Hegs and Jileanna.

"I suppose seeing your family makes you miss home?" the prince asked.

He nodded and shrugged at the same time.

"Be at peace about your decision to come with me, Remaine. You are growing up. And don't worry, you will see her again."

"Where are the rest of them?" Remaine asked, his brow scrunched. Why was his mother the only one present if the prince had sent for his whole family?

"Who?" the prince asked.

Remaine swallowed, remembering he knew about Prince Xietas's plan to send for all the Plinks only because he had spied on the prince from this very spot weeks ago. Too sheepish to admit his actions or to bring up the Rawthornes again, whom he knew the prince did not understand, he shook his head and changed his question.

"I mean, why is my mother here?"

"Ah," said the prince delicately. "Well, when you do see your mother again… you may find her… circumstances… have changed."

"What do you—"

Remaine's inquiry was cut off by a servant who poured the prince's drink into his goblet. As was the custom, Lyme Stretcher tested the drink first before handing it over to the prince. A few more members of nobility waved up to the balcony from their tables on the lower level. The prince waved back. The nobles shouted something, laughed, raised their glasses and the prince did the same.

"You'd be surprised how much time we spend doing that," sighed the prince, loosening his collar. "Talking. Just… talking. And smiling. You can sit, Remaine. Sit there." He pointed to a smooth, black chair of simple design next to the more ornate throne.

"Thank you, Your Enchanted."

"We'll be spending a lot of time together, Remaine, and I think the formalities will wear on me. 'Prince Xietas' will be just fine, and on the rare occasion, 'Your Enchanted.'" The prince rolled his eyes in the direction of Grand Pinion Stretcher and gave Remaine another wink.

"Yes, Prince Xietas," smiled Remaine, lowering himself into his seat.

"And these three you'll address as Courtiers." The prince took a sip of his drink and looked out over the balcony at the hordes of people. Remaine followed his gaze. From the prince's side he could see a hundred feathered hats and glittering diadems tipping to acknowledge three distinct figures entering the room.

The first, an older woman with silvery hair running straight down her back, swished elegantly into the room. "Courtier Rima Orchid," said the prince. "She's the Master of Festival. Perhaps you've seen her at the Pearlback dance in Windluff a time or two."

The man behind her was much younger and everything from his hair to his long nose was shiny, smooth, and polished. "That's Courtier Hoaras Fiddler, Master of Relics and Histories."

They were both spectacles to behold, but the two of them were almost forgettable in the presence of the third. He was a tall man with a pointy black beard and decorated ears. And like the Monkeywood witches, his skin was the color of fresh moss. On the green man's shoulder sat the ancient macaw of the king.

The prince saw Remaine's open mouth at the sight of the man and he chuckled. "And that's Courtier Doromund Venerack, Master of Beasts—pinion advisor to my father. He'd give his right arm to make my father happy, and he'd give his life to make my father's Singer happy. These are three of my father's most trusted allies."

The courtiers ascended the staircase. With his eyes fixed on Venerack, Remaine recalled his encounter with the macaw in the Rawthorne gardens. He had been laughing with Serae, maybe even feeling the smallest sensation of being at home. Then the Pellatrim brothers had arrived—he realized he had yet to see them tonight— and he was outside, face to face with that bird. Remaine shuddered. But now here he was, dressed like royalty, sitting with the prince, spending his final hours on the Weatherlee mainland with absolutely no knowledge of where he was going nor when he would return.

The prince, Lyme Stretcher, and the two accompanying guards prepared for the arrival of the courtiers. Remaine followed suit. When they reached the balcony, the courtiers bowed before the prince. Remaine bowed before them. That's when he saw two enormous spiders scurry across the top of his boot. He yelped and stumbled back. The prince steadied him with a firm grip.

Courtier Doromund Venerack laughed and gave a whistle. Remaine was disturbed to see the spiders—bigger than any dock spider he had ever seen back home in Windluff—scurry up Venerack's leg and onto his hand where they disappeared into his sleeve.

"So… this is the infamous Remaine Plink." Venerack's voice was as deep and dark as a dungeon. "Back from the dead."

"Welcome, Venerack," said the prince. "Yes. I've made the boy my ward. He will travel with me tonight."

In unison, the three courtiers glanced back and forth between Remaine and Prince Xietas.

"And have you recovered from your encounter with the monster in the mountains, Remaine?" queried Venerack.

Remaine couldn't be sure, but he thought he saw another spider crawl up the green man's neck and peek out above his collar. Then the spider slipped quickly out of sight, leaving no trace of its presence on his green skin.

"Y–yes. I am still a little tired, though. Prince Xietas saved my life."

"Hmm," the courtier replied, stroking his pointy beard. "Yes, we'll do well to keep you close."

Below the balcony, Belwin and Diggory, still in disguise, entered the theater balancing goblets of wine on trays held aloft. At the top of the stairs, the king's court was just visible to them, and all chins were turned upward in that direction watching as the courtiers disappeared into the recesses of the balcony.

The chatter of the crowd resumed and Belwin and Diggory returned to the task of delivering wine. Diggory flanked to the left heading towards the stage and Belwin worked his way right, slowly coming to the space beneath the overhang of the balcony.

Belwin took a deep breath, calculating the details. He did not want to make a single misstep. No mistakes. Every few minutes he returned to a room off the main hallway where the long skinny crate waited, its contents slowly diminishing as they continued to refill goblets and serve guests. Diggory was back and forth, too, checking on the contents of the crate. They glanced at one another.

Shortly the wine service turned into dinner service, and the Rawthornes followed the other servers back to the kitchen to pick up elaborate trays of food to serve.

Belwin's nerves twisted in his gut. The smell of the dinner made him gag. He was glad when the lights were finally lowered, some of the candles were extinguished, and all eyes were drawn to the stage. He gave Diggory one last nod and made his move to the back corridors which ran behind the stage. Belwin slid through the hallways quietly, efficiently, and by the time the music began, he was moving with purpose among the performers who were huddled in the dark backstage.

He found Wynnie illuminated by a slice of light that spilled in through a slim opening where the two sides of the stage curtains met. Wynnie was dressed in black. She held her hands in a tight clasp, peering out at the dancers performing on the stage.

"All is set," he whispered into her ear. Wynnie did not move.

"Second to last cell," she whispered back. "I'll bring Serae just before the finale."

"Diggory will meet you at the kitchens."

Wynnie nodded. The music swelled. The audience clapped.

Every second counted. Belwin had just turned to leave when, through the slit in the curtain, he caught sight of his daughter, fluttering on stage like a little bird in moonlight. In all the madness, all the planning, he had almost forgotten that were things to have been different on this night—he would have been among the guests watching his daughter with pride.

Belwin's eyes stung at the sight of Serae. Even in her own small way, she looked so much like Willow. Her perfect innocence floated along with the music like a wispy summer cloud, oblivious to the storms of the world. And with her hair drawn up like that, the fine lines of her small jaw and neck were visible. Belwin could see she was wearing the necklace that matched his own. Once the earrings of Willow Rawthorne, the twin jewels, now charmed, were laced with the very breath which he had so often spilled with grief in memory of his wife.

He remembered his mother, too. And then he remembered his father—in the second to last cell. He quickly departed, leaving Wynnie to protect Serae.

Serae Rawthorne held not only the loving attention of her father, but the rapt attention of the entire room. Dukes and duchesses from all over Cracklemore were captivated.

"To exhibit talent of that caliber at such a young age!"

The nobility from Ravillion Bay beamed with especial pride to see one of their own darlings shine so brilliantly.

But no one was more entranced than Remaine Plink. Having never seen anything like this before in his life, he fell into a dreamlike trance as he watched his friend.

To watch only movement, only dancing—it was not strange at all. The lack of words, the lack of explanation left no void. Remaine had heard the bards back home, had listened to the professors—he knew the story. Somehow the idea of adding words to the dance felt like a crude interruption. Tonight, it was all in the spectacle. The story was alive. It moved him. It transported him. And he understood it better than ever.

It was the story of a young girl, the princess of the Cracklemore Isles, held lovingly in the heart of her little brother and father. The performance took Remaine on a journey. Time seemed to disappear and the stage along with it, leaving a real ocean and a real ship in its place. The dancers transformed themselves into the wild waves of a murderous storm. And Serae, who played the part of the young Ravillion princess, drowned.

The curtains closed. Remaine blinked in the brightness of the room as the light returned. The room filled up with the chatter of the guests. Confused and wonderstruck, Remaine looked up at the prince.

"Did you enjoy that?" chuckled the prince.

"I've never seen anything like it," Remaine confessed. "Is that all there is?"

"No, no." The prince studied Remaine with a knowing smile on his face. "There's another act to honor my sister."

"How old were you when she died?"

"It was a very long time ago," said the prince, shaking his head slowly. "Would you care for a drink?"

Remaine agreed and followed him to the back of the balcony where everyone stood around a table laden with food and drink. The prince handed Remaine a glass of something suited for him, then clinked his glass against Remaine's. They strolled back to the balcony's edge, peering down at the sparkling crowd of people, many of whom looked up at them with adoration. Remaine briefly caught his mother's gaze, but her attention was yanked away by Jileanna's obscene laughter. One man, hands busy with a tray of drinks, all but gawked up at them. His face was familiar. Perhaps Remaine had seen him before in the kitchens. How strange it must be to see a boy, a scrawny little boy from Windluff, sitting in the most honored place in all of Cracklemore right at this moment.

"So, tell me, Remaine, what do you think so far?"

Remaine stared up at the prince, his mind still enraptured by the first act. "It feels like I'm hearing this story for the first time—like I'm *there*, in it."

The prince rested his elbows on the balustrade. "The festivals are for remembering the Ravillion heroes. Windluff, Moorington—they have the Pearlback Dance—to honor Igniro, you know. But ever since her death, the Brumaloss has always told the tale of my sister, who never should have been lost that winter day. Brumal—winter. And the loss of our princess." The Prince's gaze drifted away for a moment. He inhaled and continued with smile. "Then, of course, my father never misses the Brinky Cup—the race honors the Terrible Briskman. We will journey with him next summer—I think you will enjoy that. And the Thousand Falls Concert in the heart of the fjords—you've never heard anything like it."

At the mention of King Ignis, Remaine looked around for the king's court. He glanced back over his shoulder, peering around the balcony. The courtiers, the guards… all of them were gone.

Two full bottles remained in a skinny wooden crate, nestled inside their velvet bed. With a quiet *click*, Belwin unlatched the box and pressed on the end of the cushioned case. The false floor of the crate popped up, revealing two elegant swords in their sheaths stashed beneath the bottles. Belwin looked over his shoulder. No one. Leaving one of the swords in the container, Belwin grabbed his own blade and quickly fastened it to his belt, using his apron to cover most of the sword's length. He tapped his other hip where the gruggleblade still lay perfectly concealed. Then he was off.

Getting past the kitchens was as easy as getting through them, however Belwin's progress came to a full stop on the floor below. Guards were stationed in the corridors, and though he intended to keep to the shadows, Belwin knew his chances of getting past the guards on stealth alone were slim. The torches flickered in their sconces. One guard coughed and the echo pulsed off the cool bricks. It smelled dank down here, and the temperature felt significantly colder.

Belwin crept like a cat to a heavy wooden door. *Find the first room you can.* That was the plan. He gave the handle a shake. Locked. More coughing. Closer.

Belwin gave the jewel around his neck a twist. A click of metal. The door swung open.

The room was black as pitch. As he fumbled about, Belwin smiled with satisfaction as his hands discovered an assortment of items. A stack of wooden buckets leaned in one corner, and great bags of something squishy were piled high next to them. Brooms and mops hung on the wall. This would do well, thought Belwin.

A long wooden ladder laying on its side, caused Belwin to trip. He cursed, then pushed the door almost completely shut, careful to leave enough of a crack to spy through. A slit of light cut through the middle of his face. Belwin carefully observed the scene in the corridor.

There were three guards close by. Only three. He felt confident. Only one guard meandered into close view every few minutes. He was a tall man with a face like pinched bread-dough and he strolled casually in Belwin's direction. The guard moseyed along, as if he might fall asleep. Belwin could hear him yawn. His boots shuffled sloppily into view, inches from the supply closet where Belwin, tense and alert like an animal of prey, controlled each breath, working to keep his heart rate smooth.

Trying to minimize the squeak of the hinges, Belwin swung the door open quickly. It didn't work. The hinges sang sharply. The guard spun around.

Belwin sprang forward.

Like a monkey, Belwin launched himself onto the tall man's back. He wrapped his arms round the man bringing his dagger, laced with gruggleroot, across the guard's stubbly throat. Belwin made a shallow, but effective cut.

The shock kept the man from crying out. His hands flew to his throat. Belwin jumped off the man's back and stepped to the side. The man staggered backwards, wide-eyed. He gawked at Belwin like a fish, looking down at the blood on his hands, then back up at Belwin. Words bubbled up in his throat, or at least they began to bubble, but the man's eyes rolled back in his head and with one last dramatic step forward, the man fell to the ground. Belwin seized him by his feet and dragged him into the supply closet that welcomed Belwin's first target, who, hopefully, would sleep next to the brooms for the next few days.

Belwin's heart began to pound now. He moved methodically. He focused on his breath, just visible in the icy corridors, but he could not slow the rising heat now coursing through his veins. He harnessed the energy, though, and brought his second target down even more smoothly than the first. With two sleeping bodies stashed in the closet, Belwin made his way deeper into the dungeons of Lichenbluff Castle.

When he reached his third target, he could see the prison cells just visible at the end of the long hallway. With the closure of his mission in sight, he felt a jolt of renewed energy as he slid his blade along the neck of the last guard. The last of the guards was an unfortunately large man and Belwin breathed heavily as he began to haul him back down the corridor to the supply closet. Suddenly, the sound of voices reverberating down the hallway brought him to a cold, dead halt.

Whoever they were, they were close. He let out a low groan of frustration as he dragged the unconscious guard with greater vigor now, hustling down the hallway as swiftly as he could under the weighty circumstances. He could see the door to the closet. He was almost there. On the adjacent wall of the perpendicular hallway, the light of torches grew, and the lengthening shadows of bodies reached out to him. Belwin threw himself at the door and shoved the man inside. Then, at the last second, before the approaching party rounded the bend, Belwin slipped into the closet too and baubled the door shut once more. A tiny slice of light illuminated the base of the frame.

Judging by the footsteps and voices, the group of guards that marched by was large. Belwin guessed ten, perhaps, maybe more. They conversed as they passed, most of them seemed to be guards, though perhaps not all. It was a cacophony of clanking armor and thudding boots, swishing cloaks and clanging swords. They passed by so near to the door, and so swiftly, Belwin could hardly distinguish one sound from another. He held his breath and gripped the old handle of the door so hard he could feel the blood draining from his knuckles.

After they had passed by, Belwin became aware of another sound faintly echoing down the same hallway. It was the sound of pots and pans. The kitchens were alive once more.

Act I was over? How long had it been over? Belwin cursed again. This was taking too long. He wanted his father out well before the end of the performance. His mind raced, analyzing every possible move from here. If he left his cover now, he would almost certainly run into that small band of people deeper down the corridor, but if he didn't—

More noise came, accompanied by a fresh ensemble of dancing flames sneaking in under the doorway and undulating on the walls. Belwin pressed himself back once more, his breath involuntarily stopping in his lungs. The same band was returning from the direction of the cells, and they were moving quickly, now. Whether by a stroke of incredible luck or by some enchanted favor, Belwin heard a man say, "I'll have all three of them strung up by their fingers for this—probably off eating and drinking."

Belwin deduced the small entourage was returning the way it came having noticed the lack of personnel. Could he be that fortunate?

Inching the door open as quietly as possible, Belwin slipped out. He continued deeper into the corridor, making his way back to the cellars.

Much to his relief, the large room was clear of all the guards. Gated storerooms bordered the edge of the chamber, most of which were filled with large, unmarked barrels. There were stores of dried goods and straw. And there, at the back, was a cell that perfectly resembled the description Wynnie had given him. Yanking a torch off a nearby sconce to light the way, Belwin walked straight for the cell. In the cold, small puffs of white vapor escaped his lips as he crept along. The smell grew increasingly foul as he drew nearer to the darkest depth of the north cellars. Belwin came upon the cell, the one that held his father. He lifted the flame.

The cell was empty.

Then, as soft and as faint as the wisps of his visible breath, the sound of music drifted into the room. Belwin turned to the entrance of the cellars and tipped his head to hear. His gut twisted with the grip of stone-cold panic. Act II had begun and Terveo Rawthorne was nowhere to be found.

CHAPTER 22

FINALE OF FANGS

THE YOUNG PRINCESS, played by Serae, was gone. The princess had transformed into a mature woman. A woman dressed in white who leapt into the light of the stage. The music swelled. She was joined on stage by a troupe of others in identical white costumes.

It was a sad dance, telling the story of what could have been had the princess lived to grow into adulthood. The spectacle consumed Remaine once more. In fact, he was so engrossed in the performance that he did not even notice the sound of clinking armor behind him and the whispered conversation that followed.

"Your Enchanted," bowed High General Cottley. "You summoned me?"

"Yes, Cottley, good," whispered Xietas. "You'll accompany Remaine directly to the ship after this."

"And his sister? She is still upstairs."

"Yes. I'll collect her and bring her down when I come."

The general bowed his head. "My prince."

Remaine was too absorbed in the dance to hear the conversation, but standing within earshot, having just returned from his rotations, was Estin Merchant. Overhearing the exchange between the general and the prince, Estin Merchant slipped out of the balcony as silently and as stealthily as a dock rat from Windluff.

The prince placed his feet up on the footrest before him. Remaine copied him.

Belwin's vision had narrowed onto a singular task: get Serae and get out of Lichenbluff Castle, even if it meant leaving his father behind. He dashed through the lower levels, taking the stairs three at a time. The volume of the music grew louder as he neared the theater. He found a cart, grabbed a tray, loaded it with drinks, and as craftily as he had left, he surreptitiously returned once more to the edges of the darkened room.

While the audience was oblivious to Belwin's departure and return, Diggory saw Belwin come back. Knowing Belwin's return could mean nothing good, Diggory lowered his tray and scanned Belwin's face. Belwin shook his head, signaling more than one meaning. Diggory understood them all. The two began to circulate the room with their trays and when they finally stood shoulder to shoulder, Diggory whispered, "Transferred?"

"Probably."

"Where do you think? Wynnie said he—"

"The ships, perhaps? We might still be able to find him if we leave now, but I won't risk losing—"

"—there's something else," Diggory said.

Belwin looked at his brother.

"Remaine is here," Diggory whispered.

Belwin's jaw muscles tightened. "What do you mean *here*?"

"He's sitting fifty feet above our heads at this exact moment."

Belwin ground his teeth. How could one boy infuriate him so immeasurably? Remaine was like Diggory in that way—smack at the center of every problem. "How do you know?"

"I saw him. And he saw me."

"Did he recognize you?"

"I don't think so."

"And Levo?" Belwin asked.

Diggory shook his head. "No sign."

They stood quietly as the ballet unfolded before them. It had intensified into a dazzling, yet dizzying display of movement. Several performers twirled torches. The dangers of the stunts brought gasps from the audience.

"We need to get out of here," Belwin said to Diggory without turning his head.

"And Remaine?" asked Diggory.

"What about him?"

"Are we to leave him?" Diggory asked.

"He's chosen his path, Diggory," Belwin said, nodding upward. "I won't risk Serae's safety for one more minute, especially not for that wretched boy. Jolly's waiting. We move now."

Diggory's gaze darted quickly around the room calculating their next move. With a final, sheepish glance in Belwin's direction, Diggory slowly nodded and said, "All right…"

Belwin could see his little brother's brilliant mind in motion, his brown eyes searching for answers on the stage, in the audience, somewhere above him.

"Diggory," Belwin said calmly, yet still with a tone as solid and cold as a diamond. "I will not wait for you. Not if it means risking my daughter."

Diggory placed a hand on Belwin's shoulder, "I understand, brother. I will never ask that of you. Go get them. I'll flag down Jolly."

They parted ways. Diggory slid over to the opposite end of the theater, intending to head towards the entrance of Lichenbluff Castle where Jolly would be waiting in queue with the other carriages.

Belwin found the nearest table upon which to abandon his tray of drinks and then, with one last glance at Diggory's disappearing back, Belwin left the theater. His nervous energy propelled him. He spun around quickly, ready to make his move to backstage, and ran headlong into a frazzled red-faced man. The force of the collision knocked the poor man over, sending his spectacles flying through the air.

"JOLLY!" hissed Belwin. "What are you doing over here?! You're supposed to be over there!" He motioned across the auditorium in the direction of Diggory.

"F–f–forgive me, Master Belwin," whimpered Jolly. Belwin helped him to his feet as he dragged Jolly over to a private corner. "I h–h–had to come!"

They both noticed flickers of light at their side. They saw that Jolly wasn't the only thing that had toppled. A table of lit candles had fallen over as well. The flames were spreading.

Belwin launched himself into action. Jolly was right behind. Seizing the tablecloth together, they suffocated the flames.

They hoisted the table back onto its legs, and Belwin eyed his butler carefully. Jolly's face was as pale as parchment—it was both dripping with sweat and a sticky substance that looked like candle wax. Belwin put his hands up to his own face and found his mask melting away too.

He wanted to seize Jolly by the ear and yell at him, but the look on his butler's face stayed his hands. Jolly looked as if he had come face to face with death. "Jolly?"

"There's s–s–something out there, my lord," Jolly said, wringing his hands and wiping the dripping mask off his face. "I saw the carts— *cages*—there must have been thirty or so. They were bringing them down the back—loading them onto the king's ships." Jolly looked up, disoriented. He pointed left, then spun around and pointed in the opposite direction. "Th–that way... I mean *that* way... and—and I saw..." his eyes widened. "I saw Courtier Venerack, my lord, and the other two courtiers. Outside. Not twenty minutes ago."

"Jolly," Belwin said as calmly as he could. "What were they doing?"

But Jolly was unable to finish because a deafening applause thundered from the auditorium. Belwin and Jolly turned back to the archway and saw the audience on their feet. The show was over.

The theater began to buzz with excitement and appreciation for the performance. Remaine Plink was the first to stand on the royal balcony. His hands turned a vivid red as he slammed them together enthusiastically. It was the most beautiful thing he had ever seen. It was different from the stories of his secret perch—a different kind of hero's tale—yet somehow it was still the same—the way the story came to life.

The prince bent down and spoke into his ear, "Remaine, Cottley will escort you to my ship now. There are a few more people I need to speak with. It will take me a little while," the prince rolled his eyes. "Not much fun. Go make yourself comfortable in my quarters. We leave shortly."

At that moment, Serae took the stage to take her bow. Remaine blushed at the sight of her. He wished he could tell her goodbye—he wished she could come with him. Remaine was ushered from his seat into the care of Vector Cottley, which felt like being ushered into the care of an active volcano. The general escorted him down the back staircase of the royal balcony with a heavy hand pressed to Remaine's back. As they neared the bottom of the staircase, Remaine came face to face with two people he would have preferred never to meet again.

Hands clasped behind their backs, the Pellatrim brothers were standing next to two superior guards. Tarquin appeared to have grown yet taller, even in just the last week. Their eyes met. Tarquin's mouth fell open. The sight of Tarquin's surprise gave Remaine the smallest flutter of satisfaction.

At the base of the staircase, they rounded a bend in the large hallway and Remaine could see into the theater through an archway. The glittering audience was still standing, still applauding, and the stage was still awash with bejeweled dancers. As they passed by, Remaine noticed two men standing together. They were peering inside the theater. The smaller one was wringing his white-gloved hands together.

It took only a second for Remaine to recognize them. Jolly. Belwin. And what was all over their faces?

A tingling fire coursed beneath Remaine's skin at the sight of them. He continued to walk calmly alongside Cottley. He purposely looked away from Jolly and Belwin, but his mind was racing. That strange translucent film on their faces? Suddenly he knew. But why were they wearing Wynnie's masks? Why did Jolly look so anxious?

Cottley and Remaine rounded another corner. There was one more staircase ahead of them before they reached the entrance. Remaine's hands began to tremble. Suddenly he feared the worst. This was a mistake. The Rawthornes were going to get themselves into trouble.

"I–I forgot something!" Remaine blurted.

The general gave an annoyed bark. "What?"

"I'll be right back," Remaine said. It was only after the words had spilled out of his mouth that he registered what he had said and realized what his plan was. Without waiting for permission, he tore off in the opposite direction, back to the archway into the auditorium.

When he came upon it, Jolly and Belwin were gone. Remaine scanned the area nervously. They were not outside the auditorium.

He peeked inside where the applause had finally abated and the guests were beginning to stir at their tables, gathering their things.

Then he spotted them. There. At the back of the auditorium, the disguised Belwin and Jolly were moving swiftly but discreetly toward the opposite end of the room. Remaine could hear Cottley coming up behind him. He waited no longer. He took off through the auditorium, winding his way between guests like a dog released from its leash.

"Wait! Belwin!" Remaine said.

Belwin spun on his heels so fast it frightened Remaine. Jolly turned too; his eyes were doubly wide beneath his round glasses. Remaine caught them entirely by surprise. That much was clear on their faces. The rage in Belwin's face was animalistic, but no words escaped his lips. Beneath his disfigured disguise, Belwin's eyes darted up and down so fast, soaking in every inch of the boy. Remaine could only stand still and endure the silent examination.

But time was short. Remaine looked up at the looming figure. "Belwin—I don't know why you're here, but I saw you—your disguise—and I just came to say it's all right—it's just—there's been a misunderstanding—"

Like a snake, Belwin's hand shot out and snatched Remaine's arm. He yanked Remaine into a corner. Remaine's head jerked back. With all the venom of a viper, Belwin hissed, "You have *no* idea what you are talking about, you *fool!*"

A stir in the audience broke Belwin's rage and drew their attention back towards the stage.

"Master Belwin," Jolly whispered. "Look."

The huge doors to the auditorium were slowly closing. Several guards ushered guests back into the room, reassuring them as they did so. Remaine turned. Cottley was in the room. Remaine could see him searching frantically for him. Belwin saw him too. Belwin positioned himself between Remaine and the general. Remaine did not totally understand why, but he allowed himself to be hidden by Belwin. If it meant getting the Rawthornes out before an unnecessary conflict broke out, he would go along with this.

As the doors to the theater thumped shut, a sickening feeling crept into Remaine's stomach. He knew that whatever was happening right now, the prince had not intended for him to be present. He was meant to be climbing aboard the prince's ship right now.

The curtain rose. The murmuring of the audience ceased. The stage, previously filled with the loveliest dancers Remaine had ever seen, held a new cast of characters. At center stage stood Courtiers Orchid, Fiddler, and Venerack. But even the green-skinned Venerack was a sideshow to the creatures positioned beside him like obedient pets.

There were two of them. Pivoting their blocky heads on their thick necks, the enormous lionesses looked around the auditorium slowly, their gaping, black mouths dripping with dark, oily saliva.

At the sight of the creatures, there was a collective gasp from everyone in the room except for Remaine, Jolly, and Belwin. They stood as frozen as the statues in the alcoves. Their attention fell on the other two individuals flanking the lions. Stage left, heads drooped, hands shackled, stood Wynnie Canny and Terveo Rawthorne.

CHAPTER 23

THE BEASTS OF DOROMUND VENERACK

"HOLLOWFIENDS, MY LORDS AND LADIES," boomed Venerack. "Are they not the diamonds of your city? Your strange obsession, here before you in the flesh?"

The room crackled with terror, shock, and confusion. Women placed gloved hands over their hearts or brought them to their painted lips. The men tried to straighten themselves, trying to stand tall, taking their cue from the courtiers. But the sight of the legendary beasts, much larger than the bay lions native to Ravillion Bay, kept them low, grasping the backs of their chairs for support.

"The Ravillion family has known of their whereabouts for some time, but—" Venerack continued and as he did, one of the lions let out a rumbling growl that shook the room. Several guests let out audible gasps. A man fainted; the woman next to him crumbled in her effort to catch him. Remaine saw his mother. She gripped the back of her chair with white knuckles. Hegs watched on, plate and fork in hand. Poor Jileanna struggled to keep her posture, but the rumble from the lion's throat made her and all her ruffles sway like a sapling in the wind.

Venerack tugged at the chain to settle the disgruntled she-lion and continued. "They are, admittedly, quite violent without our presence, so we've kept them safely in the mountains. When we discovered them, not too long ago—we sought their loyalty. We have succeeded in obtaining it."

Suddenly, both monsters roared. The sound was so loud it sent half the room into a crouching position, hands over their ears. Jileanna completely tipped over. Even Courtiers Orchid and Fiddler grimaced.

"Not to worry, though, as long as I am here, and Prince Xietas, of course," Venerack's gaze turned towards the balcony staircase where a few paces from Remaine, the prince calmly descended. "No harm will come to any of you."

The nobility of Ravillion Bay made a valiant attempt to regain control of their nerves. Now that the lions had been acknowledged, everyone's attention turned first to the prince, then to Terveo and Wynnie.

"As one of the ancient beasts of Cracklemore, the Hollowfiend carries a gift—an ability—in its blood: into the flesh of its prey, the beast injects a disarming poison. Animals are paralyzed. Humans, though," Venerack paused and muttered something to the lioness on his left and she turned her square head towards Terveo, snarling. "Humans become completely defenseless. They cannot move. *And...* they cannot lie."

Belwin took a step forward.

Venerack jerked his pointy beard, and the lions nudged the prisoners forward into the light. "Behold. Terveo Rawthorne and Wynnie Canny. Traitors to the Ravillion rule and all the Cracklemore Isles. Insurrectionists. Conspirators against the royal family. Perpetrators of the collapse of our world as we know it."

The crowd stirred in discomfort—exchanging glances, adjusting wigs, covering mouths. It was as if a legion of Venerack's spiders had crawled into the room, creeping up backs and into shoes. Hegs picked daintily at his food. It was not the quantity of food he was consuming that was the marvel, although judging by the number of plates at the table it was a spectacular amount. Instead, it was, rather, the way he ate that was the wonder. Hegs was taking the tiniest, most diminutive bites, one after another in rapid succession, each perfectly speared on a delicate fork.

"Some people prove powerfully resistant against the charm of the lion," continued the Master of Beasts. It was obvious Terveo was the one of whom he spoke. "Others, however, are not so strong."

It happened quickly. The monster nearest Wynnie opened its massive jaw and snapped it like a trap on Wynnie's right leg. Wynnie's face looked frantic, but her form froze stiff. She managed to emit a blood curdling scream that was matched by shrieks of terror in the audience. Two more people fainted, dropping limply into their chairs. Remaine winced. He clapped both hands over his mouth.

"Tell us, Miss Canny, with whom are you allied?"

Wynnie screamed. Her voice was pitiful as she replied, "Terveo Rawthorne."

"Yes," said Venerack calmly. "I am aware. I saw you that night in the dungeon. And?"

"B–Belwin Rawthorne."

Belwin took another step forward, this time with more intent, yet he still kept himself in the shadows.

"Yes, I am aware of him too... and no doubt his brother, Diggory?"

Tears streamed down Wynnie's face. "Yes."

"Any others?" asked Venerack.

"D–Dasko Rawthorne," she moaned.

"Interesting. So, both old men have spurned Colony Gardens."

Several people gasped at this information as well.

"Years ago," asserted Prince Xietas, "Belwin Rawthorne was healed from the early onset of Frostblood."

Whispers hissed around the room like geysers.

"A rare sight. But it dawned on me, just this past week, *how* he did it. Miss Canny, where is the—"

"ENOUGH!"

The shout bellowed from two different locations. The king's court and the prince looked up, confused. Terveo had shouted the word, that much was certain. Belwin's identical objection, issued at the exact same instant, forced everyone to squint into the darkness, peering for the source. Even Terveo leaned forward, searching for the other who had belted out the same word.

Belwin stepped into the light, but not before shooting a pointed look towards Diggory who, like a magician, ducked his head and vanished into the crowd.

"Enough," Belwin said coolly.

"Hello, Viscount," said Venerack, seemingly unaffected by Belwin's presence. "Well I suppose you wouldn't be viscount, would you? The title still belongs to your father, who hasn't gone east afterall. No. He's been hiding out here, plotting his schemes." Venerack gave a small chuckle. "Your father fights the Hollowfiend with surprising strength… but we have learned enough about your cause to know you… and your brother, too—I assume he's around here somewhere?—would, predictably, try to rescue the man who knows the most."

"Your issue is with me and my father," said Belwin, moving slowly forward. He held his hands out in front of him to suppress an escalation.

"Yes, as I said before, I am aware of this," the courtier said. The lioness near Terveo let out a dangerous warning growl. "But what I'm here to discover is just how deep into the soil the roots of this plot go, and how widely those roots have spread."

Courtier Hoaras Fiddler wrinkled his smooth face with intensity, and hollered, "Your prince has alluded to your recovery, Viscount Rawthorne. How long have you been in possession of the Valigold?"

At that moment, to everyone's surprise, the lioness moaned heavily and painfully. Abruptly her jaws released Wynnie's leg. The massive beast toppled over. It was only then that the light of the chandelier illuminated what had happened when it sparkled off the shiny blade sticking out from the monster's neck.

The other beast roared furiously at Belwin who was standing on a chair, his hand still outstretched from the throw of the dagger.

"Choose your next move carefully, Rawthorne!" Venerack cried, enraged. Remaine watched wide-eyed as Serae was ushered onto the stage, captured in the grasp of Lyme Stretcher, his cobra-like grip tightening with every step.

Venerack motioned for the remaining beast to move towards Serae. The beast flicked its long tail and locked its gaze on the girl. Fiddler and Orchid sidestepped nervously.

Wynnie, struggling to rise up, protested at the sight of Serae. "No! NO! Please, please—I'll tell you what you want to—"

She did not get a chance to finish. A second blade whizzed through the air, burying itself deep into the second lion's neck. In the next breath, Diggory stepped on to the stage, and hurled yet a third dagger. This one was aimed at Doromund Venerack.

The room exploded in panic. Several things happened all at once.

As the Master of Beasts parried the blade, he stumbled backwards, tripping over one of the lifeless lions and knocking Orchid and Fiddler down with him. Belwin launched himself over the tables and towards the stage. The prince too sprang into action, throwing people aside as he made his way.

Amidst the confusion, General Cottley spotted Remaine. He charged through the crowd like a rhinoceros. Jolly saw him coming and grabbed Remaine's wrist, pulling him in the opposite direction.

As they ran, Remaine saw Diggory fling yet another dagger in the direction of Venerack. The dagger surprised the courtier—there was something about the precision of the throw, the way it had almost swirled through the air on its own. The blade planted itself in Venerack's shoulder. He let out a terrible scream and fell back to the ground.

 In the commotion, Diggory managed to seize Wynnie, pulling her into the shadows of the stage before pivoting and launching himself at Lyme Stretcher, who, in order to defend himself, was forced to release Serae.

Stretcher faced Diggory and reached into his robes to produce a lantern. He swung it high. A blinding flash of light exploded on the stage. Screams ripped through the room.

The shockwave was enough to give Belwin pause, but only for a second. He kept scrambling over chairs and tables until he finally reached the stage. He motioned to his father. "Give me your hand!"

Diggory was on Stretcher now, tackling him to the ground. The lantern crashed. Tiny sparks of flame like buzzing bees from a hive escaped, spilling out onto the stage or flying up into the curtains. Little fires began to grow.

"Serae!" Belwin shouted. "Follow Wynnie!"

Serae heard him. Her eyes grew even wider. "Watch out!" she screamed.

It was just enough of a warning for Belwin to duck and dodge a spear flying through the air in his direction. It stuck into the stage right by where Belwin stood. He looked up. The prince was coming for him. The prince's face was hardened with focus. Unsheathed, his longsword was in his hand.

In a burst of boldness, Remaine shouted. "Prince Xietas, wait!"

This was enough to give the prince pause. In genuine shock, he turned to see Remaine far behind him near the back of the auditorium, as well as Cottley advancing on him from the side. In a roar of fury, the prince changed course and shouted to the general. "THE BOY!"

The tiny sparks buzzing around the room had coalesced and the fire was spreading.

Several more screams erupted, and chaos ensued as the nobility of Ravillion Bay descended upon the doors to the auditorium, forcing them to open.

Jolly guided Remaine right into the current, and they were swept up in a river of silk and fur, pearls and diamonds, and a growing cloud of black smoke. Some distance behind them, Cottley and Xietas fought their way towards Jolly and Remaine. Remaine caught a brief glimpse of Duke Hegs dragging Fortis Plink and Jileanna away in the opposite direction.

The fire was an accident, but Belwin could not have planned a better screen to separate his weakened father and him from the three courtiers. They strained to get back onto their feet. Venerack was in obvious pain. Orchid was decidedly disheveled. Fiddler was wiping blood from underneath his long smooth nose.

Belwin yanked his father in the opposite direction of the king's court, but just as they began to move, Terveo Rawthorne was ripped from Belwin's arms by an unseen force. Terveo floated upward.

The smoke from the fire had fallen under a charm. It gathered together into the shape of a hazy rope. The rope coiled itself around Terveo Rawthorne's entire body. In the grip of the smoke, Terveo floated back to Venerack. Orchid and Fiddler stared, fixated on the charmed smoke they had summoned. A separate wave of the smoke pushed Diggory back, away from Lyme Stretcher, and over to Venerack. Within seconds, both Terveo's and Diggory's throats were each in the grasp of Venerack's hands. The enormous macaw's wingspan was stretched wide embracing the entire scene.

The room behind Belwin quickly emptied, leaving him standing, frozen among the flames. Lyme Stretcher scowled at the Rawthornes.

Then, eyeing the flames with a horror of his own, he slithered away into the darkness beyond the fire.

Suddenly the world slowed down. Belwin could feel every beat of his heart pounding in his chest. He felt his breath whirl in his lungs like a windstorm. Every bead of sweat left a trail of icy cold as it ran down his face before it evaporated in the heat.

Despite the growing heat of flames, no one moved. Venerack stood stoically, patiently—choking the life from Terveo and Diggory. Spiders crawled from Venerack's sleeves onto the Rawthornes' faces. Venerack was unhurried, unworried. He knew that in moments, both men would be dead and, with the help of Rima Orchid and Hoaras Fiddler, he would have little trouble capturing Belwin.

It was Terveo who moved first. He brought his old hands up to his neck. Was it an attempt to loosen Venerack's grip? Even as his face turned blue, Terveo's fingers found their way to the old pendant hanging around his neck. With a final burst of strength, he ripped the chain from his neck and flung it into the air. The locket arched high. It landed on the stage, breaking open. The shining Cat's Candle burst from its chamber and rolled to Diggory's dangling feet.

It worked. In pure shock, Orchid and Fiddler lost their grip on the charmed smoke and Venerack suddenly strained with the weight of the two Rawthornes he held suspended. The strength of his grip lessened.

"The Valigold!" sputtered Fiddler. "*He's had it all along!*"

"Run!" Terveo bellowed, his voice hoarse.

Diggory gave a great, heavy kick. Simultaneously he launched the Cat's Candle across the stage and freed himself from Venerack's grip.

The Master of Beasts returned to his senses. The flames in the room reflected in his dark eyes. Venerack wasted no more time. With a sharp whistle, four beastly spiders scurried from the sleeves of his robe and pounced onto Terveo Rawthorne. They quickly found bare flesh in which to sink their deadly venom.

Belwin and Diggory both felt the blood drain from their faces as they watched the life drain from their father's.

Had Terveo Rawthorne's last words not been a command, the sudden horror of the sight of their father's death might have brought the Rawthorne brothers to their knees in sorrow. But somehow, in a split second of clarity, Diggory grabbed the Cat's Candle and disappeared into the curtains, just as Belwin baubled the flaming curtain nearest him to collapse onto the members of the king's court. The fire escalated. In opposite directions, the Rawthorne brothers fled.

Remaine's nose burned with the smells of sooty smoke, sweet perfume, and wine-saturated breath as Jolly led him through the crowd. Smiling, nodding, bowing, gently tapping them on the shoulders— Jolley uttered sincere apologies to every person he passed.

"Jolly! Hurry!" Remaine interjected impatiently as the butler's civilities began to cloud the task at hand. Jolly apologized once more, this time to Remaine. They darted into an empty hallway.

Shouts a few paces back told them the prince and Cottley were not far behind.

"Jolly!" Remaine shouted, stopping dead in his tracks. "Go! You get out of here. I'll go to the prince. I'll ask him to stop all this."

Jolly appeared profoundly confused at this.

"Of course, that won't do at all, Master Plink," he said, shoving Remaine further down the hallway, shuttling him away from the crowds. Jolly insisted they pick up the pace. Remaine kept up, running to another intersection, adorned with enormous tapestries on the wall depicting a snow-covered mountain side and spiky pines, all beneath the wash of a white moon. It was a night like tonight and soon, Remaine thought, it would all be in flames.

"Uh… let's see now, Master Plink." Jolly squinted left and right, trying to decide the best route. "Well… if that's north back there, then we'd want to take a… left. Let's go!"

They ran down one hallway, then another, then came around one more corner, and in one of those strange, inexplicable strokes of fate where fortune smiles, they ran head-long into a breathless Diggory Rawthorne.

"Remaine!" Diggory blurted out, eyes wide. "Jolly!" A strange, oily, opaque film hung in torn sheets around Diggory's cheeks. What had once been his mask was nearly gone.

"Master Diggory!" Jolly beamed, clapping.

"You didn't see where Belwin went…" Diggory's eyes darted around, working to solve a complex problem. "Did you tell Belwin where you left the carriage?"

"I did, my lord."

"Good. He'll be after Serae and Wynnie. He'll take them there." Diggory put his hands on his knees in an attempt to control his heavy breathing.

"If we hurry, my lord, we—"

But the sound of heavy footfall approaching from the adjacent hallway behind them stopped Jolly. He looked at Remaine in panic who in turn looked at Diggory in desperation. Remaine felt sick to his core—his sister was right—the Ravillions couldn't be trusted.

"Come. This way." Diggory turned on his heel and the three of them took off down another passage.

For better or worse, their route was chosen for them. At every turn, Diggory brought them to a halt, peered around the corner and, at the sight of panicked crowds or roaring flames, he would point to the opposite hallway. Deeper and deeper into Lichenbluff Castle they fled.

One hallway was so thick with smoke they were forced down a flight of stairs. At his first sight of the lower level, Remaine suddenly recognized where he was. He knew the kitchens were close.

The sounds of their boots clopped along as they ran. They kept their sights set on a door at the end of the hallway that they knew would lead outside. Just as they neared the door, it swung open. Two, caged creatures were right there.

The lions growled and swatted at their cage. Their paws reached for the surrounding guards. Neither the lions nor the guards noticed Diggory as he brought Jolly and Remaine to a dead stop behind him. "Shh."

"The place is on fire!" one guard shouted.

"You heard him!" barked the other. "He said send in two to hunt for anyone trying to escape!"

The first guard looked genuinely pained at the idea of releasing the monsters into the smoke-filled hallway, but the other man paid no attention. With the clanking of a lock and the swift sound of sliding metal, the cage door was released. The lions took off in the only direction they could go—into the heart of Lichenbluff Castle.

But Remaine only caught a glimpse of this over his shoulder because Diggory was already pushing them back up the stairs. The sight of the lions turned Remaine's blood cold. He could still feel the growls vibrating in his feet from that first time he had heard the beasts roaring when he and the prince were in the Crack in Time. A sickening thought gripped Remaine.

"Diggory!" Remaine shouted, catching up alongside him. He could not help himself. He had to bring them to a stop once more. "Diggory! Levo's here! He's unconscious! Upstairs!"

Diggory's otherwise tanned face became ghastly pale and shiny with sweat.

"Where, Remaine? Where exactly is he?"

"The prince's chambers. He was asleep before we came down."

Diggory looked around, desperate for another choice, but they already knew what they had to do. Turning once more, Diggory led them higher into the castle.

The south end of Lichenbluff Castle was up in flames, but the north end that faced the Bay remained untouched by the fire, though that was quickly changing. They climbed up staircases void of people, but slowly filling with smoke.

They made their way to the gallery hallway and Remaine led them to the same doors he had walked through just a few hours ago with the prince. Diggory pressed his hands to the lock. Then he fumbled under his apron for his sword. Finding the hilt, he gave the handle a twist and the door unlocked. Diggory, Remaine, and Jolly burst into the prince's chambers. Much to their relief they found Levo lying there, still sleeping, unphased by the chaos in the castle.

Diggory wasted no time. He tried to wake the sleeping giant. When several slaps to the face and a few flicks to the ear failed, he simply lifted Levo's eyelids. "I don't think he's *just* asleep," he said quietly. "He's—" Diggory looked at the bedside table and saw the small bottle of liquid Stretcher had administered to Levo.

"They've been keeping him unconscious," said Diggory.

"Stretcher told me he had lost too much blood," Remaine said, indicating the bandaged area where the lioness had torn into Levo.

Diggory bent down to examine the wound.

"Maybe," said Diggory. "But not enough to warrant this much sleep." Diggory looked up at Remaine. "They wanted you to see him like this," he said quietly, "but they didn't want you talking to him. They wanted you to think they were fighting to keep him alive, Remaine. But Levo's been ready to wake up for days now."

"We need to find a stimulant of some kind," Jolly said.

Remaine stood motionless, feeling useless and painfully guilty, as Diggory and Jolly rummaged about the large chamber looking for something that might do the trick.

"Ah! Here, my lord," Jolly said optimistically, eyeing another small bottle which he found in a crystal cabinet near the washbasin. "A drop or two would safely bring him around within a few hours I imagine, but perhaps—"

"Give him a few swigs, Jolly," Diggory said. "He looks parched anyway."

Diggory propped up Levo's large, red head with his left hand, and used his other hand to pry open his mouth. Jolly did his best to be neat, but the whole thing was rather slapdash; liquid poured both in Levo's mouth and down his cheeks. Then Remaine heard a noise. Down the hall, behind them, came a sound that only a few hours ago, Remaine had told himself he might not hear again for a very long time.

Remaine's eyes grew wide. With a furrowed brow, Diggory looked back over his shoulder at Remaine. Remaine did not wait for permission. In a blink he was out the door, running down the hall.

"Silome? Silome!"

They ran headlong into each other coming around the same corner. They toppled to the ground.

They both sat up, rubbing their heads. Estin was there too. He helped them stand.

"Remaine, what are you doing up here!" shouted his sister.

"Me?!" he shouted back. "What are—"

"The big troll locked me up here when we arrived!" she yelled, as if it had been Remaine's fault. "Estin got me out. We came to find you, but now the whole place is up in flames and filled with smoke and—"

The sight of Estin, there with his sister, was sinking in. For his entire childhood, the two of them together had always been the most normal thing in his world. The one never went anywhere without the other. But things had changed when Estin joined the guard. Silome didn't like to talk about it.

"Estin?"

"Yes, sorry," Silome said with an irritated shake of her head. "He's with us."

Estin pulled Remaine in for a hug, giving him a pathetic sort of smile. "Sorry, Rem. You really threw everything off when you came aboard the *Egg*."

Remaine's blood began to boil. "You told *him* all your secrets but not your little brother?"

"Remaine! Now? Really? Let's just get out of here and I'll explain it all later."

A loud cough echoed from the end of the hall.

"Come on," Remaine said. He led them back to the others.

They came upon a scene similar to the one Remaine had left, except now Levo was on his side, retching loudly into a bowl. Diggory held Levo's head and Jolly held the bowl.

"Oh, let it spill on the bloody floor, Jolly!" roared Levo, launching more vomit, intentionally missing the bowl and aiming for the prince's rug.

Jolly could not bear the mess, even if it would all be up in flames soon enough. He held the bowl with resolve, dabbing at Levo's mouth with a rag.

Levo's eyes were closed tightly, and his face was vivid red, twisted in pain. The sight of it, oddly enough, was comforting to Remaine, just to know Levo was well.

Diggory looked up. "Silome! Estin!"

They both jumped in to help Levo. Within seconds Silome was holding a cool rag to Levo's forehead. "We can't stay here much longer," she said quietly.

Jolly flashed uneasy, anxious glances in Estin's direction. "Hello there," he said, still holding the bowl under Levo's chin. "I'm Jolly."

"Heard good things. I'm Estin."

"We need Levo mobile," Diggory said resolutely. "We can't carry him downstairs—not with the fire."

"Can you both bauble him?" asked Silome, her eyes darting between Jolly and Diggory.

Diggory looked doubtful. "He'll need to help us out a bit." Then he glanced at Silome. "Where's yours?"

"Windluff," she spat. "The big brute dragged us aboard his ship before I had a chance to grab it."

"Sorry I couldn't warn you Cottley was coming," said Estin. "I've been at the prince's side constantly, looking for Remaine."

"MERCHANT!" Cottley's voice boomed from the hallway as if saying his name had summoned him.

"Quickly!" Diggory urged. "Get him up! Up, up! Levo, come on!"

But it was too late. The hulking silhouette of High General Cottley with a hungry lion at his side filled the doorway. Behind them stood both Pellatrim brothers flanked by two other higher ranked guards.

Tarquin did his best to scowl, but it was clear he was terrified by the lion he was forced to stand beside. He managed to jeer, "Told you I saw Merchant come this way with that dock rat!"

"Traitor," breathed Cottley, burning holes into the back of Estin's head with his gaze.

Estin took a deep breath. He closed his eyes and turned around to face the monstrous man. "General," he said calmly. But no amount of negotiating could block the swift blade now descending upon Estin's head. Faster than a blink, Estin unsheathed his sword and parried the blow, transforming before their eyes into an animal-like predator, crouched low, ready for anything.

Cottley readied himself then said smoothly to both the beast at his side and the men behind him: "Get them."

The lioness leapt through the air just as Cottley thrust his blade towards Estin. Estin dodged the general's sword with ease and was prepared to dodge the lion as well, but the lion leapt past Estin, landing lightly on the smooth floor just once then leapt again in the direction of Diggory.

Having already transitioned Levo's weak head into Silome's hands, Diggory was prepared. He stood with his sword crossed in front of his body, ready to defend his friends from the monster. The lioness eyed the blade with her green eyes. With a paw as big as a frying pan, she took a swipe at the blade. Diggory tipped the blade edgewise and slid it along her flesh. It cut with ease. The beast snarled and struck once more. Vector Cottley advanced on Estin. The clash of foes rang through the room like a lightning storm. Levo hurled like thunder into Jolly's trembling bowl.

For whatever reason, the lioness suddenly turned her gaze to Remaine. She pounced.

Remaine flew backwards. From his back he stared up into the black mouth of the monster as she drooled oily saliva onto his face.

By some miracle, his hands managed to find the dagger on his belt. He held it up.

At the sight of the blade, the lion reared back, snarling.

Remaine understood at once. It was the emerald. The emerald on the blade matched the emerald on the prince's sword; it was the same color as the monster's eyes, it was the same color as the skin of Venerack, and it was the same color as the Monkeywood witches. The emerald gave the blade a charm of control against the Hollowfiends.

"The prince was controlling the lion in the cave the whole time," said Remaine, his eyes glazing over with tears. The lion stepped back. Her eyes remained fixed on the dagger. "You were right, Diggory," he said, "the prince wanted me to think he was protecting me—protecting Levo... but he wasn't... he was commanding the attack the whole time."

High General Cottley and his men watched the lioness and Remaine. Diggory held his ground.

"Can you tell it to turn around?" shrieked Silome. "Tell it to get away from us!"

Remaine held up the knife. Nothing.

The high general laughed. "They might answer to the prince, boy, but not to you. Looks like that blade keeps her back at best, but she still knows her orders."

No one had noticed Tarquin Pellatrim slowly sneaking around the perimeter of the room. Truthfully, Tarquin did not have a plan, really, but at the sight of Remaine slowly distancing himself from the lion, he seized the opportunity. Lunging at Remaine, knocking him to the ground, Tarquin snatched the blade.

"Remaine!" Silome shouted, reaching out and yanking Remaine by the arm.

There they were. The prince's men and the lion stood on one side of the room and on the opposite side Diggory and Silome, with Estin, Jolly and Remaine behind them, guarding the still struggling Levo. Diggory tossed Silome another small dagger. The two of them stood like a bladed barrier in the space between.

Launching himself at Estin, the general made the first move. The lioness jumped at Diggory and Silome. Tarquin and Torrin and the two other guards lunged at Remaine and Jolly.

But it was Levo's turn to move. With all the anger of a bear woken too early from his slumber, Levo was barbaric. With his huge hands, he seized a heavy marble bust from the nearby table and brought it crashing down on the first two soldiers who had approached his bed. He knocked them out cold, leaving the Pellatrims wide-eyed.

Levo tried to rise to his feet, but instantly he began to collapse. Jolly and Remaine caught him, barely keeping themselves upright under his weight.

"Master Chince, sir," Jolly's face was as red as a cherry and the veins on his forehead and in his neck were as thick as rigging. He fought to hold Levo upright. "Why don't you drain this sunshine juice and rise and shine for good?" He thrust the last of the bottle into Levo's mouth. Levo choked it down. It was enough to rouse him. He shook his head and took in the small war that was taking place in the room.

Furniture toppled; wine bottles shattered. There were blood stains on the floor. Blood dripped from the lion's paw, from Diggory's leg, and from Estin's forearm.

Torrin poked his head out of the door and coughed. "General! The fire's moving up! We're trapped!"

The same marble bust that had been used to fell the two guards flew through the air again, straight into Cottley's neck. The behemoth general toppled with a crash.

Estin looked in shock at Levo, who gave him a drowsy salute.

It was Remaine who saw in the window their only means of escape. As the battle raged behind him, he burst onto the balcony, searching for a way down. The steep rooflines of Lichenbluff Castle, made even more treacherous in the icy covering of the snow fall, hung quietly, menacingly on every side. But compared to the flames roaring down the hallway and licking at the doorway behind him, Remaine knew this was their only choice.

"Diggory!" Remaine shouted. He turned to see Diggory deliver a nearly deadly blow to the lion's ribs. She howled as she retreated, giving Diggory, Levo, Silome, Estin, and Jolly a chance to meet Remaine on the balcony. The waters of Ravillion Bay lay below them like a black mouth waiting to eat every flake of the delicate snow fall. The royal fleet was almost directly beneath them too.

"Let's go," Diggory breathed, without hesitation. He was first over, finding his footing as carefully as possible on the slanted surface. Meanwhile, Levo and Estin barricaded the balcony's entrance with one of the couches, buying what time they could.

One by one they followed Diggory off the balcony and down the roofline. Jolly, Remaine, Levo, Silome, and finally Estin. Just as they all cleared the balcony, their pursuers broke through. From his perch on the slanted roof, Remaine watched in horror as the lion, obedient to death, leapt from the balcony in their direction. The force of her jump met the snow-kissed roof like water on ice. Her massive paws could find no footing. She slid, plummeting to her death.

Diggory, Jolly, and Levo used their baubles to help their boots find purchase in the snow. They scurried along, helping the others, increasing the distance between themselves and Cottley and the Pellatrims who, judging by their own fear of the task at hand, would have a much more difficult time getting down.

Slipping occasionally, but like rats on the run, the six of them scurried as quickly as they could down the steep angles of Lichenbluff

Castle. They kept moving, the encroaching smoke filling their nostrils and stinging their eyes. The white world of Ravillion Bay drank in the color. Suddenly every roof of every building and every snow-covered rock on the hillside glowed bright orange. Down they climbed. Down the snow fell, swirling. From balcony to balcony, roofline to roofline, Diggory led the four of them to the foundation of the castle. They came at last to their final descent. They dropped one last time, landing at the top of a cobblestone staircase whose bottom emptied out onto the pier at the base of the cliff. Just one more staircase to go.

They were halfway down the steps. They had only a rough potential of a plan—more of an idea than a plan—in their minds. Just as they arrived at the pier, the sound of Prince Xietas' voice echoed. It bounced off the water, even rising to reverberate above the roar of the burning castle.

"Remaine! Stop!"

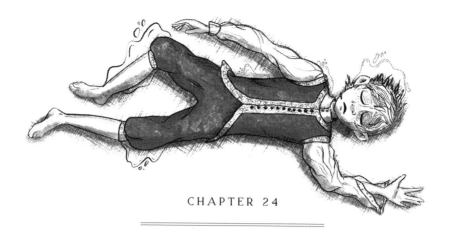

CHAPTER 24

THE GREAT CHARMING

THEY WERE ALMOST THERE. The waters of the bay sloshed below them. The ships were moored dead ahead, just there at the foot of the stairs. One by one they each stopped and turned around.

At the top of the stone stairs, in the softness of the tranquil snowfall but backlit by the menacing orange of flames and the dense gray of smoke, Prince Xietas looked down at them. "And Estin… Estin Merchant," said the prince. "I'm disappointed in you…"

Diggory cut through.

"Come," he whispered urgently, extending a hand to Remaine. "Move."

Remaine took a step down. He froze at the sight of Lyme Stretcher, suddenly appearing there at the bottom, aboard the causeway to the first of the ships. Stretcher pulled back the cover from a large, grated cube. Inside writhed a massive, tattered tangle of patchy fur. The animals were so closely smashed together in the cage that it was difficult to tell where one lioness began and the other ended.

"Remaine Plink!" The voice of Courtier Hoaras Fiddler called out. The silhouettes of the other members of the king's court appeared next to the prince.

"His Enchanted, Prince Xietas, sees in you the key to the kingdom." Fiddler's words hung strangely in the air, drifting slowly down with the snow.

Remaine blinked.

"I, however," said Fiddler, "as a sworn student of the histories and prophecies… advisor of such to His High Enchanted, King Ignis Ravillion, am not so sure."

The hulking frame of Vector Cottley, followed by the Pellatrim brothers, stepped into view as though birthed from the fire and smoke. By some miracle, although they were disheveled and they had their scrapes, it seemed they had managed to descend the castle roofs safely as well.

"We intend to discover the truth, Remaine," said Fiddler. He reached into his robes, but the prince stayed his hand.

"Wait," said Prince Xietas. "Wait a moment longer."

The prince descended a step, then another. Both groups stood motionless, too afraid to move.

"Remaine, there's nowhere to run." The prince's brow was raised with the same look of deep empathy he had given him many times prior. His voice was smooth as he continued. "Others have stolen you away before—forced your hand to evade me, to escape from a nonexistent danger. But now it's your choice."

The prince kept his words calm, his delivery even. Remaine hardly noticed him stepping closer as he spoke. "The prophecy *is* about you. The Cracklemore Isles *need* you. Your family, *my* family, the court—*they* need you. They will all come to know it in time, in a way they never imagined."

He took another step. The closer he got, the more clearly Remaine could see his face. He was no longer a shadow or a silhouette; he was the prince of Cracklemore, the Chosen Winged Warrior and, perhaps, still a friend. "*I* will need you, Remaine. But you are not yet ready for the task. You must let me help you."

"Remaine," said Diggory. Diggory's voice was weak and tired compared to the prince's confident voice, but Remaine could hear the pleading tone of warning it carried. "Don't." Diggory reached his hand up the stairs in Remaine's direction. Then his eyes widened. He froze, his gaze transfixed behind Remaine. General Cottley pushed past the court descending the wide staircase with purpose. He pushed past the prince, who stood as still as a statue with his arm also extended toward Remaine.

"Come with me, and this will end peacefully." Remaine could see that the prince's face was lined with desperation.

Remaine pressed his back against the cliff wall as the mammoth general bypassed him. Single-mindedly, Cottley headed towards Diggory, who drew his blade in defense.

"Wait!" said Remaine.

"No!" Levo shouted from farther below at the exact same moment, taking a step in Diggory's direction.

"Ah, ah, ah!" cautioned Stretcher, threatening to unlock the cage.

Cottley advanced. Diggory was quick, but the brute force of the general, like an avalanche unleashed, shoved Diggory up against the wall. The general disarmed Diggory with one hand as he simultaneously pressed his massive forearm against Diggory's throat.

Remaine's breath was painfully shallow as he looked around, unsure of what to do, where to go. But what could he do? He looked at the prince imploringly. If he took his hand, would it all end?

Courtier Fiddler made a move. He rushed down the staircase, passing Remaine without so much as a blink in Remaine's direction. He too approached Diggory. Diggory began to spasm and contort his body, desperate to get free. But it was futile. Cottley's strength, plus the return of the Fiddler's charmed smoke, restrained him fully.

In one swift motion, Fiddler reached into Diggory's coat pocket. His face suddenly illuminated in the gold glow of the Cat's Candle. "At last," he breathed. "We have the Valigold."

Diggory's head sank with regret. Fiddler held the prize up cradling it delicately.

"You have no idea what this is, do you?" Fiddler inquired sincerely.

Diggory didn't respond.

Fiddler turned away. He looked toward Venerack and nodded. Venerack gave a whistle. The lions roared in response. Stretcher unlocked the cage.

Throwing themselves at the cage door, half a dozen hungry she-lions, clawing, snarling, burst out. They exploded down the ship's rampart, streamed across the stone dock, and tore up the stairs. Levo, Silome, and Estin squatted in defense, shielding Jolly behind them.

Silome screamed. Her terror robbed Remaine of his breath. He looked to see Silome's ribs, lodged in the jaws of one of the lions. Estin launched himself to free her, but a second lion bit down on his thigh. He screamed too.

Remaine's feet left the ground. His body was tossed onto the shoulder of Prince Xietas. With nothing but the sight of Silome and the sound of her scream in his head, Remaine kicked wildly against the prince and pounded his fists on the prince's back.

The prince carried him as though he was carrying a little child with a tantrum. They passed Fiddler.

Time slowed, and Remaine's eyes were drawn to the Cat's Candle. There it was, held perfectly aloft in Fiddler's smooth hand.

Hardly thinking, gaze locked on the little source of light, Remaine acted on an instinct he didn't know he had and swiped at the Cat's Candle just as the prince carried him by.

The little ball of light shot into the air so fast that the courtier did not realize what had happened until the golden light was sinking into the waters of Ravillion Bay.

Shocked, Fiddler screamed. This startled Cottley. He loosened his grip on Diggory who, by some miracle, was ready to take advantage of the opportunity. Falling to his knees, Diggory grabbed his blade and swiped viciously at the prince's legs. Xietas crumpled. Remaine dropped to the ground.

Cottley's eyes blazed. He drew his sword. With venomous speed, he swung his blade across Diggory's belly. The wound was grievous. Diggory cried out, yet at the same moment, he launched himself like a cat in Remaine's direction. He grabbed Remaine and pulled him off the edge of the staircase with him. Together they tumbled into the water.

The cold slap of the bay hit Remaine. It was like the bewilderment of waking up from a nightmare, only this time, it was the panic of plunging into one. The icy waves had the double effect of both shocking him awake while also threatening to make him unconscious. But somewhere in his body, Plink blood began to pump. Before his mind could think, he began to swim up to the surface. He was vaguely aware of Diggory holding on to him desperately, relying on Remaine for help. Remaine kicked with such force he was afraid he might further injure Diggory. Then, with a great spray of water, they surfaced. They each took a sharp inhalation of the icy, northern air.

It was a tenuous achievement. Almost instantly, they started to sink as Diggory began to fade. Remaine kicked furiously, fighting to keep them afloat.

Then, somewhere in the chaos, another set of hands slid under Diggory's arms and worked with Remaine to hold Diggory up. It was Jolly. He must have jumped in right after Diggory and Remaine hit the water. Together they kicked against the rolling waves of the bay. The sky above them was alive with flames, the water below them was as black as midnight. They made their way to the soaring rock wall above them, clinging to the slick rock by their fingertips. They could not last long.

Suddenly Jolly's face began to glow. Remaine spat out icy water and screwed up his eyes at the sight. Jolly's spectacles, barely hanging on to his round nose, grew brighter with a little turquoise light, then a pink one, then an orange. Three darting lights reflected in the lenses. Only when they stopped, briefly, did Remaine notice they were little minnows.

Overhead, shouts of protest drew his attention. With the help of the lions, and Lyme Stretcher, Vector Cottley had overtaken Estin. He was dragging the rogue guard along the dock towards one of the ships.

"Silome!" cried Estin. "Help my mother! Don't let them—"

Just then they saw Levo leap from the staircase, a blood-soaked Silome in his arms.

As if suspended by puppet strings, the two of them froze, midair.

Remaine gasped and choked on another swallow of water.

The three courtiers held them. Silome screamed in pain. Levo cursed in frustration. They were unable to drop into the water. Then the water around Remaine began to lift taking Remaine along with it. Lyme Stretcher and the prince were drawing him back too!

"M–my blade," coughed Diggory. "J–Jolly." Diggory grabbed the rock wall and winced as he fought to give Jolly a free hand.

Jolly understood. He squinted his eyes shut and with a gloved hand that was trembling violently, Jolly clutched at his jacket pocket.

Remaine heard ringing metal. Diggory's blade, still on the steps, flew on its own, slicing across Fiddler's legs as it sailed past.

The courtier shrieked as Diggory's cutlass fell into the water.

Remaine dropped. Levo and Silome dropped.

With his free hand, Remaine grabbed Diggory's sword before it could sink.

They were all kicking together, treading the black water. Remaine knew it would only be minutes before Diggory and Silome faded.

The glowing fish returned. They darted behind Remaine.

"P–Pua!" coughed Diggory.

Three fish turned into thousands before Remaine had time to fully understand exactly what was going on. He felt a lightness in his body as the minnows surrounded them, buoying them along, carrying them away from the wall.

THE GREAT CHARMING

Lichenbluff Castle roared like a mountain on fire. Mingling with the snow a steady cascade of ash sifted down upon them.

A rocky spire in the water caught the light from the fire. Remaine nearly burst into tears as Pua, aboard a small rowboat, rounded the spire, her large, tattooed hand outstretched.

More splashes came from behind.

Remaine whirled. Three lions launched themselves into the water. Their vast, square heads bobbed in the blackness as they paddled towards the group.

"Hurry!" shouted Pua, helping to pull each of them into the boat.

Getting Diggory and Silome into the boat was a struggle and the small craft nearly tipped over twice, but eventually, they were in. Levo heaved Remaine and Jolly up over the side rail. Levo was last in the water. The lions had arrived.

Levo shrieked loudly as the first Hollowfiend sank her teeth into his foot. He used his free foot to kick it square between the eyes, freeing himself.

"Levo!" Remaine shouted. "Up!"

Jolly reached over to help Remaine with the massive man, whose girth nearly capsized the boat as he kicked at the monsters.

Pua and Jolly were whispering about Terveo and the courtiers. Then there was more splashing, hollering, snarling—Pua stood and suddenly she looked as menacing as her enemies. Her eyes blazed with anger at the lions. She muttered something Remaine couldn't decipher.

A dozen birds with rainbow feathers appeared high in the sky and descended upon the lions. They pecked and clawed their enormous green eyes. It was pandemonium. The lions roared and swatted, but by the time the birds flew away, every one of the lions was sightless—their eyes destroyed. The boat was safely underway.

Remaine wanted to sigh with relief, but then he looked over at his sister, who was coughing up more than water. Blood dripped down her chin. She laid her head back and closed her eyes.

"Silome!" Remaine sat up. He leaned over her and patted her cheek. "Silome! Silome!"

"Remaine," said Diggory. He clutched his belly, looking as bad as Silome. He grasped Remaine's hand. "Remaine," he struggled, "the Cat's Candle. Can you get it? Can you dive?" Diggory's eyes rolled back.

"W–what?"

"Laddie!" Levo barked, grabbing Remaine by the shoulders. "The bloody cat toy!"

Remaine looked back to the spot where the stone had hit the water. Just beyond, loomed one of the royal ships. Remaine could see the prince at her starboard railing. Cottley had climbed aboard with Stretcher. Aboard the other ship he could see the king's court standing on deck. Though they were disheveled and covered in soot, they all seemed eerily calm. Watchful. Waiting.

Remaine shook his head. "I–I can't…"

Silome opened her eyes. "Rem," she wheezed. "This is it. This is your Plink Dive."

Remaine's eyes filled with tears and his body began to shake so furiously he felt like he might collapse. "I failed the Plink Dive, Silome."

"You have what you need, Remaine. *You have the true, great charming.*"

Silome's head fell back. The sight of her in peril was enough to spur Remaine on.

Remaine stood. His legs were shaking violently. He stared into the black water. The irregular breathing of his sister was like a goad in his back. Remaine removed the cloak the prince had fastened around his neck only a few hours ago. Then, without another hesitation, he took three deep breaths, held the third, and dove.

In the waters of Windluff there existed, even at night, a certain color under the water. The corals and reefstone, the pale marble ruins, all of it caught the diffuse light. Here, in Ravillion Bay, the water was black as night, the obsidian stone hungrily consuming the fiery light of Lichenbluff Castle. As he swam down, he could barely see his own hands.

Remaine felt the first sting in his lungs. He swam harder, kicking furiously, ignoring the pressure building in his ears and chest. He did not know where to go. He felt the panic begin.

Turquoise light flashed in the water, followed by pink and orange. Cheering him on, the tiny fish darted this way and that, unsure themselves of where to go, but willing to stay by Remaine's side.

Remaine allowed more bubbles to escape his ballooned cheeks. He kept swimming down.

Then he saw it. The soft, golden glow of the Cat's Candle. Its light shone as faintly as the first star at sunset. It was all he needed. The pain in his chest had become agonizing, but he was close now. Remaine kicked with renewed vigor, his hand outstretched.

His fingers closed around the small crystal. He grabbed it. There was a swirl of disturbed sand. At his touch the stone's bright glow increased. Coupled with the lights from the minnows, the bottom of the black world suddenly lit up.

But then the brightly colored minnows changed. Their little bodies flashed red. Then, in a blink, they went black as pitch. They darted away, leaving Remaine with no light other than the Cat's Candle.

His heart was pounding, his head was splitting, his lungs were on fire. With the faint, golden glow, Remaine saw what lay before him.

The seafloor in the distance—a familiar, pearly pale color—moved. Diver's Spin! Remaine's heart raced.

Instead, something came into focus in the shadowy darkness. It was like a mountain in the distance drawing nearer, yet its massive bulk seemed still half-hidden in the fog of the dark waters.

Two glowing, ghost blue orbs the size of a ship's sails blinked at him in the black waters. One was fogged over, grayish in color. It squinted. Remaine's stomach did a flip as he recalled the Plink Dive. The movement he had seen was not the sea floor shifting. It had not been Diver's spin then. And it was not Diver's Spin now. The Pearlback had been beneath him in Windluff. The Pearlback. And it was the Pearlback beneath him again tonight.

The serpentine head of the monster loomed, unmoving. The rest of its girth was concealed in the dark abyss. The knowledge of its presence became a force that all but possessed Remaine. He began to swim faster than he ever had in his life. It did not matter that the minnows had gone. Remaine knew which way was up.

When Remaine surfaced it was as if he was rising from the dead. He gasped for air, inhaling and choking at the same time, hoarse screams ripped his throat as they escaped from his mouth.

Pua was there, ready to pull him up. Jolly helped. Remaine could hardly feel his own body as it flopped like a fish onto the planks of the boat. His mouth tasted ash. His body shook hard enough to rock the boat, but still, he could not feel anything. Pua took the Cat's Candle from Remaine's hand and got to work. He had no idea what she was doing as she hummed and rummaged about in her bags. Her work to heal using the Cat's Candle had begun. Remaine heard someone call his name.

"Remaine Plink!" Prince Xietas' voice echoed around the bay once more. "Chince! Rawthorne!"

"Get us out of here, Pua," Levo hissed.

"How about a trade?" yelled the prince.

Remaine pressed his elbows to the bottom of the rowboat and forced himself to sit up.

Behind the prince and his men, three figures were ushered into view at the railing. In the flaming glow of the castle, Remaine could see Belwin, Wynnie, and Serae standing like tragic beacons aboard the Ravillion ship. Their hands were tied. Their mouths were gagged.

Levo whimpered at the sight.

"Give us the boy and the Valigold… and you can have the girls."

"Not her father, too, eh? You snake!" spat Levo.

"No," said the prince. "We still have questions for the viscount."

Levo's large hands were shaking as he gripped one of the oars. His jaw hardened; his gaze was set on the captive Rawthornes.

"You don't like the deal?" asked the prince. "Fine." He motioned for them to look to the other ship. Remaine was not prepared for what he saw.

They were small in the distance, but there they stood, and he recognized them clearly. He could see his father and his grandparents.

Remaine suddenly remembered what Hegs had said to the prince at the Brumaloss. He had said something about keeping a deal… somehow, he knew, this was part of it.

"All of them," said the prince. "For the boy. And the Valigold."

There was a beat of silence.

The cold embrace of shame caught Remaine once again. He could not deny he had played a terrible role in all of this mess. Diggory and Silome lay dying beside him. Six more people were being held as prisoners besides. Eight lives were in peril. And it was all his fault. The prince stood watching patiently as the weight of the guilt began to pull Remaine down like the devil's anchor.

"L–Levo," Remaine said, his voice hardly above a whimper. "I'll go. Let me go."

"Shh, laddie."

"How about we make this a little easier," spat Courtier Fiddler, covered in sweat and clutching at his wounds. "Let us test the boy, find out if he's worth all this trouble. I have heard of this interpretation of the boy who holds his breath."

Remaine did not have time to question the courtier, nor did he have time to wonder what he meant by a test. Fiddler reached into his robes and produced a small golden box. All three courtiers placed their hands on the box, murmured something, then stepped back. Golden flakes fell from the outer cover of the box. Remaine recognized the flakes—Aureate Shells. The prince had said that the shells could preserve anything.

The box flew open in an explosion of purple light. In the sky high above them, lightning split the snowy silver sky.

Then a warm mist floated in. It came from no particular direction, but gradually the air around them thickened and sparkled. All at once, Remaine was enveloped in the familiar storm he had seen so many times but had never experienced.

And this time he did experience it. This time he *felt* it.

Remaine stood on the bow of a ship afloat a purple sea. The sky was violently slashed with a glorious sunset.

All was calm.

There was a coldness, though, around his feet.

Remaine looked down to find something like water rising above the tops of his bare feet. It was thicker than water—a bright, glowing blue wind—it rose above his knees now. Then his waist. He began to panic as his head slipped beneath...

He was back. He had received the Great Charming. Remaine inhaled so sharply it felt as if he had swallowed a sword. Then he exhaled. As he did, he realized he was once again lying on his back, snow and ash gently falling around him. From out of his lips came, to his total shock, a bluish mist, coiling like a serpent into the air. Then, inexplicably, an ancient instinct guided his hand to his belt where he removed his vial. It felt natural. It felt... healing, in a way, catching the blue mist for himself, in the same way he had seen everyone do before. Somewhere in the back of his mind, a question rang like the faint tinkling of a bell. He ignored it. For now, he had nothing to question.

Remaine stared at the sky in a daze. Then a warmth washed over him and brought with it a calm unlike any he had ever experienced before. He breathed deeply, warmly, fully. He thought he saw hints of bluish vapor swirling around him, no doubt from everyone else. It did not matter. He was ready to sleep.

"Alas!" laughed Courtier Fiddler. "Not so special."

Courtier Rima Orchid spoke for the first time. "All he needed was a stronger dose."

It was dark, but Remaine could still see the prince's face screwed up with focus.

"Come," hollered Venerack. "Enough of this bargain charade. Bring them in—they could not row if they wanted to."

The little rowboat began to move.

Something flashed gold. Out of the corner of his eye, Diggory saw it and he cried out as the Cat's Candle flew from the boat. It whizzed past their heads straight into the hands of Fiddler. Pua, who had been busy tending to Silome and Diggory, stood. The boat heaved violently beneath her shifting weight. She appeared as if she wanted to protest in some way. Instead, her eyes grew wide.

She dropped into a surprisingly lithe crouch and hissed to the others in the boat, "*Hold on!*"

A sound rippled all around, its vibrations much deeper and much louder than the crackling of flame and crumbling of wood coming from the castle. The savage lions snarled in their cages aboard the ships. Then all sound was drowned out as the noise rose from beneath them. It filled the air. Like the cry of a thousand whales or the creaking of the ocean floor. The sound resonated and repeated and reverberated. It was everywhere all at once.

The Pearlback's head surfaced out of the black water like a shining white island between the little rowboat and the Ravillion vessels. The long, pallid neck of the sea monster grew in girth as it twisted itself upward.

Levo shouted something loudly as their own boat began to ride the wall of rising water. They held onto the edges of the boat. Remaine could hardly hear anything else but the crashing of water and the deafening roar erupting from the monster's throat. Hungry for the moon itself, the Pearlback roared into the sky. Then, with horrifying speed, it brought its neck down upon the fiery structure of Lichenbluff Castle.

Smoke and flames erupted all around the monster. The small boat that held the six of them nearly overturned as an enormous wave swept them away.

Pua wailed. Silome and Diggory, splashed with seawater, coughed with what little reserves of energy they had remaining. Levo paddled furiously. Before they could compose themselves, the monster lifted its head a second time and brought it down with an ear-splitting crash. There was nothing left of Lichenbluff. A second wave rose. This one pushed them even farther away. By the time the Pearlback returned to the depths, a vast distance of black, still water lay between the rowboat and the Ravillion vessels.

"Head to the brook," Levo whispered. "There's no going back."

An arm's length from Harbor's Hand (assuming the arm were the one attached to Harbor's Hand), the Hollian Hills cascaded down to a bank with a pebbly beach. Splitting the beach was a babbling little river, its silver length mostly overgrown by large, wintery bayferns and other trees, all dusted with snow and now, dusted with ash as well.

The little beach was practically invisible from Harbor's Hand. Tonight, it was also invisible from those aboard the Ravillion ships. Unbeknownst to the Ravillion entourage, smoldering with an ancient rage and unmatched fear at the sight of the Pearlback, now gone beneath the waters of Ravillion Bay, a small rowboat cut through the midnight water and slipped onto the beach.

CHAPTER 25

THE CAVERNS OF CRACKLEMORE

REMAINE PLINK DID NOT KNOW IT YET, but this was the second time he had been to this little beach.

The first time his unconscious body (poisoned by a gruggleblade then stashed in a hideout in Harbor's Hand for some time) was hauled up on the beach, then through the woods, then stuffed into a carriage, then whisked away to Rawthorne Manor.

This time, Remaine's body threatened unconsciousness once more. The shocks of the night's events, maybe more than the shock of the cold-water dive, were taking a toll on him. He stepped out of the boat with wobbly legs.

They began to climb through the thick wood along the brook's edge. Levo, who was carrying Diggory, dropped to

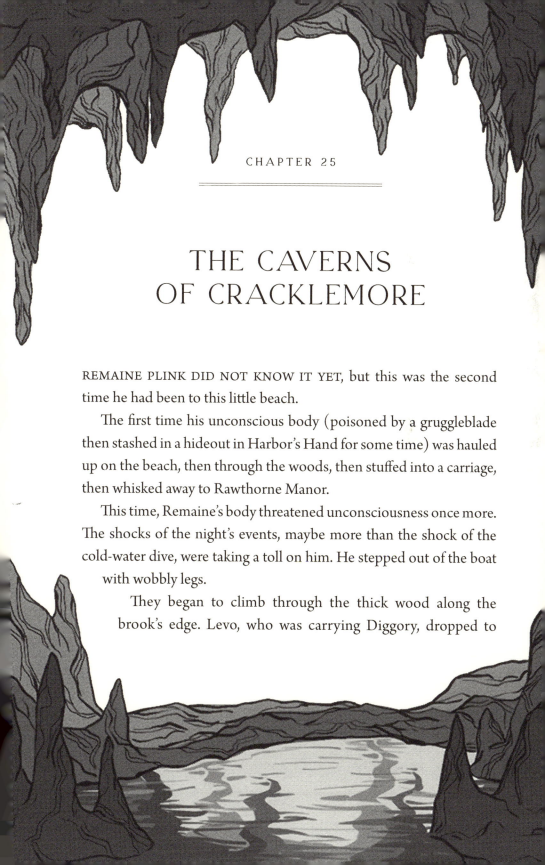

the ground. Pua and Jolly, who were struggling to hold up Silome, dropped too. Behind them, Remaine collapsed to his knees.

Silome coughed. Remaine was relieved to see there was no blood. Diggory sat up, bent forward, and held his head in his hands. Remaine stared in disbelief at the sight of Silome and Diggory. The wounds to each of them on their ribs had already begun to change. The damaged flesh that had been black with blood, was slowly replacing itself with a shiny, paler pink skin. For both of them, their breathing had deepened, widened. They all sat in silence shivering violently. Their breathing was the only sound in the world. They waited. Within a minute or two, Silome and Diggory were both sitting upright, blinking in the world. Diggory smiled.

"HAH!" burst out Levo. He leaned over, yanking Diggory and Silome both into an embrace, popping their backs and necks as he did.

Jolly took his gloves off to dry, revealing his pink hands for the first time. He fixed his glasses on his nose and gave a teary round of applause.

Diggory looked around, then slowly stood to his feet.

"Easy, Cap'n," Levo said. "No need to lead on just yet. We're safe—there's time to rest."

"Not much time," said Silome, rubbing her ribs. She winced a little. "They're eastbound. All of them."

"We don't know their plans for certain, lass."

"Colony Gardens!" spat Silome. "Whether next week or next year, our families are on Ravillion ships now. They'll end up in Colony Gardens where they'll be sucked dry."

She looked at Remaine. She looked tired, downcast. It was the first time Remaine had seen his sister look so defeated.

"It's all my fault," Remaine said.

No one spoke for a minute.

Heeding Levo's advice, Diggory crouched back down. He looked terrible. Like the rest of them, his lips were blue with cold, his face was pale with fatigue. He shivered violently. "You've made mistakes,

Remaine. We'll s–s–sort them out together, in time," a spasm shot across his chin and lip. "And mine along with them."

"Are you all well enough to swim?" Pua asked.

Remaine gawked. "We're going *back*?"

"Not back," said Pua. She pointed in the direction of the brook, which wound its way further into the wood. "In."

"Pua," said Diggory. "You're coming too."

"No. Wicked charms are at work." As she said this, a shiver ran through them. Her voice was low. "In the Hollowfiends' eyes. Wicked charms have been worked to breed those beasts—the poisoned ways of Venerack—the way of the witches—the way of dark power."

"That's why the king wanted all of Cracklemore's governors at the Brumaloss," said Diggory, staring off in deep thought. "To see the lions. To debut their power."

"S–s–so many more aboard," whimpered Jolly. "W–w–what c–c–could stand against a strength like that?"

Diggory grimaced and nodded. "What indeed?"

"The king feels pressure forming," Pua said. "A tide rises on his shores; he's fighting to reinforce the foundation of his throne. The ancient things are stirring—some by his command. But others are waking on their own." Her eyes glazed over as she squared her broad shoulders.

"The Pearlback," Remaine whispered.

Pua looked carefully at Remaine.

"I saw it when I dove down," he said, aware of her gaze. "I saw its dead eye—the one the prince speared. It followed us from the lagoon." Remaine paused, then added, "And I saw it in Windluff too."

"What?" asked Silome.

"Diver's Spin…" he said.

Pua closed her eyes, then said. "The beast destroyed the castle. The flames…"

Diggory sat up. "The fire in Broken Bottle…" he said. "You think the flames are drawing it to the surface?"

"Perhaps," said Pua. "But why now? Many fires have burned. Many fires have sunk ships. After generations, the whole world believed the monsters gone, but now here they are—the Pearlbacks, the Hollowfiends… and the prophecies." She looked at Remaine. "The old relics… alive… the harpy's song… a time long awaited has come." She was muttering to herself more than anyone else. She lifted her chin high and said, "No, I am going where you cannot come."

"Lady," protested Levo, "They've seen you. You'll be—"

Pua stood and even though she wasn't taller than Levo, she somehow managed to dwarf them all. "I am not afraid, Mr. Chince." She looked back at Diggory. "I will be fine here for the night. My pets will keep me safe. When it is clear, I will make my way. I must understand the mysteries of the Crack in Time—the connections to Mirror Pass."

"They're connected?" asked Remaine.

"Yes," breathed Diggory. "Apparently the Ravillions built a fortress around a secret opening to the Crack in Time. It's where they've been breeding the lions. Belwin and I found a way out through the other side—a side I've explored half a dozen times with no trace of any lions before."

"The winds will bring our ships to the same isle when the time is right," said Pua. "Now. Off you all get. It's only a matter of time before the Rawthorne cavern is found."

Diggory stood once more, wincing a bit.

"Stay close, everyone," he said with resolve. Then he pushed his way through the dense foliage, further into the woods. Before he followed, Remaine looked back at Pua, sitting there on the large rock. She eyed him carefully, then turned her gaze upward where the stars were sparkling.

They had only hiked a few more minutes before Diggory brought them all to a halt. They were standing in a small clearing, mostly free of snow due to the thick canopy surrounding it. The brook had become a small black pool, smooth save for the few ripples that emanated from the gentle waterfall at the far end. "The tunnel's just down here," whispered Diggory, pointing to a nondescript location in the water.

Jolly looked sick with worry. Diggory put a hand on his shoulder.

"You'll be all right, Jolly," he said. "This is the very reason we taught you to swim."

Jolly feigned confidence, bobbing his head up and down anxiously, adjusting his glasses.

"Chince?"

Levo swatted a bear claw and spat. "Bah. I'm fine." But Remaine saw him flinch a tiny bit when he put that same hand on the bandaged wound where the Hollowfiend had taken out a chunk of flesh.

"Plinks," Diggory was moving down the line, "I trust you'll be fine?"

Silome nodded. Sometime in the last ten minutes, her face had returned to its normal shark-like state. Remaine did not know what else to do, so he nodded too.

"Good." Diggory said. "Let's all catch our breath for a few moments—not too long—then we'll go."

They fell naturally into two groups. Diggory, Levo, and Jolly stood near the pool, talking quietly. Levo leaned on Diggory, who leaned on Jolly, whose loyal frame groaned beneath the taller men. On the other side of the pool, Silome and Remaine sat next to each other.

"Silome," Remaine said, bashfully hanging his head. "I'm sorry for doubting—for running away—then for lying—and—"

"I'm sorry too," Silome returned. "Sorry for not telling you. I'm sorry for not telling Mom sooner…"

"You told her everything, then?"

Silome's eyes narrowed. "She's strange, Rem. It's like she's always known—or at least she's always known *something*—but she's been too afraid to say it." She ran her fingers through her wet hair. "Turns out we're not the only ones who have been keeping secrets."

"What do you mean?"

"The night Dad came back—the night of his accident—you don't remember any of it, do you?"

He shook his head.

"I was supposed to be in bed," said Silome.

It was an endless war between Fortis Plink and her daughter—one fought over and over again, when it was time to go to bed. That's how their mother had always described it. From the moment she was born, Silome had refused to go to sleep when she was supposed to. Not a night went by in the first ten years of her life that she didn't catapult protests at their mother. As Silome recounted the night of the accident, her eyes grew glassy and her voice flattened.

"Mom kept screaming at me to go to bed—she kept begging me to leave them alone. But I couldn't help it. I just kept staring at him—the way he burst into the house, the way he fell to the floor—the way he was writhing around, shrieking, screaming—stuff about the curse that's coming for our family—screaming about Berylbones and about going east—he kept begging Mom not to let them take him east."

Remaine had managed to construct this much of the image himself, though some of it he had added quite recently. He nodded. Silome kept going.

"When I told Mom about you, though—when I told her that you were alive—told her the truth about the League, the truth about the Rawthornes—" Silome paused again and her face hardened. "Then Mom told me more."

"More?"

"When she had calmed Dad down—later that night—after I did finally fall asleep—she told me he started mumbling something else. *Not with the king*—that's what he said. *Not east. Not with the king.*"

Remaine stared wide-eyed at his sister. "Dad wasn't just scared of Berylbones. Not just a curse. Dad didn't trust the Ravillions either?"

Silome shrugged. "Apparently not. Something happened to him. He saw something. But he's never been well enough to talk about it.

It was enough to make Mom want to keep him safely locked away, but she never considered that *everything* was a lie—that the Great Charming was really a beguiling."

Remaine felt a swell of frustration. This had all been locked up for years. "Why didn't Mom tell us?"

"I was furious at first too," Silome said. "But I had the chance to think about it on the way here."

He saw her wipe something from her cheek, but she moved fast, like a shark.

"Mom's been terrified. She has never known what to do with all these secrets. What *could* she do? A curse coming for the family? And then *you*, and how... odd you've always been—"

She smirked. He pretended he didn't care.

"And Dad," she added. "It was all too much. Too many secrets in the Plink family. And she's been holding it all in, pretending it's not real. I wish we had known too—we all could have trusted each other."

Remaine shook his head slowly, trying to picture his mother and the weight she had been carrying alone for all these years. Then he looked up at Silome.

"Mom wasn't aboard the ship with Dad and Gramma and Grampa! She's—"

"—she's with Hegs," Silome finished. "I tried to find her when the fire started, but they had left. Hegs has been working something all along, Remaine. He was the one who poisoned the butterfin at the Tour of Valor."

Remaine gawked at her.

"What? Why? How do you know?"

"I beat it out of Jileanna." Silome hid a little smile at the sight of his face. "Easy—I didn't actually beat her up. After Hegs kept showing up at our house, pestering us, pestering Mom, I had to figure out why. So, I scared the paint right off Jileanna's face on the voyage here. She told me everything she knew." Silome twisted her hair one last time, ringing out more water. She gave a shiver. "Jileanna knew he poisoned the fish to weaken our family. And it worked. After the Tour, Gramma and Grampa and Dad couldn't even get up. It was time for them to go east. He's been trying to get the Plinks out of Windluff."

"Why us?"

"Well… not all of us," Silome replied. "At first, he wanted to keep you for Jileanna. Hegs has been grooming her for you—Jileanna doesn't get it though—that was apparent when she told me everything. Jileanna likes you so much because Hegs has been feeding her lies about how much you love her. It's sad, really."

It had been so long since that morning at Hegs' big house, Remaine had nearly forgotten about the marriage proposition. It was as absurd now as it was then. "But why does Hegs want us to marry?"

"I wasn't sure at first. But then it occurred to me when Hegs barely broke stride when everyone thought you died—and he just went after Mom."

"After Mom? To *marry* her?" Remaine gawked. "*Hegs* marry *Mom*? What occurred to you?"

Silome shrugged. "With the family gone, and you marrying Jileanna no longer a possibility, he's been arranging to collect her with the same sort of single-minded persistence."

Remaine recalled the exchange between Hegs and the prince back in the castle. "That's what Hegs meant when he asked the prince if their arrangement still stood," he said. "He wanted to keep one of the Plinks for himself." The question came to him once more. "But why the Plinks?"

"I don't think it's the Plinks, exactly," said Silome, knowingly. "The Plinks who stay behind in Windluff—we all have one thing in common: we've all got Diaquinn blood. Mom gave up a fortune when she left her old life. Hegs is after it."

"More money?"

"He must be up to something."

Diggory approached them. "Big breath, everyone. Don't panic. The cold will not last forever. Warmth awaits us at the end. The first air pocket is very close—you'll all make it if you stay calm and swim straight." He paused, "Oh, and follow the light."

"What light?" Remaine asked, looking around at the thick dark water.

As if it heard him, a little turquoise light appeared in the water. The tiny glowing minnow darted around excitedly.

Silome stood. "I'm not going with you, Rem."

Remaine stared at her, suddenly feeling small. "What? What do you mean?"

"Estin was right. The Ravillions will be after the Plinks, now. And the Merchants. I've got to go back and help get Mom and Cressa out."

"I'll go with you!" Remaine burst.

"No, Remaine—" she put a hand on his shoulder. "You need protection right now. Don't worry. I'll meet up with you on that island Pua talked about."

Diggory heard the exchange but did not say a word. With a deep breath, he dove quietly into the water.

One by one they followed (Jolly hesitated, but only briefly) until the last left by the pool were Silome and Remaine. Silome sighed. "Anyway, I should have told you a long time ago, Rem, and I am sorry."

"You weren't allowed," Remaine replied.

She rolled her eyes. "When did rules ever stop me? Obviously, I broke them to tell Estin. The truth is, even after you were immune, and even after I saw your hideout, and caught a glimpse into your strange head, I still counted you out."

Remaine stared at her.

"It was always going to be *me* to save our whole family," shrugged Silome. "Can you believe *I* would think that?" She smirked.

Remaine smiled. "If anyone could…"

Silome punched him in the arm. "I'm proud of you, Rem. You're a Plink through and through. The rest of them don't get it yet, but when they do, they'll all get on board. You go ahead," she said. "I'll see you soon."

She pushed him forward. "Now dive."

It was enough for Remaine.

He took a deep breath, then dove into the water. Several glowing minnows were waiting for him, darting in circles, gently illuminating the rocky floor. They led him forward, swimming deeper, then they entered into a black hole, speckled with little bits of color. He pulled himself along the tunnel. Aside from the frigid temperature of the water, he felt almost at home—like he was back in the Butterfin Caves. Sooner than he expected, he saw the shimmering ripples of the water's surface. As he neared the surface, he rose through several pairs of dangling legs kicking. Remaine broke through the surface, gasping for air, then joined them.

The pocket was small, but large enough for them to all breathe deeply for a few minutes.

"Everyone good?" Diggory asked. They all confirmed, even Jolly, though he looked a little bit uncertain. "Good. Let's not waste ourselves treading water. Deep breath. Five more to go."

"F–five!" Jolly said, but everyone else was already descending.

At last, they came to the final pool which, compared to the others, was quite large. Exhausted, Remaine kicked to the surface, gulped in the air, and rubbed the water out of his eyes. He found himself in a cavernous space of shiny black stone. It was lit with torches. Diggory hopped out of the water, then extended a dripping hand to each in turn as he helped them out of the water. Each of them collapsed onto the stone floor, shaking.

Little *mip* sounds echoed from the far end of the chamber along with a loud squawk, as Diggory's cat and bird greeted him.

"H–h–hello, Barrow. E–e–evening, S–S–Staunch." Diggory's lips had gone blue.

The pets clung tightly to their master as he walked over to a nearby trunk and pulled quilts out of it. He handed them around. The room slowly filled with the warm light of a growing fire. They huddled together, too tired to speak, too tired to sit up.

A voice came from overhead. "Where *is* she!"

Lady Solace clacked into the room with Mr. Lecky Wooling at her side. It was the fastest he had ever seen Lady Solace move. With her cane, she was pushing each one of them out of her way as they lay on their backs. Perhaps she thought her granddaughter was hiding underneath one of them.

Diggory stood. He spoke to Lady Solace in hushed tones. Remaine closed his eyes, shivering, taking deep, heaving breaths. He could make none of the conversation out, but the stifled, choking sort of moaning sounds slipping from Lady Solace let him know that Diggory had told Lady Solace about Serae. Remaine clutched the small figurine in his pocket and squeezed the game piece reverently. He was desperate to know Serae was all right.

After a while, their shivering steadied, and they began to catch their breath. Remaine sat up and looked around. He mustered enough energy to ask the obvious.

"Where are we?"

Levo swiped the water from his face with a giant hand and sighed, "Another cavern in Cracklemore, Wiggles. Ol' Terveo used to—"

But he stopped, suddenly aware that Lady Solace and Mr. Lecky Wooling were just now fully understanding what had happened to Terveo Rawthorne.

Levo hung his big red head. Tears fell into his beard. In the whirlwind of the night, Remaine had almost forgotten. Terveo Rawthorne was dead. Lady Solace's icy face broke. With his head lowered, Mr. Lecky Wooling walked away in silence.

"My father and my uncle Dasko spoke often of caverns," said Diggory, his voice thick. "Caverns tucked away—sealed off, holding all the secrets of the world. The Caverns of Cracklemore, he and my uncle would say. But they believed light must come to all, eventually." Diggory took a shaky breath.

Diggory, Jolly, and Levo, sat as still as stones. Tears left shiny streaks on their faces. The streaks shimmered in the firelight.

Diggory nodded. "He was very attached to that rock around his neck for that reason. Light in the cavern."

"And now the Ravillions have it," mumbled Levo.

"W–what is it, Master Diggory?" Jolly shivered. "The… Valigold, they called it. Why do they want it so badly?"

"Another secret in another cavern, Jolly," said Diggory.

Remaine looked around. He remembered that Pua had warned them that this very cavern would be discovered soon enough. She had said that they must hurry. It seemed like all the secrets of the world were leaking out and all the dangers of the world were creeping in.

Nothing more was said that night. Remaine did not remember how it all happened, but before too long, he was curled up in a ball by the fire, dreaming. His head filled with the strange images that had come when he had received the Great Charming earlier that evening. Then he felt vague and strange about calling it the Great Charming, but he couldn't remember why.

He awoke in a cold sweat. The vision felt as real as it had been the first time. He couldn't help it. He had to breathe out a wispy stream of blue into his vial. He capped the vial. It helped, but that made him feel strange. That's when he noticed Diggory. He was near the water, packing a few bags. Everyone else was asleep.

"You dreamed of the Beguiling?" Diggory said.

Remaine did not respond.

"It's normal," Diggory whispered. "Not all of your dreams will be like that. But many will."

"Diggory? The prince thought I was…"

"The boy in the prophecy." Diggory finished Remaine's sentence for him as he tightened the straps of his leather satchel.

"But I guess I'm not, huh? I can't hold my breath anymore."

"Interpretations can be tricky, Remaine. I don't think I'm the one to tell you whether or not the prophecy speaks of you. We'll need the help of others." He paused, then added, "time will tell what the prophecy means."

The thoughts were cloudy in his mind, but they began to solidify into more questions. "He… he thought I was special."

"He saw something in you, yes," Diggory affirmed.

"I wasn't Charmed—uh, Beguiled—but he wasn't scared by that."

Diggory nodded.

"And… Serae was different too." Remaine screwed up his face in concentration. He had known for some time Serae was like him—but it occurred to him, for the first time, to wonder if the prince would have been just as intrigued in Serae? Then another question came. "Is she Ch–Beguiled now, too?"

Diggory shook his head. "Can't say for certain." His scruffy chin moved around as he chewed his lip and stared off. "That has never happened before," Diggory continued, "at least like that. We've heard of bewitchments being contained and preserved before. And obviously we have figured out how to bottle up some magic of our own—but the Beguiling? Preserved in an Aureate Shell, sent by the king to test you? It was frightfully strong."

The whole bay had been wrapped up in a minute. Surely Serae had been enveloped too.

"But…" Remaine continued thoughtfully. "He said he'd teach me how to be brave. He saw my… abilities. He appreciated them—knew they made me special."

"He wasn't the only one who appreciates you and your gifts, Remaine."

"But what he saw was… wrong?" asked Remaine, a pitiful pit swelling in his belly. It was odd, how everything had happened slowly, steadily, without him really noticing. All his life he had longed to be Charmed like everyone else and now, he found himself disappointed that he was no longer an exception, no longer different in the slightest. The prince had changed him, made him feel courageous… but now he was nothing but a cowardly, dock dwelling bottom feeder again. "I'm not as special as he thought—I'm just like everyone else. Right?"

Diggory smiled. "Perhaps."

"But…" he tried to find the right word. "My mind? The things I see?" He recalled the incident with Vulcutta and the explosion inside Pua's home after the bird sang the prophecy. He knew that it was his presence that had triggered it all. "Is there not more to it?"

Diggory did not respond. He was lost in his thoughts, a state which manifested itself in the immediate task of loading a pack with supplies. One by one, everyone began to wake, to rub the sleep out of their eyes. Together they ate a humble breakfast of bread and cheese. Then Diggory passed around traveling cloaks that he had pulled from another trunk. He also handed out familiar black boxes.

"Bit of Wynnie's preparations," Diggory said.

A heavy cloud of gray sadness hung over them as they opened the black boxes to find strange, floppy molds of big noses and bushy eyebrows. Poor Wynnie. She was a bound and gagged prisoner, and here they were reaping the benefits of her labors. The masks lay like wet pancakes inside the boxes. They applied their disguises and before long, Remaine found himself huddling with a group of total strangers near a large door at the far end of the cavern.

"No speaking once we open the door," Diggory said. His nose now had a large scar down the middle and his brow had nearly doubled in height. "Follow Mr. Wooling. We will come out into the gardens, and from there we'll take the north trail down to the docks. As soon as we're under open sky, hoods up."

Mr. Lecky Wooling led the way. Like ants trooping up an anthill, Remaine and the others silently followed him through yet another tunnel. Up they climbed as the tunnel made its ascension. On a few occasions, they had to duck or crawl. At last, they came to a trap door.

Wooling pressed the door open, bringing it down to the ground above without so much as the squeak of a hinge.

They were in a thick hedge after that. A pebbly trail was before Remaine and each step was fraught with tree roots to trip over and rough foliage to scrape his cheeks or snag his cloak. Eventually they came to an opening in the hedge where there was a forest of snow-laden trees.

Down the hill they trudged, weaving in and out of the trees. Hating every moment of the hike, Lady Solace was forced to choose between dampening the hem of her skirts in the snow, or the indignity of riding piggyback on Diggory. Remaine guessed it was mostly because of her weak leg that she chose the latter, but whatever the reasoning, she did not ride quietly.

"Now really, is there not a road we might take—is there not a single, solitary line in this frozen earth sketched by better, civilized men?"

"We're keeping off the roads, my lady," replied Diggory, resolute in his downhill gait.

"Diggory, I will insist you keep hold of the silk. Do *not* let it drag."

Diggory adjusted his grip and gathered up the yards of fabric wordlessly.

"And this *temperature*," huffed Lady Solace. "Jolly, I'll take another blanket."

They came to a little rocky overhang. Just below them lay the docks of Ravillion Bay.

By midmorning they were on the docks. As inconspicuously as possible, they trailed behind Diggory. The docks were, as always, buzzing with activity.

"I could see the flames all the way from the point!" hollered one man.

"Nearly burned down my house!" cried another.

"I won't be sailing for the rest of my life—not with that monster out there. I swear it!"

Remaine's gut twisted. He felt responsible for it all. The smell of fish tickled his nose and a stabbing ache for home thrummed in his chest. He dropped his head. He was so tired.

Diggory led them aboard a noble vessel, a vessel that any Plink would be pleased as pickles to own. Jolly, Mr. Wooling, and Lady Solace were easily the most out of place aboard the beautiful ship—not a one of them knowing where to stand or what to do. Diggory and Levo slid comfortably into their usual positions and Remaine followed orders with the ease of a seasoned crewman. Within the hour, they were pushing away from the dock.

The sun was still to the east, but it was quickly rising directly overhead into the white, hazy winter sky. Remaine held a hand up to block the light, painful to his eyes. Ravillion Bay lay behind them and an expansive gray ocean lay before them.

"Where are we going?"

"My brother and niece have been kidnapped, along with the Plinks."

"We're going after them?" Remaine asked.

"No. We're going to find my uncle Dasko," Diggory said, taking a deep breath of sea air. "We need more help. Then we save our families, Remaine. We do our best to fix our mistakes." Diggory turned towards Remaine and put an arm around his shoulders.

The water was smooth, the wind was following, and although the darkness loomed all around and danger was certainly imminent, Remaine felt that with these friends he might finally learn to be brave.

END OF BOOK 1

ACKNOWLEDGEMENTS

A very special thanks to the following people, in no particular order:

Grandma Joanne, S,K,N&C Bull, Leslie Prewitt, Mom, The Hares, Grandma Carole, Jacob & Tori Prewitt, The Goin Family, Nate & Sarah Schwartz Family, Kaha, The Clark Family, The Getzendanner Family, The Brown Family, The Brown Family, Tilly Miller, Hazel Anderson, Andrea Stacey, Gavin & Graham Miller, Julie & Adje, Chris Choi, Far Off Games, Vancouver Thorsviks, The Chestnut Millers, Ron & Jeanne Sears, Lock & Key Adventurer's Guild, Jordyn Schwartz, Argens, Paetyn Nicole, Randy L Carlson, Layne & Laury Schwartz, Babe & Jojo, Micki & Tim Schwartz, James & Jennifer Schwartz, The Biles Family, Logan Stecker, The Carter Family, Julia & Jordan Olson, Jeff & Linda Tatarsky, Trevor & Chelsea Hostetler, Cori, Grant & Tricia Cox, Taylor & Kayla Rassi, Emerson & Sarah Eggerichs, The Nordyke Family, The Peerys, Amber McGill, Paul Garbett, Sawyer & Alissa Jones, Amy, Ben, Caitlyn & Alyssa Graham, Marty, Candace & the Miller Fam, Madison & Mason Mays, Brynnley & Maeve, Kevin & Sue Graves, Ryan & Liz Gates, Schu, Ada & Jackson Eggerichs, Brenda Lemmon, The Csak Family, The McGreene Family, Maxwell "Cat Mage" Bixler, Reg, Madison Kelsey, Cody Cox, J & G Prewitt, The Pizot Family, Forrest & Zahara Reed, Caroline Reed, King Quince, Jerry & Amy Markus, Andrew R, Sydney MacNaughton, Lorna & Michael Farra, Kaity Kelsey, Scott & Kim Reed Family, Kenny Helmes, Jeff & Susan Reed, The Hall Family, Nolan Grubbs,

The Hatton Family, Andy & Naomi Davis, Kristen Orlando, Erik Peterson, Jenny Bernick, Cody Miller, Tess Anderson, Ren Reed, Joel Wakeman

Many more helped bring this book to life. To those who proofread for me, encouraged me, invested emotionally, spiritually, intellectually and financially in me, and put up with me as I wrote this book, thank you.

ABOUT THE AUTHOR AND ILLUSTRATOR

JACE AND MIKAILA SCHWARTZ live in Vancouver, Washington, with their two small children (and a baby on the way!). Since they met in high school, Jace and Mikaila have wanted to make beautiful things together. In 2023 they established Studio J&M as *The Caverns of Cracklemore: The Great Charming* found its footing. Whether it be picture books, poetry, chapter books (and more!), Jace and Mikaila hope to populate Studio J&M with beautiful art for the whole family for years to come.

www.studiojandm.com